BIRDSONG

Sebastian Faulks was born and brought up in Newbury, Berkshire. He worked in journalism before starting to write books. He is best known for the French trilogy, *The Girl at the Lion d'Or*, *Birdsong* and *Charlotte Gray* (1989–1997) and is also the author of a triple autobiography, *The Fatal Englishman* (1996); a small book of literary parodies, *Pistache* (2006); and the novels *Human Traces* (2005), *Engleby* (2007) and *A Week in December* (2009). He lives in London with his wife and their three children.

ALSO BY SEBASTIAN FAULKS

The Girl at the Lion d'Or
A Fool's Alphabet
The Fatal Englishman
Charlotte Gray
On Green Dolphin Street
Human Traces
Pistache
Engleby
A Week in December
Faulks on Fiction

SEBASTIAN FAULKS

Birdsong

VINTAGE BOOKS
London

FOR EDWARD

Published by Vintage 2011

2 4 6 8 10 9 7 5 3

Introduction copyright © Sebastian Faulks, 1993

First published in Great Britain in 1993 by Hutchinson

Vintage
Random House, 20 Vauxhall Bridge Road,
London SW1V 2SA

www.vintage-classics.info

Addresses for companies within The Random House Group Limited
can be found at: www.randomhouse.co.uk/offices.htm

The Random House Group Limited Reg. No. 954009

A CIP catalogue record for this book
is available from the British Library

ISBN 9780099528388

The Random House Group Limited supports The Forest
Stewardship Council (FSC®), the leading international forest
certification organisation. Our books carrying the FSC label are
printed on FSC® certified paper. FSC is the only forest certification
scheme endorsed by the leading environmental organisations,
including Greenpeace. Our paper procurement policy can be found
at www.randomhouse.co.uk/environment

Printed and bound by CPI Group (UK) Ltd, Croydon, CR0 4YY

Introduction

I WAS 39 when I wrote *Birdsong*, but I had been thinking about the First World War, off and on, since the day when, as a schoolboy of 12, I was asked to read out at assembly on November 11 the names of the old boys of my school who had died in two world wars. It was a small school, but the list was so long that I was treated that night for a sore throat. Something had clearly gone on, I thought, something almost literally unspeakable. When the history teacher, so forthcoming on the Corn Laws and the Stuarts, came to the subject of the Great War, he seemed to struggle for breath; he shook his head sadly and seemed in a hurry to move on.

Many years later, in 1988, I was literary editor of *The Independent* in London when the 70th anniversary of the armistice brought a flurry of new books into the office. One in particular intrigued me, an account of tunnelling operations. I had previously had no idea that beneath no-man's-land, in tunnels so low you couldn't stand, another war had been fought: a hell within a hell. In November that year, I was sent on an assignment by the paper to the Western Front with a group of veterans on a visit organised by the historian Lyn Macdonald. I stood in the mud at Neuve Chapelle and Aubers Ridge with men who had fought there in 1915; one of them held my hand as he described picking up the pieces of his dead friend, 'each one of them no bigger than a leg of mutton', and putting them in a sandbag which he buried in a hole before advancing. And on that cold autumn morning, the war ceased to be 'history' to me and became a real, living thing: it was now; it was this old man whose warm and living hand was in mine; it was flesh, it was blood; and, for some reason I didn't understand, it was important for me to comprehend it. In the afternoon, I wandered down a row of headstones in one of the eerily beautiful battleground cemeteries with my veteran companion. He gave a start. The body of his dismembered friend, which he had believed lost, had been dug up and buried in a war grave: there in front of us was the name on a clean white stone. 'Oh, I say,' he gasped, face to face for the first time in nearly 70 years with his best friend; 'Oh, I say.'

In the next three years, I read more about the war. I had by now, however, run into a sizeable paradox. On the one hand, I felt that the experience of this war had somehow slipped from public understanding; even educated people seemed vague about it. This was in part due to the reticence of those who had been there. In the whole of human history, no one had ever seen such slaughter before, so how were these men to talk about it? Then, only 20 years later, the world had been convulsed by a second frenzy, one aspect of which had been so well memorialised at the insistence of its victims that it seemed to leave no room in the public mind for earlier holocausts. There was a gap, a blank of memory. On the other hand, the First World War had produced a great literature and was properly understood by some. I felt that if it were to detain the well-informed, I needed to bring something new to my account of the war; and the story of the tunnellers might fulfil this role. I also needed to answer another readerly question: what have these remote events to do with modern life; why should I care? I decided to confront this problem by having a more or less contemporary character in the book – Elizabeth – pose just such questions.

By the spring of 1992, I had most of the pieces in place, while the principal theme of the novel had emerged from what I had read. It was this: how far can you go? What are the limits of humanity? I had always been intrigued by the fact that at no point during the extermination of ten million men, did one of them say: enough, we can't go on and still call ourselves human. In fact, the French army did mutiny in 1917, but although the problem was widespread, it amounted to no more than a refusal to attack; some German machine gunners on July 1, 1916, did desist, appalled by what they did. But the thematic question was largely unanswered.

I made a number of visits to the Western Front, where the history seemed encouragingly forgotten; one small notice in a two-room museum in Albert reminded visitors that nations other than the French had fought in the 14–18 War, but the local people I consulted seemed surprised to learn that the British had been involved. In April, I went to the Somme front line with a battlefield map from the Imperial War Museum. I had long been interested by what infamous places were like before they acquired their terrible names: the lively port of Hiroshima, the abandoned barracks in the foothills of the Carpathians known as Auschwitz . . . What had the Somme been like before it became 'the Somme'? If the book was to be about how far the human body and spirit could be driven in killing, then it should, I felt, ask the same question of loving. From the start, I planned to have a first section set in peace-time, with flesh-and-blood sequences that would be the corollary of the bodily dismemberments that I, though not the characters, knew were coming.

I stayed in a small bed-and-breakfast in a farm behind the British front line on the Ancre. I was very nearly there, I felt, but the spark wouldn't come; I could conceive of no reason for my Englishman to be in these agricultural villages. I returned to the disappointing town of Amiens, whose tourist brochure was keen for me to visit the famous water-gardens. There, I sat despondently, with half a dozen other trippers, on a sort of punt, wondering if I would ever manage to write this book. Then I saw a rat on the canal bank, which was held up with wooden boards or 'revetting' as the trench-builders called it. Along the water's edge was decomposing vegetation – and I was there, a hot afternoon in 1910, the pressure of a woman's leg against her lover's in the boat, the war fore-shadowed in the humid, rotting waterways. When the boat trip was over, I walked up the adjacent street, the Boulevard du Cange, and I saw the house in which it might happen: formal, strong, creeper-covered; and of course Stephen would not be a farmer, he would be in the textile industry which naturally united Amiens and England.

I spent some days walking the length of the British line along the Ancre and across the pathetically small distance of the advance, bought at the cost of 60,000 casualties in a single day. I sat for hours in some of the small cemeteries. I didn't quite know what I was looking for; I was just immersing myself in this world, hoping, I suppose, to acquire the authority to write about it. Sometimes I felt choked by rage and indignation; at other times, in the spring sunshine, among the headstones, I felt oddly tranquil and at ease. In a wood behind the rising ground at Thiepval, I stumbled on a shell casing. Then I took some earth from the Sunken Road, in sight of the German guns at Beaumont Hamel and put it in a jam jar. Finally, I stood beneath the great arch at Thiepval, where the names of the missing – not the dead, just those of whom no trace was found – are like footnotes in the wind. I saw my own surname.

Stephen had to go through the war; this much I knew. The theme of the novel dictated the narrative, which in turn suggested what kind of man might be able to survive, so to some extent his nature was given to me. I decided to provide Isabelle with a family, a childhood and some depth of personal history; they seemed important if she was to represent all that I required of her. Michael Weir and Jack Firebrace provided harmonic lines in counterpoint to Stephen's: innocent when he is worldly, scared where he is cold, despondent while he remains questing. Elizabeth existed at first to ask questions for the reader and to satisfy a thematic requirement: that the past and present, the public and the private, be shown to be interdependent, a concern which dominated all three books of what became, with *The Girl at the Lion D'or* and *Charlotte Gray*, a French trilogy. For me, however, Elizabeth's most helpful contributions came in narrative: when she visits Brennan in his incurables' home or when she telephones Gray in his Scottish home and the voice of the past comes crackling down the line. These moments, I suppose, were emblems of what I and, I hoped, the reader were making: gestures of love and redemption towards the past.

I wrote *Birdsong* quickly, completing about 1,500 words each morning, then taking the Tube to the Imperial War Museum and reading documents until the reading-room closed. There were moments when I felt overcome by emotion, and at such times I stopped writing; my aim was not to flood the page with my own feelings, but to select those details that might release comparable emotions in the reader. I think the fact that the book was written at speed is evident; some ends are loose (most, though not all, deliberately so), there is a roughness, a torn-off quality in places; but I could find no way of resisting the momentum.

As an epigraph, I took the line from Rabindranath Tagore that Wilfred Owen had quoted in his final letter to his mother before his return to the Front. For the dedication, I had toyed with the idea of some inscription to the dead of the war, but felt it seemed presumptuous; so I made it out instead to my elder brother Edward, in whose borrowed study I had written every word.

In the years since 1993, the way people think about the First World War has changed. Doubtless the century's end helped refocus people's attention on what humans had gone through in those extraordinary decades, and it would be nice to think that *Birdsong* had contributed in some small way. I occasionally now meet people who seem proprietary about the book, as though they, not I, had written it; at other times, seeing it on exam syllabuses and reading lists, I feel that it has passed into a sort of common ownership. The years pass, and there will probably come a moment when I no longer remember the daily ascent to the top floor of Edward's house, pausing only to say good morning to his new-born son, Leo, on the way up; a time when I'll forget the clacking of the portable typewriter keys and the way that Jeanne Fourmentier and Captain Gray, two characters initially unknown to me, emerged from some misty hinterland to claim their places in the story. The day will come when I no longer recall the ache of fingers, the taste of tea from the white Thermos or the sight of the slowly growing pile of A4 paper; and I could wish no better fate for this or any other book than to find a life in the minds of others.

© *Sebastian Faulks, 2011*

'When I go from hence, let this be my parting word, that what I have seen is unsurpassable.'

Rabindranath Tagore, *Gitanjali*

PART ONE
FRANCE 1910

THE BOULEVARD DU CANGE was a broad, quiet street that marked the eastern flank of the city of Amiens. The wagons that rolled in from Lille and Arras to the north made directly into the tanneries and mills of the Saint-Leu quarter without needing to use this rutted, leafy road. The town side of the boulevard backed on to substantial gardens which were squared off and apportioned with civic precision to the houses they adjoined. On the damp grass were chestnut trees, lilac and willows, cultivated to give shade and quietness to their owners. The gardens had a wild, overgrown look and their deep lawns and bursting hedges could conceal small clearings, quiet pools, and areas unvisited even by the inhabitants, where patches of grass and wild flowers lay beneath the branches of overhanging trees.

Behind the gardens the river Somme broke up into small canals that were the picturesque feature of Saint-Leu; on the other side of the boulevard these had been made into a series of water-gardens, little islands of damp fertility divided by the channels of the split river. Long, flat-bottomed boats propelled by poles took the town-dwellers through the waterways on Sunday afternoons. All along the river and its streams sat fishermen, slumped on their rods; in hats and coats beneath the cathedral and in shirtsleeves by the banks of the water-gardens, they dipped their lines in search of trout or carp.

The Azaires' house showed a strong, formal front towards the road from behind iron railings. The traffic looping down

3

towards the river would have been in no doubt that this was the property of a substantial man. The slate roof plunged in conflicting angles to cover the irregular shape of the house. Beneath one of them a dormer window looked out on to the boulevard. The first floor was dominated by a stone balcony over whose balustrades the red creeper had made its way up to the roof. There was a formidable front door with iron facings on the timber.

Inside, the house was both smaller and larger than it looked. It had no rooms of intimidating grandeur, no gilt ballrooms with dripping chandeliers, yet it had unexpected spaces and corridors that disclosed new corners with steps down into the gardens; there were small salons equipped with writing desks and tapestry-covered chairs that opened inwards from unregarded passageways. Even from the end of the lawn it was difficult to see how the rooms and corridors were fitted into the placid rectangles of stone. Throughout the building the floors made distinctive sounds beneath the press of feet, so that with its closed angles and echoing air the house was always a place of unseen footsteps.

Stephen Wraysford's metal trunk had been sent ahead and was waiting at the foot of the bed. He unpacked his clothes and hung his spare suit in the giant carved wardrobe. There was an enamel wash bowl and wooden towel rail beneath the window. He had to stand on tiptoe to look out over the boulevard where a cab was waiting on the other side of the street, the horse shaking its harness and reaching up its neck to nibble at the branches of a lime tree. He tested the resilience of the bed, then lay down on it, resting his head on the concealed bolster. The room was simple but had been decorated with some care. There was a vase of wild flowers on the table and prints of street scenes in Honfleur on either side of the door.

It was a spring evening with a late sun in the sky beyond the cathedral and the sounds of blackbirds from either side of the house. Stephen washed perfunctorily and tried to flatten his black hair in the small looking glass. He placed half a dozen cigarettes in a metal case which he tucked inside his jacket. He emptied his pockets of items he no longer needed: railway

4

tickets, a blue leather notebook and a knife with a single, scrupulously sharpened, blade.

He went downstairs to dinner, startled by the sound of his steps on the two staircases that took him to the landing of the first floor and the family bedrooms, and thence down to the hall. He felt hot beneath his waistcoat and jacket. He stood for a moment disorientated, unsure which of the four glass-panelled doors that opened off the hall was the one through which he was supposed to go. He half-opened one and found himself looking into a steam-filled kitchen in the middle of which a maid was loading plates on to a tray on a large deal table.

'This way, Monsieur. Dinner is served,' said the maid, squeezing past him in the doorway.

In the dining room the family were already seated. Madame Azaire stood up.

'Ah, Monsieur, your seat is here.'

Azaire muttered an introduction of which Stephen heard only the words 'my wife'. He took her hand and bowed his head briefly. Two children were staring at him from the other side of the table.

'Lisette,' Madame Azaire said, gesturing to a girl of perhaps sixteen with dark hair in a ribbon, who smirked and held out her hand, 'and Grégoire.' This was a boy of about ten, whose small head was barely visible above the table, beneath which he was swinging his legs vigorously backwards and forwards.

The maid hovered at Stephen's shoulder with a tureen of soup. Stephen lowered a ladleful of it into his plate and smelt the scent of some unfamiliar herb. Beneath the concentric rings of swirling green the soup was thickened with potato.

Azaire had already finished his and sat rapping his knife in a persistent rhythm against its silver rest. Stephen lifted searching eyes above the soup spoon as he sucked the liquid over his teeth.

'How old are you?' said the boy.

'Grégoire!'

'It doesn't matter,' said Stephen to Madame Azaire. 'Twenty.'

'Do you drink wine?' said Azaire, holding a bottle over Stephen's glass.

'Thank you.'

Azaire poured out an inch or two for Stephen and for his wife before returning the bottle to its place.

'So what do you know about textiles?' said Azaire. He was only forty years old but could have been ten years more. His body was of a kind that would neither harden nor sag with age. His eyes had an alert, humourless glare.

'A little,' said Stephen. 'I have worked in the business for nearly four years, though mostly dealing with financial matters. My employer wanted me to understand more of the manufacturing process.'

The maid took away the soup plates and Azaire began to talk about the local industries and the difficulties he had had with his work force. He owned a factory in town and another a few miles outside.

'The organization of the men into their syndicates leaves me very little room for manoeuvre. They complain they are losing their jobs because we have introduced machinery, but if we cannot compete with our competitors in Spain and England, then we have no hope.'

The maid brought in a dish of sliced meat in thin gravy which she placed in front of Madame Azaire. Lisette began to tell a story of her day at school. She tossed her head and giggled as she spoke. The story concerned a prank played by one girl on another, but Lisette's telling of it contained a second level. It was as though she recognized the childish nature of what she said and wanted to intimate to Stephen and her parents that she herself was too grown-up for such things. But where her own interests and tastes now lay she seemed unsure; she stammered a little before tailing off and turning to rebuke her brother for his laughter.

Stephen watched her as she spoke, his dark eyes scrutinizing her face. Azaire ignored his daughter as he helped himself to salad and passed the bowl to his wife. He ran a piece of bread round the rim of the plate where traces of the gravy remained.

Madame Azaire had not fully engaged Stephen's eye. In return he avoided hers, as though waiting to be addressed, but within his peripheral view fell the sweep of her strawberry-chestnut hair, caught and held up off her face. She wore a white lace blouse with a dark red stone at the throat.

As they finished dinner there was a ring at the front door and they heard a hearty male voice in the hall.

Azaire smiled for the first time. 'Good old Bérard. On the dot as usual!'

'Monsieur and Madame Bérard,' said the maid as she opened the door.

'Good evening to you, Azaire. Madame, delighted.' Bérard, a heavily set grey-haired man in his fifties, lowered his lips to Madame Azaire's hand. His wife, almost equally well built, though with thick hair wound up on top of her head, shook hands and kissed the children on the cheek.

'I am sorry, I didn't hear your name when René introduced us,' said Bérard to Stephen.

While Stephen repeated it and spelled it out for him, the children were dismissed and the Bérards installed in their place.

Azaire seemed rejuvenated by their arrival. 'Brandy for you, Bérard? And for you, Madame, a little tisane, I think? Isabelle, ring for coffee also, please. Now then –'

'Before you go any further,' said Bérard, holding up his fleshy hand, 'I have some bad news. The dyers have called for a strike to begin tomorrow. The syndicate chiefs met the employers' representatives at five this evening and that is their decision.'

Azaire snorted. 'I thought the meeting was tomorrow.'

'It was brought forward to today. I don't like to bring you bad tidings, my dear René, but you would not have thanked me if you had learned it from your foreman tomorrow. At least I suppose it won't affect your factory immediately.'

Bérard in fact appeared to have enjoyed delivering the news. His face expressed a quiet satisfaction at the importance it had conferred on him. Madame Bérard looked admiringly at her husband.

Azaire continued to curse the work force and to ask how they expected him to keep his factories going. Stephen and the women were reluctant to give an opinion and Bérard, having delivered the news, seemed to have no further contribution to make on the subject.

'So,' he said, when Azaire had run on long enough, 'a strike of dyers. There it is, there it is.'

This conclusion was taken by all, including Azaire, as the termination of the subject.

'How did you travel?' said Bérard.

'By train,' said Stephen, assuming he was being addressed. 'It was a long journey.'

'Ah, the trains,' said Bérard. 'What a system! We are a great junction here. Trains to Paris, to Lille, to Boulogne . . . Tell me, do you have trains in England?'

'Yes.'

'Since when?'

'Let me see . . . For about seventy years.'

'But you have problems in England, I think.'

'I'm not sure. I wasn't aware of any.'

Bérard smiled happily as he drank his brandy. 'So there it is. They have trains now in England.'

The course of the conversation depended on Bérard; he took it as his burden to act as a conductor, to bring in the different voices, and then summarize what they had contributed.

'And in England you eat meat for breakfast every day,' he said.

'I think most people do,' said Stephen.

'Imagine, dear Madame Azaire, roast meat for breakfast every day!' Bérard invited his hostess to speak.

She declined, but murmured something about the need to open a window.

'Perhaps one day we shall do the same, eh, René?'

'Oh, I doubt it, I doubt it,' said Azaire. 'Unless one day we have the London fog as well.'

'Oh, and the rain,' laughed Bérard. 'It rains five days out of six in London, I believe.' He looked towards Stephen again.

'I read in a newspaper that last year it rained a little less in London than in Paris, though –'

'Five days out of six,' beamed Bérard. 'Can you imagine?'

'Papa can't stand the rain,' Madame Bérard told Stephen.

'And how have you passed this beautiful spring day, dear Madame?' said Bérard, again inviting a contribution from his hostess. This time he was successful, and Madame Azaire, out

8

of politeness or enthusiasm, addressed him directly.

'This morning I was out doing some errands in the town. There was a window open in a house near the cathedral and someone was playing the piano.' Madame Azaire's voice was cool and low. She spent some time describing what she had heard. 'It was a beautiful thing,' she concluded, 'though just a few notes. I wanted to stop and knock on the door of the house and ask whoever was playing it what it was called.'

Monsieur and Madame Bérard looked startled. It was evidently not the kind of thing they had expected. Azaire spoke with the soothing voice of one used to such fancies. 'And what was the tune, my dear?'

'I don't know. I had never heard it before. It was just a tune like . . . Beethoven or Chopin.'

'I doubt it was Beethoven if you failed to recognize it, Madame,' said Bérard gallantly. 'It was one of those folk songs, I'll bet you anything.'

'It didn't sound like that,' said Madame Azaire.

'I can't bear these folk tunes you hear so much of these days,' Bérard continued. 'When I was a young man it was different. Of course, everything was different then.' He laughed with wry self-recognition. 'But give me a proper melody that's been written by one of our great composers any day. A song by Schubert or a nocturne by Chopin, something that will make the hairs of your head stand on end! The function of music is to liberate in the soul those feelings which normally we keep locked up in the heart. The great composers of the past were able to do this, but the musicians of today are satisfied with four notes in a line you can sell on a song-sheet at the street corner. Genius does not find its recognition quite as easily as that, my dear Madame Azaire!'

Stephen watched as Madame Azaire turned her head slowly so that her eyes met those of Bérard. He saw them open wider as they focused on his smiling face on which small drops of perspiration stood out in the still air of the dining room. How on earth, he wondered, could she be the mother of the girl and boy who had been with them at dinner?

'I do think I should open that window,' she said coldly, and stood up with a rustle of silk skirt.

'And you too are a musical man, Azaire?' said Bérard. 'It's a good thing to have music in a household where there are children. Madame Bérard and I always encouraged our children in their singing.'

Stephen's mind was racing as Bérard's voice went on and on. There was something magnificent about the way Madame Azaire turned this absurd man aside. He was only a small-town bully, it was true, but he was clearly used to having his own way.

'I have enjoyed evenings at the concert hall,' said Azaire modestly, 'though I should hesitate to describe myself as a "musical man" on account of that. I merely –'

'Nonsense. Music is a democratic form of art. You don't need money to buy it or education to study it. All you need is a pair of these.' Bérard took hold of his large pink ears and shook them. 'Ears. The gift of God at birth. You must not be shy about your preference, Azaire. That can only lead to the triumph of inferior taste through the failing of false modesty.' Bérard sat back in his chair and glanced towards the now open window. The draught seemed to spoil his enjoyment of the epigram he had pretended to invent. 'But forgive me, René,' he said. 'I cut you off.'

Azaire was working at his black briar pipe, tamping down the tobacco with his fingers and testing its draw by sucking noisily on it. When it was done to his satisfaction he struck a match and for a moment a blue spiral of smoke encircled his bald head. In the silence before he could reply to his friend, they heard the birds in the garden outside.

'Patriotic songs,' said Azaire. 'I have a particular fondness for them. The sound of bands playing and a thousand voices lifted together to sing the Marseillaise as the army went off to fight the Prussians. What a day that must have been!'

'But if you'll forgive me,' said Bérard, 'that is an example of music being used for a purpose – to instil a fighting valour in the hearts of our soldiers. When any art is put to practical ends it loses its essential purity. Am I not right, Madame Azaire?'

'I daresay you are, Monsieur. What does Monsieur Wraysford think?'

Stephen, momentarily startled, look at Madame Azaire and found her eyes on his for the first time. 'I have no view on that, Madame,' he said, recovering his composure. 'But I think if any song can touch the heart, then one should value it.'

Bérard suddenly held out his hand. 'A little brandy, if you please, Azaire. Thank you. Now then. I am going to do something in which I risk playing the fool and making you think ill of me.'

Madame Bérard laughed incredulously.

'I am going to sing. Yes, there's no point in trying to dissuade me. I am going to sing a little song that was popular when I was a boy, and that, I can assure you, was very many years ago.'

It was the speed with which, having made his declaration, Bérard launched into his song that surprised his listeners. One moment they had been making formal after-dinner conversation, the next they had been turned into a trapped audience as Bérard leant forward in his chair, elbows on the table, and sang in a warbling baritone.

He fixed his eyes on Madame Azaire, who was sitting opposite. She was unable to hold his gaze, but looked down at her plate. Her discomfort did not deflect Bérard. Azaire was fiddling with his pipe and Stephen studied the wall above Bérard's head. Madame Bérard watched with a proud smile as her husband made the gift of his song to his hostess. Madame Azaire blushed and squirmed in her chair under the unblinking stare of the singer.

The dewlaps on his neck wobbled as he turned his head for emphasis at a touching part of the song. It was a sentimental ballad about the different times of a man's life. Its chorus ran, 'But then I was young and the leaves were green/Now the corn is cut and the little boat sailed away.'

At the end of each refrain Bérard would pause dramatically and Stephen would allow his eyes a quick glance to see if he had finished. For a moment there was utter silence in the hot dining room, but then would come another deep inhalation and a further verse.

'"One day the young men came back from the war,
The corn was high and our sweethearts were waiting . . ."'

Bérard's head revolved a little as he sang, and his voice grew louder as he warmed to the song, but his bloodshot eyes remained fixed on Madame Azaire, as though his head could turn only on the axis of his stare. By an effort of will she appeared to compose herself and stiffen her body against the intimacy of his attention.

'". . . and the little boat sailed away-y-y." There,' said Bérard, coming abruptly to an end, 'I told you I should make a fool of myself!'

The others all protested that, on the contrary, the song had been magnificent.

'Papa has a beautiful voice,' said Madam Bérard, flushed with pride.

Madame Azaire's face was also pink, though not from the same emotion. Azaire became falsely jovial and Stephen felt a drop of sweat run down inside the back of his collar. Only Bérard himself was completely unembarrassed.

'Now, Azaire, what about a game of cards? What shall it be?'

'Excuse me, René,' said Madame Azaire, 'I have a slight headache. I think I shall go to bed. Perhaps Monsieur Wraysford would like to take my place.'

Stephen stood up as Madame Azaire rose from her chair. There were protests and anxious enquiries from the Bérards which Madame Azaire waved away with a smile, assuring them she was perfectly all right. Bérard lowered his face to her hand and Madame Bérard kissed the still-pink skin of Madame Azaire's cheek. There were a few freckles on her bare forearm, Stephen noticed as she turned to the door, a tall, suddenly commanding figure in a blood-red skirt that swept over the floor of the hall.

'Let's go into the sitting room,' said Azaire. 'Monsieur, I trust you will join us to make up our card game.'

'Yes, of course,' said Stephen, forcing a smile of acquiescence.

'Poor Madame Azaire,' said Madame Bérard, as they settled at the card table. 'I hope she hasn't caught a chill.'

Azaire laughed. 'No, no. It's just her nerves. Think nothing of it.'

'Such a delicate creature,' murmured Bérard. 'Your deal, I think, Azaire.'

'Nevertheless, a headache can mean the beginning of a fever,' said Madame Bérard.

'Madame,' said Azaire, 'I assure you that Isabelle has no fever. She is a woman of nervous temperament. She suffers from headaches and various minor maladies. It signifies nothing. Believe me, I know her very well and I have learned how to live with her little ways.' He gave a glance of complicity towards Bérard, who chuckled. 'You yourself are fortunate in having a robust constitution.'

'Has she always suffered from headaches?' Madame Bérard was persistent.

Azaire's lips stretched into a narrow smile. 'It is a small price one pays. It is you to play, Monsieur.'

'What?' Stephen looked down at his cards. 'I'm sorry. I wasn't concentrating.' He had been watching Azaire's smile and wondering what it meant.

Bérard talked to Azaire about the strike as they laid down their cards on the table with swift assurance.

Stephen tried to concentrate on the game and to engage Madame Bérard in some sort of conversation. She seemed indifferent to his attention, though her face lit up whenever her husband addressed her.

'What these strikers need,' said Azaire, 'is for someone to call their bluff. I'm not prepared to see my business stagnate because of the gross demands of a few idle men. Some owner has to have the strength to stand up to them and sack the whole lot.'

'I fear there would be violence. The mobs would rampage,' said Bérard.

'Not without food in their stomachs.'

'I'm not sure it would be wise for a town councillor like yourself, René, to be involved in such a dispute.'

Bérard took up the pack to shuffle it; his thick fingers moved dextrously over the rippling cards. When he had dealt, he lit a cigar and sat back in his chair, pulling his waistcoat smartly down over his belly.

The maid came in to ask if there was anything further.

Stephen stifled a yawn. He had been travelling since the previous day and was drawn to the idea of his modest room with the starched sheets and the view across the boulevard.

'No, thank you,' said Azaire. 'Please go to Madame Azaire's room on your way to bed and tell her I shall look in to see if she's all right later.'

For a moment Stephen thought he had seen another half-glance of complicity between the two men, but when he looked at Bérard his face was absorbed in the cards that were fanned out in his hand.

Stephen said goodbye to the visitors when they finally got up to leave. He stood at the window of the sitting room, watching them in the light of the porch. Bérard put on a top hat as though he were some baron on his way home from the opera; Madame Bérard, her face glowing, wrapped her cape round her and took his arm. Azaire leaned forward from the waist and talked in what looked like an urgent whisper.

A soft rain had begun to fall outside, loosening the earth at the sides of the rutted tracks on the road and sounding the leaves on the plane trees. It gave a greasy film to the window of the sitting room and then formed larger drops which began to run down the glass. Behind it Stephen's pale face was visible as he watched the departing guests – a tall figure with hands thrust into his pockets, his eyes patient and intent, the angle of his body that of a youthful indifference cultivated by willpower and necessity. It was a face which in turn most people treated cautiously, unsure whether its ambivalent expressions would resolve themselves into passion or acquiescence.

Up in his room Stephen listened to the noises of the night. A loose shutter turned slowly on its hinges and banged against the wall at the back of the house. There was an owl somewhere deep in the gardens, where the cultivation gave way to wildness. There was also the irregular wheeze and rush of the plumbing in its narrow pipes.

Stephen sat down at the writing table by the window and opened a notebook with pages ruled in thick blue lines. It was half-full with inky writing that spread over the lines in clusters that erupted from the red margin on the left. There were dates at intervals in the text, though there were gaps of days and sometimes weeks between them.

He had kept a notebook for five years, since a master at the grammar school had suggested it. The hours of Greek and Latin study had given him an unwanted but ingrained knowledge of the languages that he used as the basis of a code. When the subject matter was sensitive, he would change the sex of the characters and note their actions or his responses with phrases that could not mean anything to a chance reader.

He laughed softly to himself as he wrote. This sense of secrecy was something he had had to cultivate in order to overcome a natural openness and a quick temper. At the age of ten or eleven his artless enthusiasm and outraged sense of right and wrong had made him the despair of his teachers, but he had slowly learned to breathe and keep calm, not to trust his responses, but to wait and be watchful.

His cuffs loosened, he held his face in his hands and looked at the blank wall ahead of him. There came a noise that this time was not the shutter or the sound of water but something shriller and more human. It came again, and Stephen crossed the room to listen for it. He opened the door on to the landing and stepped out gently, remembering the sound his feet had made before. The noise was of a woman's voice, he was almost sure, and it was coming from the floor below.

He took off his shoes, slid them quietly over the threshold of his room and began to creep down the stairs. It was completely dark in the house; Azaire must have turned off all the lights on his way to bed. Stephen felt the spring of the wooden treads beneath his socks and the line of the banister under his exploring hand. He had no fear.

On the first-floor landing he hesitated. The size of the house and the number of possible directions from which the noise could have come became dauntingly clear. Three passageways opened from the landing, one of them up a small step leading towards the front of the house and two going sideways along the length of it before breaking up into further corridors. A whole family and its servants, to say nothing of bathrooms, laundries or stores, was on this floor. He could wander by

15

chance into a cook's bedroom or an upstairs salon with Chinese ornaments and Louis XVI silks.

He listened intently, stifling his own breath for a moment. There was a different sound now, not identifiably a woman's voice, but a lower note, almost like sobbing, interrupted by a more material sound of brief impact. Stephen wondered if he should continue. He had left his room impulsively in the belief that something was wrong; now it seemed to him he might merely be trespassing on the privacy of some member of the household. But he did not falter long because he knew that the noise was not a normal one.

He took a passageway to the right, walking with exaggerated care, one arm in front of him to protect his eyes from harm, and one feeling along the wall. The passageway came to a junction, and looking leftwards Stephen saw a narrow bar of light coming from beneath a closed door. He calculated how close to the door he should go. He wanted to remain sufficiently near to the turn in the corridor that he would have time to double back into it and out of sight of anyone emerging from the room.

He went to within half a dozen paces, which was as close as he dared. He stopped and listened, again quelling his own breathing so he would not miss a sound. He could feel the swell of his heart against his chest and a light pulse in the flesh of his neck.

He heard a woman's voice, cool and low, though made intense by desperation. She was pleading, and the words, though indistinct because of the way she kept her voice down, were made audible in places by the urgency of the feeling behind them. Stephen could distinguish the word 'René', and later 'I implore you', and then 'children'. The voice, which he recognized even on this slight evidence as Madame Azaire's, was cut short by the thudding sound he had heard before. It turned to a gasp which, because of its sudden move into a higher register, was clearly one of pain.

Stephen moved forward along the corridor, his hands no longer raised cautiously in front of him but tensed into fists by his ribs. A step or two short of the door he managed to control his sense of confused anger. For the first time he heard a

16

man's voice. It was repeating a single word in a broken, unconvinced tone that gave way to a sob. Then there were footsteps.

Stephen turned and ran for the cover of the passageway, knowing he had advanced beyond the limit he had set himself. As he turned the corner he heard Azaire's quizzical voice. 'Is there anyone there?' He tried to remember whether there had been any hazards on his way as he ran back towards the landing without time to check that his path was clear. From the foot of the stairs going up to the second floor he could see that some light was coming from his room. He took the steps two at a time and plunged towards the switch on the table lamp, causing it to rock and bang as he reached it.

He stood still in the middle of the room, listening. He could hear footsteps reach the bottom of the stairs below. If Azaire came up he would wonder why he was standing fully dressed in the middle of a dark room. He moved to the bed and slid under the covers.

After ten minutes he thought it safe to undress for bed. He closed the door and the shutter on the small window and sat down in his nightclothes at the writing table. He read over the entry he had written earlier, which described his journey from London, the train in France and the arrival in the boulevard du Cange. It made brief comments on the character of Bérard and his wife, under heavy disguise, and gave his impressions of Azaire and the two children. He saw, with some surprise, that what had struck him most he had not written about at all.

RISING IN THE morning with a clear head, rested, and full of interest in his new surroundings, Stephen put the happenings of the night from his mind and submitted to a full tour of Azaire's business operations.

They left the prosperity of the boulevard and walked to Saint-Leu quarter, which looked to Stephen like a medieval engraving, with gabled houses leaning over cobbled streets above the canals. There were washing lines attached to crooked walls and drainpipes; small children in ragged clothes played hide-and-seek on the bridges and ran sticks along the iron railings at the water's edge. Women carried buckets of drinking water collected from the fountains in the better areas of town to their numerous offspring, some of whom waited in the family's single room, while others, mostly immigrants from the countryside of Picardy who had come in search of work, lodged in makeshift shelters in the back yards of the bursting houses. There was the noise of poverty that comes from children on the streets and their mothers screaming threats or admonishments or calling out important news to neighbours. There was the racket of cohabitation when no household is closed to another, there were voices from the crowded bakeries and shops, while the men with barrows and horse-drawn carts cried up their goods a dozen times on each street.

Azaire moved nimbly through the crowd, took Stephen's arm as they crossed a wooden bridge, turned from the shouted abuse of a surly adolescent boy, led the way up a wrought-iron staircase on the side of a building and delivered them both into a first-floor office that looked down on to a factory floor.

'Sit down. I have a meeting now with Meyraux, who is my senior man and also, as a punishment for whatever sins I have committed, the head of the syndicate.' Azaire pointed to a leather-covered seat on the far side of a desk piled with papers. He went down the internal steps to the factory floor, leaving Stephen to look out through the glass walls of the office on to the scene below.

The workers were mostly women, sitting at spinning machines at the far end of the room, though there were also men and boys in flat leather caps at work on the machines or transporting yarn or bolts of material on little wooden-wheeled wagons. There was a rhythmical clatter from the antiquated jennys which almost drowned the shouts of the foreman, a red-faced man with a moustache who strode up and down in a coat that came down almost to his ankles. At the near end of the factory were rows of workers at Singer sewing machines, their knees rising and falling as they pumped the mechanism, their hands working in flat opposition to one another, going rapidly this way then that, as though adjusting the pressure on a huge tap. To Stephen, who had spent many hours on such premises in England, the process looked old-fashioned, in the same way that the streets of Saint-Leu seemed to belong to a different century from the terraces of the mill towns of Lancashire.

Azaire returned with Meyraux, a small, fleshy man with thick dark hair swept across his forehead. Meyraux had the look of someone honest who had been driven to suspicion and a profound stubbornness. He shook hands with Stephen, though the reserved look in his eye seemed to indicate that Stephen should read nothing into the formality. When Azaire offered him a seat Meyraux hovered for a moment before apparently deciding that this did not necessarily amount to a capitulation. He sat square and unbudgeable in the chair, though his fingers fluttered in his lap as though weaving invisible strands of cotton.

'As you know, Meyraux, Monsieur Wraysford has come to

19

visit us from England. He is a young man and wants to learn a little more about our business.'

Meyraux nodded. Stephen smiled at him. He enjoyed the feeling of being unlicensed, disqualified by his age from responsibility or commitment. He could see the entrenched weariness of the older men.

'However,' Azaire went on, 'as you also know, Monsieur Wraysford's compatriots in Manchester are able to produce the same cloth as we do for two-thirds of the price. Since the company he works for is one of our major customers in England, it is only fair that we should try to impress him. I understand from his employer, who is a most far-sighted man, that he would like to see more cooperation between the two countries. He has talked about taking shares in the company.'

Meyraux's fingers were jabbing faster. 'Another Cosserat,' he said dismissively.

Azaire smiled. 'My dear Meyraux, you mustn't be so suspicious.' He turned to Stephen. 'He is referring to one of the great producers, Eugène Cosserat, who many years ago imported English workers and techniques –'

'At the cost of several jobs among local people.'

Azaire continued to address Stephen. 'The government wants us to rationalize our operations, to try to bring more of them under one roof. This is a perfectly reasonable thing to want to do, but it inevitably means greater use of machinery and a consequent loss of jobs.'

'What the industry needs,' said Meyraux, 'as the government has been saying since my father's day, is more investment and a less mean and timid attitude on the part of the owners.'

Azaire's face became suddenly rigid, whether from anger or simple distaste was impossible to say. He sat down, put on a pair of spectacles and pulled a piece of paper towards him from the pile on the table.

'We are in difficult times. We have no money to invest and we can therefore only retrench. These are my specific proposals. Employees on salaries will take a cut of one per cent. Those on piecework will be paid at the same rate but will have to raise output by an average of five per cent. Their output

20

will no longer be measured by the metre but by the piece. Those not qualified to use the new machinery, about half the work force, will be reclassified as untrained workers and their rate of pay will be adjusted accordingly.'

He took off his glasses and pushed the piece of paper towards Meyraux. Stephen was surprised by the simplicity of Azaire's assault. He had made no pretence that the work force had anything to gain from the new arrangements or that they would make up in some other way for what they were clearly being asked to forgo. Perhaps it was just a first bargaining position.

Meyraux, confronted with the details, was impressively calm. 'It's about what I expected,' he said. 'You appear to be asking us to settle for even less than the dyers, Monsieur. I need hardly remind you what situation they are in.'

Azaire began to fill his pipe. 'Who is behind that nonsense?' he said.

'What is behind it,' said Meyraux, 'are the attempts of the owners to use slave labour at diminishing levels of pay.'

'You know what I mean,' said Azaire.

'The name of Lucien Lebrun is being mentioned.'

'Little Lucien! I didn't think he had the courage.'

It was bright in the glass office, the sunlight streaming in across the books and papers on the table beneath the window and illuminating the faces of the two antagonists. Stephen watched their hard exchange but felt dissociated from it, as though they only spoke in slogans. From the subject of Azaire's wealth, his mind moved naturally to possessions, to the house on the boulevard, the garden, the plump children, Grégoire with his bored eyes, Lisette with her suggestive smile, and above all to Madame Azaire, a figure he viewed with an incompatible mixture of feelings.

'. . . the natural consequence of a production with so many separate processes,' said Azaire.

'Well, I too would like to see the dyeing done here,' said Meyraux, 'but as you know . . .'

He could not be sure of her age, and there was something in the vulnerability of her skin where he had seen the goosepimples rise on her arm in a draught from the garden.

There was something above all in the impatience he had seen in the turn of her head that concealed the expression of her eyes.

'. . . would you not agree, Monsieur Wraysford?'

'I certainly would.'

'Not if we were to invest in larger premises,' said Meyraux.

I am mad, thought Stephen, quelling a desire to laugh; I must be insane to be sitting in this hot glass office watching the face of this man discussing the employment of hundreds and I am thinking things I can't admit even to myself while smiling my complicity to . . .

'I will not discuss it further in the presence of this young man,' said Meyraux. 'Forgive me, Monsieur.' He stood up and inclined his head formally towards Stephen. 'It's nothing personal.'

'Of course,' said Stephen, also standing up. 'Nothing personal.'

In his notebook the code word Stephen used when describing a certain aspect of Madame Azaire and of his confused feeling towards her was 'pulse'. It seemed to him to be sufficiently cryptic, yet also to suggest something of his suspicion that she was animated by a different kind of rhythm from that which beat in her husband's blood. It also referred to an unusual aspect of her physical presence. No one could have been more proper in their dress and toilet than Madame Azaire. She spent long parts of the day bathing or changing her clothes; she carried a light scent of rose soap or perfume when she brushed past him in the passageways. Her clothes were more fashionable than those of other women in the town yet revealed less. She carried herself modestly when she sat or stood; she slid into chairs with her feet close together so that beneath the folds of her skirts her knees too must have been almost touching. When she rose again it was without any leverage from her hands or arms but with a spontaneous upward movement of grace and propriety. Her white hands seemed barely to touch the cutlery when they ate at the family dinner table and her lips left no trace of their presence on the wine glass. On one occasion, Stephen had noticed, some tiny adhesion caused the membrane of her lower lip to linger for a fraction of a second as she pulled the glass away to return it to its place, but still the surface of it had remained clear and shining. She caught him staring at it.

Yet despite her formality towards him and her punctilious ease of manner, Stephen sensed some other element in what he had termed the pulse of her. It was impossible to say through which sense he had the impression, but somehow, perhaps only in the tiny white hairs on the skin of her bare arm or the blood he had seen rise beneath the light freckles of her cheekbones, he felt certain there was some keener physical life than she was actually living in the calm, restrictive rooms of her husband's house with its oval doorhandles of polished china and its neatly hatched parquet floors.

A WEEK LATER Azaire suggested to Meyraux that he should bring Stephen to eat with the men in a room at the back of the factory where they had lunch. There were two or three long refectory tables at which they could either eat the food they had brought or buy whatever dish had been cooked by a woman with a white headscarf and missing teeth.

On the third day, in the middle of a general conversation, Stephen stood up abruptly, said, 'Excuse me,' and rushed from the room.

An elderly man called Jacques Bonnet followed him outside and found him leaning against the wall of the factory. He put a friendly hand on Stephen's shoulder and asked if he was all right.

Stephen's face was pale and two lines of sweat ran from his forehead. 'Yes, I'm fine,' he said.

'What was the matter? Don't you feel well?'

'It was probably just too hot. I'll be fine.' He took out a handkerchief and wiped his face.

Bonnet said, 'Why don't you come back inside and finish your lunch? It looked a nice bit of rabbit the old woman had cooked up.'

'No!' Stephen was trembling. 'I won't go back. I'm sorry.'

He pulled himself away from Bonnet's paternal hand and moved off briskly into the town. 'Tell Azaire I'll be back later,' he called over his shoulder.

At dinner the following day Azaire asked him if he had recovered.

'Yes, thank you,' said Stephen. 'There was nothing the matter with me. I just felt a little faint.'

'Faint? It sounds like a problem of the circulation.'

'I don't know. There's something in the air, it may be one of the chemicals used by the dyers, I'm not sure. It makes it hard for me to breathe.'

'Perhaps you should see a doctor, then. I can easily arrange an appointment.'

'No, thank you. It's nothing.'

Azaire's gaze had filled with something like amusement. 'I don't like to think of you having some kind of fit. I could easily –'

'For goodness' sake, René,' said Madame Azaire. 'He's told you that there's nothing to worry about. Why don't you leave him alone?'

Azaire's fork made a loud clatter as he laid it down on his plate. For a moment his face had an expression of panic, like that of the schoolboy who suffers a sudden reverse and can't understand the rules of behaviour by which his rival has won approval. Then he began to smile sardonically, as though to indicate that really he knew best and that his decision not to argue further was a temporary indulgence he was granting his juniors. He turned to his wife with a teasing lightness of manner.

'And have you heard your minstrel again in your wanderings in the town, my dear?'

She looked down at her plate. 'I was not wandering, René. I was doing errands.'

'Of course, my dear. My wife is a mysterious creature, Monsieur,' he said to Stephen. 'No one knows – like the little stream in the song – whither she flows or where her end will be.'

Stephen held his teeth together in order to prevent himself protesting on Madame Azaire's behalf.

'I don't suppose Monsieur Wraysford is familiar with the song,' said Madame Azaire.

'Perhaps Monsieur Bérard would sing it to me.' Stephen found that the words had escaped.

Madame Azaire let out a sudden laugh before she could

25

catch herself. She coughed and Stephen saw the skin of her cheeks stain lightly as her husband glared at her.

Although he was annoyed with himself for what his host might take as rudeness, Stephen's face remained expressionless. Azaire had no spontaneous reaction, like his wife, nor, like Stephen, a contrived one. Fortunately for him Lisette began to giggle and he was able to rebuke her.

'Is Monsieur Bérard a good singer, then?' asked Grégoire, looking up from his plate, his napkin tucked into his collar.

'A very distinguished one,' said Azaire challengingly.

'Indeed,' said Stephen, meeting his gaze with level eyes. Then he looked directly at Madame Azaire. She had recovered her composure and returned his look, for a moment, a dying light of humour still in her face.

'So you didn't pass the house again?' he said to her.

'I believe I walked past it on my way to the chemist, but the window was shut and I didn't hear any music.'

The Bérards came again after dinner and brought with them Madame Bérard's mother, a woman with a wrinkled face who wore a black lace shawl and was said to have great religious sensitivity. Bérard referred to her, for reasons that were not explained, as Aunt Élise, and she asked the others to do likewise. Stephen wondered whether her married name carried painful reminders of her dead husband or whether it was some social secret of his wife's family that Bérard thought it better to conceal.

On that and later occasions Stephen watched the Bérards and the role they played in the lives of the Azaires. On the terrace, when the evenings grew warm enough, the five of them sat in wickerwork chairs with the scent of honeysuckle and jasmine that lay on the lintels and window frames at the back of the house. Bérard in his stout black boots and formal waistcoat conducted his small orchestra with dogged skill, though he always kept the best parts for himself. He was an authority on the important families of the town and could speak at length on the role played by names such as Sellier, Laurendeau or de Morville in the making of its wealth and social fabric. He hinted in a long and indirect way that his own family had had connections with the de Morvilles which, through the negligence of some Bonapartist Bérard, they had failed to ratify. His manner of criticizing this errant ancestor was to belittle the ingratiating habits of Paris society, particularly in its hunger for titles, in such a way that the failure of his forebear, who had remained stubbornly provincial, was portrayed as being virtuous in a timeless manner yet possessing in addition a greater finesse than that displayed by the more artful Parisians. This early Bérard therefore seemed both sturdy and refined, while his descendants themselves were consequently presented both as the inheritors of commendable virtues and as the guileless beneficiaries of superior breeding.

It passed the time. It was a way of getting to the end of peaceful evenings, Stephen supposed, but it made him burn with frustration. He could not understand how Madame Azaire could bear it.

She was the only one who did not respond to Bérard's promptings. She barely contributed when he invited her to do so, but would speak, unbidden, on a subject of her own choice. This appeared to leave Bérard no choice but to cut her off. He would apologize with a small bow of his head, though not for some minutes, and not until he had taken the conversation safely down the path he wanted. Madame Azaire would shrug lightly or smile at his belated apology as though to suggest that what she had been about to say was unimportant.

Aunt Élise's presence was a particular benefit to Bérard, since she could be relied on to raise the tone of any conversation with her religious conviction. Her reputation as a person of patience and sanctity was based on her long widowhood and the large collection of missals, crucifixes and mementoes of pilgrimage she had collected in her bedroom at the Bérards' house. With her blackened mouth and harsh voice she seemed to embody a minatory spiritual truth, that real faith is not to be found in the pale face of the anchorite but in the ravaged lives of those who have had to struggle to survive. Sometimes her laugh seemed more ribald or full-blooded than holy, but in her frequent appeals to the saints she was able to dumbfound her listeners by invoking names and martyrdoms of the early church and its formative years in Asia Minor.

'I'm proposing an afternoon in the water-gardens next Sunday,' said Bérard. 'I wonder if I might interest you in joining us?'

Azaire agreed enthusiastically. Aunt Elise said she was too old for boating and managed to imply that such self-indulgence was not appropriate for a Sunday.

'I should think you're pretty handy with a boat, René?' said Bérard.

'I've got a feel for the water, it's true,' said Azaire.

'Listen to him, the modest old devil,' Bérard laughed. 'If it wasn't for all the evidence to contradict him, he wouldn't even admit to being any good at business.'

Azaire enjoyed being cast in the role of self-effacing joker that Bérard had created for him. He had devised a way of inhaling sceptically when some talent of his was mentioned and following the hissing intake of breath with a sip from the glass he was drinking. He said nothing, so his reputation for wit remained intact, though not to Stephen who, each time Azaire modestly rolled his eyes, remembered the sounds of pain he had heard from the bedroom.

Sometimes from the safety of the sitting room he would fix his eyes on the group and on the vital, unspeaking figure of Madame Azaire. He didn't ask himself if she was beautiful, because the physical effect of her presence made the question insignificant. Perhaps in the harshest judgement of the term she was not. While everything was feminine about her face, her nose was slightly larger than fashion prescribed; her hair had more different shades of brown and gold and red than most women would have wanted. For all the lightness of her face, its obvious strength of character overpowered conventional prettiness. But Stephen made no judgements; he was motivated by compulsion.

Returning one afternoon from work, he found her in the garden, pruning an unchecked group of rose bushes, some of which had grown higher than her head.

'Monsieur.' She greeted him with formality, though not coldly.

Stephen, with no plan of action, merely took the little pruning shears from her hand and said, 'Allow me.'

28

She smiled in a surprised way that forgave his abrupt movement.

He snipped at a few dead flowers before he realized he had no proper sense of what he was trying to do.

'Let me,' she said. Her arm brushed across the front of his suit and her hand touched his as she took the little shears from him. 'You do it like this. Beneath each bloom that's died you cut at a slight angle to the stem, like this. Look.'

The brown petals of a formerly white rose fell away. Stephen moved a little closer to catch the smell of Madame Azaire's laundered clothes. Her skirt was the colour of parched earth; there was a dog-toothed edging to her blouse which suggested patterns or frippery of an earlier, more elaborate age of dressing. The little waistcoat she wore above it was open to reveal a rosy flush at the bottom of her throat, brought on by the small exertion of her gardening. Stephen imagined the different eras of fashion and history summoned by her decorative way of dressing: it suggested victory balls from the battles of Wagram and Borodino or nights of the Second Empire. Her still-unlined face seemed to him to hint at intrigue and worldliness beyond her obvious position.

'I haven't seen your daughter for a day or two,' he said, bringing his reverie to a halt. 'Where is she?'

'Lisette is with her grandmother near Rouen for a few days.'

'How old is Lisette?'

'Sixteen.'

Without meaning to sound ingratiating, Stephen said, 'How is it possible for you to have a daughter of that age?'

'She and Grégoire are my step-children,' said Madame Azaire. 'My husband's first wife died eight years ago and we were married two years after that.'

'I knew it,' he said. 'I knew you couldn't be old enough to have a child that old.'

Madame Azaire smiled again, a little more self-consciously.

He looked at her face, bent over the thorns and dry blooms of the roses, and imagined her flesh beaten by her withered, corrupt husband. Without thinking he reached out and grabbed her hand, folding it in both of his own.

She turned swiftly to him, the blood rushing into her face, her eyes filled with alarm.

Stephen held her hand to the thick serge of his jacket. He said nothing. The satisfaction of acting on impulse had lent him calm. He looked into her eyes as though daring her to respond in a way not dictated by their social positions.

'Monsieur. Please let go of my hand.' She tried to laugh it off.

Stephen noticed that there was not much pressure of withdrawal from her hand itself to accompany her words. The fact that her other hand held the pruning shears made it difficult for her to extract herself without pulling in some way that risked making her lose her composure.

Stephen said, 'The other night I heard sounds from your room. Isabelle –'

'Monsieur, you –'

'Stephen.'

'You must stop this now. You must not humiliate me.'

'I have no wish to humiliate you. Ever. I merely wanted to reassure you.'

It was a strange choice of words, and Stephen felt its oddness as he spoke, but he let go of her hand.

She looked into his face with more composure than she had managed before. 'You must respect my position,' she said.

'I will,' said Stephen. It seemed to him there was some ambiguity in what she had said and that he had capitalized on it by using the future tense in his acquiescence.

Seeing he could not improve on this advance, he dragged himself from her presence.

Madame Azaire watched his tall figure retreat across the grass to the house. She turned back to her roses, shaking her head as though in defiance of some unwanted feeling.

SINCE HIS FLIGHT from the room in the factory where the workers took their meals, Stephen had found a café on the other side of the cathedral where he went each day for lunch. It was a place frequented by young men, students or apprentices, many of whom sat at the same tables each day. The food was prepared by a sturdy Parisian exile who had once had a café in the Place de l'Odéon. Knowing student appetites, he served only one dish, but in quantity, with bread and wine included in the price. His commonest dish was beef, with custards or fruit tart to follow it.

Stephen was halfway through lunch at a seat in the window when he saw a familiar figure bustle past, her head lowered, with a basket on her arm. Her face was concealed by a scarf but he recognized her by her walk and the tartan sash at her waist.

He left some coins spinning on the table as he pushed back his chair and went out into the street. He saw her disappear from the corner of the square and go down a narrow side street. He ran to catch her up. He drew level just as she was pulling the bell handle outside a double door with flaking green paint.

Madame Azaire was flustered when he accosted her. 'Monsieur . . . I, I wasn't expecting you. I am delivering something to a friend.'

'I saw you go past the café I was in. I thought I would come and see if I could help carry anything for you.'

She looked doubtfully at her basket. 'No. No, thank you.'

31

The door was opened by a young man with brown wavy hair and an alert expression. His face showed recognition and urgency.

'Come in,' he said and laid his hand on Madame Azaire's shoulder as he ushered her into a courtyard.

'This is a friend,' she said uncertainly, indicating Stephen, who was lingering in the doorway.

'Come in, come in,' said the man and closed the door behind them.

He led the way across the courtyard and up some stairs to a small apartment. He told them to wait in a cramped sitting room in which the shutters were closed and piles of papers and leaflets lay on the surface of every table and chair.

He returned and pulled back a curtain which let in some light on the cramped and squalid room.

He waved his hand at it and apologized. 'There are five of us living in this little place at the moment.' He held out his hand to Stephen. 'My name is Lucien Lebrun.'

They shook hands and Lucien turned to Madame Azaire. 'Have you heard the news? They have agreed to take back the ten men they sacked last week. They won't back down on the question of pay, but still, it's a start.'

Feeling Stephen's quizzical eyes on her, Madame Azaire said, 'You must wonder what I'm doing here, Monsieur. I bring food to Monsieur Lebrun from time to time and he gives it to one of the dyers' families. Some of them have five or six children – even more in some cases – and they find it hard to live.'

'I see. And your husband doesn't know.'

'He doesn't know. I couldn't involve myself with his workers one way or another but the dyers are a separate group of people, as you know.'

'Don't be apologetic!' said Lucien. 'A gift of food is just an act of Christian charity. And in any case, the injustice done to my people is outrageous. Last week at the local meeting of the syndicate –'

'Don't start on that again.' Madame Azaire laughed.

Lucien smiled. 'I despair of you, Madame.'

Stephen felt an acrid worry at the familiar way in which

Lucien addressed Madame Azaire. He did not feel particularly concerned with the politics of the strike or the ethical nicety of Madame Azaire's position. He only wanted to know how she had come to be on such easy terms with this forceful young man.

He said, 'I think it's time I went back to the factory. Your husband is going to show me the finishing process.'

'You work with Azaire?' Lucien was dumbfounded.

'I work for an English company who have sent me here for a short time.'

'You speak very good French for an Englishman.'

'I learned it in Paris.'

'And what has he told you about the dyers' strike?'

Stephen remembered Azaire's remark about 'little Lucien'.

'Not very much. I think he will be more worried when it begins to affect his own factory.'

Lucien gave a short, animal laugh. 'That won't be long, I can assure you. Madame, will you have something to drink?'

'That's very kind. Perhaps a glass of water.'

Lucien disappeared and Stephen lingered, unwilling to leave Madame Azaire.

'You mustn't think badly of me, Monsieur,' she said.

'Of course not,' said Stephen, pleased that she should care what he thought of her.

'I am loyal to my husband.'

Stephen said nothing. He heard Lucien's footsteps approaching. He reached forward, laid his hand on Madame Azaire's arm and kissed her cheek. He left at once, before he could see the blood he had raised, calling, 'Goodbye,' as though his kiss might have been merely a polite farewell.

ISABELLE AZAIRE, BORN Fourmentier, came from a family
that lived near Rouen. She was the youngest of five sisters and
had disappointed her father by not being the son he had
wanted.

As the youngest child she lived life unregarded by her
parents, who by the time their fifth daughter was born no
longer found much to charm them in the noises and changes
of childhood. Two of her elder sisters, Béatrice and Delphine,
had early in their lives formed an alliance against the remote
tyranny of their father and Madame Fourmentier's manipula-
tive indolence. They were both lively, quick-witted girls with
various talents that went unnoticed and unencouraged by
their parents. They developed a shared selfishness that
prevented them from venturing far from their own mutual
reassurance.

The eldest sister, Mathilde, was given to outbursts of temper and to sulks that could last for days. She had dark hair
and a cold eye that sometimes made even her father think
twice before crossing her. When she was eighteen she
developed a passion for an architect who worked near the
cathedral in Rouen. He was a small, shifty-looking man with
a certain weasel quickness in his movements. He had been
married for ten years and was himself the father of two girls.
Rumours of a growing friendship between them reached
the ears of Monsieur Fourmentier, and there was a noisy
confrontation. From her attic bedroom the five-year-old
Isabelle heard the first sound of adult passion as her father's

34

pleading turned to anger and her sister's well-known temper became something more wailing and elemental. She felt the house tremble as Mathilde slammed the front door behind her.

Isabelle was a child of exceptionally sweet nature. She did not question her parents' indifference. The closest thing she had to a confidante was her sister Jeanne, who was two years older. Jeanne was the most resourceful of the girls. She had not had to make the first moves into the world, like Mathilde, nor was she included in Béatrice and Delphine's alliance. When blood came one day to Isabelle, unexplained and unpredicted, it was Jeanne who explained what their mother, through idleness or prudishness, had failed to do. This blood, Jeanne said, was supposed to be shameful, but she had never thought of it that way. She valued it because it spoke of some greater rhythm of life that would lead them away from the narrow boredom of childhood. Isabelle, who was still shocked by what had happened, was suggestible enough to share Jeanne's private pleasure, though not without a qualm. She could never quite reconcile herself to the fact that this secret thing that promised new life and liberation should manifest itself in the colour of pain.

Isabelle's father was a lawyer who had political ambitions but lacked the ability to realize them or the charm that might have made connections where talent had failed. He became bored by his houseful of women and spent mealtimes reading Parisian newspapers with their accounts of political intrigue. He was unaware of the complexity or passion of the lives led by his family. He would rebuke the girls for bad behaviour and occasionally punish them severely, but he had no other interest in their development. Madame Fourmentier was driven by his indifference into an excessive concern with fashion and appearance. She assumed her husband had a mistress in Rouen and that this was the reason he no longer showed any interest in her. To compensate for this presumed slight she devoted her time to making herself look attractive to men.

A year after her failed affair with the married architect, Mathilde was married off to a local doctor, to the relief of her parents and the envy of her sisters. It was assumed that when the other girls had also left home Isabelle would stay and look after her parents.

'Is that what I'm supposed to do, Jeanne?' she asked her sister. 'Stay here for ever while they grow old?'

'I think they'd like it, but they have no right to expect it. You must find your own life. That's what I'm going to do. If no one marries me I'm going to live in Paris and open a shop.'

'I thought you were going to be a missionary in the jungle.'

'That's only if the shop fails and my lover rejects me.'

Jeanne had a greater sense of humour and detachment than Isabelle's other sisters and their conversations together gave Isabelle the feeling that the things she had read about in books and newspapers were not just the ingredients of other people's lives, as she had once believed, but were open to some extent to her too. She loved Jeanne as she loved no one else.

At the age of eighteen Isabelle was a self-reliant but gentle girl who had no proper outlet either for her natural instincts or for the exuberant energy that was frustrated by the routine and torpor of her parents' house. At her sister Béatrice's wedding she met a young infantry officer called Jean Destournel. He spoke to her kindly and seemed to value her for some quality of her own. Isabelle, who had only ever been made to feel a shadowy version of a child who should in any case have been a boy, was confused to find that someone could think she was unique and worth knowing for herself. Jean was not just anyone, either; he was attentive and handsome in a conventional way. He wrote to her and sent small presents.

After a year of courtship, most of it conducted by letter since Jean's various postings seldom allowed him to be in Rouen, Isabelle's father made one of his rare interventions into family life. He summoned Jean to see him when he came to visit Isabelle and told him he was too old, too junior in rank, too undistinguished in family and too dilatory in his courtship. Destournel, who was essentially a shy man, was taken aback by the force of Fourmentier's objection and began to question his own motives. He was entranced by Isabelle's character and her individual appearance, which was already different from that of most girls of her age. When he had spent an evening in the mess he loved to go to his room and think of this young, vital woman. He allowed his imagination to dwell on the details of her feminine home life, with the trappings of peace and domesticity and the company of her two remaining unmarried sisters, Delphine and Jeanne. He liked to evaluate their comparative worth in his mind and was pleased with his perverse judgement that the youngest one, pretty well unregarded by the others, was the most beautiful and most interesting. But while Isabelle Fourmentier and her pale skin and her fresh clothes and her laughter undoubtedly gave him a wonderful source of relief from the daily details of army life, he was not certain that in his heart he had any definite intention of marrying her. Perhaps if Fourmentier had not interfered it might have come naturally to that; but the sudden advent of self-consciousness prompted a destructive doubt.

A few months later, on his next visit, he took Isabelle for a walk in the garden and told her that he was being posted abroad and that he was not in a position to continue their friendship. He skated round the question of marriage with pleas of poverty and unworthiness. Isabelle didn't care whether he married her or not, but when he said he would not see her again she felt the simple agony of bereavement, like a child whose only source of love has gone.

For three years her loss coloured every moment of her day. When at last it became bearable it was still like a wound on which the skin would not thicken, so the least thing could reopen it. The reckless innocence of her unguided childhood was finished, but eventually a sweetness and balance in her nature returned. At the age of twenty-three she no longer seemed the baby of the house; she appeared older than her age, and began to cultivate a style and manner of her own that were not those of her parents or her elder sisters. Her mother was a little frightened by the certainty of her tastes and the assurance of her opinions. Isabelle felt herself grow, and she met no resistance.

At a party her father heard of a local family called Azaire who had gone to live in Amiens where the wife had died, leaving two young children. He manoeuvred an introduction and distinctly liked the look of René Azaire. Isabelle was not the comfort he had hoped for at home; she had become far too strong-willed to be a housekeeper, and although she was an accomplished helper to her mother she threatened at times to become an embarrassment to him. In the strict and experienced figure of René Azaire, Isabelle's father saw a solution to a number of difficulties.

The match was adroitly sold to Isabelle by both men. Her father played on her sympathy for Azaire while he in turn introduced his children, both then at captivating stages of their lives. Azaire promised her some independence in their marriage, and Isabelle, who longed to be free of her parents' house, agreed. Her interest in Lisette and Grégoire was the most important thing to her; she wanted to help them and to submerge her own disappointments in their successes. It was also agreed that she and Azaire should have children of their own. So she changed from the little Fourmentier girl into Madame Azaire, a woman of dignity beyond her age, of pronounced taste and opinion but with an accumulation of natural impulse and affection that had not been satisfied by any of the circumstances of her life.

Azaire was at first proud to have married such a young and attractive woman and liked to display her to his friends. He saw his children prosper under her attention. Lisette was taken tactfully through the awkward changes in her body; Grégoire was encouraged in his enthusiasms and forced to improve his manners. Madame Azaire was well regarded in the town. She was an affectionate and dutiful wife to her husband, and he required no more from her; she did not love him, but he would have been frightened to have aroused such an unnecessary emotion.

Madame Azaire grew into her new name. She was content with the role she had accepted and thought that her ambitious desires could be safely and permanently forgotten. It was, by a paradox she did not seem to understand at the time, the cold figure of her husband who kept those desires alive.

He saw the production of further children as an important proof of his standing in society and a confirmation that this was a balanced match in which his age and the difference in tastes were not important. He approached his wife in a businesslike and predatory manner; she reacted with the submissive indifference which was the only response he left open to her. He made love to her each night, though, once embarked on it, he seemed to want it to be over quickly. Afterwards he never referred to what they had done together. Madame Azaire, who was initially frightened and ashamed, slowly became frustrated by her husband's attitude; she could not understand why this aspect of their lives, which seemed to mean so much to him, was something he would not talk about, nor why the startling intimacy of the act opened no doors in her mind, made no connections with the deeper feelings and aspirations that had grown in her since childhood.

She did not become pregnant, and each month as the blood returned Azaire became a little more desperate. Some reflexive guilt made him blame himself. He began to believe that there might be something wrong with him, even though he had two children to prove that this was unlikely; he even suspected in some quiet moments of the night that he was being punished for marrying Isabelle, though why this should be so or what he had done wrong he couldn't say. Eventually his feelings of frustration affected the frequency with which he was able to perform. He began also to see that there was an absence of feeling in his wife, though the prospect of examining it and finding a remedy was so appalling that he could not bring himself to face it.

Madame Azaire, meanwhile, became less concerned about her husband. She was frightened of Stephen. From the day he arrived in the boulevard du Cange with his dark face and its staring brown eyes, and his swift impetuous movements, she was afraid of him. He was not like the other men she had known, not like her father or her husband, not even like Jean Destournel, who, though young and romantic, had proved in the end to be weak.

Because Stephen was nine years younger than she was, she viewed him with a little condescension; she could see in him the youth, or at least a stage of it, that she had left behind. She tried to think of him as the third child, as Lisette's brother; after all, she thought, he is only four years older. To some extent she was successful in making herself look down on him, though she noticed that this only seemed to add an element of motherly tenderness to her alarm.

On Sunday morning Stephen rose early and went downstairs to find something to eat in the kitchen. He walked along the passageways of the ground floor, his footsteps alive in the closed air. There were still rooms in the house he had not visited and others which, having once glanced into, he could not refind. From the doors of a small sitting room he let himself into the cool of the garden and walked down to the end of the lawn. Beneath a chestnut tree there was a bench where he sat chewing on the bread he had taken from the kitchen, looking back at the house.

The night before he had taken his knife and made a small sculpture from a piece of soft wood he had found in the garden. He took it from his jacket pocket and examined it in the fresh, damp air of the morning. It was the figure of a woman in a long skirt and little jacket; close indentations in the wood indicated her hair, though the features could only be represented by marks for the eyes and mouth. He took the knife and trimmed a few shavings from around the feet, to make them look more realistic where they emerged from the skirt. He saw some shutters being opened on a first-floor bedroom. He imagined the sound of voices and running water and door-handles being turned. When he judged that the whole family would be dressed and downstairs, he returned to the house.

The children were not excited by the prospect of the trip round the water-gardens. Madame Azaire leaned across Grégoire to stop him tapping his spoon on the table. She was dressed in cream linen with a blue sash and a panel in the dress with a row of buttons that neither opened nor held anything together.

Lisette eyed Stephen flirtatiously. 'So are you coming to the famous water-gardens?' she said.

'I don't know if I'm invited.'

'Of course you are,' said Madame Azaire.

'In that case I will, with pleasure.'

Lisette said, 'Well, that might make it a bit less boring.'

'It's very kind of Monsieur Bérard to invite us,' said

Madame Azaire. 'You must be very polite to both of them. And I don't think that dress is quite right, either, for a girl of your age. It's too small.'

'But it's so *hot*,' said Lisette.

'I can't help the weather. Now run and put on something else.'

'Run, run, run,' said Lisette sulkily as she pushed back her chair. Her arm brushed Stephen's shoulder on her way to the door. The dress in question emphasised the plump swell of her breasts, of which she was clearly proud.

The five of them set out towards eleven o'clock with Marguerite, the maid, helping Stephen and Madame Azaire to carry the various baskets of food, parasols, rugs and extra clothes that had been deemed necessary. It was only a short walk to the edge of the water-gardens. They went down a flight of stairs to the landing stage where Bérard was waiting in a straw hat. Madame Bérard was already installed in the stern of a flat-bottomed boat which was shaped, after long local tradition, like a punt with a raised and squared-off end.

'Madame, good morning! What a lovely day.' Bérard was at his most expansive. He held out his arm to help Madame Azaire down into the boat. Gripping his proffered arm with one hand, she raised her skirt with the other and stepped lightly into the low craft. Grégoire, no longer bored as he had been, pushed excitedly past the others and jumped in, making the boat rock. Madame Bérard let out a little scream, 'Oh, Papa!'

Bérard laughed. 'Women and children first.'

Lisette embarked with his help and sat next to Madame Azaire.

'I shall be the helmsman in the stern of the craft,' said Bérard impressively, 'so you sit facing Lisette and you, Monsieur,' he said to Stephen, 'if you sit next to Grégoire, and Madame Bérard would like to go here, opposite you, Azaire – that's right – then we shall have perfect balance.'

Stephen settled opposite Madame Azaire, as instructed, and found room for his feet on the floor of the boat while trying not to touch hers.

Bérard let out a nautical cry and clambered into the stern

41

where he pushed the boat off from the bank with a long wooden pole.

The gardens were formed by the backwaters of the Somme, which had been channelled between numerous small islands whose banks were secured with wooden plank revetting. The land was intensely cultivated for vegetables, either in small plots, where the owner lived in a simple house on the site, or in larger areas whose farmer was likely to live in town. The area was regarded by the people who had nothing to do with its work as a site of natural beauty and an object of civic pride.

Bérard worked the boat along with some skill, plunging in the pole with a vigorous thrust and moving it to the left or right to steer as he pulled it out again. They slid along beneath the overhanging trees, occasionally coming close to other Sunday pleasure-seekers who called out greetings and comments on the sunny weather from their own boats. Bérard sweated freely at his work, mopping at his forehead with a handkerchief, but was still able to give an account of the history of the water-gardens as he punted them along.

Stephen sat uncomfortably on his wooden seat with his back to the direction of the boat's movement. The stagnant water, unmoved by any breeze, seemed to emphasize the unnatural heat of the day. His polished leather shoes lay on the slatted wooden floor of the craft at the unnatural angle required by his feet if they were not to touch the white shoes of Madame Azaire, which lay together in the position dictated by the slightly sideways attitude of her closed legs. The extreme lowness of the seats, however, which were only a few inches off the floor of the boat, meant that her knees were a little raised and the pale skirt was drawn up to reveal the taut stretch of the stockings over her instep. They were of a fine, silken material that was not, Stephen thought, the product of either of her husband's factories. He noticed the delicate definition of her ankles and the beginning of her calves and found himself wondering what fastening beneath the folds of her linen skirt achieved the tension that made the stocking's fabric look so light and open on the arch of her foot.

'. . . by the Roman soldiers. But the channelling of the water

42

between the parcels of the land was to some extent a natural phenomenon and it was several centuries before the banks of the little islands were secured by planks in the way you see now. So what we have really is man and nature working in harmony and cooperation.'

Bérard's discourse was interrupted by his occasional gasps for breath, though not by any of the others, least of all Azaire, whose interjections were ignored.

Stephen looked at the water, trailed his hand in it, smiled at Grégoire and tried to engage Madame Azaire's eye. When he did, she gave a composed smile before turning to ask Lisette a question.

The broad channels of the water-gardens were public thoroughfares, though narrower strips of water, marked 'Private', led to large houses obscured from general view by thick hedges and tall, abundant flowers. When Bérard was exhausted, Azaire took over and pushed the little craft onwards until Grégoire's pleas for lunch were eventually rewarded.

Bérard had been allowed by a friend to moor the boat at the foot of a shady garden and take lunch beneath some apple trees. Azaire made great play of hanging the wine by the boat's painter into the water to cool, while Madame Azaire and Lisette laid out rugs on the grass. Grégoire ran round the garden, returning occasionally to report his discoveries, and Stephen made conversation to Madame Bérard, though her eyes were only for her husband, who settled himself at the foot of a tree with a glass of wine and some chicken which he ripped from the bone with a sideways shake of his head.

The men took off their jackets, and as he laid down Stephen felt the little wood carving in his pocket. He took it out and turned it round in his fingers.

'What's that?' said Lisette, who had placed herself near him on the rug.

'Just a little carving. I did it with this.' He took out the knife from his pocket.

'It's beautiful.'

'You can have it if you like,' Stephen said without thinking. Lisette glowed with pleasure, and looked around to make sure the others had seen. Stephen searched for some wood with which to do a carving for Grégoire, who was busily eating his lunch.

No one else seemed to have much appetite. Various cheeses and pies were produced from the hampers by Madame Azaire but were returned with only a slice or two missing. Bérard ate some jellied tongue as well as the chicken; Lisette managed a strawberry tart and some little cakes Madame Azaire had made herself. She and her brother drank orangeade while the others had wine from the Loire valley which immersion in the placid water had not chilled.

After lunch Bérard lay back against his tree and fell asleep; Azaire lit his pipe before retiring to a neighbouring part of the garden for the same purpose. Stephen carved a hard piece of wood, with difficulty, into a passably realistic man for Grégoire.

With lunch over, the afternoon lay heavy and dull on them. They clambered back into the boat and, after Stephen had been allowed a brief spell with the pole, Bérard resumed his position. The temperature had increased and the women fanned themselves vigorously. Madame Bérard, in thick formal clothes, looked disconsolate at the front of the boat, like a brooding figurehead on an ill-fated ship headed for ice and equatorial winds.

Stephen felt hot and thickheaded from the wine. He was repelled by the water-gardens: their hectic abundance seemed to him close to the vegetable fertility of death. The brown waters were murky and shot through with the scurrying of rats from the banks where the earth had been dug out of trenches and held back by elaborate wooden boarding. Heavy flies hung over the water, beneath the trees, dipping into the rotting tops of cabbages, asparagus and artichokes that had been left unpicked in their reckless prodigality. What was held to be a place of natural beauty was a stagnation of living tissue which could not be saved from decay.

Madame Azaire, also uncomfortable in the heat and torpor of the afternoon, had lost a fraction of her poise. Her skin was red at the base of her neck, where she had loosened the top of her dress. A strand of strawberry hair was stuck to her neck with moisture. One foot lay unresisting against Stephen's leg, which was outstretched beneath her seat. As Bérard propelled the boat on its slow, straight course, a tiny roll in its motion caused a perceptible pressure to form between them. While Stephen left his leg where it was, Madame Azaire was too hot or too indifferent to shift her position. He caught her eye and she looked into his with no social smile or conversational suggestion, then turned her head slowly away as though to look at the view.

A fish broke the surface of the water unremarked even by the previously excited Grégoire. The flow of the river had been slowed by the construction of a canal, Bérard told them, which was why the boats no longer had rudders; a twitch from the pole was all that was necessary to keep the thing straight.

Stephen imagined the great pools and marshes that had occurred in nature before the further channelling of the water and planting of the ground. The river's function had not been significantly changed; still it watered a cycle of superfluous decay, the rotting of matter into the turned and dug earth with its humid, clinging soil.

It had reached a stage in the afternoon when it should have started to grow cooler, but what small breeze there had been had disappeared, and the static air coagulated, thick and choking. Grégoire began to splash water at Lisette, who smacked him on the side of the face and made him cry.

Azaire took over in the stern from Bérard, who sat perspiring next to his wife. For once he was silent.

Stephen tried to drag his mind from the vision of decay the river had induced. The pressure of Madame Azaire's foot against his leg slowly increased until most of her calf rested against him. The simple frisson this touch had earlier given to his charged senses now seemed complicated; the sensation of desire seemed indistinguishable from an impulse towards death.

All of them, he thought, would be taken back by this earth: Bérard's tongue would decompose into the specks of friable soil that gardeners rolled between their fingers; its clacking would be stilled as it was reabsorbed by the thirsting roots of artichokes or cabbages. Little Grégoire and Lisette would be the mud of the banks in which the rats burrowed and mated. And Madame Azaire, Isabelle . . . The tenderest parts of her that his imagination shamelessly embodied, even these would not outlast or rise above some forlorn, unspiritual end in the clinging earth.

As the landing stage came into view, their mood lifted. Azaire began to talk about what a splendid trip they had had and Bérard refound his usual dominance in conversation. Over the last ten or fifteen minutes he managed to rewrite the story of the afternoon by ascribing opinions on its success to all the different members of the party, inviting their agreement, and cutting them off before they had time to spoil his version of harmony with actual thoughts of their own.

Madame Azaire seemed to emerge from a trance. She sat up straight, noting with apparent alarm as she did so the position of her left leg. Grégoire trawled a glass jar in the water in the hope of catching a fish.

When they disembarked and thanked the Bérards for their kindness, Stephen loaded himself with the baskets, rugs and parasols and led the way back to the boulevard du Cange. He was glad to be able to leave the baggage in the hall for Marguerite to put away while he climbed up to his room. He took off the formal collar he had guessed was expected of him and went to the little bathroom, once a maid's, at the end of the corridor. He filled the bath with cold water and soaked himself in it, sinking his head beneath the surface and letting the icy water penetrate even into the follicles at the roots of his hair.

Back in his room, wrapped in a towel, he took a pack of cards and laid them out on the table as though for a game of Patience. The sequence in which he then moved them, however, was something he had learned from a friend of his grandfather's – a superstitious old man who made a living at fairs by telling fortunes. As a child Stephen had been enraptured by him and his games, and in private moments he still found himself drawn back. If the Queen of Diamonds could be discovered on the left-hand pile before the Jack of Clubs was filed in order on the right, then Madame Azaire would . . . He shuffled and moved the cards through subtle combinations, half smiling to himself, half in earnest.

He took a book and lay down on the bed, knowing that dinner would not be for at least an hour. The church bell was tolling and from the garden there was again the sound of birds. With the noise in his ears he fell asleep and dreamed a dream that was a variation of one he had had all his life. He was trying to help a trapped bird out of a window. Its wings battered frantically on the glass. Suddenly the whole room was filled with starlings, moving with one flock instinct. They beat their wings against the window panes, flapped them in his hair, then brought their beaks towards his face.

THE NEXT DAY Stephen received a telegram from London telling him he was to return as soon as he could conclude his business. He wrote to say it would take him another month: he still had a good deal to learn about the processes that were used in Amiens, and Azaire had promised to introduce him to other manufacturers. He also needed further information about Azaire's own finances before he could report on the feasibility of investment.

He sent his reply that evening, feeling a panic as he did so that he would have to go back to England before he had resolved the conflicting passions that were threatening to overpower him. During dinner he looked at Madame Azaire in the shaded light as she served food to the family and their guests, some cousins of Azaire's, and there was a sense of desperation in the way he registered the features of her face, the loop of her hair and the certainty of her movements. He could no longer allow himself to be passively beguiled.

At work the next day he learned that there was a threat that the dyers' strike might spread to other textile workers, causing a complete halt to production. A lunchtime meeting of the workers was addressed by Meyraux, who told them they should support their colleagues in other parts of the industry by taking them food and clothes, but that it would serve no purpose for them to go on strike.

'You have your own families and lives to consider,' Meyraux told them. 'I believe the long-term future of this industry lies in bringing all processes together and in having one body to represent all workers. But for the moment we must deal with things as they are. This is not a time for vain gestures, not when we are under such a threat from foreign competitors.'

Meyraux's speech was typically cautious. He distrusted the hot-headed leaders of the strike as much as he did the proprietors. Before he could bring his remarks to a reasoned conclusion, there was a disturbance near the door on to the street. It burst open and several young men tumbled in carrying banners and chanting slogans. Meyraux called for calm from the platform as half a dozen police officers, some with dishevelled uniforms that suggested they had already been in a struggle, tried to evict the demonstrators. Many of the female workers nearest the door backed away in alarm as blows began to be exchanged.

Lucien Lebrun, who had been among the first to force his way in, now took the platform next to the reluctant Meyraux. His candid blue eyes and wavy brown hair made him an attractive figure and compensated to some extent for the suspicion many of the workers felt of his youth. He asked Meyraux with tactful appeals to their fraternity whether he could address the workers, and Meyraux finally conceded his place.

Lucien gave a compassionate description of the hardships endured by the strikers' families and of the working conditions that had driven them to their extreme action. He spoke of the poverty and exploitation throughout the plain of Picardy which was causing a large migration of people from the valley of the Somme to the towns of Amiens and Lille in the false hope of finding work.

'I beseech you to support my people,' he said. 'We must stand together in this matter or we will all fall. We must think of our children and wives. I ask you at least to sign this declaration of support for your fellow-workers.'

He produced a piece of paper which already carried a hundred or more signatures.

'Talking of wives,' called out a deep voice from the middle of the room, 'we all know what they say about you, young man!'

There was a roar of ribald agreement. Stephen felt his nerves stiffen as his heartbeat filled his chest.

Lucien shouted, 'What was that you said?'

'I'll not repeat it in front of the law, but I think you know what I mean.'

Lucien jumped down from the platform to try to find his tormentor. He shouldered his way frantically through the press.

'And another thing,' the same man called out, 'we shouldn't be having a spy from England eating with us and coming to our meetings.'

A few voices called out their agreement. The majority had obviously not been aware of Stephen's presence.

Stephen was not listening. 'What do they say about Lucien?' he asked the man standing next to him. 'What did they mean about wives?'

'They say little Lucien and the boss's wife are very good friends.' The man gave a throaty laugh.

Azaire's work force had been good-natured up to this point. They had been lectured at length by Meyraux on the need for patience and they had submitted to his advice; they had seen their meeting disrupted by workers from other factories and they had kept calm; they had been harangued by a young man who did not even come from the town and they had endured it.

When Lucien lost his self-control and began to fight his way through them, however, a shared sense of grievance overtook them, and they set about ejecting him, the whole group of them reacting spontaneously as though to rid itself of a foreign body.

Stephen found himself jostled by people, some of them responding to the hostility towards him, but most of them anxious to turn Lucien and the other dyers out of their factory.

The worker who had called out the comment about Madame Azaire was surrounded by pushing bodies as some of Lucien's friends came to his assistance. He was a tall, red-faced man whose job was to transport bolts of cloth on one of the wooden-wheeled wagons. His placid expression was turning to one of alarm as the struggle approached him. Lucien was shouting and thrashing wildly with his arms in his attempt to push through the crowd, but a wall of Azaire's men had closed his path in silent complicity.

At the edge of the skirmish the police officers began to swing their batons in a threatening way as they moved into the crowd. Meyraux climbed up on to the platform and shouted for calm. At this point one of Lucien's wilder movements with his arm caught a female worker across the face, causing her to scream. Lucien went down on the floor under a swift blow from the woman's husband. As he lay gasping, various well-aimed boots relieved the frustrations of Azaire's workers. They were not crazed blows, but Lucien cried out as they found his legs and shoulders. Stephen tried to push back some of his assailants to give him time to stand up. He received an open-handed blow on the nose from one of the men who resented being interrupted. Three or four dyers had now reached Lucien and had joined the fight to protect him. Stephen, his eyes smarting, hit out in front of him in fury. He had lost sight of his initial aim, which was to restore peace, and now wanted only to damage the man who had enraged him. He found himself pushed to one side by the tall, red-faced worker whose comment had started the commotion and he responded with a short-armed punch to the man's face. There was no room for him to make a proper swing, but the blow was well enough timed for him to feel some dim sense of retribution. There was blood on his hand.

A combination of determined women workers and police batons ended the skirmish. Lucien was taken out, bruised and breathless, but not badly hurt. The dyers were escorted out by the police, who randomly arrested two of the most disreputable-looking. Stephen's victim dabbed his bleeding mouth with a handkerchief but seemed unaware of who had hit him. Meyraux told the workers to disperse.

Stephen left the factory by the side door, wondering how affairs had moved so quickly that he could find himself on the same side as Lucien Lebrun when, like the others, he wanted never to see his bright-eyed face again.

He walked towards the cathedral and then on into the

51

town. He felt ashamed of the way he had behaved. Years ago he had promised his guardian that he would never again lose control of his feelings but would always pause and be calm. He had abjectly failed this trial, and the memory of the startled expression on the face of the man who had slandered Madame Azaire as Stephen's closed fist found his mouth was only a small compensation for this failure.

The blow must have been harder than he had thought at the time, because his hand became quite swollen in the course of the afternoon. He returned early to the Azaires' house and went up to bathe it. He held it under cold water and wound a handkerchief tightly round the knuckles.

He felt as though his existence in the boulevard du Cange, and perhaps his life in its longer perspective also, were coming to a crisis he could not control. Perhaps it would be better to do as his employer asked. He could conclude his work within a week, then return to London in the knowledge that he had done nothing to shame his company or Mr Vaughan, the guardian who had worked so hard to help him. First, he thought, he had better write to him.

Miserably, he took a piece of paper from the desk and began.

Dear Mr Vaughan, This is not the first time I have been late in writing to you, but I will try to make up for it by telling you in detail what has happened.

He stopped. He wanted to find dignified words for the rage of desire and confusion he felt.

I think I have fallen in love and I believe the woman in question, though she has not said so, returns my feelings. How can I be sure when she has said nothing? Is this youthful vanity? I wish in some ways that it were. But I am so convinced that I barely need question myself. This conviction brings me no joy.

By this time he had already gone too far; he could not, of

course, send this letter. He wrote one more paragraph for his own sake, to see what he had to say.

I am driven by a greater force than I can resist. I believe that force has its own reason and its own morality even if they may never be clear to me while I am alive.

He tore the paper up into small pieces and dropped them in the basket.

He took the handkerchief off his hand and managed to conceal it behind his back when he talked to Monsieur and Madame Azaire in the sitting room before dinner. Azaire was too concerned with events at the factory to be looking at his house guest's hand, and when Madame Azaire allowed herself a glance at Stephen it was to his face that her eyes turned.

'I understand there was some comment about your presence at the factory,' said Azaire.

'Yes. I wasn't sure if I should have been at the meeting. Perhaps I should keep away for a day or two.'

Lisette came in through the door to the garden.

'Good idea,' said Azaire. 'Allow the men time to cool off. I don't think there's going to be a problem, but perhaps you'd better lie low until things are sorted out. I can get one of my staff to bring you some paperwork. There are plenty of ways you can make yourself useful.'

'Look!' said Lisette. 'What happened to your hand?'

'I caught it in one of the spinning machines when I was being shown how to work it this morning.'

'It's all swollen and red.'

Madame Azaire let out a little cry as Lisette held up Stephen's damaged hand for her inspection. He thought he saw a flicker of concern in her face before she managed to resume her usual detachment.

'Dinner is served,' said Marguerite at the door.

'Thank you,' said Madame Azaire. 'After dinner, Marguerite, will you please find a dressing for Monsieur Wraysford's hand?' She led the way into the dining room.

The next day when Azaire left to go to work, Stephen stayed

in the house like a sick child who has been excused school. A messenger arrived from the factory with some papers which Stephen put to one side in the sitting room. He took up a book and settled himself in a corner by the doors to the garden. He could hear the sounds of the house in its morning routine, and he felt like an eavesdropper on this female life. Marguerite came in with a feather duster which she plied with exemplary lightness over the china ornaments and polished table tops, displacing eddies of dust which rose in tiny spirals in the clear morning sunshine before settling elsewhere on the chairs or the polished wooden floor. Grégoire's footsteps came pounding down the stairs and through the hallway until his progress was checked by an audible tussle with the locks and chains of the front door. A cry of, 'Shut the front door after you,' was not answered by any sound of compliance, and Stephen pictured the rectangular glimpse of the garden, the paved path and the solid iron railings giving on to the boulevard, that would have become visible in the space left by the unclosed door.

There was a sound of crockery as Marguerite carried out a tray full of breakfast cups and plates from the dining room to the kitchen and the soft bump of her hip against the door as she pushed it open. In the moment before it swung shut came the louder, more purposeful clanking of pans being scoured or set on the stove filled with stock that would simmer through the morning.

Madame Azaire's voice was audible from her place in the dining room, where she remained until eleven o'clock, either talking to Lisette or giving instructions to the various people who called on her. Among these was Madame Bonnet, wife of the elderly man in the factory, who came each day to do the cleaning Marguerite considered too menial or too strenuous. Madame Azaire would tell her which rooms were to be done and if there were special preparations to be made for guests. The old woman's heavy, rolling step could be heard as she trundled off to her prescribed task. Lisette sat in the sunlight that splashed into the room beneath the spokes of clematis at the window, watching the shadows on the polished table, listening to the way her step-mother ran the household. She enjoyed this shared morning routine; it made her feel trusted and important, and it had the further advantage of excluding Grégoire with his uncouth behaviour and his childish remarks which, even at their most despicable and banal, sometimes threatened her precarious adult poise.

There were further, smaller parts to be played in the gently rolling drama of the morning. There was a second maid, though, unlike Marguerite, she did not live in the house; there was a cook, who had a room somewhere on the first floor; and there was a boy from the butcher's who came to take an order and one from the grocer's who delivered two heavy boxes to the back door.

Shortly after midday Madame Azaire asked Stephen if he would be taking lunch with her and Lisette. Grégoire would still be at school, she said. Stephen accepted and spent the next hour working through the papers that had been sent from Azaire's office.

Madame Azaire returned a little after one o'clock to tell him lunch was ready. Three places had been set at the end of the table, by the window. The room looked quite different from the place of formal shadows with stiff-collared guests in the lowered evening lights that Stephen had seen at dinner. Lisette wore the little white dress her step-mother had forbidden on their visit to the water-gardens. Her dark brown hair was tied back with a blue ribbon and her legs were bare. She was a good-looking girl, Stephen thought, as she looked up at him from under thick lashes; but he registered her looks quite dispassionately because his thoughts were elsewhere.

Madame Azaire wore a cream skirt with a dark red patterned waistcoat over a white blouse with an open neck.

'You can take off your jacket if you like, Monsieur,' she said. 'Lisette and I don't consider lunch to be a formal occasion, do we?'

Lisette laughed. Stephen said, 'Thank you.' He could see that Madame Azaire felt protected and emboldened by Lisette's presence.

Marguerite brought in a dish of artichokes. 'Perhaps we'll have some wine,' said Madame Azaire. 'We don't normally drink wine, do we, Lisette? But perhaps today. Marguerite, bring a bottle of white wine, will you? Not one my husband is saving.'

After the artichokes there was a small dish of mushrooms and then some sole. Stephen poured the wine for Madame Azaire and, at her insistence, for Lisette. For want of something to say, Stephen asked how they came to know Monsieur and Madame Bérard.

Lisette began to giggle at the name and Madame Azaire told her to be quiet, though she herself was smiling. 'I'm afraid Lisette is very impolite about Monsieur Bérard,' she said.

'It's so unfair,' said Lisette. 'Did your parents always make you be polite about all their silly friends?'

'I didn't have parents,' said Stephen. 'At least not ones that I knew. I was brought up by my grandparents, then in an institution until I was taken away from it by a man I'd never met before.'

Lisette blushed and swallowed hard; Madame Azaire's face showed a momentary concern as she said, 'I'm sorry, Monsieur. Lisette is always asking questions.'

'There's nothing to apologize for.' He smiled at Lisette. 'Nothing at all. I'm not ashamed.'

Marguerite brought some fillet of beef on a blue-patterned dish which she set down in front of Madame Azaire. 'Should I bring some red wine?' she said. 'There's some from last night.'

'All right.' Madame Azaire put a slice of the bloody meat on each of three plates. Stephen refilled their glasses. In his mind he was remembering the press of Madame Azaire's leg against his own in the water-gardens. The skin on her bare arms was a light brown; her mannish waistcoat and open neck made her look even more feminine than usual.

'I shall be returning to England soon,' he said. 'I had a telegram telling me I was wanted back in London.'

Neither of the others spoke. The atmosphere had thickened. He thought of the sound of her pain from the bedroom.

'I shall be sorry to leave,' he said.

'You can always come back and visit us another day,' said Madame Azaire.

'Yes, I could come back another day.'

Marguerite brought in a dish of potatoes. Lisette stretched and smiled. 'Oh, I feel sleepy,' she said happily.

'That's because of all the wine you've been drinking.' Madame Azaire also smiled and the air seemed to lighten again. They finished lunch with some fruit, and Marguerite took coffee to the sitting room. They sat around the card table where Stephen had played on his first night in the house.

'I'm going to go out for a walk in the garden,' said Lisette. 'Then I might go to my room for a little sleep.'

'All right,' said Madame Azaire.

Lisette's light step crossed the room and disappeared.

At once the atmosphere changed, and this time it was beyond recall. Madame Azaire could not meet Stephen's eye. She looked down at the card table and played with the silver spoon in the thin china saucer. Stephen could feel his chest contract. He was finding it difficult to breathe.

'Have some more coff –'

'No.'

The silence returned.

'Look at me.'

She would not raise her head. She stood up and said, 'I'm going to do some sewing in my room, so –'

'Isabelle.' He had grasped her arm.

'No. Please no.'

He pulled her to him and wrapped both arms around her so she could not escape. Her eyes were closed and he kissed her mouth, which opened. He felt her tongue flicker and her hands press his back, then she pulled herself away from his tight grip, tearing the white blouse as she did so, revealing a thin satin strap beneath. Stephen's body convulsed with desire.

'You must. For God's sake, you must.' He raged at her.

Madame Azaire was crying through her closed eyes. 'No, I cannot, I hardly . . . I hardly think it would be right.'

'You were going to say "I hardly know you".'

'No. Just that it's not right.'

'It is right. You know it's right. It's as right as anything can ever be. Isabelle, I understand you. Believe me. I understand you. I love you.'

He kissed her again and her mouth once more responded to his. He tasted the sweetness of her saliva then buried his face against her shoulder where the flesh was visible.

She pulled away from him and ran from the room. Stephen went to the window and held on to the frame as he looked out. The force that drove through him could not be stopped. The part of his mind that remained calm accepted this; if the necessity could not be denied, then the question was only whether it could be achieved with her consent.

In her room Madame Azaire wept as she paced back from one side to the other. She was choking with passion for him, but he frightened her. She wanted to comfort him but also to be taken by him, to be used by him. Currents of desire and excitement that she had not known or thought about for years now flooded in her. She wanted him to bring alive what she had buried, and to demean, destroy, her fabricated self. He was very young. She was unsure. She wanted the touch of his skin.

She went downstairs and her step was so light that it made no sound. She found him clenched in combat with himself, leaning against the window. She said, 'Come to the red room.'

By the time Stephen turned round she had gone. The red room. He panicked. He was sure it would be one of those he had once seen but could never refind; it would be like a place in a dream that remains out of reach; it would always be behind him. He ran up the stairs and saw her turn a corner. She went down the main corridor to a narrow passage, down again through a little archway. At the end of the corridor was a locked door that led into the servants' part of the house. Just before it, the last door on the left, was an oval china handle that rattled in the ill-fitting lock. He caught her as she opened the door on to a small room with a brass bedstead and a red cover.

'Isabelle.' He too was in tears. He took her hair in his hands and saw it flow between his fingers.

She said, 'My poor boy.'

He kissed her, and this time her tongue did not flee from his.

He said, 'Where is Lisette?'

'The garden. I don't know. Oh God. Oh please, please.' She was starting to shake and tremble. Her eyes had closed. When she opened them again she could barely breathe. He began to tear at her clothes and she helped him with urgent, clumsy actions. The waistcoat was caught on her elbow. He pushed back her blouse and buried his face in the satin slip between her breasts. There was so much delight in what he saw and touched that he thought he would need years to stop and appreciate it, yet he was driven by a frantic haste.

Isabelle felt his hands on her, felt his lips on her skin and knew what he must be seeing, what shame and impropriety, but the more she imagined the degradation of her false modesty the more she felt excited. She felt his hair between her fingers, ran her hands over the bulge of his shoulders, over the smooth chest inside his shirt.

'Come on, please, please,' she heard herself say, though her breathing was so ragged that the words were barely comprehensible. She ran her hand over the front of his trousers, brazenly, as she imagined a whore might do, and felt the stiffness inside. No one upbraided her. No one was appalled. She could do whatever she wanted. His intake of breath caused him to stop undressing her and she had to help him pull down her silk drawers to reveal what she suddenly knew he had long been imagining. She squeezed her eyes tight shut in shame as she showed herself to him, but still no guilt came. She felt him push her backwards on to the bed, and she began to arch herself up from it rhythmically as though her body, independent of her, implored his attention. She felt at last some contact, though she realized with a gasp that it was not what she expected; it was his tongue, lambent, hot, flickering over and inside her, turning like a key in the split lock of her flesh. This shocking, new sensation made her start to sigh and shudder in long rhythmic movements, borne completely away on her passion, feeling a knot of pressure rising in her chest, a sensation that was impossible to sustain, to bear, though all its momentum seemed to be onwards. In this conflict she thrashed her head from side to side on the bed. She heard her voice crying out in denial as from some distant room, but then the sensation broke and flooded her again and again, down through her belly and all her limbs, and her small voice, close to her head this time, said, 'Yes.'

When she opened her eyes she saw Stephen standing naked in front of her. Her eyes fixed on the flesh that stuck out from him. He had still not made love to her; the joy was yet to come. He climbed on top of her and kissed her face, her breasts, pulling the nipples upwards with his lips. Then he rolled her over, ran his hands up the inside of her legs, above the silk stockings that her speedy undressing had not had time to remove, and between the cleft where her legs were joined. He kissed her from the small of her back over the pink swell of divided flesh, down to the back of her thighs where he rested his cheek for a moment. Then he began again at her ankles, on the little bones he had seen on the boat in the water-gardens, and up the inside of her calves.

Isabelle was now beginning to breathe fast again. She said, 'Please, my love, please now, please.' She could no longer bear his teasing. In her left hand she grasped the part of him she wanted to feel inside her and the shock of her action stopped him in his caressing. She opened her legs a little further for him, to make him welcome, because she wanted him to be there. She felt the sheet beneath her as her legs spread out and she guided him into her.

She heard him sigh and saw him take the rumpled sheet between his teeth and begin to bite it. He barely moved inside her, as though he were afraid of the sensation or of what it might produce.

Isabelle settled herself, luxuriously, on the feeling of impalement. It rolled around the rim, the edges of her; it filled her with desire and happiness. I am at last what I am, she thought; I was born for this. Fragments of childish longings, of afternoon urges suppressed in the routine of her parents' house, flashed across her mind; she felt at last connections forged between the rage of her desire and a particular attentive recognition of herself, the little Fourmentier girl.

She heard him cry out and felt a surge inside her; he seemed suddenly to swell in her so that their flesh almost fused. The shock and intimacy of what he had done, leaving this deposit of himself, precipitated a shuddering response in her, like the first time, only shorter, fiercer, in a way that made her lose contact with the world.

When she had recovered enough to open her eyes, she found that Stephen had rolled off her and was lying face down across the bed, his head tilted awkwardly to one side, almost as though he were dead. Neither of them spoke. Both lay quite still. Outside was the sound of birds.

Tentatively, almost shyly, Isabelle ran her fingers down over the vertebrae that protruded from his back, then over the narrow haunches and the top of his thighs with their soft black hair. She took his damaged hand and kissed the bruised and swollen knuckles.

He rolled over and looked at her. The hair was disarrayed, its different shades milling over her bare shoulders and down to the stiff, round breasts that rose and fell with her still-accelerated breathing. Her face and neck were suffused with a pink glow where the blood was diluted by the colour of the milky young skin with its tracery of brown and golden freckles. He held her gaze for a moment, then laid his head on her shoulder where she stroked his face and hair.

They lay, amazed and unsure, for a long time in silence. Then Isabelle began also to think of what had happened. She had given way, but not in some passive sense. She had wanted to make this gift; in fact she wanted to go further. This thought frightened her. She saw them at the start of some descent whose end she could not imagine.

'What have we done?' she said.

Stephen sat up and took her by the arms. 'We have done what was right.' He looked at her fiercely. 'My darling Isabelle, you must understand that.'

She nodded without speaking. He was a boy, he was the dearest boy, and now she would have him always.

'Stephen,' she said.

It was the first time she had used his name. It sounded beautiful to him on her foreign tongue.

'Isabelle.' He smiled at her and her face lit up in reply. She held him to her, smiling broadly, though with tears beginning again in the corners of her eyes.

'You are so beautiful,' said Stephen. 'I won't know how to

look at you in the house. I shall give myself away. When I see you at dinner I shall be thinking of what we did, I shall be thinking of you as you are now.' He stroked the skin of her shoulders and laid the back of his hand against her cheek.

Isabelle said, 'You won't. And nor shall I. You will be strong because you love me.'

Stephen's level gaze, she thought, was not afraid. As his hands stroked her breasts she began to lose her concentration. They had talked only for a minute but what they had said, and what it meant, had made her tired of thought. A feeling, more compelling, began to rise through her body as his hand worked over these soft and privately guarded parts of her. Her breath began to come unevenly again; the low exhalations were broken and she felt herself begin to slide again once more, willingly, but downwards where there was no end in sight.

AZAIRE WAS IN a sprightly mood that evening. Meyraux had come close to accepting his new pay offer to the workers, and although the strike had spread among the dyers, there seemed little chance of its infecting other parts of the industry. His friend Bérard, who had not called for more than a week, had promised to look in with his wife and mother-in-law for a game of cards after dinner. Azaire ordered Marguerite to fetch up two bottles of Burgundy from the cellar. He congratulated Isabelle on her appearance and asked Lisette what she had been doing.

'I went for a walk in the garden,' she said. 'I went down to the end where it joins the others, where it grows all wild. I sat down under a tree and I think I fell asleep. I had a very strange dream.'

'What was that?' Azaire began to pack some tobacco into his pipe.

Lisette giggled. 'I'm not going to tell you.'

She seemed disappointed when he did not press her but turned instead to his wife. 'And how have you whiled away the day? Some more pressing errands in town?'

'No, just the usual things,' said Isabelle. 'I had to speak to the butcher's boy. They sent the wrong kind of steak again. Madame Bonnet was complaining about all the work she has to do. Then in the afternoon I read a book.'

'Something educational, or one of your novels?'

'Just a silly thing I found in a bookshop in town.'

Azaire smiled indulgently and shook his head at his wife's

frivolous tastes. He himself, it was assumed, read only the great philosophers, often in their original languages, though this arduous study must have taken place in private. When he settled in beneath the glow of the lamp after dinner, his hand invariably reached for the evening paper.

Isabelle's eyes flickered upward from the sofa, where she sat with her pre-dinner sewing, at the sound of a man's footsteps descending the stairs. Stephen stood in the doorway.

He briefly took Azaire's offered hand and turned to wish Isabelle good evening. She breathed a little less uneasily as she saw the sternness of his dark and steady face. His self-control appeared unshakeable.

She noticed at dinner that he did not address her, nor even look at her if he could avoid it. When he did, his eyes were so blank she feared that she could see indifference, even hostility, in them.

Marguerite came backwards and forwards with the food, and Azaire, in a lighter mood than usual, talked about a plan for a day's fishing that he was going to put to Bérard later. They could take the train to Albert and then it might be enjoyable to rent a little pony and trap and take a picnic up to one of the villages beside the Ancre.

Grégoire became animated at the thought of it. 'Will I be allowed my own rod?' he asked. 'Hugues and Édouard both have their own. Why can't I?'

Isabelle said, 'I'm sure we can find you one, Grégoire.'

'Do you fish, Monsieur?' said Azaire.

'I did when I was a child. Just with worms and bits of bread. I would sit for hours by a pool in the gardens of a big house near where we lived. I went there with a few other boys from the village and we would sit there and tell stories while we waited. It was rumoured that there was an enormous carp. One of the boys' father had seen it, in fact he had almost caught it, or so he claimed. There were certainly some large fish in the pool because we caught some of them. The trouble was that we were always being ordered off the land because it was private property.'

Isabelle listened with some astonishment to this speech, which was easily the longest Stephen had addressed to her husband since he had been in the house. Apart from his brief disclosure to herself and Lisette at lunchtime, it was the first time he had admitted to anything so personal as a childhood. The more he spoke, the more he seemed to warm to the subject. He fixed Azaire with his eye so that he had to wait for Stephen to finish before he could resume eating the piece of veal that was speared on the end of his fork.

Stephen went on, 'When I went to school there was no time for fishing any more. In any event I'm not sure I would have had the patience. It's probably something that appeals to groups of boys who are bored most of the time anyway but prefer to be together so that they can at least share the new things they are discovering about the world.'

Azaire said, 'Well, you're welcome to join us,' and put the piece of veal into his mouth.

'That's very kind, but I think I have imposed enough on your family outings.'

'You *must* come,' said Lisette. 'They have famous "English teas" at Thiepval.'

'We don't have to decide now,' said Isabelle. 'Would you like some more veal, Monsieur?'

She felt proud of him. He spoke the language beautifully, he was elegantly polite, and now had even told them something of himself. She wanted to take the credit for him, to show him off and sun herself in the approval he would win. She felt a pang of loss when she reflected how very far she was from being able to do this. It was Azaire who was her choice, her pride, the man in whose glory she was bound to live. She wondered how long she could maintain the falsity of her position. Perhaps what she and Stephen were attempting, the denial of truth on such a scale, was not possible. Although she was frightened by the drama of pretence, she was also excited by the exhilaration of it, and by the knowledge that it was a shared venture.

They had left the red room at five in the afternoon and she had not spoken to him since. She had no way of telling what had passed through his mind. Perhaps he was already regretting what had happened; perhaps he had done what he wanted to do and now the matter was finished for him.

65

For her, in the delirium of joy and fear, there were still practical matters to attend to. She had to dress and conceal the torn front of her blouse when she left the red room. She had to take the sheets and the cover from the bed and deliver them unseen to the laundry room. She had to check and recheck the room for signs of the adultery.

In her own bathroom she took off her clothes. She was known to have baths twice a day and often at this time, but the blouse was beyond repair and would have to be thrown away secretly. Her thighs were sticky where the seed she had felt so deeply planted in her had later leaked. It had stained the ivory silk drawers that had been bought for her by her mother from the rue de Rivoli in Paris as part of her wedding trousseau. When she washed in the bath there were more traces of him between her legs and she scoured the enamel afterwards. The major problem was still the bed covers. Marguerite was particular about the linen and knew which rooms needed to be changed and when, even if it was Madame Bonnet who usually did the work. Perhaps she would have to take one of them into her confidence. She decided to give Marguerite the next afternoon off and to wash and iron the sheets herself, replacing them before anyone had been into the red room. She would throw the red cover away and say she had suddenly grown tired of it. This was the sort of impulsive behaviour which annoyed her husband, but which he thought characteristic. She felt no revulsion for the stains and physical reminders of their afternoon, not even for the flecks of her own blood that she had seen. She had learned from Jeanne not to be ashamed, and in this shared mark she saw the witness of an intimacy that pressed her heart.

Marguerite went to answer the front door the to Bérards. Azaire thought it proper to continue the evening in the sitting room, or even in one of the small rooms on the ground floor, where he sometimes instructed Marguerite to lay out coffee and ices and little cakes. However, Bérard was ponderously considerate.

'No need for us to disturb this delightful family scene, Azaire. Let me rest my bulk on this chair here. If little

66

Grégoire would be so kind . . . That's it, then Madame Bérard can sit on my left.'

'Surely you would be more comfortable if –'

'And then we shall not feel that we have inconvenienced you. Aunt Élise would only accompany us on the condition that we were just neighbours dropping in on you, not guests who were to be specially treated in any way at all.'

Bérard settled himself in the chair vacated by Lisette who was given permission by her step-mother to take Grégoire up to bed. Lisette kissed her father briefly on the cheek and skipped out of the room. Although she had been pleased with her grown-up role that morning, there were times when it still paid to be a child.

Stephen envied her. It would have been easy for him to leave the families together; in fact they might have preferred it. While he could look at Isabelle, however, he wanted to stay. He felt no particular impatience with the falsity of their position; he was confident that what had occurred between them had changed things irrevocably and that the social circumstances would adjust in their own time to reflect this new reality.

'And you, Madame, have you heard any more of your phantom pianist with his unforgettable tune?' Bérard's heavy head, with its thick grey hair and red features, was supported by his right hand as he leaned his elbow on the table and looked towards Isabelle. It was not a serious enquiry; he was merely tuning up the orchestra.

'No, I haven't been past that house since we last saw you.'

'Ah-ha, you wish to keep the melody as a treasured little memory. I understand. So you have chosen a different walk for your afternoon exercise.'

'No. I was reading a book this afternoon.'

Bérard smiled. 'A romance, I'll bet. How charming. I read only history myself. But tell us about the story.'

'It was about a young man from a modest family in the provinces who goes to Paris to become a famous writer and falls in with the wrong kind of people.'

Stephen was taken aback by Isabelle's unembarrassed fluency. He watched as she spoke and wondered if he could have told that she was lying. Nothing in her manner was different.

One day she might lie to him and he would never know. Perhaps all women had this ability to survive.

From the subject of Isabelle's book the conversation moved on to the question of whether the families who lived in the provinces could be as important in their way as those who lived in Paris.

'Do you know the Laurendeau family?' asked Azaire.

'Oh yes,' said Madame Bérard brightly, 'we've met them on several occasions.'

'I,' said Bérard weightily, 'don't consider them to be friends. I have not invited them to our house and I shall not be calling on them.'

Something mysterious but noble lay behind Bérard's rejection of the Laurendeau family, or so his manner implied. No amount of interrogation from his friends would extract from him the delicate reasons for his stance.

'I don't think they ever lived in Paris,' said Azaire.

'Paris!' said Aunt Élise, suddenly looking up. 'It's just a big fashion house, that city. That's the only difference between Paris and the provinces – the people there buy new clothes every week. What a lot of peacocks!'

Azaire picked up his own thoughts on the importance of family. 'I have never met Monsieur Laurendeau, but I've heard that he's a very distinguished man. I am surprised that you haven't built up your acquaintance, Bérard.'

Bérard pursed his lips and wagged his index finger backwards and forwards in front of them to show how sealed they were.

'Papa is not a snob,' said Madame Bérard.

Isabelle had grown increasingly quiet. She wished Stephen would catch her eye or give some indication in his manner towards her that everything was all right. Jeanne had once said that men were not like women, that once they had possessed a woman it was as though nothing had happened and they just wanted to move on to another. Isabelle could not believe this of Stephen, not after what he had said and done with her in the red room. Yet how was she to know, when he gave her no sign, no smile of warmth? At first his self-control had been reassuring; now it worried her.

Under Azaire's instruction they left their coffee cups and made to transfer to another room for the advertised game of cards.

Isabelle searched for reassurance in Stephen's eyes in the safe mêlée of movement. He was looking at her, but not at her face. In the act of rising from her chair, in her characteristically modest movement, she felt his eyes on her waist and hips. For a moment she was naked again. She recalled how she had shown herself to him in her hot afternoon abandonment and how perversely right it had then seemed. Suddenly the shame and guilt belatedly overpowered her as she felt his eyes pierce her clothes, and she began to blush all over her body. Her stomach and breasts turned red beneath her dress as the blood beat the skin in protest at her immodesty. It rose up her neck and into her face and ears, as though publicly rebuking her for her most private actions. It cried out in the burning red of her skin; it begged for attention. Isabelle, her eyes watering from the heat of the risen blood, sat down heavily on her chair.

'Are you all right?' said Azaire, impatiently. 'You look very warm.'

Isabelle leaned forward on to the table and covered her face with her hands. 'I don't feel well. It's so hot in here.'

Madame Bérard put an arm round her shoulders.

'It's a circulation problem, without a doubt,' said Bérard. 'It's nothing to make a fuss about, it's quite a common ailment.'

As the blood retreated beneath her dress, Isabelle felt stronger. The colour remained in her face, though the beating of the pulse was less.

'I think I shall go to bed, if you don't mind,' she said.

'I'll send Marguerite up,' said Azaire.

Stephen could see no chance of speaking to her privately so merely wished her a polite good night as Madame Bérard took her by the elbow at the foot of the stairs and helped her up a step or two before rejoining the others.

'A circulation problem,' said Bérard, as he shuffled the cards in his plump fingers. 'A circulation problem. There it is. There it is.' He looked at Azaire, and his left eyelid slid down over the eyeball, remaining in place long enough for the broken blood vessels beneath the skin and the small wart to be visible before it was rotated smoothly back to its home beneath the skull.

Azaire gave a thin smile in response as he picked up his cards. Madame Bérard, who was searching in her handbag for her spectacles, saw nothing of the confidential male exchange. Aunt Élise had retired to the corner of the room with a book.

Upstairs Isabelle undressed quickly and slipped beneath the covers of her bed. She pulled up her knees to her stomach as she had done when she was a small girl in her parents' house and she had heard the whistling of the wind from the surrounding fields of Normandy as it worked the wooden shutters loose and sighed in the space beneath the roof. She prepared herself for sleep by filling her mind with the reassuring picture of peace and certainty she had always relied on; it contained an idealized version of her parents' home in a slightly fanciful pastoral setting, in which the sensuous effects of sun and flowers helped make analysis or decision seem unnecessary.

When she was almost in the arms of this vision there came a small knocking which at first seemed like something in the dream, then switched from one world to another to be identifiable as a soft but urgent tapping on the door of her room.

'Come in,' she said, her voice uncertainly sliding back into wakefulness.

The door opened slowly and Stephen appeared in the dim light from the landing.

'What are you doing?'

'I couldn't bear it downstairs.' He raised his finger to his lips and whispered. 'I had to see how you were.'

She smiled anxiously. 'You must leave.'

He looked about the room. There were her photographs of her sisters, her hairbrushes, a gilt mirror on the dressing table, her clothes laid across the chair.

He leaned over her bed, and felt his hand sink into the rich pile of covers beneath the quilt. A sweet smell rose up from the bed. He kissed her on the lips and touched her hair before leaving.

Isabelle shuddered as he went, fearing the noise of his foot-steps in the echoing corridor. Stephen moved, soundlessly to his own ears at least, to the main junction of the first-floor landing, then went downstairs to rejoin the game he had left.

The following morning Stephen went into town. Azaire told him he should not return to the factory for another day or so, but he found it difficult to stay quietly in the house with Lisette, Marguerite and various other visitors or members of the household preventing Isabelle from being alone or available to talk.

He thought of his life as a wood of confusion with two or three clear tracks on which he could orientate himself. From their directions he could remember and look forward with something like clarity. While they were straight enough and discernible to him, they also felt like scars that had been cut into the undergrowth, and he had no desire to reveal them to other people. For Isabelle he felt great gratitude and admiration; in the pressure of his emotions towards her there was an impulse to disclosure, a natural movement towards trust. He did not fear this nakedness but he did not feel pleasure at the prospect of it.

He was standing at the back of the cold cathedral, looking towards the choir stalls and the window in the east. It was quiet enough to think. There was the sound of a brush on the tiled floor as a cleaner worked her way down the side of the nave, and the occasional bang of the small entrance, set into the main doors, through which visitors arrived from time to time. A handful of people were praying in the body of the church. A medieval bishop was commemorated in Latin on a stone beneath his feet, his name still not erased by the traffic of the years. Stephen felt sorry for whatever anguish had caused the urgent prayers of the scattered worshippers, though also mildly envious of their faith. The chilly, hostile building offered little comfort; it was a memento mori on an institutional scale. Its limited success was in giving dignity through stone and lapidary inscription to the trite occurrence of death. The pretence was made through memorial that the blink of light between two eternities of darkness could be

71

saved and held out of time, though in the bowed heads of the people who prayed there was only submission.

So many dead, he thought, only waiting for another eyelid's flicker before this generation joins them. The difference between living and dying was not one of quality, only of time.

He sat down on a chair and held his face in his hands. He saw a picture in his mind of a terrible piling up of the dead. It came from his contemplation of the church, but it had its own clarity: the row on row, the deep rotting earth hollowed out to hold them, while the efforts of the living, with all their works and wars and great buildings, were no more than the beat of a wing against the weight of time.

He knelt forward on the cushion on the floor and held his head motionless in his hands. He prayed instinctively, without knowing what he did. Save me from that death. Save Isabelle. Save all of us. Save me.

He arrived back too late to have lunch with Isabelle and Lisette, both of whom in their different ways were disappointed. He walked through the cool, quiet house, hoping to hear voices. Eventually he heard the sound of feet and he turned to see Marguerite going into the kitchen.

'Have you seen Madame Azaire?'

'No, Monsieur. Not since lunch. Perhaps she's in the garden.'

'And Lisette?'

'I think she's gone into town.'

Stephen began to look in all the rooms downstairs. Surely she must have known that he would return. She could not have gone out without leaving a message.

He turned the handle on a door that led to a small study. Isabelle was sitting inside, reading a book. She put it down and stood up as he came in.

He went over to her, not sure if he should touch her. She put her hand on his.

'I was in the cathedral. I lost track of time.'

She looked up at him. 'Is it all right? Is everything all right?'

He kissed her and she pressed herself close to him. He found his hands at once searching beneath her clothes.

Her eyes looked up into his. They were wide and enquiring, full of urgency and light. Almost at once they closed as she let out a little sigh of excitement.

They were leaning against the wall of the room and he had slipped his hand through the fastening at the back of her skirt. He could feel the satin under his fingers, then a round soft swell beneath. He felt her fingers on the front of his trousers.

'We must stop.' He pulled himself back.

'Yes. Lisette has gone.' Isabelle was breathless. 'But Marguerite.'

'The red room?'

'Yes. You go first and go up to your room. Give me ten minutes before you come down.'

'All right,' he said. 'Let me kiss you goodbye.'

He kissed her deeply and she began to sigh again and rubbed herself against him. 'Please,' she said, 'please.'

He did not know if she meant him to stop or to continue. He had lifted her skirts as she stood with her back to the wall and now had his fingers between her legs. 'Come to me,' she whispered, her breath hot in his ear. 'Into me, now.' He removed her fumbling fingers from his trousers and freed himself. His shoulder was next to the polished wood of a glass-fronted bookcase. Behind Isabelle's head was a framed picture of flowers in a terracotta pot. He had to lift her a little, clasping her legs around his waist so that he could not move but had to bear her weight. The flowers moved half a turn on their hook as her shoulder nudged them.

She opened her eyes again and smiled at him. 'I love you.' She covered his face with kisses, keeping his body captive by her weight. Then she put her feet on the ground again and gently pulled him out of her. His flesh was rigid and swollen with blood. She ran her hand up and down it until he began to pant and give way at the knees, then spurted on to the floor, then against her dress, before she could take the last three or four spasms in her mouth. She appeared to do this from instinct, almost from a sense of tidiness, not because it was something she had known about or done before.

'The red room,' she said. 'In ten minutes.'

Her clothes had fallen back into place. She seemed unaware

of any mark on the front of her dress. Stephen watched her as she moved from the room, her walk, as always, a modest sway beneath the skirt. He felt awkward, half-undressed; it was as though she had treated him like a boy and taunted him, though he did not dislike the feeling. He rearranged his trousers and shirt and took his handkerchief to the polished parquet.

He walked briefly in the garden, trying to cool his head, then, as instructed, went up to his room. He watched the minute hand crawl round on his pocket-watch. If he added three minutes for the garden, that gave him only seven to endure. When it was time, he removed his shoes and went silently to the first floor. Down the main corridor to a narrow passage, down again and through a little arch . . . He remembered the way.

Isabelle was waiting inside. She wore a robe with some oriental pattern in green and red.

She said, 'I was so afraid.'

He sat down next to her on the stripped bed. 'What do you mean?'

She took his hand between both of hers. 'When you wouldn't look at me last night I was afraid that you'd changed your mind.'

'About you?'

'Yes.'

He felt invigorated by Isabelle's concern. It still seemed improbable to him that she could really want him so much.

He took her hair and all its colours in his hands. He felt grateful to her also. 'After all we said and all we did. How could you doubt?'

'You wouldn't look at me. I was frightened.'

'What could I have said? I would have given us away.'

'You must smile or nod. Something. Promise me that.' She had started to kiss his face. 'We'll work out a signal. Promise me, won't you?'

'Yes. I promise you.'

He let her undress him, passively standing by as she took off his clothes and folded them on the chair. He braved the exposure of his gross excitement and she affected not to notice.

74

'My turn,' he said, but there was only the silk robe to take off and then the beauty of Isabelle's skin. He laid his cheek against the whiteness of her chest and kissed her throat where he had seen the flush of exertion when she had been gardening. The skin was young and new and almost white, with its patterning of little marks and freckles that he tried to taste with the tip of his tongue. Then he laid her gently down on the bed and buried his face in the fragrance of her hair, covering his own head with it. Next, he made her stand up again while he worked slowly over her body with his hands and his tongue. He let his fingers trail only briefly between her legs and felt her stiffen. At last, when he had touched every part of her skin, he turned her round and bent her forwards on to the bed, then moved her ankles a little further apart with the pressure from his foot.

When they had finished making love they slept, Isabelle beneath a blanket with her arm draped over Stephen, he uncovered, on his front, at an angle across the mattress. She had not yet had time to wash and return the sheets.

When he awoke he at once rested his head on her splayed hair and breathed in the perfume of her skin where his face was against her neck and the soft underline of her jaw. She smiled as she felt his skin and opened her eyes.

He said, 'I was convinced when I came down the stairs that I wouldn't be able to find this room again. I thought it wouldn't be here.'

'It won't move. It's always here.'

'Isabelle. Tell me. Your husband. One night I heard sounds from your room as though he was . . . hurting you.'

Isabelle sat up, pulling the blanket over her. She nodded. 'Sometimes he . . . becomes frustrated.'

'What do you mean?'

Her eyes filled with tears. 'We wanted to have children. Nothing seemed to happen. I used to dread each month . . . you know.'

He nodded.

'The blood was like a rebuke. He said it was my fault. I tried for him, but I didn't know what to do. He was very

75

brusque, he wasn't cruel to me but he just wanted to do it quickly so I would be pregnant. It was not like with you.'

Isabelle suddenly looked shy. To mention what they did seemed more shameful than to do it.

She went on, 'Eventually he began to doubt himself, I think. To start with he was so sure it was nothing to do with him because he had two children. Then he was not so sure. He seemed to grow jealous of me because I was young. "You're so healthy, of course," he would say. "You're just a child." And things like that. There was nothing I could do. I always made love to him, though I didn't enjoy it. I never criticized him. He seemed to build up this disgust with himself. It made him talk to me sarcastically. Perhaps you've noticed. He began to criticize me all the time when other people were here. I think that for some reason he felt guilty about marrying me.'

'Guilty?'

'Perhaps towards his first wife, or perhaps because he felt he married me under false pretences.'

'Because he took you away from someone of your own age?'

Isabelle nodded, but did not speak.

'And then?'

'Eventually it became so bad that he could no longer make love to me. He said I castrated him. Naturally this made him feel worse and worse. So he would try to make himself excited by doing . . . strange things.'

'What?'

'Not, not like the things you and I . . .' Isabelle stopped in confusion.

'Did he hit you?'

'Yes. To begin with it was to try to make himself excited. I don't know why this was supposed to help. Then I think it was out of frustration and shame. But when I protested he said it was part of making love and I must submit to it if I wanted to be a good wife and to have children.'

'Does he hit you very hard?'

'No, not very hard. He slaps me on the face and on the back. He takes a slipper sometimes and pretends I am a child.

76

Once he wanted to hit me with a stick, but I stopped him.'

'And he has hurt you badly?'

'No. I have occasionally had a bruise, or a red mark. It isn't the damage I mind. It's the humiliation. He makes me feel like an animal. And I feel sorry for him because he humiliates himself. He is so angry and so ashamed.'

'How long has it been since you made love?' Stephen felt the first twinge of jealous self-interest cloud his sympathy.

'Almost a year. It is absurd that he still pretends that's why he comes to my room. We both know he comes only to hit me now, or to hurt me. But we pretend.'

Stephen was not surprised by what Isabelle had told him, though he was incensed at the thought of Azaire hurting her.

'You must stop him. You must end this. You must tell him not to come to your room.'

'But I am frightened of what he would do, or what he would say. He would tell everyone that I was a bad wife, that I wouldn't sleep with him. I think he already tells stories to his friends about me.'

Stephen thought of Bérard's secret glances. He took Isabelle's hand and kissed it, then held it against his face. 'I will look after you,' he said.

'Dear boy,' she said. 'You are so strange.'

'Strange?'

'So serious, so . . . removed. And the things you make me do.'

'Do I make you do things?'

'No, not like that. I mean, I do things of my own accord but it is only because of you. I don't know if these things are right, if they are . . . allowed.'

'Like downstairs?'

'Yes. I know, of course I know, I am unfaithful, but the actual things. I've never done them before. I don't know if they are normal, if other people do them. Tell me.'

'I don't know,' said Stephen.

'You must know. You're a man, you've known other women. My sister Jeanne told me about the act of love but that's all I knew. You must understand more.'

Stephen was uneasy. 'I've known only two or three other

women. It was quite different with them. I think what we do is its own explanation.'

'I don't understand.'

'Nor do I. But I know you mustn't feel ashamed.'

Isabelle nodded, though her face showed dissatisfaction with Stephen's answer.

'And do you?' he said. 'Do you feel guilty?'

Isabelle shook her head. 'I think perhaps I should feel guilty. But I don't.'

'And do you worry about that? Do you worry that you have lost something, lost the power to feel ashamed, lost touch with the values or the upbringing that you would have expected to make you feel a sense of guilt?'

Isabelle said, 'No. I feel that what I have done, that what we are doing, is right in some way, though it is surely not the way of the Catholic Church.'

'You believe there are other ways of being right or wrong?'

Isabelle looked puzzled, but she was clear in her mind. 'I think there must be. I don't know what they are. I don't know if they can ever be explained. Certainly they are not written down in books. But I have already gone too far now. I can't turn back.'

Stephen folded his arms around her and squeezed her. He lay back on the bed with her head resting on his chest. He felt her body go limp as the muscles decontracted into sleep. There was the sound of doves in the garden. He felt his heart beat against her shoulder. The smell of roses came faintly from her scented neck. He settled his hand in the curve of her ribs. His nerves were stilled in the sensuous repletion of the moment that precluded thought. He closed his eyes. He slept, at peace.

RENÉ AZAIRE HAD no suspicions of what was happening in his house. He had allowed his feelings towards Isabelle to become dominated by anger and frustration at his physical impotence and by what he subsequently experienced as a kind of emotional powerlessness towards her. He did not love her, but he wanted her to be more responsive towards him. He sensed that she felt sorry for him and this infuriated him further; if she could not love him then at least she should be frightened of him. At the root of his feeling, as Isabelle had guessed, was a sense of guilt. He remembered the pleasure he had taken in being the first man to invade that body, much younger than his, and the thrill he could not deny himself when she had cried out in pain. He remembered the puzzled look in her eyes when she gazed up at him. He could feel that she, more than his first wife, had the capacity to respond to the physical act, but when he saw the bewildered expression in her face he was determined to subdue it rather than to win her to him by patience. At the time Isabelle, though too wilful for her father's taste, was still docile and innocent enough to have been won over by a man who showed consideration and love, but with Azaire these things were not forthcoming. Her emotional and physical appetites were awakened but then left suspended as her husband turned his energy towards a long, unnecessary battle with his own shortcomings.

He meanwhile had no reason to mistrust Stephen. The Englishman clearly knew a good deal about the business for a man of his age, and he handled himself well with Meyraux

79

and the men. He did not exactly like Stephen; if he had asked himself why, he would have said there was something cold or withdrawn in him. Although in Stephen they expressed themselves in different ways, these were in fact the qualities Azaire disliked in himself. Stephen seemed too private and too self-contained to be the sort of man who would chase women, in any event. In Azaire's imagination such men would always declare themselves with flirtatious talk; they would be handsome and much wittier than he was and would charm women in an obvious and seductive manner. Bérard, for instance, would no doubt have been a ladies' man when younger, he thought. Stephen's quiet politeness was not threatening, and although he did seem old for his age he was, nevertheless, still a boy. His English suit sat well on him and he had a full head of hair, but he was not what Azaire would have called handsome. He was a lodger, a paying guest who was a notch above Marguerite in his claims on Azaire's attention but not quite a full member of his household.

Azaire was in any case preoccupied by his factory. In the clatter of machinery and the irritation of paperwork and decisions, he seldom thought of home or of his children, or of Isabelle.

A week after the disturbance he told Stephen it would be all right for him to return to work, though he should not attend any meetings Meyraux might call. The danger of a strike seemed to have lessened; little Lucien, Azaire was pleased to see, was unable to arouse the passions of his workers. Azaire was surprised when Stephen said he would wait another day or so; he thought he must be bored staying in the house with only Isabelle and Lisette for company, but he agreed to postpone the return until the beginning of the following week.

Stephen's telegram to London had been answered in detail by a letter from his employer. He was to stay until the end of the month, but would then be expected to deliver written reports to Leadenhall Street. Stephen felt he had done well to be granted even three extra weeks and sent a reassuring telegram back. He didn't mention the date of his departure to Isabelle; it seemed sufficiently distant for him not to have to worry, and the days were so full that his life seemed to change from one to the next.

At the weekend came the fishing expedition to the Ancre. The Bérards were unable to accompany them because Aunt Élise had been taken ill, so it was only the Azaires with Marguerite and Stephen in attendance who set out to take the train to Albert.

The station had a vast cobbled forecourt and central glass arch crowned by a pointed clock tower. It was said to have prefigured the work of Haussmann in Paris. While the rest of Amiens consciously imitated the capital, the people were proud that their station had shown the way. Horse-cabs waited in a line to the right of the huge glass-topped entrance and a row of small horseless carts were parked beneath two gas lamps set into the cobbles. To the left of the entrance was a formal garden with three oval patches of grass at various angles which unhinged the balanced vista that should have greeted passengers approaching from the street.

The ticket hall was busy with families negotiating excursions to the countryside. Trolleys with clanking wheels were pushed up and down the platform by vendors offering wine and loaves of bread filled with cheese or sausage. By the time the Azaires arrived, the windows of the large restaurant were already steamed up with the vapour from the kitchen where the soup was boiling for lunch. An aroma of cress and sorrel was just discernible when the swing doors pushed open to reveal the waiters in their black waistcoats and long white aprons carrying trays of coffee and cognac to the tables at the front and shouting back orders to the bar. At the end furthest from the kitchen was a tall cash desk at which a grey-haired woman was making careful entries in a ledger with a steel-nibbed pen.

Two locomotives were panting on the polished rails, their tenders piled high behind them. The black of the coal, and smudged faces of the driver and fireman, spoke of engineering toil and industrial work that had driven the tracks out west to Paris and north to the coast; this contrasted with the glossy flanks of the painted carriages and the bright display of local cloth among the women and children who thronged the platforms in pastel dresses with coloured parasols. Grégoire had to be dragged from his ecstatic admiration of the Paris express

81

and over to the platform where the small train was waiting to take the branch line to Albert and Bapaume.

On the hot plush of the carriage seats, they watched the centre of the city recede slowly behind them. The spire of the cathedral flickered into view as the train heaved itself east to Longueau where it juddered over the lines of crossing rails before it found its course northwards and began to pick up speed, the wheeze of exhausted steam gradually replaced by the repeated sound of the wheels on the track beneath.

Lisette sat with her hands in her lap next to her step-mother in the middle of one bench seat with Grégoire on her other side and Azaire, flanked by Stephen and Marguerite, opposite.

'So are you going to catch the biggest fish?' she said to Stephen, her head on one side.

'I shouldn't think so. I expect you need special local knowledge. French fish are cleverer than English ones.'

Lisette giggled.

'Anyway, it doesn't matter how big the fish is. It's the sport of catching it.'

'I'll catch the biggest one,' said Grégoire. 'You wait.'

'I bet you don't catch a bigger one than Stephen,' said Lisette.

'Who?' said Azaire.

'You mean Monsieur Wraysford, Lisette,' said Isabelle primly, her voice snagging slightly on her own hypocrisy.

Lisette looked at her step-mother with calm, quizzical eyes. 'Do I? Oh, yes, I suppose I do.'

Isabelle felt her heart whisper and beat. She dared not catch Stephen's eye, though had she looked she would not have found it, since at the first sound of his Christian name he had anticipated embarrassment and fixed his eyes on the landscape of green downland revealed in streaming rectangular frames by the windows of the train.

Neither Azaire nor Grégoire made anything of Lisette's slip, and Isabelle embarked on an urgent and insistent cross-examination of Marguerite about whether she had brought changes of clothes in case the children wanted to swim in the river.

'Anyway,' Lisette said to Grégoire, 'no one would want to eat anything you caught, would they, Ste – Monsieur?'

'What? Why not? I expect you're a good fisherman, aren't you, Grégoire? That's a fine new rod you've got there.'

Lisette looked angrily at her brother who appeared to have stolen Stephen's attention and said nothing for the rest of the journey.

A second train took them from Albert out along the small country line beside the Ancre, past the villages of Mesnil and Hamel to the station at Beaucourt. The sun appeared from behind clouds banked high above a wooded hill, and lit up the green valley of the river. There were some meadows between the railway line and the water and some large areas of unkempt grass. They picked their way down a dry path and through a gate in the fence that lay twenty yards or so back from the river. They could see other anglers on the opposite bank, solitary men and a few boys perched on stools or sitting in some cases with their feet in the water. The Ancre was sometimes no wider than a strong stone's throw and in other places broad and forbidding enough for only a confident swimmer to contemplate crossing. In the wide stretches there seemed barely any agitation of the surface that licked the margins marked by rushes and rotting logs which had caught in the weeds; in the narrower reaches the water occasionally showed white where a small current split the surface.

Azaire installed himself on a canvas stool and lit his pipe. He was disappointed that the Bérards had not been able to accompany them; conversation was never more enjoyable than when Bérard was there to bring out the best in him. These days there was not much to say to Isabelle, and the children bored him. He baited his line and cast it carefully into the water. With or without Bérard, it was not a bad way to pass a summer's day, beside a river in pleasant countryside, with the sound of rooks in the trees and the peaceful swell of the downs all round him.

Stephen helped Grégoire to bait his new rod and then settled himself at the foot of a tree. Lisette stood and watched him, while Isabelle and Marguerite set out a rug in the shade.

By one o'clock no one had caught anything. The river's surface had been undisturbed by fish of any kind, though they could just make out the figure of a small boy some way down the opposite bank whose home-made float seemed barely to touch the water before the line was whisked in again with a flashing, heavy creature on the end. They walked back to the station and took a pony and trap up the hill to the village of Auchonvillers which had been recommended by Bérard as having a passable restaurant. He had not been to it himself but had been told it was well known in the district.

Azaire straightened his tie outside the door. Isabelle ran her eye quickly over the children to make sure they were respectable. Auchonvillers was a dull village consisting of one principal road and a few tracks and lesser streets behind it, most of them connected to farms or their outbuildings. The restaurant was more accurately a café, though its dining room was full of local families taking lunch.

They had to wait by the entrance until a young woman showed them to a table. They settled down at last and Isabelle smiled encouragingly at Grégoire, whose hunger had made him sulky.

'At least people seem to be properly dressed,' said Azaire, looking round the room.

Marguerite was nervous about eating with her employers and could not decide what she wanted to eat when the waitress returned. She asked Isabelle to decide for her. Azaire poured wine for himself and, after she had fractiously insisted, for Lisette.

Stephen looked over the table at Isabelle. Six days earlier she had been Madame Azaire, the distant and respected object of his passion. Now she was grafted to him, in flesh and in feeling. There was the high collar of her dress with the dull red stone at the throat, the formal arrangement of her hair and the eyes turning this way and that in social concern but keeping always that point of light at the centre that seemed to him to speak so clearly of her hidden life that he sometimes felt amazed that other people could not read her infidelity with a single glance. He watched her talking to Grégoire or reassuring Marguerite, and he wanted to be alone with her, not making love, but talking to a truer version of her. When he judged there was a safe moment, he sought out her eyes with his and inclined his head in a gesture of affirmation so small that only

Isabelle could have seen it, and he saw by the fractional softening of her expression that she had.

At this moment Stephen knew he would not return to England. There had been the possibility, he now conceded, that his feeling for Isabelle could have been discharged or relieved by what they did in the red room. But it had become clear to him that it was not a contained appetite that could be exhausted or satisfied. It split and spread and changed its shape and entered areas of his thought and feeling far removed from the physical act itself. It had become more important to him than the maintenance of his livelihood or his career; he could not rest until he knew where it would end. Almost as decisive as his tenderness towards Isabelle was an overpowering sense of curiosity.

Although his mind worked clearly and had never had any difficulty in dispatching the tasks set for it by schoolmasters or employers, Stephen had not developed the habit of analysis. His confidence in himself was not checked by judgement; he followed where nothing more than instinct took him, and relied on some reflexive wariness to help. Looking at Isabelle, he knew also that the feeling he had for her was of a kind seldom experienced, and therefore he was obliged to follow it.

A strong, metallic-tasting trout was succeeded by a watery stew which they managed to eat with the help of quantities of bread. Isabelle, engrossed with making Grégoire eat his food, looked serene when she turned periodically to the rest of the table. Stephen guessed that it was the deliberate destruction of the basis of her family role that made her able to resume it with such apparent contentment. No sarcasm of her husband, no suggestive remark of Lisette or pointless tantrum of Grégoire could now disturb her charming equilibrium.

After lunch they returned to the river. Azaire went back to his stool and Grégoire to a small tree trunk he had found at the edge of the water. Stephen walked down the bank in the direction of Beaucourt. The big sky over the rolling farmland had now cleared and was filled with the sound of larks, which made him shudder in distaste. He sat down at the foot of a tree and idly began to bait the hook on the rod Azaire had lent him. He felt a hand lightly touch his shoulder and another cover his eyes. He started, but then relaxed at the gentleness of the touch. He placed his own hand over the fingers on his shoulder and stroked them. They were slender and feminine. He gripped the hand and turned round. It was Lisette. She gave a little cry of triumph.

'You didn't think it would be me, did you?'

Knowing his eyes had already betrayed his surprise, Stephen merely said, 'I didn't hear you creep up behind me.'

'You expected it to be someone else, didn't you?' Lisette had a coquettish but determined look.

'I wasn't expecting anyone.'

Lisette walked around him, her hands behind her back. She was wearing a white dress and her hair was tied back with a pink ribbon.

'You see, Monsieur Stephen, I know everything about you and my step-mother.'

'What do you mean?'

Lisette laughed. Stephen remembered the wine she had drunk at lunchtime. She lowered her voice and said huskily, '"My darling Isabelle,"' then sighed and panted as though with longing or desire, before beginning to laugh again.

Stephen shook his head and smiled in feigned incomprehension.

'That day after lunch I went out into the garden and I fell asleep on a bench. When I woke up I walked back to the house. I still felt a little dizzy when I got back, so I sat down on the terrace and I heard sounds from an open window upstairs. They were very quiet, but they were such funny sounds.' Lisette began to laugh again. 'And that evening after dinner I heard someone creeping oh-so-quietly along the corridor to her room then tiptoeing back downstairs.'

She looked at Stephen with her head on one side. 'Well?' she said.

'Well what?'

'What do you say?'

'I think you're a girl with a strong imagination.'

'Yes, I'm certainly that. I've been imagining all the things you've been doing and I think I would like to try them.'

Stephen laughed in genuine amusement.

'It isn't funny. You don't want my father to know what I've been hearing.'

'You're a child,' said Stephen, feeling himself begin to sweat.

'No I'm not. I'm almost seventeen. I'm nearer your age than *she* is.'

'Do you like Isabelle?'

Lisette looked taken aback. 'No. I mean yes, I used to.'

'She's been kind to you.'

Lisette nodded.

'Think about that,' said Stephen.

'I will. But you shouldn't have led me on.'

'Shouldn't have what?'

'When you gave me that carving, I thought . . . You know, you *are* the right age for me. Why shouldn't I have wanted you for myself?'

Stephen began to see that she was not a child who was making trouble for its own sake, but someone whose feelings had been hurt. There was some truth in the things she said.

'I'm sorry about the carving,' he said. 'You were sitting next to me. If it had been Grégoire I would have given it to him. I meant nothing by it. In fact I did make one for Grégoire later.'

'So it meant nothing at all?'

'I'm afraid not.'

Lisette put her hands on his arm. 'Stephen, I'm not a child, even if they treat me as one. I'm a woman – at least almost a woman. My body is a woman's body, not a child's.'

He nodded. He thought by keeping calm he might placate her. 'I understand. It's difficult for you, especially without a mother.'

'What do you know about my mother?'

'Don't be angry, Lisette. I have no mother, either, and no father. I do know, I do understand.'

'All right. Perhaps you do. But I meant what I said. I want you to do those things to me.'

'I can't do that, Lisette. You must know that. Be fair to me. Be fair to yourself.'

'Is it that I'm not pretty enough? Am I not as pretty as her?'

He looked at her. Flushed with wine and confusion, she

was attractive. She had deep-set brown eyes with thick lashes, coarse hair and a slim waist.

'Yes, you're pretty.'

'Touch me, then, touch me as you touch her.'

She held on to his arm with both hands. He realized how affected she was by the wine; her eyes did not quite focus as she looked up into his.

She took his hand and rubbed it between her breasts. Despite himself, Stephen felt the reflex of desire.

'Lisette,' he said, 'this is very foolish. Your parents are just round the bend in the river. I am not going to let you tease me or humiliate yourself. What I will do, if you like, is to kiss you, just very quickly, if you promise that you will go away and never say another word about this.'

She said, 'No.'

'What do you mean, "no"?'

'I mean you have to touch me.'

She took his hand again and rubbed her breasts then guided it to her waist. Something in the perversity of the situation had started to arouse him and he did not at once withdraw his hand when she placed it beneath her lifted skirt, at the top of her thigh. Then she slid it inside her drawers where he felt fine hair and wet parted flesh.

He pulled it away at once because his inclination was to leave it there and he knew if he did so it would be the start of something more awful and more hopeless than he had already begun.

Lisette had frozen at his touch; it seemed to have sobered and frightened her. She started to move away but he took her by the wrist.

He looked fiercely into her eyes and said, 'Now you understand. You must never begin these things. And you will never, never mention a word of what you were saying earlier, not to your father, not to anyone.'

Lisette nodded. 'No. I promise. I want to go now. I want to go home.'

She had forgotten about the English teas at Thiepval.

FOR A FURTHER week Isabelle and Stephen lived their strange existence in the boulevard du Cange, going through the daily rituals of normal behaviour even though their minds existed elsewhere. Each noticed, with admiration and some misgiving, how easily the other was able to pretend.

Stephen found that their hurried and clandestine couplings were made more powerful to him by their element of fear. They made love where they could: in the red room, in temporarily deserted sitting rooms, on the grassy bank at the foot of the garden. The urgency of limited time removed all inhibitions.

He did not pause to think. His mind was disarrayed by passion. It had become capable of only one desire or thought: that things should continue. The calm nature of his public behaviour was given to him by this imperative.

Isabelle was bemused by the power of the physical life that had suddenly opened up in her and found equal excitement in their fast and dangerous exchanges. But she missed the intimacy of conversation that they had first had in the red room; this seemed to her as delicate an art of closeness as any physical touch they had yet discovered.

One day, following a whispered consultation in the hall, Stephen contrived to come back from the factory early when Isabelle had dispatched Marguerite and Lisette for the afternoon.

He found her already waiting for him in the red room. Afterwards, as he sat back against the pillows, he stared at the picture of a medieval knight above the mantelpiece. In the grate there was a fire laid with neatly chopped kindling and coal. Against the far wall was a large country wardrobe in which were stored unused curtains, rugs, winter coats and various vases, clocks and boxes with no place in the house. The wood of the window frame was stripped and unpainted. Some white flowers of clematis moved in a light breeze against the glass.

It was the first chance Stephen had had since their excursion to the river to tell Isabelle about Lisette. In the reckless trust of his passion he told her everything, expecting her to value his honesty above any meaner feeling of unease.

Isabelle seemed curious. 'I don't understand where she could have learned about these things.'

'I suppose she's older than we thought. Didn't you feel such things at that age?'

Isabelle shook her head. 'Jeanne had told me what would happen one day, but I had no feelings of desire, not in the way you describe Lisette.'

'I think she feels the loss of her mother. She wants attention.'

'Was she excited? Was she . . . I don't know how to ask.'

'You mean would she be ready to make love to a man?'

'Yes.'

'Yes, she would be ready as a woman, in her body, but she would almost certainly choose the wrong man.'

'You.'

'Or worse.'

Isabelle shook her head. 'Poor Lisette.'

She looked over at him. She said, 'Did you want to . . . with her?'

'No. For a moment there was a reflex, like an animal. But no. I only ever want to do it with you.'

'I don't believe you.' Isabelle laughed.

Stephen smiled at her. 'You're teasing me, Isabelle.'

'Yes, of course I am.' She ran her hand down his abdomen. 'You are wicked,' she whispered in his ear.

Sometimes Stephen felt his body was no more than a channel for exterior powers; it had no proper sense of fatigue or proportion. He thought of Lisette as he lay on top of Isabelle again. He believed Isabelle had found the story of Lisette's indiscretion in some perverse way arousing.

Later he said, 'I am worried that she'll tell your husband.'

Isabelle, who had recovered her composure, said, 'I'm more worried that I have a duty to stay and look after her.'

'To stay?'

'Yes. Instead of . . .'

'Instead of coming with me to England?'

Isabelle, confronted with the thought at last in words, nodded dumbly.

Stephen felt a quiet elation; although he had supplied the words, the idea had been hers.

'But that's what you will do,' he said. 'You will leave the husband who beats you and go with the man who loves you. Lisette is not your child. You've already done well by her, you've been helpful to her. But you must live your own life eventually. You have one chance only.'

He heard the declamatory note in what he had said but did not disown it. He wanted Isabelle to remember the words so that they would count with her when she was alone, making her decision.

'And what would we do in England?' she teased him, not yet willing to think about it properly.

Stephen breathed in slowly. 'I'm not sure. We'd go and live somewhere remote, not in London. I would find work in a business of some kind. We would have children.'

This seemed to take the lightness out of Isabelle's manner. 'And Lisette and Grégoire . . . They would lose another mother.'

'And if you stay you will lose your life.'

'I don't want to think about it.'

'But you must. I'm supposed to return to London next week. You could come with me. Or we could go away together somewhere in France.'

'Or you could stay and work here in the town. We could meet.'

'Not that, Isabelle. You know that wouldn't work.'

'I must dress again. I must go downstairs to be ready for when Lisette comes back.'

'Before you go, I want to ask you something. Lucien Lebrun. There was a rumour that you and he . . .'

'Lucien!' Isabelle laughed. 'I like him. I think he's admirable, but really . . .'

'I'm sorry. I shouldn't have asked. It's just that . . . I was worried.'

'Don't worry. Don't ever worry. There's only you. Now really I must get dressed.'

'Let me dress you, then.'

He went to fetch her clothes from the chair where she had left them. 'Put your foot here and the other one here. Now stand up. And does this come next? How does this fasten? Let me just straighten this. You're breathing so hard, my love. Was it here that I touched, was it here?'

Isabelle was half-dressed, half-revealed. She stood holding Stephen's head as he sank to his knees in front of her.

As she began to sigh again, he stood up in front of her and said, 'You will come with me, won't you?'

Her answer was hissed between closed teeth.

The front door banged as Azaire made his way down the hall with a copy of the evening paper in his hand.

'Isabelle!' he called. 'The strike is finished. The dyers return tomorrow.'

She appeared at the top of the stairs. 'That's good news.'

'And tomorrow Meyraux will recommend my new terms to the men.'

'I'm very pleased.'

At least it meant Azaire would be in a good mood, she thought; he would not persecute her with words or come to her room later to air his frustration.

'And when will you be leaving us, Monsieur?' said Azaire at dinner, pouring a small measure of wine into Stephen's glass.

'At the end of the week, as we planned.'

'Good. It has been interesting for us at the factory, as I was saying to you this morning. I hope you've enjoyed your time with us.'

'It has been a pleasure to stay with your charming family.'

Azaire looked contented. His eyes for once lost their wounded look. The prospect of a return to normal routine in all aspects of his life evidently pleased him.

Isabelle saw his relief at Stephen's imminent departure and the end of the strike, but she could not understand how he could so happily contemplate a resumption of his life as it had been. The way he treated her might, at some stretch of his imagination, be viewed as a painful and provisional transition towards a better feeling, but not as a desirable way of behaviour that he was anxious to begin again. She was not frightened of him, but his attitude depressed her. Winters of loneliness stretched out in front of her; if he was content not to change, then she would find deeper isolation in his presence than in her own.

Meanwhile there was Stephen, an alternative she could not consider with any kind of calmness. There was too much danger in her feeling and in the practical details of what they could do. She felt she might avoid the fallibility of her own judgement by depending on his; though he was younger, he seemed sure of what was right.

Lisette had been subdued since the excursion to the river; she no longer enlivened dinner with sulks or suggestive remarks. She would not catch Stephen's eye, though he tried to meet hers with some reassurance. She sat in silence over her food as the sound of the clock on the small marble-topped serving table became louder in the room.

'I heard the strangest story,' said Azaire abruptly.

'What was that?' said Isabelle.

'They told me that at the height of the strike someone was visiting little Lucien and was taking him parcels of food to give to the dyers' families.'

'Yes, I heard that,' said Stephen. 'A number of sympathetic people in the town helped the strikers. There was one man in particular who wanted to be anonymous. So I was told at the factory.'

'Oh dear me no,' said Azaire. 'This wasn't a man, this was a woman, who used to go along disguised to wherever Lebrun lives.'

'The strikers had help from many sources, I expect.'

'But the strangest thing about this woman was that she was married to the owner of a factory.' Azaire paused and looked round the table. Neither of the children were listening. Isabelle was motionless.

'Now isn't that a strange thing?' said Azaire raising his glass to his lips. 'I couldn't believe it when I heard it.'

'I don't think it's strange,' said Isabelle. 'It was me.'

Stephen looked at her uncomprehendingly. Azaire replaced his wine glass heavily on the table.

'But my dear –'

'I took them food because they were hungry. I had no idea of whether they should be on strike or not, but I had seen their children asking for bread, running along behind the carts bringing in vegetables to the market. I had seen them going through the dustbins in Saint-Leu and I felt sorry for them.'

Isabelle's voice was surprisingly calm. She said, 'I would do the same again, whether the people made cloth or shoes or anything else.'

Azaire was white; his lips were a shade of pale purple as though even this soft membrane had repelled his blood.

'Leave the room,' he said to Lisette. 'And you.'

Grégoire pushed his chair noisily back on the wooden floor, pausing to take a piece of chicken from his plate.

Azaire stood up. 'I discounted these rumours. I did not believe them, even though it was your name that was attached to them and I suppose I should have learned about you by now. However wilful and selfish you are I could not believe that you would ever, ever behave towards me in such a way. And you, Monsieur, you had better leave the room.'

'No. Let him stay.'

'Why? He's –'

'Let him stay.'

A look of panic passed over Azaire's face. He tried to speak, but failed. He drank again from his glass. His imagination seemed to be supplying more appalling possibilities than his previously controlled and teasing anger could admit.

He struggled towards the worst question. He began it, 'You . . .?' He looked towards Stephen, then down at the table. His courage visibly failed him. He fought with himself, then regained control by resuming his previous manner.

'I did not believe my wife could let me down in such a way. The further reason I would not believe the rumours was that there was another piece of tittle-tattle that went with them, which said that the lady in question was also . . .' He waved his hand, as though swatting the thought away. '. . . enjoying some liaison with Lebrun.'

'Not with Lucien,' said Isabelle.

Azaire's face seemed to collapse. His voice had so pitifully requested a complete dismissal of the rumour that Isabelle's partial denial appeared worse than a confirmation of what he feared.

She saw this and moved to end his uncertainty even if she could not stop his anguish. 'Not with Lucien. With Stephen.'

Azaire looked up from his seat. 'With . . . him?'

'Yes.' Stephen looked evenly back at him. 'With me. I pursued your wife. I seduced her. You must hate me not her.'

He wanted to protect Isabelle as far as he could, though he was astounded to find himself in this position: Isabelle could easily have prevaricated. His slow heart was beating hard. He looked at Azaire, whose jaw had gone loose, causing his mouth to open. There was a dribble of wine on his chin. Stephen pictured the misery from the way it affected the muscles of his face. He felt pity for him. Then, in the interests of preserving something for Isabelle and himself, he hardened his heart. It was an act of almost physical willpower, as he compelled the compassion to go out of him.

Isabelle was no longer able to be cold towards Azaire. The brief sentences with which she had informed him of her unfaithfulness seemed to have drained her resolve and she began to weep and to apologize to him for what she had done. Stephen listened carefully to what she said. He did not begrudge Azaire his wife's apologies but he did not want her to retreat too far.

Azaire was incapable of saying more than, 'With him? Here?'

Isabelle said, 'I'm sorry . . . so sorry, René. I meant you no harm. It is a passion for Stephen. It was not done to hurt you.'

'This . . . boy, this English boy? In my house? Where? In your bed?'

'It doesn't matter, René. It doesn't matter where.'

'It does to me. I want to know. Did you . . . in which room?'

'For God's sake,' said Stephen.

Azaire sat silently at the table, his hand still clutching the base of his glass. His mouth dropped open again and he screwed up his eyes in puzzlement, as though looking into a bright sun.

'And your father, Monsieur Fourmentier, what can he do . . . ? What will they say? My God, my God.'

Isabelle looked at Stephen and there was fear in her eyes. Stephen could see that she had not calculated what effect her sudden honesty would have on her husband. The fear was no doubt partly for Azaire's well-being but also seemed to be for herself: there was a chance that in the crisis she might lose her resolution and follow some older code of conduct which would compel her to put herself once more at Azaire's mercy. It made Stephen feel uneasy as he looked at the wreckage of this suddenly precipitated storm. He felt he needed to keep Isabelle's determination in place, but this could not be done if Azaire collapsed completely.

He was muttering to himself: 'Bitch . . . Your father told me and I never listened. In my own house. And now my children. What will become of them? Bitch.'

'Listen.' Stephen moved swiftly round the table and took him by the shoulders. 'What can you expect from a woman you have treated as you have treated Isabelle? Did you expect her to humiliate herself for your pleasure, to sit meekly at your table in the knowledge that you would beat her later?'

Azaire was rejuvenated. 'What did you tell him?'

'It doesn't matter what she told me. This is a house where everything can be heard. How can you sit there and call her names after what you've done to her? This is a woman with her own life and feelings and look what you have done to her. What have you *done*?' He pushed Azaire violently back into his chair.

Azaire seemed inspired by Stephen's anger. He stood up and said, 'You will leave my house within the hour. If you have any sense you will never let me see you again.'

'Certainly I will leave your house,' said Stephen. 'And I am taking your wife with me. Isabelle?'

'I don't want this.' Isabelle shook her head. The words came from her mouth without thought or calculation in their purity of feeling. 'I don't know what to do or how to behave now. I could be happy in the simplest way, like any other woman with a family of her own, without this terrible pain I've caused. I won't listen to either of you. Why should I? How do I know that you love me, Stephen? How can I tell?' Her voice fell to the low, soft note Stephen had heard when she spoke on his first evening in the house. It was a beautiful sound to his ears: pleading and vulnerable, but with a sense of strength in its own rightness. 'And you, René, why should I trust you when you have given me so little reason even to like you?'

Both men watched her in silence. Stephen believed in the strength of feeling between them, and believed it would persuade her.

Isabelle said, 'This is not a situation anyone can be prepared for. Nothing I have learned in religion, or from my family or my own thoughts is any help to me. I won't be painted as some sort of whore by you, René. I'm a frightened woman, no more than that – not an adulterer, or a harlot or anything else. I'm just the same person I ever was, but you never took the trouble to find out what that was.'

'Forgive me, I –'

'Yes, I do forgive you. I forgive you any wrong you've done me and I ask you to forgive me the wrong I've certainly done to you. I am going upstairs to pack.'

She left the room with a rustle of her skirt and a barely discernible trace of roses.

'You go with him,' Azaire shouted after her, 'and you are going to hell!'

Stephen turned and left the room, trying to still the exultation of his heart.

Isabelle placed the framed photograph of Jeanne on top of the clothes she had piled in her case. She paused for a moment, then added the family group with her parents in their Sunday best, Mathilde, dark-haired and womanly on her father's right hand, herself, a little fair-haired child on her mother's left, with Delphine, Jeanne and Béatrice standing behind. The photograph had been taken in a park in Rouen; among the plane trees in the background an oblivious couple were strolling over the gravel. In the foreground at her father's feet was the Fourmentiers' small white dog.

She looked into the staring face of her father, the eyes dark and remote above the thick moustache. How hard he would find it to understand what she was doing, she thought. How little he had ever tried.

She packed two more dresses and the blouse with the dog-toothed edging. She would need more practical clothes for travelling: a coat, and shoes she could walk in. Presumably she could send for others when they arrived wherever they were going.

Isabelle did not pause for thought. She wanted to be out of the house, alone with Stephen, before the certainty deserted her and she began to consider the practical details.

She heard footsteps in the corridor leading to her room and turned to see Stephen in the doorway. She ran to him and he held her close against his chest.

'You are a wonderful woman,' he said.

'What shall I say to the children?'

'Say goodbye to them. Tell them you'll write.'

'No.' Isabelle stepped back from him and shook her head. Tears flowed from her eyes. 'I have done wrong to them. I can't pretend otherwise. I must just leave them.'

'No goodbyes?'

'No. Quickly, Stephen. We must go. I'm ready to leave.'

'Wait here. I must get my papers.'

As Stephen ran up the stairs to his room he heard the sound of a woman's voice shouting and sobbing on the floor below. There came the noise of a door slamming and he heard Grégoire's voice asking what was going on. He threw his passport, his notebooks, work reports, razor and a change of clothes into a small leather bag. As he descended to the first landing, he saw Lisette standing in her nightgown outside her bedroom. She looked pale and shocked.

'What's happening?' she said. 'Why is everyone shouting?'

Stephen felt a rush of pity for the girl. He turned speechlessly from her and ran to Isabelle's room. She had put on a coat and a green hat with a feather. She looked touchingly young.

'All right?' said Stephen. 'Shall we go?'

She took his hand between hers and looked up into his grave face. She smiled and nodded as she picked up her case.

Each space and unexpected corridor beneath the plunging roof with its conflicting angles was alive with voices and the sound of feet, heavy, hesitant, running or turning back. The door to the kitchen banged and rolled repeatedly on its hinges as Marguerite and the cook shuttled back and forth to the dining room under the pretext of clearing dinner, then lingered, listening, in the hallway. At the top of the stairs Stephen appeared with his arm round Isabelle, guiding her past the stricken looks and questions.

'To hell,' Azaire repeated from the doorway of the sitting room.

Isabelle felt the pressure of Stephen's hand on the small of her back as they passed. She turned on the threshold of the house and saw the pale figure of Lisette at the bend of the stairs. She shuddered, and led Stephen out into the night.

Back inside the house Azaire ordered the children to wait on the landing while he went to Isabelle's room. He pulled back the cover on the bed and looked at the sheets. He ran his hands over them. They were clean, starched, barely touched by the weight of his wife's body. He went upstairs to his lodger's room and ripped back the blanket. The narrow bed was more disarrayed than Isabelle's, as though Stephen had slept less soundly or the maid had spent less time making it, but it bore no signs of adultery: the sheets were clean, with the ridge of the crease running neatly up the centre.

Azaire went back to the first floor and began to go through each room in turn. He raged with a desire to see the filth and shame of what they had done to him. He wanted to see the marks of his wife's betrayal, the stains of her degradation. In

99

the midst of his anger and his humiliation, he noted the return of a low urge he had not felt for many months.

Grégoire stood terrified on the landing as his father scrutinized his bed. Lisette clutched her brother's hand as they watched the wretched emotions of adulthood. Azaire held the sheets from Marguerite's bed up to the light, believing he had seen a mark, but it was no more than beeswax or polish from her hand where she had not washed properly. He ran his fingers over the linen in the guest rooms and laid his head on it, inhaling deeply. There was only the smell of camphor.

Eventually he stood defeated and flushed beneath the light at the top of the stairs. The doors to all the rooms stood open, their beds uselessly wrecked. Azaire was breathing heavily. In his haste and rage he had not thought of the red room. He had forgotten the narrow corridor with its plain wooden boards that doubled back from the garden side of the house towards the back stairs. Since he had first bought the house he had had no cause to visit it, had never in fact seen its finished shape, such as it was, after it had been cleared of the previous owners' unwanted belongings and modestly redecorated by Isabelle. It was a place he had not refound, but which had stayed, as Stephen had feared it might for him, beyond the reach of memory.

Stephen sat opposite Isabelle in the train going south towards Soissons and Reims. He felt the simple elation of his victory, the fact that it was he who had won, who had persuaded Isabelle against the weight of convention and sound argument to do the difficult and dangerous thing. And there was the deeper happiness of being with this woman, whom he loved, and the undeniable evidence, for the first time, that she was his. Isabelle smiled, then shook her head incredulously from side to side with closed eyes. When she opened them again they had a look of resignation.

'What will they say? What will he say to Bérard and to his friends?' Her voice was intrigued but not anxious.

'It's not the first time a wife has left her husband.' Stephen had no idea what Azaire would say, but he did not feel inclined to imagine. He felt it was important that he and Isabelle concentrated on themselves.

The train was the last of the evening, so they had had little choice of destination. At the station Isabelle had wrapped a shawl over her face, fearing recognition as she clambered on to the train. As it made its way south over the flat landscape, she relaxed; there might be years of regret, but the prospect of immediate drama and reverse had gone.

The train stopped at a dimly lit station and they looked out of the window at a porter unloading mail and pushing a trolley full of boxes to a wooden building that gave on to the empty stockyard. The man's face showed pale in the darkness. Behind him was the ordered black swell of a street, leading uphill into a town where the occasional yellow light showed hazily from behind curtains and shutters.

The train shrugged and clanked out of the station and made its way south through the tranquil night. The summer was almost at an end and there was an edge of cold to the air. To the east was the Forest of the Ardennes, and beyond it the Rhine. After a stop at Reims they followed the line of the Marne through Joinville. Occasionally the gloomy river would be caught by moonlight when the railway travelled alongside before retaking its own course through cuttings and embankments whose high sides enclosed it in darkness.

As they moved south, Isabelle came and sat next to Stephen, resting her head against his body. The rolling motion of the train made her eyes heavy; she slept as it picked out its set course, nosing its way south where the Marne joined the river Meuse, whose course linked Sedan to Verdun – a flat, unargued path through the lowlands of her native country.

She dreamed of pale faces beneath rose-coloured lights; Lisette at the corner of the stairs, the bloodless features in the red glow, a lost girl, and others like her caught in some repeated loop of time, its pattern enforced by the rhythmic motion of the train; many white-skinned faces with dark eyes, staring in disbelief.

They stayed in a hotel in the spa town of Plombières. It was a grey building with wrought-iron balconies and thick ivy.

Their room was on the first floor; it overlooked a damp garden with a broken summerhouse and a number of outsized cedar trees. Behind the wall at the far end were the baths themselves, whose waters were held to have curative properties for people with rheumatism, chest complaints and certain diseases of the blood. There were a dozen or so other residents in the hotel, mostly old couples, who ate in the ornate dining room. For the first three days Stephen and Isabelle barely left their room. Isabelle was tired by the journey and the strain of what she had done. She slept in the large wooden bed with its boat-shaped ends, and Stephen would sit beside her for hours, reading a book, smoking a cigarette or standing on the balcony, looking over the peaceful little spa.

A shy maid left trays outside their door at dinnertime and hurried back along the passageway. On the third day Stephen went down to the dining room on his own, and sat by the window that overlooked the square. The owner of the hotel brought him a menu.

'Is Madame your wife quite well?' he asked.

'Quite well, thank you. Just a little tired. I expect she'll come down tomorrow.'

Various residents nodded their greetings to Stephen as they took their places at table. He smiled back and drank from the bottle of wine he had ordered. A waiter brought fish in a heavy cream sauce. Stephen drank again and let himself slip into the tranquil atmosphere of this foreign world: nothing, he imagined, had changed for years in the ordered routine of the hotel, in the thin air or the rich food that was based on recipes from the eighteenth century, or in the probably imaginary qualities of the waters and the genteel, restrictive lives their presumed properties had supported in the town.

On the fourth day Isabelle ventured out with him for a walk. She took his arm like a long-married wife as they explored the streets, sat for a time in an almost grassless park and drank coffee in a square opposite the boys' school.

Stephen was endlessly curious. He asked Isabelle to describe her early life in the smallest detail; he never seemed to tire of stories of her days in Rouen.

'Tell me more about Jeanne.'

'I've told you everything I can think of. Now you tell me how you came to be in this place, this institution.'

Stephen exhaled slowly. 'There's not much to tell. My father worked for the post office in a flat part of England called Lincolnshire. My mother worked in a factory. They were not married, and when she became pregnant he disappeared. I never met him. From what I heard of him later he seemed an ordinary man, someone who took what he could find and preferred not to pay for it.'

'Is that what you think is ordinary?'

'It's how people live. My father probably had some charm, though he was not a handsome man, not what you would think of as a seducer. He was just a man who liked women and I should think I have half-brothers and sisters in England, though I've never met them. My mother left the factory and went back to live with her parents, who worked in a village. Her father was a farm labourer. My mother eventually got a job in service, as a maid in a big house. Like Marguerite.'

Isabelle watched Stephen's expression as he spoke. There seemed to be no emotion in his voice, though the line of his jaw had tightened a little.

'But my mother was not a strong character either. When I was a small child I wanted her to prove herself independent of my father, so that he could be dismissed from our minds. In fact she got pregnant again, by someone who worked at the house. She was fond of me but never looked after me much. I was brought up by my grandfather, who taught me to fish and catch rabbits. I was a real farm boy. He also taught me how to steal and how to fight. He was quite young, still in his fifties, and very fit. He regarded it as proper that any labouring man should augment his income in whatever way he could. He would have bare-knuckle fights for money, if enough was offered, and he stole from the larger houses in the district. Mostly food or animals he'd trapped.

'My mother went off with the man she'd met at the house. I heard that they went away to Scotland. Soon after this my grandfather was arrested on some small charge and was sent to prison. Part of his defence was that he needed to stay at home to look after me. The court ordered that I should be taken into a home in the local town since he was not fit to be my guardian. I'd been quite happy running wild, living with my grandmother, and the next thing I was dressed in a sort of tunic and set to work scrubbing floors and tables in this huge brick building. We had to do lessons as well, something I hadn't done before.

'There are things I remember about the place that will be with me even on the day I die. The smell of the soap that we used to clean the floors and the feel of the uniform against the skin. I remember the big room with a ceiling that was so high it was almost lost to view and the long tables we ate from. I'd been happy enough with my grandmother. I'd never seen so many people in one place before and it seemed to me each one of us was diminished by it. I had feelings of panic when we sat there, as though we were all being reduced to numbers, to ranks of nameless people who were not valued in the eyes of another individual.

'Those of us who had family or people to see were allowed out from time to time. I would spend the day with my grand-parents. He was back from prison by now. One day I had a fight with a local boy, and I hurt him much more than I meant to. I can't remember who started the fight or what it was about. It was probably my fault. I remember seeing him sink to the ground and wondering what I had done.

'His parents called the police and there was a fuss. I was sent back to the home because I was too young to stand trial. The incident was reported in the local paper and a man I had never heard of called Vaughan must have read about it. My grandmother was excited because this man was rich and said he wanted to help. He came to see me in the home and talked to me for a long time. He was convinced I was clever and needed to be given a chance to improve myself. He asked if I was willing to let him be appointed my guardian by the court. I'd have done anything to escape from the institution, and my grandparents were happy for someone else to take the responsibility.

'It took a year for all the legal things to be gone through. He was quite well known locally. He'd been a magistrate but hadn't married or had children himself. He insisted that I go to school during the day and he taught me himself in the evenings. I lived in his house and he somehow procured me a place in the grammar school.'

'What's that?'

'A school where they teach you Latin and Greek and history. And how to use a knife and fork.'

'Didn't you know how before?'

'Not with any finesse. But I learned all the lessons they gave me. It was difficult enough to begin with because I was so far behind. But the teacher was encouraging.'

'So he was your great benefactor, like the good genie in a story.'

'Yes. Except for one thing. I didn't like him. I thought he would treat me like his son. But he didn't. He just made me work. He was a social reformer of some kind, I suppose, like the priests who went into the slums of London to work with the boys there. I think his interest in my learning was a substitute for other things in life. He never showed me any affection, he just wanted to know how much progress I'd made with my studies.'

'But you must have felt grateful to him.'

'Yes, I felt grateful. I still do. I write to him from time to time. When I finished at the school he found me an interview for a job with a firm in London who paid for me to go to Paris on their behalf to learn the language and find out more about the textile industry. Then I worked in London, living in lodgings in a place called Holloway. Then I was dispatched to Amiens.'

He looked at her with relief. The self-revelation was over. 'That's it.'

Isabelle smiled at him. 'That's all? That's all your life? You seem so old to me, I think of you sometimes as being older than I am. It's your eyes, I think. Those big, sad eyes.' She stroked his face with the tips of her fingers.

When they returned to the hotel Isabelle went ahead to the bathroom. She noticed with dismay that, despite her elaborate carelessness, the blood had returned at its appointed time.

After a week in Plombières they travelled south. Stephen wrote to his company in London, enclosing his reports and explaining that he would not be returning. In Grenoble they celebrated his twenty-first birthday and he wrote to Vaughan thanking him for his guardianship, which was now ended. They stayed until some money arrived for Isabelle, wired from Rouen by Jeanne, whom she had contacted by letter. Stephen still had two large English bills which had been given to him by his guardian for use in case of emergency.

In October they arrived in St-Rémy-de-Provence, where Isabelle had a cousin on her mother's side. They rented a small house and Isabelle wrote to Marguerite, enclosing some money and asking her to send a trunkful of clothes. She specified exactly which ones she needed; the occasional item purchased en route had been no substitute for the outfits put together so carefully from shops in Amiens, Paris and Rouen or for the things she had added or sewn herself.

Resplendent again in her oxblood skirt and linen waistcoat, Isabelle read Marguerite's letter to Stephen as they sat over breakfast in the living room overlooking the street.

Dear Madame, I did not recognize your writing, perhaps you asked Monsieur to write it for you. I have sent the items you requested with this letter. Lisette is very well, thank you, and is being very good to Monsieur and is looking after him very well, she seems happy. Little Grégoire is also well, though he has not been to school every day. I am keeping well enough though we do miss you terribly, all of us, it's not the same without you. Monsieur and Madame Bérard have been to call on Monsieur most evenings and I sometimes hear the two gentlemen having long conversations. I have done what you asked and not shown your letter to anyone so they won't know that you are in St-Rémy. I wonder what it is like there and if you are keeping well. Everything is going along fine in the house but we hope you will come back soon. With warm wishes from Marguerite.

Stephen walked through the streets of the almost-deserted town. The fountain in the square round which people gathered in summer played coldly into its stone surround. The loose shutters on the houses were blown violently back against the buildings by the autumnal wind that was rolling in from the south. Stephen did not mind the feeling of loneliness, nor the tedium that awaited him in his work. He had found a job as an assistant to a furniture maker. He did the preliminary sawing and planing, and was occasionally allowed to do some of the more skilled work in design and carving. At midday he and the other four men employed in the business would go to a bar and smoke and drink pastis. Although he could see they thought him curious and he tried not to outstay his welcome, he was grateful to them for accepting him into their company.

In the evenings Isabelle would prepare some dinner from what she could find in the market. She was critical of what was on offer. 'Rabbit and tomatoes, that's all they seem to eat,' she said as she set down a large pot on the table. 'At least at home I could have a choice between a dozen different kinds of meat.'

'Though Picardy itself is not the gastronomic centre of France,' said Stephen.

'Didn't you like the food?'

'Yes, I did. I liked the lunches with you and Lisette especially. But I don't think a gourmet from Paris would have found much to cheer about in the local restaurants.'

'Well, he needn't come then,' said Isabelle, nettled at what she took to be a criticism of her own cooking.

'Don't be cross,' he said, laying his hand across her cheek.

'I'm never cross with you, dear boy. What are these cuts on your hand?'

'The chisel. It was different from the ones I've used before.'

'You should be more careful. Now sit down and have some rabbit.'

After dinner they read books on either side of the fire. They went to bed early in the room at the back of the house. Isabelle had painted it and sewn new curtains. Her photographs stood on top of the cheap chest of drawers and the huge carved wardrobe bulged with her dresses. There were not many flowers to buy in the market, though there was always lavender to put in the numerous blue pots around the house. Compared to the bourgeois opulence of the boulevard du Cange, the room was stark. The presence of Isabelle's things in it, however, gave it in Stephen's eye something of

107

the atmosphere of her old bedroom. The silk stockings that sometimes trailed from an open drawer and the piles of soft undergarments, the finest fabric the trade could provide, mitigated some of the harshness of the bare boards. In that shared bedroom Stephen felt a privileged proximity to these small intimacies that even her husband had never been permitted. In sleep they were also together, though Stephen found the closeness of Isabelle's unconscious body made him feel uneasy, and he often took a blanket to the sofa in the living room.

He would lie alone, looking up at the ceiling and across to the big fireplace, over to the kitchen range and its black, hanging implements. His thoughts and dreams did not fill up with the big skies of Lincolnshire or the memories of refectory tables and inspections for head lice; nor did he give a backward thought to having abruptly left his employment, to import licences, dockets, or bales of cotton unloaded at the East India Docks. He thought about the moment and the next day and the capsule of existence in which he and Isabelle lived, contained within a town and a world of kinds outside. It was an existence he felt had been won by him but in some wider judgement would not be allowed.

He thought about what he would make at work the next day. Sometimes he thought about nothing at all, but merely traced with his eyes the lines of the timber in the beams above his head.

TWO MONTHS PASSED and winter calmed the worst of the winds with an icy stillness that made the pavements dangerous and stopped the water in the fountain. Isabelle stayed in the house for most of the day when Stephen was at work. She spent the time altering the decorations to suit her taste and cooking soup or stew for him to eat when he came home. She did not miss the comfortable life she had had in Amiens with the attentive delivery boys from the milliner or the grocer. It did not matter to her that much of her day was spent in performing tasks that even Marguerite preferred to leave to Madame Bonnet. Her cousin, whose husband ran the pharmacy, came to visit her frequently, and she was not lonely.

At the end of December no blood came. She looked at the small black diary in which she marked the days and saw that it was due. By the end of January there was still none. This seemed appropriate to Isabelle. It had been hard to think of blood as the mark of new life, of hope, as Jeanne had told her when she first ran to her sobbing in alarm; now in the withholding of it there was a sense of being healed. She had stopped haemorrhaging herself away; her power was turned inwards where it would silently create. She said nothing to Stephen.

One Saturday at noon she went to meet him after he had finished work, and they went for a walk in the town. They stopped briefly at a café so he could eat after his morning's exertion, then carried on past the town hall and out along a narrow street of shops towards the outskirts of the place.

Their breath left thinning trails behind them as they climbed a slight gradient leading out of town. They arrived in a square, which was the last before the street became a road and vanished into the grey and purple countryside.

Isabelle felt light-headed and went to sit down on a bench. A slight moisture had come up on her forehead, which was now turning cold against her skin under the winter wind.

'I'll find you some smelling salts,' said Stephen, and set off in search of a pharmacy.

Isabelle sat quietly, not sure whether to loosen her coat and allow the cool air to reach her or to wrap it more tightly around her to keep out the chill.

She intended to tell Stephen about the child she believed she was expecting, but something made her delay. She wished she could present it to him whole without the long toil of pregnancy. She had no wish to be cared for or treated with special regard. She did not feel that the minute organic changes taking place inside her were the concern of anyone else, even of the man who had caused them.

Yet she already loved the child. She imagined it to be a boy and could picture his smiling, open face. She didn't see a swaddled baby but a young man, with a guileless manner, rather larger than herself, who would fling his arm protectively round her before returning to some undemanding task in the fields. He was never an infant in her imagination, nor a man of substance or achievement for whom she felt ambitious, but always just this ageless, happy male.

She thought of all the mothers who lived in the villages that lined the narrow road leading from the town. Out there were millions of young men, strong, smiling, as her boy would be, working on the land. They never knew each other, never met, never considered any kinship or allegiance they might have to each other or to the country they lived in, because such things existed only in time of war.

Isabelle began to look with regret towards her parents and their continuing lives. The coming child had already begun to still her most restless expectations. The need satisfied in her was so deep that she had not previously been aware of it; it was as though she had become conscious of a starving hunger

110

only after having eaten. It seemed to alter the levels and balances of her needs. She felt closer to the girl she had been at home; a broken circle had been rejoined. Although this was a soothing thought, it brought with it some doubts about what she had done; it made her want to be reunited with her family, or at least with her sister Jeanne. It was to her more than to anyone that she wanted to talk. It was she, Isabelle thought, who must be the first to know about the child.

She had started to feel uneasy about the things she and Stephen had done in Azaire's house. Stephen seemed so sure of everything and she had been so overcome by desire that she had trusted him. She had followed her instincts and where there was doubt she was reassured by his certainty and by the tenderness of her feeling for him. Without the stimulus of fear and prohibition, her desire had slackened.

In the southern winter the excesses of their brazen love affair seemed to belong to a different season. She went into a church in St-Rémy to confess to the local priest, but found she could not bring herself to describe in detail the extent of what had passed between them. The priest cut her off soon after she confessed to the adultery herself. The penance seemed to bear no relation to the sin; it was a formality plucked from the register where such commonplace transgressions were graded. Isabelle felt unsatisfied, and although she did not regret what had happened she began to feel guilty.

Stephen returned with a bottle of salts and sat beside her on the bench.

'I wonder what it is,' he said. 'Perhaps you haven't been eating well enough at home. Sometimes that makes people feel faint. I brought you a little cake as well.'

'No, I don't think it's that. It's nothing serious.' She laid her hand on his arm. 'Don't worry about me.'

She was smiling at him in a sweet, indulgent way that made it seem as though it was he who needed to be cared for or protected. She broke the cake in half and offered some to him. A shower of yellow crumbs fell on to the wooden seat between them.

There was a whirring and banging of a bird's wings above them as a fat pigeon, attracted by the sight of the crumbling cake, descended from the gutter of the building behind them and landed impudently between them on the bench.

'Jesus Christ!' Stephen leapt up from his seat in horror.

Isabelle, who had been amused by the bird's fearlessness, looked up in alarm. 'What is it?'

'That bird, that bird. For God's sake. Get rid of it.'

'It's only a pigeon, it's just –'

'Get rid of it. Please.'

Isabelle clapped her hands, and the plump bird managed to heave itself back into the air, across the square and into the branches of a tree, where it waited in sight of the crumbs.

'What on earth is the matter, my darling? You're trembling.'

'I know, I know. I'm sorry. I'll be all right.'

'It's just a fat old pigeon, it wouldn't do you any harm.'

'I know it wouldn't. It's not that I think it'll attack, it's just some strange fear.'

'Come and sit down now. Come on. Sit next to me and let me put my arm round you. That's right. My poor boy. Is that better? Shall I stroke your hair?'

'No, I'm fine. I'm sorry to have made a fuss.'

'The noise you made.'

'I know.'

Stephen gradually stopped trembling. 'I've always hated birds. That time I told you about when I hit that boy and they made me go back into the institution. He had been taunting me about some crows that the gamekeeper had nailed up to a fence. I went up and stroked one to show I was not afraid. It had maggots under its wings and drooling, milky eyes.' He shuddered.

Isabelle said, 'So birds make you think of having to go back to that place?'

'It's partly that. But I had always hated them, from long before that. There's something cruel, prehistoric about them.'

She stood up and took his arm. For a moment she looked into his dark brown eyes, into the symmetrical beauty of his pale face. She nodded a little and smiled.

'So there is something that frightens you,' she said.

A week later Isabelle was chopping vegetables on the table when she felt a pain just below the waistband of her skirt. It

112

felt as though she was being penetrated by a knitting needle with large walnuts midway up its shaft. She pressed her hands flat over the pain and sat down heavily at the table. If she kept still and concentrated she would keep the baby; she would not allow it to escape. Her manicured fingers tenderly aligned themselves on the area she imagined the barely visible thing to be. Her pulse was transmitted through the fabric of the dress and the soft skin beneath to the chamber where the life was balanced. She willed it to stay, trying to reassure it through the gentleness of her palms, but she felt further sharp probes going right up into her womb. She went to the bedroom and lay down, only to find there was bleeding she could not stop.

In the afternoon she took her coat and found a doctor whose name had been given to her by her cousin. He was a bald man with a deep voice and a roll of fat that almost obscured his stiff white collar. He seemed unmoved by her anxiety and talked in brief, cheerful sentences as he examined her and gestured her to a door off his surgery where she would find a glass container. He told her the result of the test would be available to him within a week and she was to call back then. In the meantime, he said, she should take things quietly and not exert herself. He pressed a large, folded piece of paper into her hand and told her to pay the receptionist as she left.

On the way back to the house, Isabelle stopped at the church and sat in a pew at the back. She had no further desire to confess to the priest, but she wanted to admit, if only to herself, her feelings of guilt about the way she had abandoned herself to physical pleasure. Lurid images of afternoons in the boulevard du Cange came into her mind inside the wintry cold of the church. She could see Stephen's blood-swollen flesh in front of her face, her mouth; she could feel it probing and entering each unguarded part of her, not against her will but at her hungry and desperate insistence.

She opened her eyes and shook the sacrilegious pictures from her mind, feeling ashamed that she had entertained them in a church, even if it had been only to confess them. She looked at the altar where a wooden crucifix was lit by candles, the waxy flesh below the ribs pierced and bleeding from the Roman soldier's spear. She thought how prosaically physical this suffering had been: the punctured skin on forehead, feet, hands, the parting of flesh with nails and steel. When even the divine sacrifice had been expressed in such terms, it was sometimes hard to imagine in what manner precisely human life was supposed to exceed the limitations of pulse, skin and decomposition.

Isabelle wrote:

My dearest Jeanne, I have missed you so much, not only in the past few weeks but in the years before when we never seemed to meet. How much I regret that now. I feel like a child who has been absorbed in her own game all day and suddenly stops, only to see that it is growing dark and she is far from home with no idea of how to get back.

I terribly want to see you to talk about what has happened. I am pregnant, though I thought last week that I had lost the child. I have strange pains and bleeding, though the doctor says these are quite common. He says there may be a bruise inside which is bleeding and could dislodge the baby. I am to rest and not exert myself.

I have still not told Stephen about it. I don't know why I can't do this. I truly love him, but he frightens me a little. I'm not sure he would understand my joy at being pregnant or how worried I am at the thought of losing it. He hardly talks about such things. Even when he has mentioned his own childhood he speaks as though it were something that happened to someone else. How could he feel attached to something that does not yet exist?

There is something worse, Jeanne. When we were young and I was the baby, no one ever paid me much attention (except you, of course) and I was allowed to do what I liked as long as my dress was kept clean and I was polite at mealtimes. I wanted to explore. Do you remember how I said I would go to Africa? Now I feel I have explored in some other way. It has damaged René, though I owe him very little after the way he treated me. It has also damaged Lisette and Grégoire, and of course you and Mama and Papa, though whether Papa takes much notice of anything these days I don't know. Although I will love the baby and protect it with all my strength, I will not be the ideal mother, compromised as I am.

At the worst moments I feel we have gone too far. Stephen and I were fearless – or unscrupulous you might say – and we had no doubts that what we were doing was right: it was its own justification, Stephen used to say. I feel we have lost our bearings. I am alone, like the child, on the verge of nightfall. Although I am lost I still think I can find my way home if I go now.

This must sound feeble, I know. She has made her choice, you must be saying to yourself, she can't expect to change her mind now. But I want so desperately to see you. I want so very much that you should hold the baby when it comes, take it in your arms. I want to sit on the bed in your room and feel your hand on my head as you start to comb my tangled hair. What mad thoughts and impulses have pushed me out so far from you?

Isabelle was crying too much to carry on with the letter. Jeanne had been trusting enough when Isabelle first wrote to ask for money. She had never met Stephen, but out of love for her sister had sent funds of her own. It was not fair, Isabelle thought, to ask more of her.

She laid her head on her arms as she sat at the kitchen table. She felt as though she had been tricked. She had believed herself to be one thing, then turned out to be another. How was she to know whether to trust her latest inclinations, or whether to suspect they too might be superseded by other more compelling ones? In her confusion the only constant emotion was her devotion to the child inside her. For reasons she could not disentangle, its well-being could not be guaranteed in the life she was living, far from home, with Stephen, in this frozen town.

Stephen also thought of home. His grandfather's cottage had been at the end of a village with a view to the church, some ugly new houses behind it, and the big road going north. In the other direction were flat fields, very pale green in colour, running out into deciduous woods in which the local farmers shot.

He thought how he would take Isabelle to see them one day. He had no sentimental attachment to the idea of home, he did not weep for his thieving grandfather or his absent mother, but he wanted to see Isabelle against this different background, so that the ages of his life would be united.

He had surprised himself by the gentleness he had discovered, all of which was now directed towards Isabelle. When he worked the wood in the mornings he imagined how smooth it would need to be if she were to walk barefoot on it. When the tedium of the work lowered his spirits he thought about her face lighting up at his return in the evening. In his affections she had moved from the object of fearful passion to someone whose well-being was his life's concern, though in that transition he had not lost his sense of her dignity, of her superior age and position.

Meanwhile Isabelle privately made plans to visit Jeanne in Rouen. She would tell Stephen that she would be gone only a few days, then when she was there she would decide whether or not to return. The moment would come, she told herself, when she would tell Stephen.

Another week passed and her pregnancy became visible. Stephen noticed that she was heavier, but some new-found modesty meant that he never had a chance to examine her properly without her clothes. He noticed that she talked to him less and he wondered why. She seemed troubled and removed. There had been another episode of pain and bleeding.

One day when he was at work she packed a small suitcase and sat down at the table to write a note of explanation.

'I feel we have gone too far and I must turn back,' she began, then tore up the sheet of paper and put the pieces in her pocket. There was nothing she could say to explain herself. She looked round the front room with its open range and the heavy wooden mantelpiece that had so much delighted her at first. She went upstairs to take one final look at the rough floorboards of the bedroom and the curtains she had made. Then she left the house and walked to the station.

When Stephen returned in the evening he saw at once that some clothes and personal things, her photographs and jewellery, were gone. He opened the wardrobe. Most of her dresses were still there. He took out one she had worn soon after he had arrived at the boulevard du Cange. It was cream-coloured with a rustling skirt, ivory buttons and a ribbed bodice. He held it against his face, then crushed it in his arms.

He felt like the blocks of wood they sometimes split in the back yard at work when the axe was first embedded, then raised and driven to the ground, so the wood was cloven in half, from top to toe. No shred or fibre escaped the sundering.

In the days that followed he returned to work. He arrived on time in the morning and exchanged pleasantries with the other men. He swore and spat at the snagging teeth of the saw as the blade caught in the grainy timber. He rolled off the long curls beneath his plane. He sanded with three grades of paper, feeling the surface of the finished wood beneath the soft skin of his fingers. He felt the sweet taste of aniseed on his tongue at midday and watched the viscous liquid cloud over in the glass as he poured in water. He talked and told jokes with the men and showed no sign that anything had changed.

In the evening he laboured with the range, conjuring what he could from the food available, from the variations of rabbit and tomatoes. Then he sat in front of the fire and drank bottles of wine as he looked at the embers.

She had returned because she felt she could save her soul. She had gone home because she was frightened of the future and felt sure a natural order could yet be resumed. He had no choice but to continue with what he had begun.

When he had drunk the wine he went upstairs and lay on their bed, his boots on the white cover. He could think of nothing.

He lay and stared at the night beyond the window.

He felt himself grow cold.

PART TWO
FRANCE 1916

JACK FIREBRACE LAY forty-five feet underground with several hundred thousand tons of France above his face. He could hear the wooden wheezing of the feed that pumped air through the tunnel. Most of it was exhausted by the time it reached him. His back was supported by a wooden cross, his feet against the clay, facing towards the enemy. With an adapted spade, he loosened quantities of soil into a bag which he passed back to Evans, his mate, who then crawled away in the darkness. Jack could hear the hammering of timbers being used to shore up the tunnel further back, though where he worked, at the face, there was no guarantee that the clay would hold.

The sweat ran down into his eyes and stung them, making him shake his head from side to side. At this point the tunnel was about four feet across and five feet high. Jack kept sticking the spade into the earth ahead of him, hacking it out as though he hated it. He had lost track of how long he had been underground. He found it easier not to think when he might be relieved, but to keep digging. The harder he worked, the easier it seemed. It must have been six hours or more since he had seen daylight, and even then not much of it, but a thin green haze across the lowlands of the French–Belgian border, lit by the spasmodic explosion of shells.

His unit had not been able to return to its billet in the local village. So intense was the activity in this part of the line that the surface troops would not stay in their trenches without the protection of the men underground. The miners had to sleep,

121

for the time being, in chambers at the top of their shafts or in the trenches with the infantry.

Jack felt a hand clutch his elbow. 'Jack. We need you. Turner's heard something about twenty yards back. Come on.'

Evans pulled him off the cross, and Jack turned stiffly, easing the sweat-soaked vest off his shoulders, and following Evans's crawling buttocks until he could stand. Even the murk of the timbered tunnel was bright to him after the clay face. He blinked in the gloom.

'Over here, Firebrace. Turner said it sounded like digging.'

Captain Weir, a startling figure with disarrayed hair, in plimsolls and civilian sweater, pushed him over to where Turner, a tired, frightened man, shivering with fatigue in the hot tunnel, was resting against his pick.

'It was just here,' said Turner. 'I'd got my head close up to this timber and I could hear vibrations. It wasn't our lot, I can tell you.'

Jack placed his head against the wall of the tunnel. He could hear the rhythmic gasp of the bellows in the overhead hosepipe draped from the ceiling. 'You'll have to turn off the air-feed, sir,' he said to Weir.

'Christ,' said Turner, 'I can't breathe.'

Weir dispatched a message to the surface. Two minutes later the noise ceased and Jack knelt down again. His exceptional hearing was frequently in demand. The previous winter, two miles south of Ypres, he had lowered his ear to rat-level in the trench into a water-filled petrol can and held it there until his head lost all feeling. He preferred the airless quiet of the tunnel to the numbing of his skull.

The men stood motionless as Weir held his finger to his lips. Jack breathed in deeply and listened, his body rigid with effort. There were sounds, distant and irregular. He could not be sure what they were. If they evacuated the tunnel as a precaution and the noise turned out only to have been shellfire or surface movement then time would be lost on their own tunnel. On the other hand, if he failed to identify German digging coming back the other way, the loss of life would probably be greater. He had to be sure.

'For God's sake, Firebrace.' He heard Weir's hissing voice in his ear. 'The men can hardly breathe.'

Jack held up his hand. He was listening for the distinctive knocking made by timber when it was hammered into place against the wall. If a tunnel was very close it was also sometimes possible to hear the sound of spades or of bags of earth being dragged back.

There was a thumping noise again, but it did not sound hollow enough for wood; it was more like the rocking of the earth under shellfire. Jack tightened his nerves once more. His concentration was interrupted by a noise like the delivery of a sack of potatoes. Turner had collapsed on to the tunnel floor. Jack made up his mind.

He said, 'Shellfire.'

'Are you sure?' said Weir.

'Yes, sir. As sure as I can be.'

'All right. Tell them to turn the air-feed on again. Firebrace, you get back on the cross. You two, get Turner on his feet.'

Jack crawled back into the darkness, feet first, where Evans helped him regain his position and passed him the spade. He sank it into the earth ahead of him, feeling glad of the resumption of mechanical toil. Evans's grubbing hands worked invisibly beside him. Towards the end of his shift he began to imagine things. He thought for a second that he was standing in the lighted bar of a London pub, holding up his beer glass to the lamp, looking at the big gilt mirror behind the bar. The bright reflection made him blink, and the flickering of his eyes brought back the reality of the clay wall ahead of him. Evans's hand scraped. Jack struck out ahead of him again, his arms grinding in their joints.

Evans swore beneath his breath and Jack reached out and gripped him in rebuke. Evans had tried to light a candle but there was not enough oxygen. The match burned bright red but would not flame. The two men stopped and listened. They could hear the roar of their breathing magnified in the silence. They held their breath and there was nothing. They had dug to the end of the world. Jack could smell the damp earth and the sweat from Evans's body. Normally he could hear the timbers behind them being put into place by hand, pushed quietly

123

against the clay. There was not even this cautious sound. The narrow tunnel closed round them. Jack felt Evans's hand grip his arm. His breath rasped out again. Something must be happening behind them.

'All right,' Jack said. 'Get me off this thing.'

Evans pulled the wooden support away and helped roll Jack over. They crawled back until they saw lamplight. Weir was half-standing in the low tunnel. He clutched his ear, then gestured them to lean against the side walls. He began to mouth an explanation but before he could finish there was a roar in the tunnel and a huge ball of earth and rock blew past them. It took four men with it, their heads and limbs blown away and mixed with the rushing soil. Jack, Weir and Evans were flattened against the side wall by the blast and escaped the path of the debris. Jack saw part of Turner's face and hair still attached to a piece of skull rolling to a halt where the tunnel narrowed into the section he had been digging. There was an arm with a corporal's stripe on it near his feet, but most of the men's bodies had been blown into the moist earth.

Weir said, 'Get out before another one goes.'

Back towards the trench someone had already got a fresh lamp down into the darkness.

Jack took Evans's shoulder. 'Come on, boy. Come on now.'

It was dusk on the surface and the rain was falling. Stretcher-bearers pushed past Jack as he stood blinking at the top of the tunnel, breathing the damp air. Weir dismissed the men and went to find a field telephone. Jack walked from the tunnel head to his place in the trench.

'Letter for you, Jack,' said Bill Tyson. 'Mail came this morning.'

They sat huddled beneath a wooden frame with a ground-sheet stretched over it. Arthur Shaw, the third man who shared their shelter, was trying to make tea on a primus stove.

Jack's letter was from his wife in Edmonton. 'My Dearest Jack,' it started. 'How are you keeping?'

He folded it away inside his pocket. He could not bring his mind to bear on the distant world her handwriting suggested. He was afraid he would not understand her letter, that she

124

would be telling him something important his mind was too tired to register. He drank the tea Shaw had conjured from the gloom.

'Turner's dead,' he said. 'And at least two others.'

'Didn't you hear anything?' said Tyson.

'Yes, but I thought it was shellfire. There must be a tunnel.'

'Don't worry,' said Tyson. 'Anyone can make a mistake.'

There was a whining sound in the air about a hundred yards to their right as another shell came over.

'Any news about when we're getting out of here?' said Jack.

'Supposed to be tomorrow,' said Shaw, 'but I can't see us getting down the line while this shelling's going on. Did Weir say anything?'

'No, I don't think he knows.'

The three men looked at each other with expressionless, exhausted eyes. Tyson and Shaw had been together for a year, since they had been drawn to enlist by the six shillings pay on offer to men with experience of working underground. Both had been miners in Nottingham, though Tyson had done little work beneath the surface, having been chiefly concerned with the maintenance of machinery. Shaw claimed to be thirty-one, but might have been ten years older. He would work like a packhorse in the tunnel but had little enthusiasm for the military discipline imposed on them by the infantry.

In Jack's life they had replaced two fellow-Londoners with whom he had worked on the construction of the Central Line. Both these men, Allen and Mortimer, had died in an explosion on the Messines Ridge near Ypres the year before. Jack, already immune to death, let their white faces drift from his memory. He had succumbed only with reluctance to the friendship of Tyson and Shaw, but found to his dismay that their company had grown important to him. When they lay down to sleep, he let Shaw rest his head on his knees, which were folded inwards to keep out of the line of the trench itself. Sometimes he awoke to find a rat had crawled across his face. At other hours he lay rocked between the fear of being buried by a shell, consumed in the earth they had crawled under, and the overpowering need to lose consciousness of the noise that assailed them. There were wooden planks beneath them

125

which seemed to lie against their bones. Even Shaw's big flanks and shoulders gave him no cushioning of flesh as he rolled and tossed in half-sleep.

Captain Weir's face appeared round the corner of the groundsheet. He was wearing a waterproof cape over his white sweater and had changed into knee-length rubber boots.

'Shaw, you're needed in the tunnel,' he said. 'I know you were in this morning, but they need help to clear the debris. You'd better report for duty, too, Tyson.'

'I'm on sentry duty at ten, sir.'

'Firebrace will have to do it for you. Come on, move yourselves. Sergeant Adams is in charge of the working party. Go and report to him.'

'Finish my tea, Jack,' said Shaw. 'Don't let the rats have it.'

With the others gone, Jack tried to sleep. His nerves were too stretched. He closed his eyes but could see only the dark of the tunnel face. He kept hearing the sudden quiet that had made him and Evans stop and hold their breath. He did not berate himself for failing to identify the sound of a German tunnel. He had done his best, and the men might have died anyway, perhaps in a worse way, with gas in their lungs or lying beyond help in no man's land. They would find that part of Turner's face and head and they would bury it beneath the earth with any other bits of bone and uniform they could bring back from underground. He thought of Shaw's big hands sifting through the blown soil. For a moment he relaxed into sleep, but then the decontraction of his body made him jump and he awoke again, his body tensed and ready to fight.

Abandoning sleep, he took out the letter from his breast pocket and lit a stub of candle he found in the side compartment of Tyson's pack.

My Dearest Jack, How are you keeping? All our thoughts and prayers are with you. We read the newspapers each day, we look at the casualty columns first. There doesn't seem to be any news of where you are. We have had Mother staying and she says to tell you she got your letter and she

126

is sending another parcel with some soap and cigarettes and some gooseberries from the garden. I hope they won't be too ripe by the time they get to you.

I am very sorry to have to tell you little John has been taken ill. He has been very poorly indeed and the doctor says it is diphtheria. He was in hospital in Tottenham last week and he is a little better, but his temperature is still very high. As you will imagine it is not easy getting medicine and the doctors to look after him with so much going to the men at the front which is how it should be.

He is in good spirits when he is awake and we have seen him in the hospital. He asks me to send you his love. I am sorry to bother you with this news but I think it is for the best. He does miss you very much and I know he loves you. Our prayers are with you and I send my love to you, From Margaret.

With the mail had come rations. There were some tins of stew and bully beef which were held over to midday, but there was bread and jam to go with half a mug of tea. Hungry from his work underground, Jack ate quickly at an improvised station at the head of the communication trench. Sometimes the men who brought the rations had unreliable news of troop movements and plans from behind the lines; today there was no word. Jack ate in silence before returning to his position.

His son John had been born eight years before, when Margaret was nearly forty and they had almost despaired of having children. He was a bright-eyed boy, thin and fair, with a vacant expression that often gave way to shrill laughter. His physical frailty was compounded by the simplicity of his mind. He was tolerated by the other boys in the street when they needed someone to make up numbers. He was the goalkeeper in their unrefereed games of football and was allowed to bat at cricket only in an emergency.

Jack looked closely at his wife's careful handwriting and tried to bring the boy's face to mind. In the murk of the rainy evening, with only Tyson's piece of candle for light, it was difficult to see. He closed his eyes and pictured his son's knees beneath the ragged grey shorts, the big teeth he revealed when he smiled, the untidy hair through which he would sometimes run a fatherly hand.

At the front he hardly ever thought of home. In his wallet was a picture of Margaret, but none of John. There was always too much to think of to allow his mind to dwell on inessentials. He had not been home for almost a year. He found it unbelievable when Shaw told him that if the atmospheric conditions were right the guns could be heard in London. The place in which he often found himself, often underground, with no clear idea of where the nearest village was, seemed as distant from those streets and houses as if he now inhabited another world.

That night he stood on the firestep at the end of the trench on sentry duty for Tyson, who had still not returned from underground. The miners were not supposed to do sentry duty, but their officer had struck a deal with his opposite number in the infantry. In view of enemy activity and the consequent danger underground, the infantry would provide fighting cover in the tunnels in return for the miners doing some of their fatigues. For Jack the days and nights had ceased to be distinct. There was the darkness of the tunnel, the twilight of late afternoon under the intermittent light of shellfire and the blackness of the trench at night beneath the curtain of a groundsheet.

He listened for noises from the no man's land in front of him. German night patrols had been out, with the aim of checking on enemy movements and spreading anxiety. Jack imagined that his side, too, had men in listening posts who would hear anything before he did, but in his trench the sentries were never told in case it made them complacent. The infantry battalion came from London; they referred to the tunnellers as 'sewer rats' and were anxious to prove how ineffective they were as soldiers.

Jack was so tired that he had passed the stage when sleep was possible. His body had found some automatic course, powered by what source of wakefulness he couldn't say, that kept him awake if not alert while other men nodded and dozed on the ground, some slumped as though dead on the floor of the trench, some leaning with their backs to the wooden boards. From further down the line he could hear trench repair parties at work.

John's face was now in his mind quite brightly: the wan, solitary boy at the tail of the street gang, the stumbling baby with his troublesome steps. He could hear his piping London voice with its parrot greetings and unfounded optimism. He pictured his boy in the high-ceilinged hospital ward with the yellow smudge of gas lamps, the starched headdresses of the nurses and the smell of soap and disinfectant.

Sleep came to him like an unseen assailant. It was not the sinister light of the ward but the lamps of a huge bar in a pub on Lea Bridge Road: the men in suits and flat caps, smoke rising, ale glasses held aloft. There were other pictures, end to end: the kitchen of his parents' house in Stepney; a park, a dog; the lit pub again, thronged with people; John's face, the dear boy. He was aware of a great temptation being offered, some ease of mind, some sleep for which he would sell the lives of his comrades, and he embraced the offer, not aware that he was already slumbering, head slumped forwards, cradled between the aching shoulders that had dug out French earth for hours without respite.

He did not know he was asleep until he was awake again, feeling himself slump forwards as a boot cracked into his ankle.

'What's your name?' It was an officer's voice.

'Firebrace, sir.'

'Oh, it's you, Firebrace.' He recognized Captain Weir's surprised tone.

'Were you asleep?' The first officer's voice was cold.

'I don't know, sir. I just wasn't listening and –'

'You were asleep on duty. It's a court-martial offence. See me tomorrow at six. Your sergeant will bring you. You know the punishment.'

'Yes, sir.'

Jack watched the two men walk on and swing left at the end of the firebay, the red ends of their cigarettes glowing.

He was relieved by Bob Wheeler, another tunneller. He went back to find Tyson and Shaw asleep beneath their wooden frame. There was no room for him with them, so he took a handful of cigarettes from his pack and went back down the communication trench, past the half-hearted challenge of a sentry. He climbed over the back of the support trench and found himself in an area where piles of ammunition and supplies lay strapped under tarpaulin in the drizzle. There was a group of men, including a sergeant, on guard near by and he went to make himself known to them. He told them he was going to the latrines, and they let him pass.

He found a tree that had not been damaged by shellfire and sat down beneath it, lighting a cigarette and sucking in the smoke. Before the war he had never touched tobacco; now it was his greatest comfort.

If he was found guilty by court martial he could be shot. The tunnellers had become more and more part of the army; although they had not undergone the humiliating drills and punishments handed out to the infantry before they were deemed ready to fight, they had lost the separate status they had had at first. When Jack had arrived at Ypres with his fellow-Londoners Allen and Mortimer, he was told they would spend the war there while different divisions of infantry came and went, but to begin with they found themselves in a constant and bewildering state of movement, the very trouble the organization had been designed to prevent. They had become soldiers and were expected to kill the enemy not only by mining but with bayonet or bare hands if necessary.

This was not the life Jack had envisaged when he volunteered. At the age of thirty-eight he could reasonably have avoided service, but he had no work in London. Margaret was ten years older than him and had enough to do looking after John. She managed cleaning jobs from time to time, but the money was not enough for them. Jack didn't think the war would last long; he told Margaret he would be home within the year, having saved half his pay.

She was a practical woman of Irish descent who was drawn to Jack by his humour and his kindliness. They had met at the wedding of one of her eight sisters, who was marrying a workmate of Jack's. At the party after the service Jack was drinking beer and doing conjuring tricks for a group of

130

children. He had a big, square face with hair parted in the middle. She liked the way he talked to the children before he began joking with the other men who had come along to see their friend married.

'I'm an old maid,' she told Jack when he went round to visit her a week later. 'You don't want to be walking out with me.' But he seemed to know exactly what he wanted and they were married three months later.

Lighting another cigarette beneath his tree, listening to the screech of a shell going over the British line about half a mile south, Jack Firebrace began to tremble.

He had thought himself immune to death; he thought he had hardened himself against it, but it was not so. If they found him guilty they would take him alone at daybreak to some secluded place behind the lines – a glade in a forest, a yard behind a farm wall – and shoot him dead. They would ask members of his own unit, miners and diggers, men who had not even been trained to fire on the enemy, to do the job. Some would have blanks and some would not; no one would know whether the fatal shot had been fired by Tyson or Shaw or Wheeler or Jones. He would fall like the millions of the dead who had gone down into the mud: baker's boys from Saxony, farm labourers from France and factory workers from Lancashire, so much muscle and blood in the earth.

He could not look on this possibility without shaking. When there was a battle or a raid, they expected to die; it was the losses through sniper fire, through shells and mortars, the blowing of the tunnel, the continuous awareness that any moment could bring death in a number of different ways that had been harder to understand. Slowly Jack had become accustomed even to this. It took him a day of sleep each time they went into rest before he could adjust to not being in constant fear; then he would begin to laugh and tell stories in the surging relief that overcame them. The indifference he had cultivated, however, was to the extermination of the enemy, his colleagues and his friends; he was not, he now admitted to himself, indifferent to the prospect of his own death.

He held his face in his hands and prayed to God to save him. There was no task he wanted to complete, no destiny by which he felt impelled: he merely wanted to see Margaret again. He wanted to touch John's hair. My son, he thought, as he sat in the rain, my darling boy. It would make no difference to the outcome of the war whether he himself lived or died; it made no difference whether today it was Turner whose head was blown from his body, or whether tomorrow it was his or Shaw's or Tyson's. Let them die, he prayed, shamefully; let them die, but please God let me live.

Through the night he sat unchallenged and alone, forcing his exhausted mind to bring out memories of his life, pictures of what he had done that might go with him and comfort him if he had to face the line of rifles pointed at his heart. There were games of football on Hackney Marshes, the comradeship of workers on the construction of the London Underground; odd faces and voices from childhood; his son. There was nothing to make it seem a life worth saving. In the end his memory offered him only fragments of early childhood: sitting in front of the kitchen range, the smell of his mother as she kissed him in his bed. With them came a desire to sleep, to surrender.

He stood up and stretched his stiff arms and legs, then slunk back to his position in the trench and crept in beside Tyson and Shaw. Shortly before dawn he went to look for Sergeant Adams.

'Come along, then,' said Adams. 'Smarten yourself. Get your belt on straight.'

He was not the kind of sergeant most men feared. He had a mocking sense of humour and seldom shouted. The men privately admired him.

'I've heard all about you, sleeping on the job,' he said.

Jack said nothing. He was ready to die.

'You may be lucky. Some of these young officers blow hot and cold. Mr Wraysford is the strangest one I've seen. Law unto himself. This way.'

Adams walked him down a narrow trench in the rear of which were several dugouts. He pointed to an entrance at the end of the line and told him to go down on his own.

Jack looked up at the rim of the world that was appearing

through the grey light: the burned and blasted trees, the once-green fields now uniformly brown where all the earth had been turned by shells. He was reconciled to leaving it.

He went down the wooden ladder and found a gas curtain across a home-made door. He knocked and waited.

A voice told him to come in and he wrenched the door open. There was a strong smell of paraffin inside. Pipe smoke obscured the contents of the room. Jack was able to make out a wooden bunk in the lower half of which a figure lay hunched in sleep, and a makeshift table and chairs. It was better made than most of the squalid arrangements he had seen, though the primitive boarding that made the walls and the tinker's use of odd cups, candles, wicks and nails to do duty for missing essentials gave it a primitive appearance.

'Who are you?' He was addressed by a lieutenant, who was one of two officers sitting at the table. The other was Jack's own company commander, Captain Weir, on a visit to the infantry.

'Firebrace, sir. You told me to report to you at six this morning.'

'Why?'

'I was asleep on sentry duty.'

The officer stood up and walked over to where Jack was standing. He brought his face up close. Jack saw a man with dark hair that was going grey at the sides; he had a thick moustache that obscured his upper lip and big brown eyes that stared thoughtfully at him. He might have been any age from twenty-five to forty.

'I have no recollection at all.'

'I think you were going to put me on a charge, sir.'

'I don't think I could do that. You're not in my unit. You're a tunneller, aren't you?'

'Yes, sir.'

'One of yours, Weir.'

Jack looked towards Weir and noticed the almost empty bottle of whisky that stood on the table. There were only two glasses.

'Sit down, Firebrace. Have a drink,' said Weir.

'No thank you, sir. If I –'

'Sit down anyway.'

Jack looked round. He didn't want to sit on a chair that might belong to the officer commanding the infantry, an irascible man called Gray whom he had heard giving orders. He wondered where he was: bullying the sentries, perhaps.

Jack took the chair that Weir kicked towards him. Weir was back in his soft shoes and white sweater. He looked unshaven and his eyes were bloodshot. Jack looked down, afraid to meet his gaze. Also on the table were five playing cards laid out in the shape of a star, face down, with thin trails of sand between them. In the centre of the formation was a carved wooden figure and a stump of candle.

'This is Lieutenant Wraysford,' said Weir. 'His platoon is next to your section in the line. His are the men we are protecting against mines. Last night he had two men out in a listening post. Perhaps he was worried about them. Is that right, Wraysford?'

'No. Brennan and Douglas would be all right. They know what they're doing.'

'Don't you want to talk to this man?' said Weir.

'I would if I could remember who he was.' He turned to Jack. 'There'll be some tea in a minute if you don't want whisky. I'll tell Riley to make an extra cup.'

As Jack's eyes grew accustomed to the smoky dugout he saw that parts of the walls were covered with fabric. It looked like expensive foreign silk or cotton. On top of a small locker were more wooden carvings of human figures. There were no photographs on the bookshelves in the corner, though there were some amateurish sketches of heads and bodies. He became aware that the lieutenant had been following his gaze.

'Do you draw?'

'A bit,' said Jack. 'I don't get enough time now. Or the quiet.'

A tray with three mugs of tea was brought in by Riley, a small grey-haired man in neat uniform. He reached up to a bag suspended from the ceiling, out of range of rats, and produced some sugar.

Jack watched the lieutenant go over to the shelves and take down a sketch. 'The human anatomy is extraordinarily simple,' he said. 'The construction of the legs for instance: two long bones with a simple joint for flexing, and the proportions always the same. But when you draw them it's difficult to suggest the shape. Everyone can see this muscle on the thigh, the quadriceps. I never knew there was another one here, inside, the sartorius. But if you emphasize it too much the figure looks muscle-bound.'

Jack watched the lieutenant's finger trace the lines of the leg on the drawing as he spoke. He was not sure whether the man was teasing him, extending his agony, or whether he really wanted to talk about drawing.

'Of course,' the lieutenant said with a sigh, 'the war has provided all of us with daily lessons in anatomy. I could write a paper on the major organs of the British private soldier. Liver in section. Bowel, extent of, when eviscerated. The powdery bone of the average English subaltern.'

Jack coughed. 'Excuse me, sir. Can I ask about the charge?'

'The charge?'

'For God's sake, Wraysford,' said Weir. 'You told this man to report to you because he was asleep. He wants to know if you are going to have him court-martialled. He wants to know if he's going to have an art lesson or whether he's going to be shot.'

'There's no charge. You are not under my command.'

Jack felt a hot stinging in his eyes.

'I'm sure your own company commander will punish you if he wants to.'

Weir shook his head. 'No further action.'

'Thank you, sir. Thank you.'

Jack looked at the two men with love and gratitude. They understood the difficulties of a man who had been stretched too far. He felt sure that their mercy sprang from compassion for him. He took out Margaret's letter. In his enthusiasm for living he wanted to share the burden of his son's illness.

'You see here, sir. I had this letter from my wife. Our boy's been taken poorly. I was worried about him. I'd not slept when I came up from the tunnel, I was so worried about him.'

He handed the letter to Weir, who nodded. 'See this, Wraysford?' he said, pushing it across the table.

'Yes,' said Stephen. 'I see it. Diphtheria, it says. That's serious.'

'Will I be allowed leave to go and see him?'

Stephen raised an eyebrow towards Weir. 'I doubt it. We're undermanned as it is,' said Weir.

Jack said, 'Have you got children, sir?'

Weir shook his head. 'Not married.'

'You, sir?'

'No,' said Stephen.

Jack nodded a few times to himself. 'I suppose it's funny when I'm out here with men getting killed all round me and it's him that's in danger.'

Stephen said, 'Every one of the men we've killed is someone's son. Do you think of that when you see them dead? Do you wonder what their mothers thought when they first held them to their breast – that they would end like this?'

'No, sir. I hadn't thought of it like that.'

The three men drank their tea. From the outside came the whining of shells. They could feel the reverberation of the explosions in the dugout. Fragments of dried earth fell from the ceiling.

Stephen said, 'Two of my men were in a shellhole listening for eight hours last night in no man's land. What do you think they were thinking about all that time? It's not as if they're allowed to talk.' He was looking at Jack.

'I don't know, sir. Perhaps it's like when we're in the tunnel. You stop thinking at all after a bit. It's as though you've stopped living. Your mind goes dead.'

'I'd like to go down your tunnel,' said Stephen.

'No you wouldn't,' said Weir. 'Even the miners don't like it.'

'I'd like to see what it feels like. Some of my men think you don't work fast enough down there. They think you don't hear the noise of the enemy. They're terrified of being blown up from underneath.'

Weir laughed. 'We know that all right.'

Jack shifted in his chair. There was something strange about the two officers. He suspected they were drunk. He had always thought of Weir as dependable. Like all the tunnelling company commanders, he was a Regular Engineer who had been transferred. He was careful and reliable underground, even though he had had no experience of it before the war. But his eyes looked wild and red with whisky. The brownish stubble on his cheeks and chin was surely the result of more than one morning's missed shave. The lieutenant, Jack thought, looked more sober, but in some ways even stranger. You could not be sure whether he was serious. He seemed forgetful and distant, but also enthusiastic about going underground. It was as though he was not all there, Jack thought. The affection and gratitude he had felt at first began to evaporate. He didn't want to share any more of his personal feelings with them. He wanted to be back with Tyson and Shaw, or even Wheeler and Jones with their irritating chatter. At least with them he would know where he was.

'Any idea when we'll get some rest, sir?' he asked Weir.

'Tomorrow, I should think. They couldn't keep us here longer than that. What about your men, Wraysford?'

Stephen sighed. 'God knows. I hear rumours all the time from battalion headquarters. We will have to attack sooner or later. Not here though.'

'Are we going to have to lose a few lives just to placate the French?' Weir laughed.

'Yes. Oh, yes. They want to feel they're not alone in this. But I believe they will reap the whirlwind.'

Riley appeared from the back of the dugout. 'It's nearly six, sir. Stand-to in ten minutes.'

'You'd better go, Firebrace,' said Weir.

'I'll see you in that tunnel,' said Stephen.

'Thank you, sir.'

Jack climbed back out of the dugout. It was almost light outside. The low sky of Flanders met the earth at a short horizon, only a few miles behind the German lines. He breathed in deeply on the morning air. His life had been spared; the last trace of elation came to him as he looked towards the back of the trench and saw the plumes from cigarettes and steam from the tea that cold hands were now clasping. He thought of the stench of his clothes, the lice along the seams, the men he was frightened to befriend in case their bodies came apart the next

137

day in front of his eyes. It was the hour of Tyson's ablutions when he would empty his bowels into a paintpot and throw the contents over the top.

From the officers' dugout behind him came the sound of piano music, a rising melody under the scratch of a thick gramophone needle.

WHEN THEY WERE finally relieved the miners were allowed to go to a village further back than their usual billets for a rest. The men were so tired they found it hard to march. Three miles behind the front line they were on a prepared road with ditches on either side. The order 'march at ease' had been given, and some men smoked as they walked. Jack Firebrace concentrated on keeping a straight line under the weight of his pack with its extra digging tools. There was a village visible dimly at the end of an avenue, but he found that if he focused on it he lost the ability to coordinate his feet. He felt as though he were walking across a ravine and the road was a hundred feet below. Twice he jerked awake, realizing he had been walking in his sleep. A few ranks behind him, Wheeler had to be pulled from the ditch. Jack closed his eyes for a moment against the brightness of the daylight, but quickly reopened them as he felt a sensation of nausea at his loss of balance.

There were things he had thought he might never see again, signs that life had persisted outside the narrow inferno of his existence. A curate rode towards them on a bicycle and raised his flat hat as he passed the column of men. Beside the road was grass that was still green, that had not been uprooted. There was blossom in the trees.

When they stopped in the village square, Sergeant Adams gave them leave to sit down while officers went in search of billets.

Jack leaned against the stone surround of the village water pump. Tyson was staring at him with blank eyes, unable to

139

register the change in his surroundings. There were columns of smoke coming from the houses in the small street behind the square. They could see a food shop and a butcher's in the doorway of which two small boys were playing.

Then Jack heard the sound of a woman's voice. It spoke an unfamiliar language with a harsh accent that was strange to his ears, but there was no mistaking its femininity. It belonged to a stout woman of about thirty who was talking to a fair-haired girl. The miners listened as the high voices came to them on the thin air of the morning like consoling memories of a lost life.

Two other members of Jack's unit, O'Lone and Fielding, had fallen asleep where they lay on the cobbles. Jack allowed the feeling of rest to come up to him slowly, trying to adjust himself to the lack of fear.

He turned to look at Shaw, who sat beside him. His unshaved face was black with dirt and his eyes showed white and fixed below the grime. He had not spoken since they had begun the march and his body seemed to have frozen.

In the corner of the square a white dog began barking. It ran around in front of the butcher's shop until the butcher himself came out and clapped his hands fiercely at it. Then it went up and sniffed at the feet of the men who were nearest to it. It wagged its tail in excitement at the presence of so many people. It had a sharp, pointed face and a feathery tail that arched over its back. It licked Jack's boot, then rested its head on Shaw's motionless knee. Shaw looked down at the bright eyes that searched his face for any sign that he might feed it. He began to stroke the dog's head. Jack watched Shaw's big miner's hands run down the animal's soft back. Gently, Shaw laid his head against the dog's flank and closed his eyes.

Captain Weir directed them to a barn on the outskirts of the village. The farmer had grown used to billeting troops and drove a hard bargain. Many men dropped their packs and slept on the first piece of straw they could find. Tyson found a clean corner, to which he invited Shaw and Firebrace. They disliked each other's habits, but they were familiar with them and feared worse.

In the afternoon, Jack woke from his sleep and went out into

140

the farmyard. The company cooker, a kitchen range on wheels, was being stoked up. A horse-drawn cart had come to deliver disinfectant and delousing powder under the critical eye of the quartermaster.

Jack walked down the lane towards the village. He spoke no word of French and viewed all buildings, fields and churches as profoundly alien. The comfort of not being under fire was diluted by a growing homesickness. He had never been abroad before the war, and only two or three times had he left the reassuring noise and pattern of the London streets in which he had been brought up. He missed the clank and rattle of trams, the long terraces of north London and the names that took him towards his home territory, Turnpike Lane, Manor House, Seven Sisters.

There was also an infantry battalion at rest: the village was taken over by the racket and movement of an army regrouping, resting and trying to restore itself. Jack went among the snorting horses, the shouting NCOs and the little groups of smoking, laughing soldiers like a boy in a dream. What happened a few miles away was kept secret. None of these men would admit that what they saw and what they did were beyond the boundaries of human behaviour. You would not believe, Jack thought, that the fellow with his cap pushed back, joking with his friend at the window of the butcher's shop, had seen his other mate dying in a shellhole, gas frothing in his lungs. No one told; and Jack too joined the unspoken conspiracy that all was well, that no natural order had been violated. He blamed the NCOs, who blamed the officers; they swore at the staff officers who blamed the generals.

The company cooker disgorged hot stew, coffee and a second helping, for the keenest, of fat and water mixed to an imitation gravy. With a piece of fresh bread in his other hand, Jack spooned it all down hungrily. Wheeler complained that the food was disgusting, nothing like the teas his wife cooked for him, or the fish and chips he sometimes ate for supper on his way back from the pub. O'Lone had memories of meat pies and new potatoes, followed by sponge pudding. Tyson and Shaw were not given to complaining, though neither had much relish for the food. Jack finished what Tyson didn't want. He was too ashamed to admit that the army food, though irregular and sometimes contaminated when it arrived at the front, was generally better than what they would afford at home.

Shaw had revived. His strong back helped shift fresh bales of straw in the barn; his bass voice once more joined in the repetitive sentimental songs that broke out after feeding. Jack was glad to see it; he depended on the resilience of certain men to nerve himself to his unnatural life, and Arthur Shaw with his handsome, heavy head and calm manner was his greatest inspiration.

In good humour, braving the barely understood jeers of the washerwomen who stood by to take their clothes, the men queued naked for the baths that had been set up in a long barn. Jack stood behind Shaw, admiring his huge back, with the muscles slabbed and spread out across his shoulder blades, so that his waist, though in fact substantial enough, looked like a nipped-in funnel by comparison, above the dimple of the coccyx and the fatty swell of his hair-covered buttocks. Inside the barn the men roared out in song or in shouted abuse, throwing cakes of soap and splashing water from the baths of variable temperature that had been improvised from wine barrels and animal feeding troughs. By the doorway stood Sergeant Adams with a cold hose over the end of which he placed his finger to intensify the pressure and drive the men into the air where they would recover clothes which, though clean, still contained the immovable lice.

They collected their pay in five-franc notes in the evening and looked for ways of spending it. Since he had been cast as the joker in their section, Jack Firebrace was also regarded as the man who should be in charge of entertainments. Newly shaved, with combed hair and cap badges polished, Tyson, Shaw, Evans and O'Lone presented themselves to him. 'I want you back by nine o'clock, and sober,' said Sergeant Adams as they swung out through the gates of the farm. 'Will you settle for half-past?' called out Evans.

'Half-past and half-pissed,' said Jack. 'That'll do me.' The men laughed all the way to the village.

Queues were drifting and forming outside a shop where an

improvised bar, which they called an estaminet, had been set up. Using his gifts as master of revels, Jack lighted on a cottage with a bright kitchen and a small queue. The men followed him and waited outside until there was space for them to crowd round a table where an elderly woman produced plates full of fried potatoes from a pan of seething oil. There were litre bottles of unlabelled white wine passed around among the diners. The men disliked the dry taste of it and one of the younger women was prevailed on to fetch sugar which they stirred into their glasses. Still pantomiming their disgust, they managed to swallow it in quantity. Jack tried a bottle of beer. It was not like the pints that memory served him in the Victorian pubs at home, made with Kentish hops and London water.

Sleep took them all by midnight, when Tyson extinguished his last cigarette in the straw. In the loud noise of snoring they forgot what was unforgivable. Jack noticed how men like Wheeler and Jones treated each day as though it were a shift at work and talked to one another in the evening in the nagging, joking way they would have done at home. Perhaps in some way he did not understand, that was what the two officers had been doing; perhaps all that talk about life-drawing was just a way of pretending everything was normal. As he began to drift towards sleep, he concentrated hard on the thought of his home; he tried to imagine the sound of Margaret's voice and what she would say to him. The health of his son became more important than the lives of the company. No one had even raised a glass to Turner in the estaminet; no one remembered him or the three others who had been taken with him.

The night before they were to return to the front there was singing. The men knew no shame. Wheeler and Jones sang a mawkish duet about a girl worth a million wishes. O'Lone recited a poem about a little house with roses at the gate and a bird in the tree that went tra-la-la.

Weir, who had been prevailed on to play the piano, blanched with embarrassment as Arthur Shaw and the rest of his section, men he knew had been responsible personally for the taking of at least a hundred lives, longed over several

143

verses for the touch of their mama's kiss. Weir promised himself he would never again socialize with other ranks.

Jack Firebrace told a series of jokes in the style of a music-hall comic. The men joined in with some of the punchlines, but kept laughing at his performance. Jack's solemn face glistened with the effort of his comedy, and the men's determined response, whistling and slapping each other in mirth, was a token of their determination, and their fear.

Jack looked out over the hall that had been borrowed for the occasion. There were waves of red faces, smiling and shiny in the lamplight, their mouths open as the men roared and sang. Each one looked to Jack, from his vantage point on an upturned box at the end of the hall, indistinguishable from the next. They were men who could each have had a history but, in the shadow of what awaited them, were interchangeable. He did not wish to love one more than the next.

Towards the end of his routine he felt the low onset of dread. The leaving of this undistinguished village now seemed to him the most difficult parting he had had to make; no sundering from parents, wife or child, no poignant station farewell, could have been undertaken with heavier heart than the brief march back through the fields of France. Each time it grew more difficult. He did not become hardened or accustomed. Each time he seemed to have to look deeper into his reserves of mindless determination.

In a rage of fear and fellow-feeling for the mass of red faces he concluded his act with a song. '"If you were the only girl in the world,"' he began. The tinkling words were gratefully taken up by the men as though they expressed their deepest feelings.

STEPHEN'S SECTION OF the line had been shelled off and on for three days. They assumed a large attack was imminent. On the third morning he rose wearily in his dugout and pushed aside the gas curtain. His eyes felt heavy with fatigue. His body was running not on natural energy given by food and sleep but on some nervous chemical supplied by unknown glands. His mouth felt burned and sour all the way down to the gut. His skull was throbbing beneath the surface with a broken, accelerated pulse. A tremor was starting in his hand. He needed to go and reassure the men in his platoon.

He found Brennan and Douglas, two of the most experienced, sitting on the firestep white-faced, with perhaps sixty cigarette ends on the ground beside them.

Stephen exchanged pleasantries with them. He was not a popular officer. He found it difficult to think of words of encouragement or inspiration when he himself did not believe there was a purpose to the war or an end to it in sight. He had been reprimanded by the company commander, Captain Gray, a shrewd and forceful man, for telling one soldier he believed the war would grow very much worse before there was a chance of its getting better.

Brennan's comments on the shelling contained his usual quotient of obscenity. His favourite adjective appeared so often in his sentences that after a time Stephen had stopped noticing it. It was the same with all the men.

Stephen had been promoted from the ranks because he had a better education than most of the others and because those of the university subalterns who were not dead had taken on companies. Gray picked him out and sent him back to England for a spell with an officer cadet training unit. On his return to France he was given further instruction by staff officers in Béthune, though as far as he could see, the only decisive moment came during a game of football in which he was supposed to show his mettle. He obliged by fighting with a player on the other side and was taken on a hasty three-week tour of the front line by an asthmatic major who was making his first excursion from brigade headquarters. The major was insistent that Stephen should not see any of the men with whom he had joined up; he was to be re-presented to them as a different and superior being who had magically acquired the attributes of an officer. The major wheezed his farewells and Stephen found himself the possessor of a shiny belt, new boots and a deferential batman. He had not met any of his platoon before, though the men with whom he had trained and fought were only a hundred yards or so down the line.

'No word of when this will stop, then?' said Douglas.

'They never tell me. What do you think?'

'I wish they'd give it a break.'

'Just as well they stop for lunch.' It was the cheeriest thing Stephen could think of to say. 'You can't keep a German gunner from his sausage.' His dry mouth did not relish the forced jollity.

There was a tearing sound in the air as a gun was fired. It was a medium-sized piece whose shell made a clanking, rattling noise that at first sounded quaint, then suddenly alarming as it accelerated closer to them. Brennan and Douglas flattened themselves against the front of the trench as it went over. The ground shook and small pieces of earth rained down gently on their heads. Stephen saw that Douglas's hands were now shaking badly as he rubbed his face.

He nodded to the two men. 'It can't last for ever.'

Normally shelling was aimed at night towards the rear areas, at the guns and ammunition and stores. The pounding of the front line in daylight was usually the prelude to an attack, though Stephen suspected it could be a variation of tactics, or just inaccuracy.

He made his way along the trench and talked to other members of the platoon. They took their orders from the NCOs and regarded Stephen as little more than a symbol of some distant authority in front of whom they were supposed to behave well and be respectful. Because of his friendship with Weir, Stephen had learned almost as much about the tunnellers as about his own men. He realized when he spoke to them under the continuing shellfire that he was ignorant of their lives. They were mostly Londoners who had belonged to the Territorials before the war.

The ones he liked best were Reeves, Byrne and Wilkinson, a sardonic trio who, unlike Brennan and Douglas, never volunteered for anything dangerous but retained a compelling and relentless dislike for the enemy.

He found them together, as usual, though uncharacteristically silent. A battery of field guns had been increasing in activity over the last hour, Reeves reported. While he was talking they heard the spanking report of one being fired, followed by the screeching sound of the shell.

'We're getting those all the time now,' said Reeves. 'Listen.'

The three men lay close together. They feared shell wounds more than bullets because they had seen the damage they did. A direct hit would obliterate all physical evidence that a man had existed; a lesser one would rip pieces from him; even a contained wound brought greater damage to the tissue of the body than a bullet. Infection or gangrene often followed.

A sharp wailing began a few yards down the trench. It was a shrill, demented sound that cut through even the varying noises of gunfire. A youth called Tipper ran along the duckboards, then stopped and lifted his face to the sky. He screamed again, a sound of primal fear that shook the others who heard it. His thin body was rigid and they could see the contortions of his facial muscles beneath the skin. He was screaming for his home.

Byrne and Wilkinson began swearing at him.

'Help me,' said Stephen to Reeves. He went and took the boy's arm and tried to sit him down on the firestep. Reeves gripped him from the other side. His eyes were fixed on the sky and neither Stephen nor Reeves was able to unlock the muscles of his neck and make him look downward.

Tipper's face appeared to have lost all its circulation. The whites of his eyes, only a few inches from Stephen's face, bore no red tracery of blood vessels; there was only a brown circle with a dilated pupil floating in an area of white which was enlarged by the spasmodic opening of the eye. The pupil seemed to grow blacker and wider, so that the iris lost all light and sense of life.

With no idea of where he was, the boy repeatedly and imploringly called out some private word that might have been a pet name for his father or mother. It was a noise of primitive fear. Stephen felt a sudden loosening of compassion, which he quelled as quickly as he could.

'Get him out,' he said to Reeves. 'I don't want this here. You and Wilkinson, get him to the MO.'

'Yes, sir.' Reeves and Wilkinson dragged the rigid body to the communication trench.

Stephen was shaken. This eruption of natural fear brought home how unnatural was the existence they were leading; they did not wish to be reminded of normality. By the time he returned to his dugout, he was angry. If the pretence began to break, then it would take lives with it.

There seemed to be no way in which they could confront this dread. At Ypres and in other actions they had been able to prepare themselves to die, but the shellfire unmanned them all again. Men who had prepared themselves to walk into machine guns or defend their trenches to the last could not face death in this shape. They pretended that it was more than this; it was the evidence of what they had seen. Reeves had searched for his brother but had found no trace to bury, not a lock of hair, not even a piece of boot. He told Stephen this with bitterness and disbelief. The shell that had taken him was of a size that had to be loaded by crane from a light railway; after flying six miles at altitude it had left a crater large enough to house a farm with outbuildings. It was no wonder, Reeves said, that there was no trace of his brother. 'I wouldn't mind,' he said, 'but he was my own flesh and blood.'

By the afternoon of the third day Stephen began to be

worried about the effects on all the men in his platoon. He felt like a useless and unused link in the chain. The senior officers would not confide in him; the men took direction from the NCOs and comfort from themselves. The bombardment continued.

Stephen talked briefly to Harrington, the lieutenant who also shared Gray's dugout, then drank the tea Riley produced promptly at five. He went out to look at the late afternoon light. It had begun to rain again, but the shells kept coming along the blackened skyline, their flares like unexpected stars, in the grey-green, turbulent darkness.

Towards midnight Weir came to the dugout. He had run out of whisky and wanted some of Stephen's. He waited till Gray had gone out.

'How was your rest?' said Stephen.

'A long time ago,' said Weir, drinking deeply from the flask Stephen pushed over to him. 'We've been back for three days.'

'So you've been underground. It's the safest place to be.'

'The men come out of the hole in the ground and they find themselves under this. They don't know which is worse. It can't go on, can it? It just can't.'

'Take it easy, Weir. There's not going to be an attack. They're there to stay. Those big guns take almost a week to dig into their pits.'

'You're a cold bastard, aren't you, Wraysford? Just tell me something that'll make me stop shaking, that's all.'

Stephen lit a cigarette and put his feet up on the table. 'Do you want to listen to the shells or do you want to talk about something else?'

'It's that idiot Firebrace with his trained hearing. He's taught me how to distinguish between each gun. I can tell you the size of it, the path of the shell, where it's going, the likely damage.'

'But you liked the war when it started, didn't you?'

'What?' Weir sat up in his chair. He had a round, honest face with receding fair hair. What was left of it was generally standing on end, or uncombed after he had removed his cap. He was wearing a pyjama jacket and a white naval jersey. He settled back a little on his seat as he contemplated what Stephen had said. 'It seems impossible to believe now, but I suppose I did.'

'It's nothing to be ashamed of. We all had our reasons for joining up. Look at Price, our CSM. He's flourished here, hasn't he? What about you? Were you lonely?'

'I don't want to talk about England,' said Weir. 'I've got to think of staying alive. I've got eight men underground with a German tunnel coming at us the other way.'

'All right,' said Stephen. 'I'm going out to check on my men in half an hour anyway.'

The dugout shook with the reverberations of a huge shell. The lantern swung on the beam, the glasses jumped on the table, and bits of earth fell from the ceiling. Weir gripped Stephen's wrist.

'Talk to me, Wraysford,' he said. 'Talk to me about anything you like.'

'All right. I'll tell you something.' Stephen blew out a trail of cigarette smoke. 'I'm curious to see what's going to happen. There are your sewer rats in their holes three feet wide crawling underground. There are my men going mad under shells. We hear nothing from our commanding officer. I sit here, I talk to the men, I go on patrol and lie in the mud with machine guns grazing my neck. No one in England knows what this is like. If they could see the way these men live they would not believe their eyes. This is not a war, this is an exploration of how far men can be degraded. I am deeply curious to see how much further it can be taken; I want to know. I believe that it has barely started. I believe that far worse things than we have seen will be authorized and will be carried out by millions of boys and men like my Tipper and your Firebrace. There is no depth to which they can't be driven. You see their faces when they go into rest and you think they will take no more, that something in them will say, enough, no one can do this. But one day's sleep, hot food and wine in their bellies and they will do more. I think they will do ten times more before it's finished and I'm eager to know how much. If I didn't have that curiosity I would walk into enemy lines and let myself be killed. I would blow my own head off with one of these grenades.'

150

'You're mad,' said Weir. 'Don't you just want it to be over?'

'Yes, of course I do. But now that we have come this far I want to know what it means.'

Weir began to shake again as the sounds of the shells came closer. 'It's a mixed barrage. The field gun alternating with heavy artillery at intervals of –'

'Be quiet,' said Stephen. 'Don't torture yourself.'

Weir held his head in his hands. 'Talk to me about something, Wraysford. Talk to me about anything but this war. England, football, women, girls. Whatever you like.'

'Girls? What the men call their sweethearts?'

'If you like.'

'I haven't thought about them for a long time. Constant shellfire is a cure for impure thoughts. I never think of women. They belong to a different existence.'

Weir was silent for a moment. Then he said, 'You know something? I've never ever been with a woman.'

'What? Never?' Stephen looked to see if he was serious. 'How old are you?'

'Thirty-two. I wanted to, I always wanted to, but it was difficult at home. My parents were very strict. One or two of the girls I asked out for the evening, well they . . . they always wanted to get married. Then there were the working girls in the town, but they would have just laughed at me.'

'Aren't you intrigued to know what it's like?'

'Yes, yes, of course. But now it's become such an issue, it's assumed such an importance in my life that it would be difficult.'

Stephen noticed that Weir had stopped listening to the shellfire. He was staring down at the glass in his hands, deep in concentration.

'Why don't you go to one of those places all the men go to in the villages? I'm sure you could find someone friendly, not too expensive.'

'You don't understand, Wraysford. It's not that easy. It's different for you. I suppose you've been with hundreds of women, have you?'

Stephen shook his head. 'Good God, no. There was a girl in

151

my village who'd do it with anyone. All the boys lost their innocence with her. You had to give her a present – chocolate or money or something. She was a simple girl but we were all very grateful. She got pregnant of course, but no one knew who the father was. Some fifteen-year-old youth, probably.'

'Was that all?'

'No. There were some other girls. Boys expected to do it. They thought it was unhealthy to store it up. Even their mothers thought so. That's the difference between a Lincolnshire village and a town like – what was your home?'

'Leamington Spa.'

'Exactly! The price of respectability.' Stephen smiled. 'It was bad luck for you.'

'You're telling me.' Weir began to laugh.

'Well done.'

'What do you mean, "well done"?'

'You're laughing.'

'I'm drunk.'

'It doesn't matter.'

Weir poured another drink and tipped his chair back. 'So all those girls, Wraysford, tell me –'

'Not that many. Perhaps four or five. That was all.'

'However many. Tell me, was there one you loved? Was there one you did it with again and again?'

'Yes, I think there was.'

'Just one?'

'Yes, just one.'

'And what was that like? Was it different from the others?'

'Yes, I suppose it was. It was quite different. It became confused with other feelings.'

'You mean, you . . . you were in love with her, or what?'

'That's what you would call it. I didn't know at the time what it was. I was just aware of some compulsion. I couldn't stop it.'

'What happened to this woman?'

'She left.'

'Why?'

'I don't know. I went home one day and she hadn't even left a note or a message.'

'Were you married?'

'No.'

'What did you do?'

'Nothing. What could I do? I couldn't pursue her. I let her go.'

Weir was quiet for a moment. Then he said, 'But when you . . . you know, with her, was it a different feeling, a different experience from with the girl in the village? Or is it always the same?'

'By the time she left I don't think I was thinking about that. It felt more as though someone had died. As though you were a child and your mother or father had died. As though you were a child and your mother or father had vanished.' Stephen looked up. 'You must find out for yourself. Your next leave. Or maybe we can get you down the line somehow. One of my men will know.'

'Don't be ridiculous,' said Weir. 'Anyway, this woman. Do you think of her now? Do you have a keepsake?'

'I had a ring that belonged to her. I threw it away.'

'Don't you ever think of her when you're lying here at night hearing the guns outside?'

'No. Never.'

Weir shook his head. 'I don't understand. I'm sure I would.'

There was a momentary stillness outside. The two men looked at each other in the dim light, their faces grey and weary. Stephen envied the innocence still visible beneath the strain that showed in Weir's open features. He felt he had already lost all connection with any earthly happiness that might persist beyond the sound of guns. The scattered grey hairs at his temples and above his ears seemed to remind him that he was changed and could not return.

'So,' he said. 'Before the war. Were you lonely?'

'Yes, I was. I was still living with my parents, I didn't seem to be able to get away. The only thing I could think of was to join the army. My father knew someone in the Engineers, so that was it. I joined up in nineteen-twelve. You were right. I liked having a role. And I liked the comradeship. It was as simple as that. I had had no friends before, and suddenly I found that I had, if not the friendship then at least the

153

company of hundreds of men of my age. When I was commissioned I found that some of them even looked up to me. It was a grand feeling.'

'You've done well,' said Stephen. 'They respect you.'

'No,' said Weir dismissively, 'they'd follow anyone who –'

'I mean it. You've done well with them.'

'Thank you, Wraysford.'

Stephen poured more whisky. He always hoped it would make him sleep, but in fact it made little difference. If sleep came it was as a gift and was as likely to come after tea as after alcohol.

'My men don't respect me,' he said. 'They respect Sergeant Price. They're frightened of him, anyway. And they do what the corporals tell them, Smith and Petrossian. But I'm irrelevant to them.'

'Nonsense,' said Weir. 'You're in there with them just as much as any other subaltern. You go on patrols. They must admire you.'

'But they don't respect me. And they're right not to. Do you know why? Because I don't respect them. Sometimes I think I despise them. What do they think they're doing, for God's sake?'

'You're a funny chap,' said Weir. 'I remember a major I met outside Ypres, in the Salient, who –'

The door to the dugout was pushed open. It was Hunt. 'You'd better come, sir,' he said to Stephen. 'Shell in our setion. There's a lot of casualties. Reeves, Wilkinson, I think.'

Stephen took his cap and followed Hunt out into the night.

The sandbags that made up the parapet had been blown away on a front of about twenty yards. The wall of the trench had caved in and barbed wire had been blown back and was hanging over the churned earth. There was a sound of groaning. Stretcher-bearers were trying to clear the debris to get to the wounded men. Stephen took a trenching tool and began to dig. They pulled out a man by his shoulders. It was Reeves. His expression was more vacant than usual. His ribcage was missing on one side where a large piece of shell casing stuck out from under his breastbone.

A few yards further on they disinterred Wilkinson. His dark profile looked promisingly composed as Stephen approached. He ran through his mind for Wilkinson's personal details. He remembered. He had just married. He worked as a book-maker. There was a baby on the way. He prepared words of encouragement as he came alongside. But as the stretcher-bearers lifted him, they turned his body and Stephen saw that his head was cut away in section, so that the smooth skin and the handsome face remained on one side, but on the other were the ragged edges of skull from which the remains of his brain were dropping on to his scorched uniform.

He nodded to the stretcher-bearers. 'Take him away.'

Further on was another casualty, Douglas, whom he had seen that morning and thought indestructible. Douglas was alive and had been left leaning against the trench wall. Stephen went up and sat beside him.

'Cigarette?' he said.

Douglas nodded. Stephen lit one and put it in Douglas's mouth.

'Help me up,' said Douglas, 'just so I can sit.'

Stephen lifted him further with his arm round his shoulders. Douglas's blood was pumping from a shrapnel wound in his shoulder.

'What's that white on my leg?' he said.

Stephen looked down. 'It's a bone,' he said. 'It's the femur. It's all right, it's just bone. You've lost some muscle.'

Douglas's blood was all over Stephen. It had a peculiar smell, not unpleasant in itself, though cloying in such quan-tity. It was fresh. It was like the smell in the back of a butcher's shop, only stronger.

'Is Tom all right?' said Douglas.

'Who?'

'Tom Brennan.'

'Yes, I think so. Don't worry, Douglas. Hold on to me. We'll get you some morphine. Try and stop this bleeding. I'm going to put something on your shoulder. It's just a field dressing.'

As he pressed it to the wound he felt Douglas's flesh slipping under his hands. A rib or two had collapsed and his

155

hand was going in towards the man's lung. He stopped the pressure.

'Hunt!' he shouted. 'For Christ's sake get a stretcher here. Get me some morphine.'

Douglas's blood had run up inside the arms of Stephen's uniform. It was on his face and in his hair. His trousers were saturated. Douglas was hanging on to him.

'Have you got a wife, Douglas?'

'Yes, sir.'

'Do you love her?'

'Yes.'

'Good. I'll tell her. I'll write to her. I'll tell her you're the best man we've got.'

'Am I going to die?'

'No, you're not. But you won't be able to write a letter. I'll tell her all the things you did. The patrols and so on. She'll be proud. Where's that morphine? Hunt, for Christ's sake! You love your wife, Douglas. You'll see her again. Think of her when you get to hospital. Hold on to that thought. Don't let go of it. It's all right, it's all right, they're coming. Hold my arm there. That's right. I'm going to take that cigarette or it'll burn you. Don't worry, I'll give you another one. There you are.'

Stephen did not know what he was saying. He was close to choking on Douglas's blood. By the time the stretcher-bearers reached them Douglas had lost consciousness. They levered the inert body up, trying not to make the wound worse.

As they moved off there was a screaming metal sound overhead. Another shell landed with an explosion of light. For a moment Stephen saw the whole line of the trench, straight for twenty yards, then dog-toothed to prevent blast, then straight again. He saw the land behind it stretching out for miles; trees, a distant farmhouse. For an instant it was calm: rural France lay bathed in radiant light.

Then, with the earth and shrapnel flying, he was blown forward. The rear stretcher-bearer had been hit in the head. Douglas lay tipped out on the duckboards. Stephen, unhurt, shouted, 'Get him out. Hunt! Get him out!' Feeling the stickiness on his face, he held his head in his hands and called out, 'Get this man's blood off me.'

WHEN THEY WERE relieved at the front, Stephen's company had three days' rest in Béthune, a town much liked by the men because of the friendliness of the French girls and the large number of bars and estaminets. Stephen was billeted in a doctor's house on the edge of the town. It had a formal front garden with gravel triangles and small yew hedges. Although there were five other officers, Stephen had his own bedroom for the first time since the war had started. It overlooked the lawn at the rear of the house which was of a coarse grass with some untended flowerbeds and a horse chestnut at the end.

It was mid-afternoon when he finally went off duty. He laid his kit on the polished floor, pulled off his boots and sank on to the bed, which had been made up with clean sheets. The smell of dried herbs rose up from the bedclothes. It was always impossible to sleep at first, he found, because his body relaxed so quickly that the muscles jumped and woke him. The medical officer had given him a box of pills, but they made him sleep so heavily that he didn't want to take one until the night.

The fatigue he felt was in his limbs and organs, an aching heaviness like gravity. His mind remained clear. Although he had little idea of time, the burned images of the preceding days lived in his memory with static clarity. He saw Weir's anxious open face, desperate for reassurance; Wilkinson's soft, beautiful lips in profile and the absence that was the other side of his face. Douglas's blood, the smell of which still came to him, though he had died of his wounds, pouring

157

himself away through the slats of the duckboards; the casing of the shell, the manufacturer's serial number legible if he had cared to read it, that stuck out from Reeves's heart. The others they had buried next day when the shelling finally lifted, the wooden crosses sent up from stores, little piles of stones laid by their friends. In the wonderful quiet, when the German guns had stopped, they heard the song of a blackbird.

Stephen screwed up his eyes. Nothing he had foreseen, nothing he had dreamed of could have bodied forth the shape and taste of this existence. He drank some whisky from the flask in his pack. Suddenly he was asleep.

He did not wake until seven the following morning. He looked in amazement at his watch. He had slept for twelve hours, unmoving, still in his uniform. No one had called him for dinner; he had heard no movement in the big house.

He found a bathroom and shaved while the water ran. When he had finished, he dressed in the clean clothes Riley had put in his bag and returned to his room, where he sat on the bed, resting himself against the pillows. He pushed open the window on to the garden. It was a dull day, but the air was fresh and there was no sound of shells; it was good enough. Stephen found that he had been the victim of the harlot's trick that he despised in the men: sleep had healed.

He began to think about breakfast. There would be eggs, but would there be meat? He remembered Bérard's insistence that all English people ate roast meat for breakfast each day. And where was Bérard now? Somewhere safely behind the lines he presumed. Although Amiens had been taken by the Germans before being recaptured, he imagined that Bérard would have found a comfortable existence for himself; he had no anxieties for his well-being.

Relaxed by sleep, he allowed his mind to conjure up the big house on the boulevard du Cange. It was almost six years since he had stepped out into the night, leaving the front door open, taking Isabelle on his arm. What had taken place beneath that placid irregular roof seemed to him to belong to a world as peculiar and abnormal as the one in which he now lived. He remembered the uncontrollable fury of his desire, fully reciprocated by Isabelle. He could envisage her head thrown back against the wall, moving a framed picture of flowers a half-turn on its hook. He could taste her flesh on his tongue. If he tried very hard he could see a vague outline of her face, but very vague, not really coming into focus. What had gone completely from his mind was the memory of what made her human, her ways and her thoughts. The withholding of these details was like a torment. When he tried to bring her back to mind, he could not hear the voice, he could not imagine one aspect of her, the way she looked or talked, the expression of her face, her walk, her gestures. It was as though she were dead and he bore the responsibility for killing her. What he and the men endured was the punishment for what he had done.

He stayed for a year in St-Rémy after she left. If she were to change her mind, he reasoned, she would need to know where to write. She might need him, she might want his help in her dealings with her family or with her estranged husband. No word came, and he knew, when he could bear to admit it, that she would never write.

Eventually he said goodbye to the men at the furniture makers and took a train to Paris. He rented a room in a house off the rue de Rennes and set about finding work. He had no wish to present himself in his old guise as a businessman; he wanted to forget his knowledge of weaving and tariffs and taxes. He was employed by a builder who needed woodwork done.

In the room along the landing was a bright-eyed young student up from Tours called Hervé, who was excited about living on his own in the capital. He invited Stephen to meet his friends in various cafés near the Place de l'Odéon. He went, and drank rum or coffee, but could not share Hervé's nervous exhilaration. He thought of returning to England, but with no fixed idea of what he might do, found it easier to be in a foreign country. He wrote briefly to his former guardian to assure him he was well. No letter came back.

In the next-door house was a family with a daughter of eighteen called Mathilde. The father, who worked in a lawyer's office, found Stephen a job as a clerk, which, while tedious, was better paid than sawing wood. He dined occasionally at their house and was encouraged to take Mathilde out to the Jardins du Luxembourg at the weekend. They became friends in the course of their long walks, and Stephen confided to Mathilde the story of his affair with Isabelle.

Since he did not describe the physical aspect of what had taken place, the story sounded incomplete. Mathilde was puzzled by Isabelle's apparent change of heart. She said, 'There must be more to it than you know.'

His friendship with Mathilde was a new experience. The boys in the institution had all been on their guard, searching for a way out. Although there was a fellow-feeling in the face of shared difficulties each was too interested in his own self-preservation to be generous to the others. At work in Leadenhall Street there had been colleagues, but none of his own age except two office boys from Poplar who kept to themselves. In his visits to docks and factories Stephen had seen men of his own age and had craved their company, but there was never time enough to get to know them.

Mathilde had strong teeth and brown hair which she wore pulled back with a ribbon. Her large eyes had an earnest expression which frequently gave way to laughter. She took Stephen for walks along the river and he showed her the places he had visited when he had first been sent to Paris by his company. Mathilde's friendship was uncomplicated and undemanding, with no element of passion or competition. It was easy to make her laugh, and Stephen found that when she was there to tease it out of him he, too, was able to be frivolous. Still he missed Isabelle; for all Mathilde's qualities she seemed no more really than a pale version of what womanhood could achieve. Stephen viewed all women in this way. He felt sorry for men who were married to creatures who were so obviously inferior; even the men who were happy and proud of the imagined beauty of their wives had, in his eyes, made a desperate compromise. He even pitied the women themselves: their vanity, their looks, their lives were poor things in his eyes, so far short of what could exist.

The strain of his anguish lasted for another year, then went cold in him. He had no sensation of healing, no awareness that time had soothed him or lent him a longer perspective in which to view his passion. He experienced it only as a loss of memory. Her presence, which he had felt permanently in his mind, abruptly disappeared. He was left with the feeling of emotions undischarged, of a process uncompleted.

The coldness enabled him to live more easily, to respond with some degree of conviction to other people; he began to regard them as something more than second-best, acting out lives that were impoverished. However, the sudden chill loss of her also made him uneasy. Something had been buried that was not yet dead.

When the war came Stephen was relieved. He contemplated joining the French army, but although it would have entailed killing the same people and fighting for possession of the same land, it was not the same as fighting with other Englishmen. He read in the papers of British regiments mobilizing in Lancashire and London; of men flocking to recruiting stations in Suffolk and Glasgow, all for the defence of Belgium. Nothing in the French or British newspapers gave cause for alarm. While the scale of the war quickly became apparent, there was still no reason to think it would last more than a year. The accounts of the British retreat from Mons in August stressed how an outnumbered British force had proved themselves the equal of anything the vaunted German infantry could throw at them. Pulling out, wiring up the bridges across the canal, they had shown initiative and bravery; in the Salient they had got their rifles off so fast that the Germans thought they were facing machine gunners. Stephen was moved by the thought of his fellow-countrymen fighting this foreign war.

He returned to London with a renewed feeling for England. The suppressed frustrations and unexpressed violence of his life were turned into hatred of the Germans. His desire to defeat and kill them was something he cherished; he nurtured and fed the feeling carefully: the enemy was in sight.

At Victoria he met a clerk he had known called Bridges, who was in the Territorials. 'We can't raise a full battalion,' he said. 'We're a few short. If you join us you can be out there by Christmas. Be a sport.'

'I won't have had the training,' said Stephen.

'You'll go on a weekend in the New Forest. The sergeant'll turn a blind eye. Go on. We're desperate to get at them.'

Stephen did what Bridges suggested. They did not make it to France by Christmas, but crossed the following spring. They were attached to two regular battalions and quickly came to think of themselves as professionals.

At first he thought the war could be fought and concluded swiftly in a traditional way. Then he watched the machine gunners pouring bullets into the lines of advancing German infantry as though there was no longer any value accorded to a mere human life. He saw half his platoon die under the shells of the enemy's opening bombardment. He grew used to the sight and smell of torn human flesh. He watched the men harden to the mechanical slaughter. There seemed to him a great breach of nature which no one had the power to stop.

He could protest or he could go with it. He tuned himself to killing. He tried to be fearless in the hope that it would comfort the other men, whose dazed and uncomprehending faces he saw through the blood and the noise. If this was to be permitted, reported, glossed over, then at what level of activity, he wondered, could they stop? He came to believe that much worse was to come; that there would be annihilation on a scale the men themselves had not yet dreamed of.

Breakfast was already on the table when Stephen went downstairs. Captain Gray was adept at finding good billets for himself and his officers; he had also acquired a batman called Watkins who had once trained as a chef in the kitchens of the Connaught Hotel in London. His skill was of little use on the rations at the front or on the limited supplies available in the villages, but Gray always approached his offerings with enthusiasm. He was the first to the table.

'Good sleep, Wraysford?' he said, looking up from his plate. 'Harrington went up to have a wee look at you last night but said you were dead to the world.'

'Yes, I slept like a child. It's all that fresh air, I suppose.'

Gray laughed. 'Help yourself. Fried eggs on the side there. I've got Watkins out looking for bacon but you'll have to make do without for the time being. French bacon's pretty vile at the best of times.'

Gray was an unorthodox officer. The men feared him; but although he had borrowed the brisk manner of the regular soldier he spent much of his spare time reading. He carried volumes of verse in his pocket and his dugout always had a small shelf of books above the bed which were augmented or replaced by parcels from England. After university he had become a doctor and had qualified as a surgeon when the war broke out. Some of the works of the Viennese school of psychiatrists would appear on his shelf next to the novels of Thomas Hardy. He was viewed as a disciplinarian after he had chaired a court martial which passed the death sentence on a young private, but he also talked about motivation and understanding the men. A childhood in the Scottish Lowlands had given him a dry sense of mockery and tempered his more abstract military and psychological theories with practical caution.

He chewed vigorously through the last of his bread and fried eggs and poured himself another cup of coffee.

'Nice little house, this, isn't it?' he said, pushing back his chair and lighting a cigarette. 'You can always rely on a doctor to make himself comfortable. Do you know France well?'

'Quite well,' said Stephen, sitting down with a plate of fried eggs. 'I spent some time here before the war.'

'How long?'

'About four years.'

'Good heavens. So you speak the language like a native?'

'I should think it's a bit rusty by now, but it used to be all right.'

'Could be useful to us. Not that we have any contact with the French at the moment. But you never know. As the war progresses . . . How's your platoon doing? Do you like being in charge?'

'We've had a bad time of it. A lot of casualties.'

'Yes of course. What about you? You getting on well with the men?'

Stephen drank some coffee. 'Yes, I think so. I'm not sure that they really respect me.'

163

'Do they obey you?'

'Yes.'

'Do you think that's enough?'

'Probably.'

Gray stood up and went over to the marble fireplace. He stubbed out his cigarette in the fireplace. 'You've got to make them love you, Wraysford, that's the secret.'

Stephen grimaced. 'Why?'

'They'll fight better. And they'll feel better about it, too. They don't want to have their brains blown out in the service of some stuffed shirt.' Gray's wiry body was twitching with animation; his keen eyes searched Stephen's face for signs of agreement. His head was nodding up and down with excitement.

Stephen said, 'Perhaps so. I try to set an example.'

'I'm sure you do, Wraysford. I know you go out on patrol with them and bind up their wounds and so on. But do you love them? Will you give your own life for them?'

Stephen felt himself closely scrutinized. He could have said, 'Yes, sir,' and closed the conversation; but Gray's informal, hectoring manner, although unsettling, permitted frankness.

'No,' he said. 'I suppose not.'

'I thought so,' said Gray, with a small triumphant laugh. 'Is that because you value your own life too much? You think it's worth more than some simple footsoldier's?'

'Not at all. I'm a simple footsoldier myself, don't forget. It was you who promoted me. It's because I don't value my life enough. I have no sense of the scale of these sacrifices. I don't know what anything is worth.'

Gray sat down at the table again. 'There's something about you I don't understand,' he said. He screwed up his face in mock perplexity as he examined Stephen, then laughed. 'But I'll find out what it is, never worry. You could be a good soldier if you wanted to. You aren't yet, but you could be.'

Stephen said nothing for a moment, then, 'Price is a good soldier.'

'Price is a wonderful man. Another of my promotions, if you will allow me to bask a little in his glory. That fellow was a clerk in a warehouse before the war. He just sat at a table ticking off numbers all day long. Now the company couldn't function without him. He runs their lives for them. And do you ever see him flustered?'

'No, thank God. I depend on him as much as the men do.'

'Of course you do,' said Gray. 'Now tell me about these clay-kickers. You see a lot of them, don't you?'

'Yes. Their tunnel starts in our part of the line. They're a good lot on the whole. They work hard underground. It's not a job many people could do.'

'What's the name of that laddie in the plimsolls?'

'Weir? The company commander?'

'Yes. What's he like?'

'He's a strange man, but perhaps no stranger than anyone else in the circumstances. He's not a miner by profession, he's an Engineer who was put in charge of the miners.'

'He looks pretty odd to me. I've no time for these clay-kickers myself. After months of digging they finally get their mine in place. They blow it up and what have they got? A nice little crater with a raised lip that the enemy can occupy.'

Lieutenant Harrington, a tall, mournful man with a slight stammer, came into the dining room.

'Good morning, sir,' he said to Gray. His manner was deferential, though his expression was one of almost permanent surprise, as though he could not quite believe where he had found himself. Stephen wondered how he managed to be so punctilious when he clearly found it difficult to remember which day of the week it was.

'We were just talking about the miners,' said Gray.

'Oh yes, sir.'

'Wraysford is a friend of their company commander, Weir.'

'I believe they're inseparable, sir,' said Harrington.

Gray laughed. 'I knew it. Hear that, Wraysford?'

'I'd no idea Lieutenant Harrington took such an interest in my life.'

'Only teasing you, Wraysford,' said Harrington, piling his plate with the fried eggs, which had started to congeal beneath the cover.

'Of course,' said Stephen. 'I'm going to have a look round the town now. Excuse me.'

165

'Good idea,' said Gray. 'I've given up all hope of that bacon. Tell Watkins if you want more coffee, Harrington.'

'Thank you, sir.'

Gray went up to his bedroom to find a book and Stephen stepped outside. He walked down the garden to the road and closed his eyes as he felt the pale sunshine on his face. He breathed deeply and began to walk.

JACK FIREBRACE'S APPLICATION for leave to visit his son was turned down. 'I've thought about it,' said Weir. 'I'm sympathetic to the fact that you haven't been home for a year. But the truth is that with so many men out here now it's a hell of a job shifting them backwards and forwards. The roads are jammed with supplies as it is. You'll have to wait your turn.'

Jack went back underground. The tunnel head in the trench concealed a vertical timbered shaft from which two tunnels had been dug. The first, at thirty feet, had run into trouble with German mining efforts. There had been fighting at close quarters underground. It was better being in clay than chalk. Frequent explosions caused the chalk to fragment; it mixed with water that had seeped down from shellholes in no man's land to make a viscous liquid that was sometimes coloured with the leaking blood of miners who had been pulverized by blasts.

Following instructions from his superiors, Weir ordered a second tunnel to be driven at a level of seventy feet. It was, according to the rule book, to be only three feet wide.

'I don't like it,' said Tyson, who was lying flat on the ground behind Shaw and Evans. 'I've never seen anything as narrow as this in all my life.'

Where they pressed the timbers in a little further back the men had lanterns, but at the face it was dark.

Jack tried not to imagine the weight of earth on top of them. He did not think of the roots of the trees, stretching down through the soil. In any case they were too deep now.

He had always survived in London by picturing the tunnel in which he worked as a railway compartment at night: the shutters were closed over a small space, you could not see anything, but outside a wide world of trees and fields beneath an open sky was whistling safely by in the darkness. When the space was no more than three feet wide and he had the earth pressing in his mouth and eyes, the illusion became difficult to sustain.

Evans's hands scrabbled away tirelessly behind him: Jack heard his rasping breath sucking in what oxygen the air-feed had managed to deliver. Evans's presence was a comfort to him. On the surface he cared little for his ferrety face and sarcastic jokes, but here their breathing and their hearts worked as though in one body.

Shaw came to relieve him at the face. He had to crawl over Evans's body, then haul Jack off the cross and flatten himself on the tunnel floor so Jack could get over him and go back down the tunnel. Even twenty yards back they could not stand up, but they could crouch and stretch each limb in turn. The air was bitter and the lamps showed the timbering to have been done with reassuring precision.

'Ten minutes' rest,' said Weir. 'Make the most of it.'

'Shouldn't you be in your dugout having a nice cup of tea?' said Jack. 'I bet none of the other company commanders go underground.'

'I've got to keep an eye on you lot,' said Weir. 'Until this thing's going properly anyway.'

The men were allowed to speak without deference to the officers underground. It was a way of acknowledging that conditions in the tunnel were difficult. By talking as though they were in a civilian mine they were also able to remind themselves of the differences between them and the infantry; they might be sewer rats, but they were better paid.

'Let's play Fritz,' said Evans. It was a superstitious game that was popular with the miners though incomprehensible to the officers.

'I wish you wouldn't,' said Weir. 'Be very quiet, if you must.'

'Right,' said Evans. 'I say he's twenty-five, married with two kids. He's ten feet from the chamber.'

'I say there's four of them,' said Jack. 'They're in the fighting tunnel now. Ten feet by teatime says we'll get there first.'

Evans had a scoring system based on the number of feet the tunnel was driven in a day. The purpose of the game was to predict where the enemy was. The winner would see him dead; the loser could only secure his safety by paying the others in cigarettes. Weir understood neither the rules nor the scoring, but allowed it on the grounds that it distracted the men and increased their awareness of the enemy. Turner, significantly in his colleagues' eyes, had lost five days running, including a game on the morning of his death.

That afternoon Weir had a message to see Captain Gray, whom he found inspecting supplies in the rear.

'We haven't met, have we?' said Gray. 'Your men are doing a good job. It must be bloody awful under there.'

'No worse than being shelled. We just don't want to be caught. Your men are frightened of being blown up from below, mine are scared of being trapped in a tunnel three feet wide with people firing at them. Did you get my request?'

'Yes I did. Of course you must have proper defence. I appreciate that. But you must understand that my men are not used to being underground. Have they done all right so far?'

'Yes, they've done fine. But we need a regular rota.'

'And you really can't spare your own men?'

'Not now we've got a lower tunnel. They're working round the clock. It's only a patrol at a time. Three or four men would do it.'

'All right,' said Gray. 'As you may know I have some doubts about how useful it is blowing craters for the enemy to occupy, but I'm not going to quibble over your men's safety. I'm going to ask Wraysford to take charge. You know him, I think.'

'Yes, I do.'

'Sound man?'

'I think so,' said Weir.

'Bit of an odd fish,' said Gray. 'I'll speak to him later. They can start tonight.'

Stephen asked for volunteers. 'We'll take a sewer rat to show us the way, but I need two others. We'll be in a fighting tunnel. We won't have to crawl.'

No one offered. 'All right, I'll take Hunt and Byrne.'

He went to see Sergeant Adams to ask which of the diggers would go with them.

'They're sending up a volunteer right away, sir. It'll be the man who lost at Fritz.'

It was Jack who, in addition to giving Evans five cigarettes, was required to escort the men down into the tunnel. They took gas masks and attached grenades to their belts. At ten o'clock they went to the tunnel head.

Stephen gave a final look at the sky before following Jack down the shaft. He had never been underground before. He felt a brief wave of tenderness towards the open world under its endless sky, perverted though it was by the twisted rolls of barbed wire over the shell-torn earth.

The rungs of the ladder that led down the shaft had been made for durability; his hands felt no fine sanding on the splintery wood. They were set at irregular intervals so that it was difficult to achieve any rhythm in the descent. He had to struggle to keep up with Jack Firebrace. At first he was careful not to tread on his fingers, but soon all he could see was the occasional bobbing and gleam of a helmet far below.

Stephen eventually stepped off the ladder where Jack was waiting. For a moment the darkness and silence reminded him of childhood games when he and the other boys would dare each other to enter some long-closed cellar or disused well. He was frightened by the dank smell of the earth and the implacable weight of matter. The shell craters on the surface were no more than scratches compared to this crushing volume. If it moved or slipped there would be no second chance, no possibility of fighting back or escaping with only a wound. Even Reeves's younger brother, under the full blast of a howitzer shell, had stood a better chance.

Hunt and Byrne looked round uneasily. They carried rifles and had borrowed miners' helmets in place of their soft service caps. Stephen had a revolver and all of them had grenades, which Weir told them were likely to be their most effective weapon in case of trouble.

170

Jack spoke in a low voice. 'I've heard German movement coming this way. We need to protect our men laying the charge and also the lower tunnel which they won't know about. We're going through this entrance here which leads into a long gallery. Off that there are two fighting tunnels with listening posts. We should all stick together.'

Byrne looked at what Jack described as the entrance.

'I thought there was going to be no crawling.'

'It gets bigger,' said Jack.

Byrne swore and ran his hand along the packed earth and clay.

'La France profonde,' said Stephen. 'This is what we're fighting for.'

'Not for one shilling a day I'm not,' said Byrne.

Jack went ahead into the darkness. His eyes were accustomed to working in the murk, and his body moved in a shuffling, automatic crouch. When they had been going for about ten minutes, the narrow tunnel came to a junction with the lateral gallery that Jack and his company had dug two months earlier. To the right was the entrance to a parallel tunnel which would lead eventually to a chamber in which the men were laying the charge. To the left were the two fighting tunnels from one of which they had heard the sound of enemy digging.

Byrne and Hunt had stopped swearing. Hunt looked terrified.

'Are you all right?' said Stephen.

Hunt shook his head slowly from side to side. 'I don't like it. Being underground. Being closed in like this.'

'It's quite safe,' said Stephen. 'They're professionals. Look how well they've done the timbering.'

Hunt had started to shake.

'It's not right,' he said. 'I'm infantry. I'm not supposed to do this. I'll take my chances in the trench, not in a bloody hole. What if the earth falls in? Christ.'

'Be quiet,' said Stephen. Hunt was gripping his arm in panic. 'For Christ's sake, Hunt. You go down that tunnel or you'll be on a charge. I'll send you on every patrol until you've cut the wire from here to Switzerland.'

Stephen could feel Hunt's fear begin to infect him. He himself had a long horror of being in a space so narrow that he could not turn round.

Jack disappeared down the entrance to the fighting tunnel and Stephen looked at Hunt's pathetic face in the darkness. For a moment he pictured the man in his civilian life. He was a labourer who worked on building sites in London and Hertfordshire; he did not want to die forty feet below the ground of a foreign country. Stephen felt a softening of compassion.

He said, 'Get in there, Hunt. I'll follow you.'

'I can't, I can't.' Hunt began to jabber.

'If you don't do it you're going to get us all killed.' Stephen took out his revolver and cocked it. 'You hate the Germans, don't you?'

'Yes.'

'They've killed your friends. They're trying to kill you. They killed Reeves and his brother. Wilkinson. Douglas. All your friends. This is your chance to help kill some of them. Get in there.' He pointed the gun at the opening and then at Hunt's head. He was surprised at his own brutality; he assumed it was caused by fear.

Hunt went slowly into the tunnel and Stephen followed. Hunt's boots were in front of him and he could hear Byrne crawling behind him. If there was a problem he would be stuck. He could not go forward or turn back. He squeezed his eyes shut and swore silently to give himself courage.

The roof of the tunnel was a foot above his head. He kept repeating to himself the vilest words in the most terrible combinations he could think of; he shaped obscenities against the world, its flesh and its imaginary creator.

Eventually the tunnel widened. They could half-stand. Byrne had taken a cigarette from his pocket and was sucking on it. Stephen nodded to him in encouragement. Byrne smiled.

Jack whispered to Stephen. 'We think there's a German tunnel very near by. Our men laying the mine are frightened they'll dig through into their chamber. I'm going up to the listening post. I'll take one with me for cover. You keep one here.'

'All right,' said Stephen. 'You'd better take Byrne.'

He watched them move up ahead and turned to Hunt, who was sitting on the floor of the tunnel with his arms round his knees.

He was whimpering quietly. 'That narrow bit we've just come through. Suppose they blow that. We can't get back. We're stuck.'

Stephen sat down next to him. 'Listen,' he said. 'Don't think about it. This patrol will last two hours while our men are laying their charge. Two hours will pass. Think how quickly it passes. Think of the times you've wanted it to go on longer. It's the length of a football match by now – we've been down for half an hour already.' He was gripping Hunt's arm. He found that talking to him helped to keep some of his own fear from running over.

Hunt said, 'Do you hate the Boche?'

'Yes,' said Stephen. 'Look what they've done. Look at this world they've created here, this kind of hell. I would kill them all if I could.'

Hunt began to moan. He took his head in his hands and then lifted his face to Stephen. He had bland, open features with fleshy lips and smooth skin. His pleading, scared face was cupped between large work-roughened hands on which the nicks and burns from countless jobs were scored in the skin.

Stephen shook his head in despair and held out his hand. Hunt took it between his palms and began sobbing. He crawled into Stephen's arms and laid his head against his chest. Stephen felt Hunt's lungs pump and blow with the sobs that shook his body. He hoped that Hunt would somehow discharge the terror that had got inside him, but after a minute the noise of his sobbing began to grow louder. Stephen pushed him away and raised his finger to his lips. Hunt lay with his face to the floor, trying to stifle his own nose.

Stephen heard the sound of boots coming back from in front of them. Byrne's lanky figure, bent double but still scurrying, came into view.

His tobacco-heavy breath blasted into Stephen's face. 'Fritz has dug through into our tunnel. Firebrace is thirty yards up there listening. He says you've got to come.'

173

Stephen swallowed. 'All right.' He took Hunt by the shoulder and shook him. 'We're going to kill some Germans. Get up.'

Hunt got to his knees and nodded his head.

'Come on then,' said Byrne.

The three men set off deeper into the darkness. It took them five minutes to reach the point where Jack was crouching with his ear to the wall. At the end of the timbered tunnel they could see a ragged hole where German diggers had burst through.

Jack raised his finger to his lips, then mouthed the word 'Fritz' and pointed to the hole.

There was silence. Stephen watched Jack's face as he listened. He was wearing a faded shirt with the sleeves rolled up and the fabric was damp with sweat. Stephen saw the bristles on the back of Jack's broad neck where the barber had shaved the hair.

There was the sound of an explosion with rocks and earth falling from behind them. The men stayed motionless. They could hear feet in a tunnel parallel to their own. They seemed to be going away from them towards the British line.

Hunt began screaming. 'We're trapped, we're trapped, they've blown the tunnel. Jesus, I knew it, I –'

Stephen clasped his hand over Hunt's mouth and pushed his head back against the tunnel wall. The footsteps stopped, then started to come back towards them.

'This way,' said Stephen, moving back the way they had come. 'Cut them off before they get to our men.'

Towards the end of the fighting tunnel, before it rejoined the gallery, the way down which they had come was blocked where the camouflet they had heard had smashed the timbering and dislodged the earth. Stephen and Jack managed to force their way through the debris as gunfire broke out behind them.

'They're through, they're through, they've come through the hole,' Hunt was screaming.

Stephen pulled Byrne over the rubble. He saw Hunt rolling a grenade before he too made it to the site of the explosion. Rifle fire began at about thirty yards. There were four Germans visible when Hunt's grenade went off with a dense, shattering report. Stephen saw two of them flung backwards and a third twist sideways into the wall, but within a few seconds the firing began again. Stephen climbed on top of the pile of earth and began to fire into the gloom. Byrne found a position and manoeuvred his cumbersome rifle into place. Both men fired repeatedly, guided by the occasional flash of a rifle ahead of them. Stephen reached down to his belt for the grenades. It was impossible to hit anything with a rifle; a grenade would do more damage and might block the tunnel, which would enable the men laying the charge in the parallel tunnel to get out. As he fumbled with his belt he shouted out to the others to throw their grenades. His own seemed to have become entangled. Grappling desperately with his fingers, he was aware of renewed firing ahead, then suddenly of a sensation of having been hit by a falling house. He was thrown backwards by the force.

Hunt stood on Stephen's body and levered himself up so that he could throw his grenades through the space where Stephen had been standing. He and Byrne let off three each in quick succession with a long rolling sequence of explosions that caused the roof of the tunnel to cave in twenty yards away. The German rifles stopped firing and Byrne, who had picked up some words of German, heard a command to evacuate the tunnel. With Jack leading the way, they dragged Stephen along the tunnel back towards the gallery, cursing and grinding as they doubled up their limbs with the muscular effort of pulling the extra weight of his slack body. In the gallery they met other diggers coming up from the tunnel and four men who had been laying fuses in the explosives chamber.

There was a commotion of shouting and misunderstood reports of what had happened. The men took it in turns to drag Stephen along the tunnel back to the foot of the ladder, but his hot slippery blood made it difficult for the tired men to keep their grip.

They emerged to find chaos. Further shelling had caused casualties in the trench and had destroyed the parapet over a length of fifty yards. They took what cover they could find.

Byrne dragged Stephen's body to a relatively unscathed section while Hunt went in search of help. He was told that the regimental aid post, supposedly impregnable in its dugout, had been wiped out by a direct hit.

Stephen lay on his side, with the wood of the duckboards against the skin of his face, his legs bent up double by Byrne to keep him out of the way of men moving up and down. His face was covered with dirt, the pores plugged with fragments blown into them by the explosion of a German grenade. He had a piece of shrapnel in his shoulder and had been hit by a rifle bullet in the neck; he was concussed by the blast and unconscious. Byrne pulled out his field-dressing kit and emptied iodine into the hole in Stephen's neck; he found the tapes that pulled open the linen bag and freed the gauze dressing on its long bandage.

Rations came up at ten o'clock. Byrne tried to force some rum between Stephen's lips, but they would not open. In the bombardment priority was given to repairing defences and to moving the wounded who could walk. Stephen lay for a day in the niche dug for him by Byrne until a stretcher-bearer finally got him out to a forward dressing station.

Stephen felt a profound weariness. He wanted to sleep in long draughts of days, twenty at a time, in perfect silence. As consciousness returned he seemed able to manage only shallow sleep. He dipped in and out of it and sometimes when he awoke he found his body had been moved. He was unaware of the pattering rain on his face. Each time he awoke the pain seemed to have intensified. He had the impression that time had gone into reverse and he was travelling back closer to the moment of impact. Eventually time would stop at the moment the metal pierced his flesh and the pain would stay constant at that level. He yearned for sleep; with what willpower he could muster he forced away the waking world and urged himself into the darkness.

As infection set in, he began to sweat; the fever reached its height within minutes, making his body shake and his teeth rattle. His muscles were convulsed and his pulse began to beat with a fierce, accelerated rhythm. The sweat soaked through his underclothes and mud-caked uniform.

By the time they transported him to the dressing station the fever had started to recede. The pain in his arm and neck had vanished. Instead he could hear a roaring sound of blood in his ears. Sometimes it would modulate to a hum and at others rise to a shriek according to how hard his heart was pumping. With the noise came a delirium. He lost touch with his physical being and believed himself to be in a house on a French boulevard in which he searched and called the name of Isabelle. With no warning he was in an English cottage, a large institution, then back in the unremembered place of his birth. He raved and shouted.

He could smell the harsh carbolic soap of the orphanage, then the schoolroom with its dust and chalk. He was going to die without ever having been loved, not once, not by anyone who had known him. He would die alone and unmourned. He could not forgive them – his mother or Isabelle or the man who had promised to be a father. He screamed.

'He's shouting for his mother,' said the orderly as they brought him into the tent.

'They always do,' said the medical officer, peeling back the field dressing Byrne had applied almost thirty hours before.

They put him out of the tent to await transport to the casualty clearing station or death, whichever should come first.

Then under the indifferent sky his spirit left the body with its ripped flesh, infections, its weak and damaged nature. While the rain fell on his arms and legs, the part of him that still lived was unreachable. It was not his mind, but some other essence that was longing now for peace on a quiet, shadowed road where no guns sounded. The deep paths of darkness opened up for it, as they opened up for other men along the lines of dug earth, barely fifty yards apart.

As the fever in his abandoned body reached its height and he moved towards the welcome of oblivion, he heard a voice, not human, but clear and urgent. It was the sound of his life leaving him. Its tone was mocking. It offered him, instead of the peace he longed for, the possibility of return. At this late stage he could go back to his body and to the brutal perversion of life that was lived in the turned soil and torn flesh of the war; he could, if he made the effort of courage

177

and will, come back to the awkward, compromised and unconquerable existence that made up human life on earth. The voice was calling him; it appealed to his sense of shame and of curiosity unfulfilled: but if he did not heed it he would surely die.

THE BOMBARDMENT CAME to an end. Jack Firebrace and Arthur Shaw sat on the firestep smoking cigarettes and drinking tea. They discussed rumours that the division was to be moved south for an attack. They were in a reflective frame of mind, brought on by the knowledge that they had survived the shelling and the fighting underground. They felt a little self-congratulatory.

'Any news of your boy, Jack?' said Shaw.

'Still poorly. I'm hoping for another letter.'

'Cheer up. Our lad had something like it and he was all right in the end. Good hospitals at home, you know.' Shaw clamped his hand on Jack's shoulder.

'What happened to that lieutenant who got wounded underground with you?'

'I don't know. They got him down the line eventually, but he was raving by then.'

'It was him that put you on a charge, wasn't it? Good riddance, I say.'

Jack looked wistful. 'He was all right in the end. He didn't do anything.'

'Gave you a sleepless night.'

Jack laughed. 'Had a few of those anyway. We could ask Captain Weir what happened.'

'Go down and find out,' said Shaw. 'It's all quiet now. If the sergeant wants to know where you are, I'll cover for you. Get down and have a look at what's gone on down there.'

Jack thought for a moment. 'I'm a bit curious about that

fellow, I must admit. I think I might just go and have a look. I might even get a souvenir.'

'That's a good lad,' said Shaw. 'Get one for me and all.'

Jack finished his tea and put some cigarettes from his pack into his top pocket. He winked at Shaw and set off to the communication trench that led back to the rear area. There was a good deal of rebuilding going on after the bombardment. Jack found it strange how quickly the roads and fields seemed to lose their French agricultural identity and become railheads, dumps, reserves, or just what the men called 'transport'. The shelling had briefly made the ground look more like something that grew crops and vegetables, but this would not last long.

He asked a man digging new latrines where the dressing station was.

'Don't know, chum. But there's some medical tent over that way.'

He went back to his work. Jack found an orderly with a list of wounded and they went down the names.

'Wraysford. Yes. Here we are. They put him over the wall.'

'You mean he's dead?'

'They didn't take him to the clearing station. He must have had it. It was only an hour ago. There's a couple of dozen behind that wall there.'

I'll say a prayer for him, thought Jack: I will at least do my duty as a Christian.

It was twilight. Jack went down a rutted, muddy track to a low stone-built wall behind which was a ploughed field. There were rows of crumpled rags with dark stains. Some faces shone white in the moonlight that was coming up behind a copse. Some bodies were bloated, bursting their uniforms, some were dismembered; all had a heaviness about them.

As Jack looked out behind the row of dumped flesh into the furrows of the ploughed field behind, his astonished eyes widened at the sight of a figure he had not previously noticed. Naked except for one boot and a disc round his neck, his body tracked with the marks of dirt and dried blood, Stephen loomed from the half-light towards him. From his lips came dry words which sounded like, 'Get me out.'

180

Jack, recovering from his fright, climbed over the wall and went closer. Stephen took one short step forwards, then pitched into Jack's arms.

BACK IN HIS usual billet in the village, Michael Weir sat at the little table by the window and looked out at the rain on the grey, poplar-lined street. He was trying not to think of Stephen. He knew that he had been taken back to a clearing station, but no further word had reached him. He believed that Stephen would survive because there was some untouchable quality of good fortune about him. He breathed out heavily: this was the stupid, superstitious way the infantry thought.

He made a list of things he needed to do. Normally he enjoyed these housekeeping sessions, when he could escape from the worst of the shellfire and turn his mind to practical tasks.

He was worried by the parapet of the trench where they were working. Too often the sandbags were disturbed by men coming back from patrol, slithering hurriedly in before they could be illuminated by a German flare. In places where the bags were not properly replaced this meant that there was insufficient protection against enemy snipers, whose eyes were focused on them throughout the hours of daylight. The unexpected bullet through the head provided a quiet, relatively clean death, but it was demoralizing to the nerves of the others.

Weir tried to persuade Captain Gray that the infantry should look after themselves more, or at least have the Engineers' field companies to do it for them, but in return for having the protection of the infantry in the tunnel he found he had agreed to do more and more of their fatigues. He

182

wondered whether this was the price he paid for such generous access to Stephen's whisky.

At the top of his list he wrote 'check plates'. The loopholes used by the sentries were masked by iron plates, but some of these had been damaged by shells or by the attrition of enemy machine guns and snipers. There was also wire to be maintained, though this was a job from which he had so far successfully excluded his men. The infantry tied empty tins to the wire to act as alarm bells, but they were only ever sounded by rats. When it rained, the water would drop off the wire into the empty tins below. The different rates at which they filled were naturally a source of gambling to the infantry, as one man backed his tin against another, or of superstitious dread at the significance of whose might fill first.

Weir heard something different in the sounds. Once, during a period of calm, he sat on the firestep waiting for Stephen to return from an inspection and listened to the music of the tins. The empty ones were sonorous, the fuller ones provided an ascending scale. Those filled to the brim produced only a fat percussive beat unless they overbalanced, when the cascade would give a loud variation. Within his earshot there were scores of tins in different states of fullness and with varying resonance. Then he heard the wire moving in the wind. It set up a moaning background noise that would occasionally gust into prominence, then lapse again to mere accompaniment. He had to work hard to discern, or perhaps imagine, a melody in this tin music, but it was better in his ears than the awful sound of shellfire.

It was the middle of the afternoon, and Weir wanted to sleep before their nocturnal activities began. That night they were to help the infantry carry up ammunition and dig new sumpholes. There would also be repairs to the traverses and walls of the trench, quite apart from the work they were doing underground.

Before lying down to rest, he went to visit some of the men. He found them smoking and making repairs to their kit. The miners' clothes needed particularly frequent attention, and although each man had his own way of sewing, they had all become expert with needle and thread.

After some cheering words to them, Weir went back to his billet and lay down. There had been no word on Stephen from battalion headquarters when he went to check that morning. If he had been alive, he would somehow have got word to him, Weir believed. Even if his own commanding officer had not been formally notified by the medics, Stephen was resourceful enough to have let his friend know.

Weir closed his eyes and tried to sleep. He would want to write a letter to Stephen's next of kin, if such a person existed. Some phrases began to form in his mind. He was quite fearless . . . he was an inspiration . . . he was my closest friend, my strength and shield. The empty expressions that had filled so many letters home did not seem enough to describe the part Stephen had played in his life. Weir's eyes filled with tears. If Stephen was gone, then he himself would not be able to continue. He would court death, he would walk along the parapet, he would open his mouth to the next cloud of phosgene that drifted over them and invite the telegram to be delivered to the quiet street in Leamington Spa where his parents and their friends carried on their lives with no care or thought for the world that he and Stephen had known.

STEPHEN WRAYSFORD REINHABITED his body cell by cell, each slow inch bringing new pain and some older feeling of what it meant to be alive. There was no sheet on the bed, though against the skin of his face there was the rough comfort of old linen, washed and disinfected beyond softness.

In the evening the pain in his arm and neck grew worse, though it was never more than he could tolerate and it was never as bad as that of the man in the next bed, who could apparently visualize the pain: he could see it hovering over him. Each day they removed more of the man's body, snipping ahead of the gangrene, though never taking quite enough. When they unplugged his dressings, fluid leapt from his flesh like some victorious spirit that had possessed him. His body was decomposing as he lay there, like those that hung on the wire going from red to black before they crumbled into the earth leaving only septic spores.

One morning a boy of about nineteen appeared at the end of the ward. His eyes were covered with pieces of brown paper. Round his neck was a ticket, which the senior medical officer, a short-tempered man in a white coat, inspected for information. He called out for a nurse, and a young English girl, herself no more than twenty, went over to help him.

They began to undress the boy, who had clearly not had a bath for some months. His boots seemed glued to his feet. Stephen watched, wondering why they did not even bother to put up a screen. When he himself had arrived he calculated that he had not taken off his socks for twenty-two days.

When they finally prised the boy's boots off, the smell that came into the ward made the nurse retch into the stone sink beside them. Stephen heard the MO shout at her.

They peeled the boy's clothes from him and when they came to the undergarments the MO used a knife to cut them off the flesh. Finally the boy stood naked, except for the two brown eye patches. The top layer of skin had gone from his body, though there was a strip round the middle where the webbing of his belt had protected him.

He was trying to scream. His mouth was pulled open and the sinews of his neck were stretched, but some throat condition appeared to prevent any sound from issuing.

The MO peeled the brown paper from the boy's face. The skin of his cheeks and forehead was marked with bluish-violet patches. Both of his eyes were oozing, as though with acute conjunctivitis. They rinsed them in fluid from a douche cap into which the nurse had tipped some prepared solution. His body stiffened silently. They tried to wash some of the grime from him, but he would not stay still while they applied the soap and water.

'We've got to get the filth off you, young man. Keep still,' said the MO.

They walked down the ward, and when they came closer Stephen could see the pattern of burns on his body. The soft skin on the armpits and inner thighs was covered in huge, raw blisters. He was breathing in short fast gasps. They persuaded him on to a bed, though he arched his body away from the contact of the sheet. Eventually the doctor lost patience and forced him down with hands on his chest. The boy's mouth opened in silent protest, bringing a yellow froth from his lips.

The doctor left the nurse to cover him with a kind of improvised wooden tent, over which she draped a sheet. Finally she had time to bring a screen down the ward and conceal him from the others.

Stephen noticed that she was able to tend the wound of the man in the next bed and even to rebuke him for his noise, but whenever she emerged from behind the screens she would wring her small hands in a literal gesture of anguish he had never seen before.

He caught her eye and tried to comfort her. His own wounds were healing quickly and the pain was almost gone. When the doctor came to inspect them, Stephen asked what had happened to the boy. He had apparently been caught by a gas attack some way behind the front line. Blinded by the chlorine, he had stumbled into a house that was burning after being hit by a shell.

'Stupid boy didn't get his mask on in time,' said the MO. 'They have enough drills.'

'Will he die?'

'Probably. He's got liver damage from the gas. Some post-mortem changes in his body already.'

As the days went by Stephen noticed that when the nurse approached the screens behind which the gassed boy was lying her step would always slow and her eyes would fill with foreboding. She had blue eyes and fair hair pulled back under her starched cap. Her footsteps came almost to a halt, then she breathed in deeply and her shoulders rose in resolution.

On the third morning the boy's voice came back to him. He begged to die.

The nurse had left the screens slightly apart and Stephen saw her lift the tent away with great care, holding it high above the scorched body before she turned and laid it on the floor. She looked down at the flesh no one was allowed to touch, from the discharging eyes, down over the face and neck, the raw chest, the groin and throbbing legs. Impotently, she held both her arms wide in a gesture of motherly love, as though this would comfort him.

He made no response. She took a bottle of oil from the side of the bed and leaned over him. Gently she poured some on to his chest and the boy let out a high animal shriek. She stood back and turned her face to the heavens.

The next day Stephen woke to find the boy had gone. He did not come back in the evening, or the next day. Stephen hoped his prayers had been answered. When the nurse came to change his dressing, he asked her where he was.

'He's gone for a bath,' she said. 'We've put him in colloidal saline for a day.'

'Does he lie against the bath?' Stephen asked incredulously.

'No, he's in a canvas cradle.'

'I see. I hope he'll die soon.'

In the afternoon there was the sound of running feet. They could hear the MO shouting, 'Get him out, get him out!'

A bundle of screaming blankets was carried dripping down the ward. Through the night they contrived to keep the boy alive. The next day he was quiet, and in the evening they tried to lever him into the body cradle to get him back in the bath. His limbs dangled over the sides of the canvas. He lay motionless, trailing his raw skin. His infected lungs began to burble and froth with yellow fluid that choked his words of protest as they lowered him into the stone bath outside.

That night Stephen prayed that the boy would die. In the morning he saw the nurse, pale and shocked, making her way towards him. He raised his eyes interrogatively. She nodded in affirmation, then burst into shuddering tears.

Stephen was allowed to go outside in the afternoons and sit on a bench where he could watch the wind in the trees. He did not talk; he had no urge to say anything. Soon he was walking again and the doctors told him he would be discharged at the end of the week. He had been there twenty days.

'Visitor for you,' said the fair nurse one morning.

'For me?' Stephen spoke. His voice uncurled in him like a cat stretching after a long sleep. He was delighted by the unaccustomed sound. 'Is it the King?'

The nurse smiled. 'No. It's a Captain Gray.'

Stephen said, 'What's your name?'

'Nurse Elleridge.'

'Your first name.'

'Mary.'

'I want to tell you something, Mary. Can you come here for a moment?'

She went over to his bed, a little reluctantly. Stephen took her hand.

'Sit on the bed for a second.'

She looked round doubtfully but perched on the edge of the bed. 'What did you want to tell me?'

188

'I'm alive,' said Stephen. 'That's what I wanted to tell you. Did you know that? I'm alive.'

'Well done.' She smiled. 'Is that all?'

'Yes. That's all.' He let go of her hand. 'Thank you.'

Captain Gray came down the ward. 'Good morning, Wraysford.'

'Good morning, sir.'

'I hear you're walking. Shall we go outside?'

There were two wrought-iron benches set against the wall of the hospital which overlooked a lawn that dropped down to a cedar tree and a large stagnant pond. Occasional figures were moving tenderly about the grounds with the aid of sticks.

'You seem to have made a pretty good recovery,' said Gray. 'They told me you'd had it.'

He took off his cap and placed it on the bench between them. His crinkly hair was a glossy brown colour still unmarked by grey; his moustache was neat and trim. Although Stephen was pale, unkempt and showing grey hairs in places on his head, his face retained a youthfulness that Gray's had lost. The light in his large eyes still promised something unpredictable, while Gray's expression, though animated, was steady. He was a man who had mastered himself, and although his manner was informal he was manifestly the superior officer.

Stephen nodded. 'Once they got rid of the infection I made good progress. The wounds themselves were not that bad. This arm's going to have slightly restricted movement, but otherwise it's all right.'

Gray took a cigarette from the case in his breast pocket and tapped it on the end of the bench. 'You've got two weeks' home leave from the moment you leave this place,' he said. 'After that you're being promoted. I want you to go on a course at Amiens. Then you'll have a spell on brigade staff.'

Stephen said, 'I'm not going.'

'What?' Gray laughed.

'I'm not going home and I'm not going on some staff job. Not now.'

Gray said, 'I thought you'd be delighted. You've been in the front line for over a year, haven't you?'

'Exactly,' said Stephen. 'A year of preparation. I don't want to leave at the vital moment.'

'What vital moment?' Gray looked at him suspiciously.

'Everyone knows we're going to attack. Even the doctors and nurses know it. That's why they're trying to get those men walking.'

Gray pursed his lips. 'Perhaps, perhaps. But listen, Wraysford. You've done well with your platoon. They haven't achieved much yet, but which of us has? You've kept them together under fire. You've earned a rest. No one's going to say you're shirking anything. For God's sake, they gave you up for dead only three weeks ago. Did you know that? They dumped you with the corpses.'

Stephen was appalled at the idea of being separated from the men he had fought with. He despised the war, but he could not leave until he had seen how it would end. He had become, in some way he did not understand, wedded to it: his small destiny was tied to the larger outcome of events.

'To begin with,' he said, 'I have no home in England. I wouldn't know where to go. Would I loaf around in Piccadilly Circus? Should I go to the seaside in Cornwall and sit in a little cottage? I'd rather stay in France. I like it here.'

Gray smiled with indulgent curiosity. 'Go on. And promotion? You don't want that either? It would mean promoting Harrison instead.'

Stephen smiled. 'Even that, sir. I think there will be other opportunities for promotion. I don't think the killing is going to stop directly.'

'Probably not,' said Gray. 'But listen, Wraysford, these are my orders. There's not much I can do about it.'

'You could speak to the commanding officer.'

'Colonel Barclay?' Gray shook his head. 'I don't think so. He plays it by the book. I think he *wrote* the book.'

Stephen was encouraged. The idea of the unorthodox clearly appealed to Gray, for all his dapper appearance and military keenness.

The two of them were silent. A lorry brought stretcher cases to the side of the hospital and two orderlies went out to help. Some of the men they unloaded were fit only to die; the worst wounded were always left to last by the stretcher-bearers on the grounds that they were less likely to be of future use. It must, Stephen have reflected, seem like a self-fulfilling judgement to those who lay in shellholes, waiting, watching the infection begin.

'Do you know where we're being moved?' he said.

'Yes I do,' said Gray. 'Though I'm not supposed to tell you yet.'

Stephen said nothing, but opened his hands in a slight shrug.

'Albert,' said Gray. 'Then we'll have precise instructions. Brigade headquarters will be in a village called Auchonvillers, if that's how you pronounce it. The Colonel called it Ocean Villas.'

'I know it!' said Stephen excitedly. 'I've been there. It's just by the river Ancre. I know the area well. And I speak French. I would be –'

'Indispensable,' laughed Gray.

'Exactly.'

'Tell me about it, then.'

'It's nice countryside. Not flat, more like downland, I think you'd call it. Good fishing in the Ancre – not that I ever caught anything. Open fields with some large woods and copses. Quite heavily farmed for crops and vegetables. A lot of sugar beet, I think. The villages are dull. The railway from Albert stops at Beaucourt. There's a pretty village called Beaumont Hamel.'

'You won't see much of that. It's a German fortress. What else?'

'That's about all. There's a problem, though. It *is* hilly. It depends who has the high ground. You wouldn't want to attack uphill; that would be suicide.'

'I don't suppose we *want* to attack at all, but we have to draw the fire from Verdun. If they break through there we're finished.'

'And will we attack uphill?'

'The Boche have been there for a year. I don't suppose they chose the low ground.'

Stephen said nothing, then, 'And who else is going?'

191

'It's mostly the new boys, Kitchener's Army, just a few regulars like ourselves to stiffen them up.'

'They're sending them to attack there?' Stephen was incredulous.

Gray nodded. Stephen closed his eyes. He remembered from the day he had spent fishing the way the ground rose from the river. He had a dim recollection of a large wood on a hill that lay beneath a village called, if he remembered rightly, Thiepval. He knew what the German defences would be like after a year of preparation; even after a week they built better trenches than the British. The thought of waves of businessmen and labourers, factory hands and clerks in their first taste of war going up to meet them was absurd. They would not allow it.

'Had second thoughts?' said Gray. 'Piccadilly Circus is not such a bad place. You'd get a decent meal at least. You could go to the Café Royal.'

Stephen shook his head. 'Do you think you'll be able to do something for me? Persuade them to let me stay?'

'Anything is possible. It's always easier in the long run to tell a commanding officer that you are offering him troops rather than taking them away. I can tell his second-in-command, Major Thursby.'

'And what about the staff job? Can you delay that, or send someone else?'

Gray said, 'If you make yourself indispensable. And if you toe the line a bit more.'

'What do you mean?'

Gray coughed and ground out his cigarette under his heel. 'You're superstitious, aren't you?'

'We all are.'

'Officers are not superstitious, Wraysford. Our lives depend on strategy and tactics, not matchsticks or card games.'

'Perhaps I'm still a private at heart.'

'Well, stop it. I've seen that rubbish in your dugout. The wee carved figures, cards and candle ends. Chuck it out. Trust to preparation and good leadership. Trust your men. If you want something supernatural go and see the chaplain.'

Stephen looked down. 'I'd never thought of Horrocks as particularly supernatural.'

'Don't be funny, Wraysford. You know what I mean. If I help you, you've got to repay me. Cut out the mumbo-jumbo and believe in yourself.'

Stephen said, 'I don't really believe in that stuff, you know – cards and fortunes and so on. But everyone does it.'

'No they don't, Stephen. You do it because of what happened to you when you were a child.' Gray's voice had softened a little.

'What do you mean?'

'I don't know your life history, but I think children need to believe in powers outside themselves. That's why they read books about witches and wizards and God knows what. There is a human need for that which childhood normally exhausts. But if a child's world is broken up by too much reality, that need goes underground.'

'What ridiculous Austrian quak –'

'Be quiet.' Gray stood up. 'I'm your company commander. I'm supposed to know things you don't. If I help keep you here at the front, God help you, you will do things my way in future.'

He held out his hand. Stephen shook it briefly and went back into the hospital.

'YOU MAD BASTARD, Wraysford,' said Michael Weir. 'You mean you chose to stay when you could have gone home?'

'Home?'

'You know what I mean. England. It's so lovely at this time of year. I used to go and spend Whitsun with an aunt who lived in Sheringham on the coast of Norfolk. In late May the air was so pure you could get drunk on it. The fields and hedgerows were alive. It was the most beautiful time. And there was a little pub in Burnham Thorpe where –'

'Take me when it's finished, not before. I'll show you something in the meantime. The place we're going next. Have you had your orders?'

'Yes, though they're not very detailed. We move out on Friday and down to Albert. Just our luck. I thought we'd spend the rest of the war here, but they've got so much mining on down there that corps staff's asked for two extra companies. And guess who got chosen. Albert's the place with the Virgin hanging off the tower, isn't it?'

'Yes. It's going to be a squash. Half the bloody BEF's going to be there. Whisky?'

'All right,' said Weir.

'On Thursday night when the rear area's full of transport I'm going to take you into the village for a farewell treat.'

'What do you mean?'

'You wait and see. Something you've waited a long time for.'

Weir looked suspiciously at Stephen but said nothing. He

guessed what Stephen was planning. He had heard from men returning from rest that there was a farmhouse on the other side of the village where a light shone in the window all night. A woman and her daughter, it was said, would work through a whole platoon.

The thought of it filled Weir with anxiety. He had first touched female flesh when only seventeen and had recoiled from the possibility it offered. The girl was a year older but had seemed to belong to a different generation. When he felt inhibited and much too young for what she was suggesting, she had a humorous worldliness, as though her long experience made her view the act as the simplest and most natural thing imaginable. What he had heard about and what he wanted to do seemed to him so shameful and so private that he would not want to be seen doing it by anyone at all, even the girl herself. He declined her invitation; he told himself he would wait until he was older.

Meanwhile he looked with bewilderment at the married people he knew, particularly his parents. When they sat in the sitting room of their roomy brick house, reading books or playing cards, he gazed at them with big eyes, picturing scenes of debauchery. When his mother turned to him with a quizzical tilt of her head and laid down her sewing to ask him what he was thinking, he had to focus quickly on her parted hair, her beads and modest layers of clothes, and put from his mind the picture of inflamed organs and the interplay of flesh. Clearly these acts were natural, this was the way the world renewed itself and carried on, but even so when he watched his parents talking to their married friends he wondered at the strange conspiracy that kept their actions hidden beneath their demure public behaviour.

He began to invite women to dances or to tea at his parents' house, but there never seemed to be a question of sex. He held hands occasionally or, if he was lucky, was granted a goodnight kiss on the cheek. He went to university where the small number of women were educated separately with only brief and tightly chaperoned meetings with the men. If he had done it just once, he would have known how to do it again. At the age of twenty-three he thought of trying to contact the girl

195

again to ask if she was still interested but saw that this was a ridiculous thing to contemplate. He later discovered she was married.

He joined the Royal Engineers two years before the war broke out. The chaste male comradeship offered camouflage. Here at last he would be like everyone else: a man who wanted women but who was – regretfully, but with, in his case, some relief – denied them by circumstances. He could make rueful jokes with the others about their absence and his remarks would be tinged with real remorse.

For the first six months of the war he found the relief made him euphoric. He gained a reputation as an eccentric but dependable officer of unquenchable high spirits. With his university background he was quickly promoted and the men warmed to his ebullience. But as the fighting grew and the shelling intensified, his nerves began to wear. He had not been trained to live in tunnels three feet wide at great depths underground. He did not like the feeling that at any second in the trench he might be killed.

At the age of thirty his lack of physical contact with women became less like an absence in his life than a positive presence. He became tired by his ignorance, no longer envious of other people. He convinced himself that what he had missed could not, by definition, be extraordinary. It was a simple function, unremarkable, and easy for him now to ignore. The thought of ending his abstinence became more and more bizarre and full of practical pitfalls he could never overcome; it became, in the end, unthinkable.

The heavy bombardment had not preceded a major advance by the enemy, as many had feared. It had been the signal only for another short bombardment, and then a resumption of relative quiet.

Patrols went out at night and listened to the sound of German housekeeping: the mending of wire, the sewing on of buttons, the visits of the orderly with his lice powder, and an old Bavarian barber. They were better dug in than their British counterparts and better provided for by mobile kitchens and barrels of beer that came up as far as the reserve trenches. Occasionally at night there would come the sound of a folk song. These were not of the sentimental kind favoured by the British soldiers but strong, mournful evocations of a loved land.

Stephen, lying in a shellhole with Byrne, felt his body tense with hatred at the sound of them. Many of the men in his platoon felt respect for the Germans, a tolerance in quiet times that seemed to him to border on affection. He felt nothing but an urge to violence; he wanted to answer them with steel and explosive, with metal tearing into soft tissue and spinning on the bone. When the war was over there would be a place for contemplation, even generosity, but in the meantime he treasured his hatred as a means of saving his own life and those of his men.

He turned towards Byrne's cork-blackened face and pressed his lips to his ear, where he whispered so softly that the creak of his tongue against teeth and palate was louder than the words themselves.

'Machine gun at the far end. No activity. All asleep. May as well go back.'

The night was helpfully starless; the moon was buried deep behind banks of rain cloud. A fretful wind was not enough to open them and shed light on the ruptured earth in which they lay. Above the occasional rush and murmur of the breeze was the sound of a nightingale.

Stephen fingered his unused knife regretfully. Byrne nodded his head. He carried a two-foot club he had made from a piece of oak. With a short arm swing and a snap of the wrist he had once shattered a German sentry's skull with it.

They eased out of the shellhole and began the crawl back to their own lines where, in the most hazardous part of the excursion, they had to cross four rows of wire and roll into the trench without attracting fire, either from German machine guns that were permanently trained on the lip of the British trench, or from their own sentries, startled from a guilty slumber and loosing off at the first sound they heard.

Hunt was the sentry when they returned to the trench. They heard his rifle cock as Byrne knocked against a tin can that dangled on the wire.

Stephen felt Hunt's hand reach out and help him into the trench. Byrne slithered in after him.

'Well done, Hunt,' said Stephen. 'I'm going to give this man a drink now. Do you like whisky, Byrne?'

'Not half.'

'If Petrossian wants to know where Byrne is, tell him he's with me.'

'All right.' Hunt watched the men move off over the duckboards.

A few yards down the trench Jack Firebrace was sitting on the firestep with a cup of tea. He was regaining his strength after six hours underground. His thoughts turned towards home. Eight and a half years earlier when his wife had given birth to a son, Jack's life had changed. As the child grew, Jack noticed in him some quality he valued and which surprised him. The child was not worn down. In his innocence there was a kind of hope. Margaret laughed when Jack pointed this out to her. 'He's only two years old,' she said. 'Of course he's innocent.'

This was not what Jack had meant, but he could not put into words the effect that watching John had on him. He saw him as a creature who had come from another universe; but in Jack's eyes the place from which the boy had come was not just a different but a better world. His innocence was not the same thing as ignorance; it was a powerful quality of goodness that was available to all people: it was perhaps what the Prayer Book called a means of grace, or a hope of glory.

It seemed to Jack that if an ordinary human being, his own son, no one particular, could have this purity of mind, then perhaps the isolated deeds of virtue at which people marvelled in later life were not really isolated at all; perhaps they were the natural continuation of the innocent goodness that all people brought into the world at their birth. If this was true, then his fellow-human beings were not the rough, flawed creatures that most of them supposed. Their failings were not innate, but were the result of where they had gone wrong or been coarsened by their experiences; in their hearts they remained perfectible.

This love Jack felt towards his son redeemed his view of

human life and gave substance to his faith in God. Where his piety had been the reflex of a fearful man, it was transformed into something that expressed his belief in the goodness of humanity.

He was aware that John was an unlikely vehicle for such a change in his own beliefs, but it didn't matter to him: his son was all he cared about. He had not had the chance to say goodbye when he left and had corresponded with the boy through messages in Margaret's letters. At the front and underground he was often too preoccupied to think of John and Margaret, to form exact pictures of them in his mind, but when he lay on the cross at the tunnel face or strained his ears on sentry duty there was always a sense in which they were with him. His endurance was for them; the care he took to try to stay alive was so that he would see the boy again.

He watched as Byrne and Stephen disappeared, then prayed hard for John's life. The smell of the earth in the trench wall reminded him of his own boyhood, when he would fall in the mud during a game of football or play at building a dam in the stream that ran through the open ground behind the factory: there was this enduring smell of soil and boyhood. He was quite alone, as he had been always, but now with the urgent life of another boy in his heart.

The next day there was a letter for Jack from Margaret. He decided not to open it until he had come back from underground. He might be killed in the tunnel and it would be better to die in ignorance if the news from the hospital was bad. If it was good, then it would seem all the better for having been kept.

It was a quiet day. Some of the division was already packing up to leave. In the morning Jack took out a sketchbook and made some drawings of his friend Arthur Shaw. His big head had a sense of weight and shadow that yearned for the soft lines of the pencil. Shaw sat placidly while Jack went to work, his eyes flickering up and down from paper to face and back again, the pencil held lightly in the tips of his fingers. Tyson came and looked over Jack's shoulder and made a short, appreciative grunt. The drawing was simple and lacking in refinement, but Jack had the ability to make a likeness and this impressed Tyson, who wanted to be drawn himself. Jack was mysterious in his choice of subjects, however. There were a few pictures of lorries and stores, some of the villages in which they went to rest, the occasional group scene taken from memory of a concert hall or estaminet, but most of his sketchbook consisted of portraits of Arthur Shaw.

In the late afternoon Sergeant Adams came up with Jones and O'Lone, and the men formed up to go underground.

Michael Weir had detailed Adams to be in charge while he spent the evening in his dugout with a book. At about eight o'clock Stephen pulled back the gas curtain and let himself in. He was in a state of nervous excitement.

'Let's go,' he said.

'Go where?'

'The surprise I told you about. Come on. Bring that whisky bottle.'

Weir stood up hesitantly. He was afraid of what Stephen was planning. He swallowed an inch of whisky from the bottle and felt it add its small effect to the several he had already drunk. He guessed from his manner that Stephen had also been drinking. Weir breathed in deeply as they emerged into the darkness. It was a dry summer night and there was only the distant sound of some half-hearted shelling a mile or so down the line, like a routine metal lullaby to warn the forgetful that death could come to them even in their sleep.

He followed Stephen down the communication trench, through the reserve line and out into the rear area where the headlights of lorries were approaching from the tree-lined roads, illuminating the large piles of kit that had been laid under tarpaulin for transport. CSM Price strode about at the railhead, where a huge artillery piece was being laboriously winched on to a train. With clipboard and checklist he had temporarily resumed his old warehouse occupation.

Stephen hung back for fear of being seen by Price and ushered Weir over to a muddy area at the end of a line of poplars where two men were standing next to a motorcycle, smoking.

'I need that bike,' he said. 'Major . . . Watson needs it urgently.' He nodded towards Weir.

200

'Major Who?' said the man, looking doubtfully at Weir, who was wearing his white pullover and soft shoes with no sign of rank.

'Special operations,' said Stephen. 'Take these and say no more about it.' He held out a tin of fifty Capstan cigarettes.

'Can't do that, mate,' said the private, taking the cigarettes anyway. 'But there's a bike down there, behind the shed, that no one's using. Dispatch rider got hit in the arse by a farmer. By a bloody shotgun!' He laughed.

Stephen found the bike and shook it to and fro to see if there was petrol in it. There was a faint but adequate sound of liquid from the tank. He kick-started the machine and stamped it into gear. Weir climbed cautiously on to the back and held on. The bike had only one seat so he had to perch on a rack that had been fitted over the rear wheel. His legs hung loose on either side.

As they accelerated over the rutted track and down towards the road, Stephen felt a leap and surge of exhilaration. They had left behind the death and turmoil and filth; they were breaking free into the darkness of normality, with food and drink, the sound of women and the sight of men whose first thought would not be to kill them. The bike roared its way on to the road.

They saw the lights of the village, sparse and dimmed, and a lit window on the extreme western edge which had become famous in rumour. Stephen felt Weir's fingers digging into the flesh between his ribs.

The building was a farm with a low brick house on one side and barns for livestock and straw making up a square. Stephen propped up the bike at the entrance while Weir took the bottle from his pocket and sucked thirstily.

'Listen, Wraysford, I don't think I want to go on with this. Look at this place, it's pretty squalid and –'

'Come on. It's a woman, a soft creature who will be kind to you and make you feel well. It's not someone with a gun.'

He took Weir's arm and led him across the courtyard. Weir missed his footing as they neared the door. At the entrance he began to tremble.

'Christ, Wraysford, just let me get out of here. Let me go home. I don't want this.'

'Home? Home? A trench filled with rats?'

'If the red hats find us we'll be shot.'

'Of course we won't be shot. Disciplined, perhaps. Made to resign our commissions. Pull yourself together.'

They went through into a dim parlour with a stove in the middle of the floor. An old woman was sitting smoking a pipe. She nodded at the two of them in the doorway. She shook her head when Stephen began to speak and pointed to her ear.

'I want to leave,' Weir hissed.

Stephen gripped his wrist. 'Wait.'

The old woman let out a screech towards the door that led into the house. They heard footsteps, then a female voice. A woman of perhaps fifty appeared on the dark threshold.

'I wasn't expecting people tonight,' she said.

Stephen shrugged. 'My friend was anxious to come and see you. I'm worried that he may be a little nervous. He wants you to be very patient.' Stephen spoke as fast as he could in the hope that Weir would not understand.

The woman smiled grimly. 'Very well.'

'You have a daughter, Madame?'

'What is that to you?'

'I understand that she also . . .'

'That is none of your business. Tell your friend to come with me.'

'Go on.' Stephen pushed Weir in the back and watched him go faltering and afraid into the darkness on the other side of the door.

Stephen turned to the old woman and smiled. He made a drinking gesture and took out a five-franc note from his pocket. She went stiffly to the corner of the room and produced a bottle of wine and a dusty glass. Stephen took a chair beside the stove and rested his elbow on the long flue that ran across the wall. He raised his glass towards the old woman and drank the bitter white wine.

He wanted Weir to know what it felt like to be with a woman, to feel that intimacy of flesh. It made no difference to him whether Weir died in all innocence, but he felt it was in some way necessary for him to understand the process that had brought him into being.

Escaped from extermination, Stephen feared nothing any more. In the existence he had rejoined, so strange and so removed from what seemed natural, there was only violent death or life to choose between; finer distinctions, such as love, preference or kindness, were redundant. The flesh of a widowed farmer's wife, paid for in the wages of killing, was, in the reduced reality inhabited by him and Weir, a better choice than the flesh of Wilkinson, shell-shattered in section, its banal brain cell and membrane dripping memory and hope out on to his shoulder.

He stretched out his legs and saw his heels mark the beaten earth of the farmhouse floor. He had almost finished the bottle of wine and could feel it extinguish his last trace of caution, his last recognition of the spurious ways and codes of peacetime behaviour. He felt aged and weary but very calm.

The older woman had fallen asleep. Stephen went softly to the corner of the room and found another bottle in the cupboard. He poured himself a glass and took his seat again, waiting in the dim light.

When Weir returned he looked shaken and pale. The black marks beneath his eyes were visible even in the gloom of the parlour. Stephen looked at him interrogatively. Weir shook his head. 'You go.'

'No, thank you. This is your expedition. I have no interest in her.'

'She wants you to go. Go and see her. Go and see her, you bastard. You started this. You finish it.'

Weir was more agitated than he had been even during the bombardment.

Stephen had a sudden feeling of panic. 'What have you done?' he said. 'What have you done, you raving idiot?'

Weir sat down heavily in a chair and held his face in his hands.

Terrible pictures formed in Stephen's mind as he ran through the door. He was confronted by a junction with four passageways. He called out.

The lighting was so bad he could barely see where he was going. He fumbled down a wall and pushed open a door. There was a fluttering of chickens inside. He slammed it closed with a shudder. He ran down a second passage, pushing open doors, closing them in relief when no fearful sight met his eyes, but pressing onwards in desperation.

He heard a woman's voice from behind him. 'Monsieur?' It was a young, dark-haired woman. She had large, soft eyes and her hair was tied back with a red ribbon. Stephen stood speechless.

'What do you want?'

'I'm looking for . . . for your mother.'

'This way.'

She took him by the arm. They went into a room with a red lamp and screens with oriental decorations. Around the door was a wooden cut-out shaped like a minaret. The floor was of the same beaten earth as in the parlour. Stephen looked aghast. The young woman took him behind a screen where a double bed lay beneath a home-made canopy of purple silk. There were half a dozen candles on the floor and one in the window.

'Don't be alarmed. It's all right. Give me the money now.'

The last sentence restored a kind of normality.

'It's all right. I don't want to . . . I just came to see that everything was all right.'

He heard a laugh from the other side of the screen. It was the middle-aged woman who had taken Weir off with her. 'All right. As good as it will ever be.' She came and stood beside Stephen. He could smell some sweet scent on her. 'Your friend is very strange. I take him like this' – she cupped her hand in Stephen's groin – 'and he backs away.' She laughed. 'It is long and soft, and when I touch it, he begins to cry.'

She was older than Stephen had thought. In the candlelight he could see her more clearly than in the parlour. She sat on the bed and pulled up her skirt to her waist, then lay back and spread her legs. Stephen had never seen someone of that age naked. She put her hand into a bowl of disinfectant, then ran her fingers through the gash between her legs, through the

204

coarse hair and the scarlet flesh that parted at her familiar touch.

Stephen began, like Weir, to back away. Then he laughed. He reached out to the young woman and took her arm. 'You, Mademoiselle, yes. Otherwise, nothing.'

The older woman got off the bed and came towards him, pulling down her skirt. He felt her hands on the front of his trousers. She slid her fingers inside, and pulled out what she wanted, a piece of limp flesh, like a butcher taking something from display and laying it on the wooden board. When he felt her mouth close on it, Stephen braced himself not to back away from her slavering attention. He looked up and saw the young woman undressing. The candlelight caught the round white curve of her buttocks as she stepped out of her underclothes and Stephen felt himself stir in the woman's mouth.

She stood up and smiled, holding his stiffening flesh in her hand. 'You English,' she said, and vanished behind the screen.

It did not cross Stephen's mind how ridiculous he must look. His skin was bursting, stretched almost to transparency by the blood pumped down into it.

The girl smiled at him from the bed. She had small round breasts. She sat with her legs straight out in front of her and her arms folded across her stomach. There was no sheet on the bed.

'Take off your clothes,' she said.

Stephen dumbly did what she told him. He stood naked in front of her. The girl was patient, as though she was accustomed to dealing with awkward soldiers.

Stephen looked at her. Almost six years had passed since he had touched a woman. She was beautiful. There was light in her dark brown eyes; there was air and life in her limbs. The flesh was young and unwounded. He wanted to drown himself in her, to bury deep into the cells of her skin and to forget himself there. She was peace and gentleness; she was the possibility of love and future generations.

As he took a step towards the bed he remembered a day when another woman had lain naked like this, her legs parted in front of his eyes, and he had kissed her there, allowing his tongue to open her, as though this unlocking would provide a way into her deepest self. He remembered her gasp of surprise.

He had obliterated himself in her; he had purged her longing and desire; he had lodged and invested himself in her body. In her trust and love for him, he had deposited the unresolved conflicts of his life. Perhaps his self was still in her – betrayed and unhealed.

The body was only flesh, but she had taken hers away from him; and in her physical absence there was more than missing flesh: there was abandonment.

The tenderness he had felt towards the dark-haired girl was gone. She smiled at him and rolled on to her side, so he saw again the swell of her hip, too curved to allow the passage of her arms in running or aggression.

When he looked at the girl's upper body, the ribs and spine, he thought of the shell casing that stuck from Reeves's abdomen; he thought of the hole in Douglas's shoulder where he had pressed his hand through almost to the lung.

His tenderness was replaced at first by a shuddering revulsion. Then his mind emptied. There was only this physical mass. He was losing control. The old woman smearing disinfectant between her legs was unlike anything he had seen before. The daughter's body was no more than animal matter, less dear, less valuable than the flesh of men he had seen die.

He did not know whether to take the girl or kill her.

In the pocket of his trousers beside his feet was the knife he had carried on patrol. He bent down and took it out, opening it against the palm of his hand. He went over and sat on the edge of the bed.

The girl looked at him, her eyes wide, her mouth open but unable to produce a sound. He felt no pity for her ignorant fear.

He turned the knife so that the blade was in his palm, then ran the handle of it down between her breasts and over her thighs.

He did not know what he was doing. He hated her for not having seen what he had seen. He felt the skin on her legs give a little under his pressure. The knife left a thin white trail where the flesh was momentarily parted before the blood

206

rushed in again beneath the skin. He wanted there to be more than just this flesh. He rested the handle on the hair between her legs, the blade pointing up towards her abdomen. The girl looked down in horror at the reflections of light on the steel.

Stephen took his hand off the knife. It lay balanced. The girl was too frightened to move. Eventually she slid her hand slowly up her thigh and took it in her hand, her eyes on Stephen all the time. She took the blade in her fingers, closed the knife and threw it to the far side of the room, where it landed on the earthen floor.

Stephen looked down at the bed. His mind, which had been blank, was flooded with thoughts and recriminations.

The girl had regained her calm. She did not scream for help or remonstrate; she looked at Stephen's broken attitude on the bed, his head bowed, his excitement shrunk. Her relief made her generous.

She touched his hand.

Stephen jumped and looked up. He could not believe her touch. It was tender. She should have killed him.

He shook his head in bewilderment. 'What . . . ?'

She raised her finger to her lips. She seemed to grow stronger by the second, feeding on her relief and his despair.

She said, 'It is very difficult. The war.'

He said, 'I'm sorry. I'm so sorry.'

'I understand.'

He looked at her with incredulous eyes, then took up his clothes and dressed hurriedly behind the screen.

IN THE TURMOIL of a division preparing to move, no one noticed the temporary absence of two officers in the night. They left the motorbike where they had found it and made their separate ways back to the front line, both feeling more sober than they had expected.

The next day Weir had his orders. They would move the following evening to a billet not yet specified, then march to Albert. They were expected to help complete the digging that had already begun near the village of Beaumont Hamel. There was no indication of whether this was part of a larger strategy or merely a routine redeployment. Since the whole division was on the move, however, it appeared that the rumours were true: they were going to attack.

Weir slumped down on the lower bunk in his dugout. He ran his hand back over what remained of his hair. So this was the attack at last. No more peace and tranquillity. The Big Push. He managed a snort of dry laughter. No more the quiet sector with its friendly routine patrols. With the men of the New Army, he would sweep the Germans out of France.

He was resigned to it. He felt that he had lost control of his own life: when he had finally tried to alter some central part of his existence it had come to nothing but humiliation. The guns would not be much worse.

Returned from his night-time shift underground, Jack went to a quiet part of the trench with a cup of tea and took out

Margaret's letter. He read it very slowly, not allowing his eyes to glance ahead.

My Dearest Jack, How are you? We think about you all the time and our prayers are for you. Thank you for your letters which have been a great comfort to us. It is good to know you are keeping cheery and well.

I have to tell you that our boy died this morning. The doctors said he suffered no pain and was very restful at the end. There was nothing they could do for him. I saw him in the hospital but they would not let me take him home. I do believe they cared for him to the last and did not let him suffer.

I am sorry to have to tell you this my dear Jack because I know how much you loved him. You must not let it get you downhearted. You are all I have left now and I pray God will send you home to me safe.

I am to collect his little body this afternoon, the funeral will be on Friday. I will light a candle from you in the church.

I will write again but I haven't the heart to go on now. Please do take care of yourself and come home to me. With love from Margaret.

Jack put the letter down on the ground and stared in front of him. He thought: I will not let this shake my faith. His life was a beautiful thing, it was filled with joy. I will thank God for it.

He put his head in his hands to pray but was overpowered by the grief of his loss. No polite words of gratitude came, but only the bellowing darkness of desolation. 'My boy,' he sobbed, 'my darling boy.'

They arrived at Albert in the first week of June. The tunnellers were at once dispatched to the front, but the infantry were allowed to pass the time in rest, with fewer drills and inspections than usual and a suspiciously improved diet that included oranges and walnuts.

Captain Gray took Stephen to see Colonel Barclay, who was staying in a large house on the west side of town.

'He's an irascible fellow,' said Gray. 'But you shouldn't be taken in by his manner. He's a fine fighter. He enjoys hardship and danger.' Gray raised an eyebrow as though to question Barclay's judgement.

They discovered the Colonel looking at maps in the converted study. He was younger than Stephen had expected; although grey, he had a lean, ferrety presence.

'Pretty nice house, isn't it?' said Barclay. 'But never you mind, I'll be in the trench with you chaps when you go over the top.'

'Are you actually going to go over the top yourself, sir?' said Gray, with a note of surprise.

'I should bloody well think so,' said Barclay. 'I've been stuck on my arse with creeping-Jesus staff officers for the last six weeks. The day the balloon goes up I'm aiming to have dinner off the regimental silver in Bapaume.'

Gray coughed. 'That would indeed represent a remarkable advance.' His accent seemed to have become more Scottish in Barclay's presence.

'And do you know who I'll be having it with? The C-in-C of the Second Indian Cavalry.'

'I had not appreciated that the cavalry would be involved.'

'Of course they are. We punch a hole, they pour through. Haig's dead set on it.'

'I see.' Gray nodded his head slowly. 'This is Lieutenant Wraysford, who has some knowledge of the terrain. You may remember I mentioned him to you.'

'Yes, I remember,' said Barclay. 'The Somme expert. Well you'd better sing for your supper.'

They went out into the gardens of the house for a stroll, and Barclay asked Stephen about the lie of the land. At Gray's suggestion, he had refreshed his memory by looking at a map and was able to tell him of the marshy flanks of the river Ancre, the rising ground towards Thiepval on one side and the ridge on the other.

'Hawthorn Ridge,' said the Colonel. 'That's what they call that. We're attacking on that line towards Beaumont Hamel. They're going to blow a bloody great hole in the ridge first.'

'I see,' said Gray. 'So that will give the enemy plenty of

warning and a nice bit of natural fortification.'

Barclay looked at him with a stern pity. 'We'll get to it first, Gray. But it's going to be a long day. I expect we may be asked to reinforce other units at various stages depending on how it goes.'

'But we will be in the first wave of attack?'

'Oh, yes,' beamed the Colonel. 'Over at dawn, don't worry. Regroup and take a breather at midday. Back in the early evening to put the shoulder to the wheel if necessary. Your men ready for it?'

'Oh, I think so,' said Gray. 'What do you think, Wraysford?'

'I think so, sir. Though I'm a little worried about the terrain. Also they've been here a long time, haven't they, the enemy? They will have built defences like –'

'Good God,' said Barclay, 'I've never come across two such faint-hearts. There is going to be a six-day bombardment which is going to cut every bit of German wire from here to Dar-es-Salaam. If there's any Boche left alive after that he'll be so bloody relieved it's over that he'll come out with his hands up.'

'That would certainly constitute an unexpected bonus,' said Gray.

'And another thing,' said Barclay. 'I don't need tactical advice from a platoon commander. I've got Rawlinson breathing down my neck already, as well as brigade orders every day. You just do what you're told. Now let's go and have lunch.'

Barclay's second-in-command, Major Thursby, and the three other company commanders joined them at an elegant table in a room with long windows at the side of the house. Stephen wondered if he should not offer to do the waiting rather than converse with these superior officers, but there seemed to be ample mess waiters, augmented by an elderly French couple.

'What's this stuff?' said Barclay holding up a bottle to the light. 'Gevrey-Chambertin. Hmm, tastes all right, though I don't know why we can't have white wine with fish.'

'There was no white wine in the cellar, sir,' said the

Colonel's batman, a small white-haired Londoner. 'But I knew you were partial to a bit of fish. Trout, sir. From the local river.'

'Very well, Davis,' said Barclay, refilling his glass.

A thin stew followed, then ripe cheese and fresh bread. Lunch went on past three o'clock, when they went to the sun-filled sitting room with coffee and cigars.

Stephen felt the softness of the chair beneath him and allowed his hand to linger on the brocade. One of the company commanders, a tall man called Lucas, was talking about the fishing on the river Test in Hampshire near his parents' home. The others were discussing a battalion football match. An Edinburgh unit who were coming into the line nearby contained the entire Heart of Midlothian professional team and had proved unbeatable.

The Colonel's batman brought brandy, and Stephen thought of the men in his platoon and the way they conjured cups of tea on tiny spirit stoves in damp trench walls. A sullen decorator called Studd used to fix a piece of cheese on his bayonet to entice the rats, then pull the trigger. Stephen felt that he was betraying them by eating and drinking in this elegant house, though in fact the men themselves believed you took what was available. They would barter and scrounge what they could in rest or in the line; food parcels were common property and a recent one addressed to Wilkinson, some weeks dead, had been the cause of particular celebration.

Stephen smiled to himself, aware that his brief flight from reality would soon be ended.

THE BATTALION MARCHED to a village called Colincamps. They sang on the road and swung their arms. It was a warm June day and the sun lit up the pallid green of the countryside. In the elms the rooks were calling dreamily, and in the plane trees and chestnuts was the constant sound of blackbirds and thrushes. The village was a babel of accents from Ulster, London, Glasgow and Lancashire. The men overwhelmed the resources of the local families in their search for billets. They played football in the evening and their sweat awakened the memories of action in their unwashed, lice-filled clothes.

Stephen took his platoon to a barn where Gray was attempting to make a deal with a reluctant woman and her son. By nightfall they had got the men inside with clean straw and a hot meal from the mobile cooker.

That night the guns began. Stephen was reading a book by candlelight in the hayloft of the barn when he heard them. A howitzer was embedded not far behind and was shaking down the dust of centuries from the rafters.

The bombardment was not much to begin with; it was like a clearing of the throat, but the echoes went on and on over the soft downland, on a ringing bass note. When the echo was starting to become so deep it was no longer audible, another low boom could be made out in the continuous murmur of sound, then another, so that the walls of the barn began to tremble. Stephen could feel the vibrations run through the wooden floor of the loft. He pictured the gunners beginning to warm to their task, stripping off their shirts in the deep-dug emplacements, pressing the protective wax deeper into their ears. He was awed by the sound the guns were making; so many of them in rolling sequence on a line of sixteen miles, the heaviest providing the continuous rumble like a sustained roll of timpani, and the lighter adding unpredictable pattern and emphasis. Within an hour the whole line was pouring out shells, filling the night sky with a dense traffic of metal. The noise was like thunder breaking in uninterrupted waves.

There was some consolation to be taken from the evident power of the bombardment, though none at all from the scale of the conflict it portended. Stephen felt that the odds had been dramatically increased; there seemed to be no question any longer of escape or compromise; it was only a matter of hope, that his own side should prove stronger than the enemy.

They stayed in Colincamps for two more days before moving off towards the front line.

'Won't be long now, sir,' said Byrne, grinding out his cigarette and taking his place next to Hunt. 'I never thought you'd be with us when we went down in that tunnel.'

'Nor me neither,' said Hunt. 'I wish we'd all bloody well stayed underground.'

Stephen smiled. 'You didn't much like it at the time. Never mind. This'll be different. Get Studd and Barnes over here, will you? Leslie, you've had two days to clean your rifle. Don't do it when you're just about to start marching.'

The platoon fell in under the eye of CSM Price, who strutted from one edge of the ragged square to the other before taking instructions from Captain Gray. Price was the only man who seemed to know which cart track would take them to the right place and which long defile would ultimately bring them to their appointed position in the front-line trench. The countryside was shaking beneath their feet as the bombardment entered its third day.

The company had a nervous joie de vivre as it set off on the prepared road towards Auchonvillers. The traffic of ammunition and supplies was so heavy that the men were obliged to take a farm track across the fields.

Stephen felt his skin and nose begin to itch with the dust and seed that was blowing from the crops and hedgerows.

214

Beneath their laden packs the men began to sweat, and the smell of them rose on the warm summer air. They sang marching songs with banal, repeated words of home. Stephen looked down at the ridge of grass along the centre of the track where the cartwheels had not pressed. He thought of the generations of farmers who had worked their way along it on such clear summer days.

As they rounded a corner, he saw two dozen men, naked to the waist, digging a hole thirty yards square at the side of the path. For a moment he was baffled. It seemed to have no agricultural purpose; there was no more planting or ploughing to be done. Then he realized what it was. They were digging a mass grave. He thought of shouting an order to about turn or at least to avert their eyes, but they were almost on it, and some of them had already seen their burial place. The songs died on their lips and the air was reclaimed by the birds.

They moved in silence, back on to the prepared road and down into Auchonvillers. Everything had changed in readiness for battle. The café where he had had lunch with the Azaires had been converted into a temporary hospital. On the main street of the village, flanked by piles of hay and carts full of animal feed, Colonel Barclay was sitting on a bay horse with shiny, barrelled flanks. As the companies formed a square and stood in silence, gazing at him, he coughed and told them what they had guessed, but had not until then officially known. He looked like a character from comic opera with his attempted grandeur and indolently snorting horse.

'You are going to attack. I know you'll be relieved to hear it because that's what you've come for. You are going to fight and you are going to win. You are going to inflict such a defeat on the enemy that he will never recover. You can hear the artillery going to work on his defences. The bombardment will stop tomorrow and you will attack. The enemy will be utterly demoralized. His defences have been shattered, his wire is cut, his dugouts are obliterated. I confidently expect that only a handful of shots will be fired at you. The enemy will be relieved to see someone to whom he can surrender.'

He overcame an initial nervousness that made him bark. His enthusiasm and simple belief in what he said was communicated to the men. Some of the younger ones began to shed tears.

'However, I have to warn you that you must be extremely careful about accepting any such surrender. My instructions from the Chief of the General Staff are that it lies with the enemy to prove his intention to surrender beyond possibility of misunderstanding. If you have any doubts, then I think you know what to do. The bayonet remains in my view an extremely effective weapon.

'I need hardly remind you of the glorious history of this regiment. We acquired our nickname, the Goats, in the Peninsular War when we proved our worth in rocky terrain. We did not retreat; and the Duke of Wellington himself commended our bravery. I can say to you no more than this: that you must honour the memory of those men who bore the colours before you. In your conduct in battle you must be worthy of the great deeds of this regiment's history. You must strive to win for your families, for your King and your country. I believe you will do so. I believe we shall take dinner in Bapaume. God bless you all.'

An outbreak of cheering was instantly quelled by the military police, who began to shout a list of instructions to each company. The strictest discipline would be enforced. Any man shirking his duty would be shot on the spot. There would be no questions in the heat of battle. As the men's enthusiasm faltered, the police concluded with a list of men who had been executed for cowardice. 'Kennedy, Richard, desertion in the face of the enemy, executed; Masters, Paul, disobeying an order, executed . . .'

Stephen turned his head from the sound of the list, looking at the baffled, fear-filled faces of Hunt, Leslie and Barnes. Tipper, the boy who had been carried screaming from the trench, had been brought back just in time, with the same vacant expression. Even Byrne's long, sanguine features had gone pale. Many of the men had the look of questioning boys, torn between excitement and a desire to be back with their mothers. Stephen closed his ears to the sound.

'Simpson, William, desertion, executed . . .'

When they left the village of Auchonvillers Stephen's mind

flickered back to that hot day by the river with the Azaire family. They had encountered other families who came from as far away as Paris for the famous fishing in the Ancre. Perhaps tomorrow he would finally taste 'English teas' in the pâtisserie at Thiepval.

He thought of Isabelle's open, loving face; he thought of the pulse of her, that concealed rhythm of her desire that expressed her strange humanity. He remembered Lisette's flushed, flirtatious look and the way she had taken his hand and placed it on her body. That day of charged emotion seemed as unreal and bizarre as the afternoon that was now taking them across the field to the reserve trenches.

As Stephen listened to the sound of men beginning to move off, he looked down at his feet, where the scuffed riding boots were taking him forward. At that moment, as they left the village and its trappings of normality, time seemed to stall and collapse. The passage of the next three days passed in the closing of an eye; yet the images retained a fearful static quality that stayed in the mind until death.

On the way up they were given wire-cutters.

'I thought the guns would cut the wire,' said Byrne. 'Two gas masks? Why two?'

Tipper was smiling madly while Price attached a tin triangle to his back. 'So the observers at the rear can see you, young man,' said Price. The air overhead was solid metal, the ground trembling with the bombardment.

There were new images even for experienced men. The reserve and communication trenches like railway carriages in the rush hour, and only Price's barked instructions keeping some thread of order. Harrington's platoon on a wrong turning, heading in the direction of Serre. B Company, under Lucas, completely lost. The sweat of moving packs of eighty pounds through the crush of bewildered, nervous men. A sudden summer storm coming in from Pozières, drenching the German lines then drifting west and turning the earth to mud beneath the press of British feet. All of these things happening at once.

There was Michael Weir standing on raised ground, gazing towards Hawthorn Ridge. Stephen pulled himself out of the trench and went to him. Weir's face was lit by a strange excitement. 'There's going to be a bang there the size of which will make you gasp,' he said. 'We've just laid the fuses. Firebrace is underground burying the cable.'

Stephen had a moment of lucidity. 'What will you do tomorrow? Where will you be?' His voice was puzzled, concerned.

'Watching from a safe distance.' Weir laughed. 'Our work is done. A few of my men have volunteered to be stretcher-bearers if manpower gets short. We're hoping to join you for a hot dinner. Don't the German lines look beautiful?'

Stephen saw yellow gorse and weed along the long-established lines, with white chalk marks across the hills where the main defences were dug. A towering red mist hung over them where the brick of the villages was pulverized by the bombardment. Cones of shrapnel exploded with white and yellow light. A faint rainbow was coming up above them as the sun began to press back the stormclouds.

Weir grinned. 'Happy?'

Stephen nodded. 'Oh yes.'

He rejoined the flow of men through the trench. He thought: this thing has its own momentum now; I am being borne away by it. 'Poor Fritz,' said a voice. 'He must be mad by now under those guns.'

Hunt was at his side, panting beneath his pack. A small wooden cage was attached to it. It contained two pigeons. Stephen looked at their blank, marbled eyes.

There was just the night to negotiate, then it would begin. They were in position. Somehow Price had found their place, and Corporal Petrossian with his mania for detail had got the platoon lined up correctly. The trench was a good one. 'Best parados I've seen,' said Petrossian. 'And at last a front with full wooden revetting.'

'Look, it's the reserve padre!'

Horrocks in white cassock over khaki trousers, bald head gleaming, was standing with bands and prayer book on raised ground like a useless earthbound bird; the real and only padre but known as the reserve because he never ventured beyond the back lines. Some jittering movement among the men, non-believers finding faith in fear. A shameful flock formed round the padre.

Stephen Wraysford joined them. He saw the still-earth-grimed face of Jack Firebrace. Arthur Shaw, a big solemn man, beside him.

His own men, those who would attack in the morning, knelt on the earth, faces hidden behind one hand, in an agonizing tunnel of their own, a darkness where there was no time but where they tried to look on death. The padre's words hard to distinguish against the bombardment.

Stephen found something more than humility, a feeling of complete inconsequence. He pressed his hand against his face, particles of flesh, pathetic Lincolnshire boy. He felt no fear for his blood and muscle and bone, but the size of what had begun, the number of them now beneath the terrible crashing of the sky was starting to pull at the moorings of his self-control.

He found the word Jesus in his mouth. He said it again and again beneath his breath. It was part prayer, part profanity. Jesus, *Jesus* . . . This was the worst; nothing had been like this.

The wafer was in his mouth and the sweet wine, but he wanted more. Communion was over, but some men could not stand up again. They stayed kneeling. Having communed with their beginnings they wanted to die where they were without enduring the day ahead of them.

Stephen returned to the trench to find the men in disarray.

'It's been postponed for two days,' said Byrne. 'It's too wet.'

Stephen closed his eyes. Jesus. Jesus. He had been ready to go.

Gray's face was a line of whipped anxiety. They went together to a small hill made by the excavation of earth from a tunnel.

'Let us be calm,' said Gray. Stephen could see how hard he was finding it. 'Let me recap the plan. The artillery lays down a protective barrage in front of you. You advance at walking pace behind the barrage. When it lifts, you take your objectives, then wait for it to begin again. It provides protection for you all the way. The German wire is already cut and many of their guns destroyed. Casualties will be ten per cent.'

Stephen smiled at him. 'Do you think so?'

Gray breathed in deeply. 'I am giving you our orders. We are on the flank of the main attack. Our battalion is to be flexible. We are in the midst of great fighting units. The Ulsters, the Twenty-Ninth Division – the Incomparables, fresh from Gallipoli.'

'Fresh?' said Stephen.

Gray looked at him. 'If I die, Wraysford, and you are still alive, I want you to take charge of the company.'

'Me? Why not Harrington?'

'Because you are a mad, cold-hearted devil and that is what we are going to need.'

The light was going down and Gray raised his binoculars to his face for perhaps the twentieth time that day. He passed them to Stephen. 'There's a banner over there above the enemy front-line trench. Can you see what it says?'

Stephen looked. There was a huge placard. 'Yes. It says "Welcome to the Twenty-Ninth Division".' He felt sick.

Gray shook his head. 'The wire isn't cut, you know. I don't want you to tell your men, but I've been up and down with these things and I can assure you that for stretches of hundreds of yards there is no shell damage at all. The shells have just not gone off.'

'I thought it was cut from here to Dar-es-Salaam.'

'It's a staff cock-up. Haig, Rawlinson, the lot. Don't tell your men, Wraysford. Don't tell them, just pray for them.'

Gray held his head in his hands. His wisdom and his shelves full of books were no good to him here, Stephen thought.

In their forty-eight hours of unwanted reprieve the men had more time to ready themselves.

The first rifle fire came with a falsetto crack. Barnes had shot himself through the palate.

At nightfall they wrote letters.

Michael Weir wrote:

Dear Mother and Father, We are going to attack. We have been making preparations for some days underground. My own unit has been involved and we have now done our bit.

Some of the men have volunteered to help as stretcher-bearers on the day. Morale is very high. We expect that this push will end the war. It is unlikely that many of the enemy will have survived our bombardment.

Thank you for the cake and the strawberries. I'm glad the garden is such a joy to you. We certainly all enjoyed the fruit. I think often of you both and of our quiet life at home, but I ask you not to worry about me. May your prayers be with the men who will go over the top. Thank you for the soap, Mother, which I assure you was put to good use. I was pleased that your evening with the Parsons was such a success. Please pass on my sympathy to Mr and Mrs Stanton. I have only just heard about their son.

I am sure I paid the account at the tailor's when I was on leave but do settle it on my behalf if I am mistaken and I will repay you on my next leave. Don't worry about me, please. It is warm enough here. A little too warm if anything – so there is nothing further I need, no more socks or pullovers. From your son, Michael.

Tipper wrote:

Dear Mum and Dad, They sent me back to join my pals and I am so proud to be back with them. It's a terrific show with all the bands and the men from other units. Our guns are putting on a display like Firework Night. We are going to attack and we can't wait to let Fritz have it! The General says we don't expect no resistance at all because our guns have finished them off. We were meant to go over yesterday, but the weather was not so good.

The waiting is awful hard. Some of the chaps are a bit downhearted. That fellow Byrne I told you about, he come up and told me not to worry. I'm pleased to hear Fred Campbell has kept safe so far. Good show.

Well, my dear Mum and Dad, that's all I've got to say to you. Tomorrow we will know if we will be seeing each other again one day. Don't worry about me. I am not frightened of what is waiting for me. When I was a little lad you were very good to me and I won't let you down. Please write to me again, I do like so much to hear the news from home. Please send me a couple of views of St Albans. Give my love to Kitty. You have been the dearest Mum and Dad to me. From your Son, John.

Stephen choked when he read the letter and sealed the envelope. He thought of Gray's face and its experienced foreboding. He felt a terrible anger coming over him. He tore a page from his notebook and wrote:

Dear Isabelle, I am sending this to you at the house in Amiens where it will probably be destroyed, but I am writing to you because I have no one else to write to. I am sitting beneath a tree near the village of Auchonvillers where we once came to spend the day.

Like hundreds of thousands of British soldiers in these fields I am trying to contemplate my death. I write to you to say that you are the only person I have ever loved.

This letter will probably never find you, but I wanted to tell someone what it feels like to be sitting on this grass, on this Friday in June, feeling the lice crawl against my skin, my stomach filled with hot stew and tea, perhaps the last food I will eat, and hearing the guns above me crying out to heaven.

Some crime against nature is about to be committed. I feel it in my veins. These men and boys are grocers and clerks, gardeners and fathers – fathers of small children. A country cannot bear to lose them.

I am frightened of dying. I have seen what shells can do. I am scared of lying wounded all day in a shellhole. Isabelle, I am terribly frightened I shall die alone with no one to touch me. But I have to show an example.

I have to go over first in the morning. Be with me, Isabelle, be with me in spirit. Help me to lead them into what awaits us.

With my love always, Stephen.

Jack Firebrace wrote:

Dear Margaret, Thank you for your letter. My words cannot say how sad I am. He was our boy, he was the light of our life.

But dear Margaret, we must be strong. I worry about you so much, what it must be like for you. There are things here to take my mind off it all right.

I believe it was God's will. We would have kept him, but God knew best. Do you remember how he used to chase the dandelion seed down by the canal and the funny words he had for things he couldn't say when he was a baby?

I think about these things all the time and God is merciful. He has given back to me memories of him when he was a little boy, lots of little things have come back to me. I think about them when I lie down at night and they are a comfort to me. I imagine he is in my arms.

His life was a blessing to us, it was a gift from God. It was the best gift we could have had. We must be thankful.

Tomorrow the men are going to attack and I think we will win a big victory. Soon the war will be over and I will be home again to look after you. With love from your husband, Jack.

Byrne, who was not, like the other men, a regular correspondent, found a small piece of paper on which to write to his brother. He wrote very neatly in blue ink.

Dear Ted, These are a special few lines for you in case we don't meet again. We are going to attack tomorrow, everything is absolutely thumbs-up merry and bright and trusting to the best of luck.

I ask you to remember me to my very many, very dear friends.

Please give my fondest love to Ma, to Tom and Daisy and the babies.

Here's hoping it is au revoir and not goodbye. Your loving brother, Albert.

When he had finished he could not bring himself to seal the envelope. He took the letter out again and wrote diagonally across the bottom: 'Cheer-oh, Ted, don't worry about me, I'm OK.'

Eight hours before the revised time of attack the guns went quiet, preserving shells for the morning.

It was night-time, but no man slept. Tipper gazed with incredulity at Leslie and Studd. No magic or superstition could get him out now. His last chance had gone. He had only to hold himself together until dawn.

Stephen looked deep into Byrne's face beside him. When Byrne looked back, Stephen could not meet his gaze. Byrne had guessed.

He went to Hunt, who was kneeling on the trench floor, praying. He touched his shoulder, then laid his hand on his head. He came to Tipper and punched him on the shoulder, then shook his hand vigorously.

Smith and Petrossian, the corporals, were checking kit, pushing among the reluctant men.

Brennan was sitting alone, smoking. 'I was thinking of Douglas,' he said. Stephen nodded. Brennan began to sing an Irish song.

He saw Byrne reach out his arm and gather Tipper to his chest. 'Not long to go now, not long to go.'

Towards four, the lowest time of the night, there was a mortal quiet along the line. No one spoke. There was for once no sound of birds.

There was at last a little light over the raised ground and mist down by the river. It began to rain.

Gray, urgent, sour-breathed at the head of the communication trench. 'The attack will be at seven-thirty.'

The platoon commanders were stricken, disbelieving. 'In daylight? In *daylight*?' The men's faces cowed and haunted when they were told.

Breakfast came with tea in petrol cans. Hunt's earnest features bent over bacon on a tiny stove.

Stephen felt the acid of a sleepless night run from his stomach to his tongue.

Then came the rum, and talk began again. Men drank greedily. Some of the younger boys staggered and laughed.

German artillery fire, which had been sporadic, began to build, to the surprise of the men who had been told that the German guns had been destroyed.

The British reply started up. At last the men were close enough to see what it did and were cheered by it. Studd and Leslie, breathing rum, waved their arms in the air and shouted. They could see the earth ripped up in fountains in front of the German trenches.

The noise overhead began to intensify. Seven-fifteen. They were almost there. Stephen on his knees, some men taking photographs from their pockets, kissing the faces of their wives and children. Hunt telling foul jokes. Petrossian clasping a silver cross.

The bombardment reached its peak. The air overhead was packed solid with noise that did not move. It was as though waves were piling up in the air but would not break. It was like no sound on earth. Jesus, said Stephen, Jesus, Jesus.

The mine went up on the ridge, a great leaping core of compacted soil, the earth eviscerated. Flames rose to more than a hundred feet. It was too big, Stephen thought. The scale appalled him. Shock waves from the explosion ran through the trench. Brennan was pitched forward off the firestep and broke his leg.

We must go now, thought Stephen. No word came. Byrne looked questioningly at him. Stephen shook his head. Still ten minutes.

German fire began at once. The lip of the British trench leapt and spat soil where machine guns raked it. Stephen ducked. Men shouting.

'Not yet.' Stephen screaming. The air above the trench now solid.

The second hand of his watch in slow motion. Twenty-nine past. The whistle in his mouth. His foot on the ladder. He swallowed hard and blew.

He clambered out and looked around him. It was for a moment completely quiet as the bombardment ended and the German guns also stopped. Skylarks wheeled and sang high in the cloudless sky. He felt alone, as though he had stumbled on this fresh world at the instant of its creation.

225

Then the artillery began to lay down the first barrage and the German machine guns resumed. To his left Stephen saw men trying to emerge from the trench but being smashed by bullets before they could stand. The gaps in the wire became jammed with bodies. Behind him the men were coming up. He saw Gray run along the top of the trench, shouting encouragement.

He walked hesitatingly forward, his skin tensed for the feeling of metal tearing flesh. He turned his body sideways, tenderly, to protect his eyes. He was hunched like an old woman in the cocoon of tearing noise.

Byrne was walking beside him at the slow pace required by their orders. Stephen glanced to his right. He could see a long, wavering line of khaki, primitive dolls progressing in tense deliberate steps, going down with a silent flap of arms, replaced, falling, continuing as though walking into a gale. He tried to catch Byrne's eye but failed. The sound of machine guns was varied by the crack of snipers and the roar of the barrage ahead of them.

He saw Hunt fall to his right. Studd bent to help him and Stephen saw his head opening up bright red under machine gun bullets as his helmet fell away.

His feet pressed onwards gingerly over the broken ground. After twenty or thirty yards there came a feeling that he was floating above his body, that it had taken on an automatic life of its own over which he had no power. It was as though he had become detached, in a dream, from the metal air through which his flesh was walking. In this trance there was a kind of relief, something close to hilarity.

Ten yards ahead and to the right was Colonel Barclay. He was carrying a sword.

Stephen went down. Some force had blown him. He was in a dip in the ground with a bleeding man, shivering. The barrage was too far ahead. Now the German guns were placing a curtain of their own. Shrapnel was blasting its jagged cones through any air space not filled by the machine guns.

All that metal will not find room enough, Stephen thought. It must crash and strike sparks above them. The man with him was screaming inaudibly. Stephen wrapped his dressing round the man's leg, then looked at himself. There was no wound. He crawled to the rim of the shellhole. There were others ahead of him. He stood up and began to walk again.

Perhaps with them he would be safer. He felt nothing as he crossed the pitted land on which humps of khaki lay every few yards. The load on his back was heavy. He looked behind and saw a second line walking into the barrage in no man's land. They were hurled up like waves breaking backwards into the sea. Bodies were starting to pile and clog the progress.

There was a man beside him missing part of his face, but walking in the same dreamlike state, his rifle pressing forward. His nose dangled and Stephen could see his teeth through the missing cheek. The noise was unlike anything he had heard before. It lay against his skin, shaking his bones. Remembering his order not to stop for those behind him, he pressed slowly on, and as the smoke lifted in front of him he saw the German wire.

It had not been cut. Men were running up and down it in turmoil, looking for a way through. They were caught in the coils where they brought down torrents of machine gun fire. Their bodies jerked up and down, twisting and jumping. Still they tried. Two men were clipping vainly with their cutters among the corpses, their movement bringing the sharp disdainful fire of a sniper. They lay still.

Thirty yards to his right there was a gap. He ran towards it, knowing it would be the focus of machine gun fire from several directions. He breathed in as he reached it, clenching for his death.

His body passed through clean air and he began to laugh as he ran and ran then rolled down into a trench, bumping his heavy pack on top of him. There was no one there.

Alive, he thought, dear God, I am alive. The war lifted from him. It is just a piece of field beneath a French heaven, he thought. There are trees beyond the noise, and down in the valley is the fish-filled river. He was aware of a thirst that was flaying his throat, and he took his water bottle. The warm, shaken fluid ran down inside and made him close his eyes in ecstasy.

There was no one in the trench. He moved along the

duckboards. It was beautifully made with high parapets, revetting as neat as Sussex weatherboards, and tidy entrances to deep dugouts. He looked back towards the British line, each foot of which was pathetically exposed to fire from this superior position. Through the smoke of the German barrage he could see the scruffy line still straggling on, driven by some slow, clockwork purpose into the murder of the guns.

The trench was dog-toothed after twenty yards or so. He could not see what lay beyond. He crept up and threw a grenade over the traverse, then ducked down. No answering fire came. He stood up and the lip of the trench spat earth in his eyes where a machine gun was firing from the second line. Stephen presumed that most of the men who had begun the attack with him were dead. The second wave had not reached this far and perhaps never would. He reasoned that he should try to retire and join a later attack, but his orders were to press on past Beaumont Hamel as far as Beaucourt, on the river. The soldier's motto, Price had told the men: when in doubt go forward.

He moved down the trench and found a ladder. As the machine gun fire licked at the earth ahead of him, he crawled forward on the open ground, then ran, crouching, to a shell-hole. Six men of the Lancashire Fusiliers were firing doggedly at the German reserve trench. He was almost impaled on a bayonet as he slithered into the hole.

A man firing looked at him and mouthed something Stephen could not hear. The lips seemed to be saying 'fucking dead'. The man plucked at Stephen's regimental badge, then cut his throat with his finger and pointed back over his shoulder towards the carnage of no man's land. They had a Lewis gun on the floor of the shellhole and from what Stephen could gather were trying to get it up behind some trees from where they would sweep the trench.

Stephen took a rifle from a corpse, placed it on the rim of the shellhole and began firing. An hour, perhaps two, passed under the growing return fire from the second-line trench. There was barely any damage to the defences. The wire was uncut, the dugouts intact. The counterattack would shortly begin.

Stephen looked round the shellhole at the exhausted faces of the Lancashire men. They knew they were trapped.

Something moved beneath his feet. It was the face of a man whose head was horribly wounded. He shouted out to be killed, but since he was not of his own regiment, Stephen demurred. He gave him his second water bottle, and when he bent down with it the man begged to be shot. In the noise of the battle, Stephen thought, no one would know. He fired twice down by his feet. It was the first life he had taken that day.

Jack Firebrace stood with Arthur Shaw on raised ground near what they had called One Tree Hill, watching. They expected a swift passage, almost unopposed.

Jack was muttering, Shaw saying nothing at all. They saw the Scots coming up out of their burrows like raving women in their skirts, dying in ripples across the yellowish-brown soil. They saw the steady tread of the Hampshires as though they had willingly embarked on a slow-motion dance from which they were content not to return. They saw men from every corner walking, powerless, into an engulfing storm.

Their own contribution to the day, the vast hole that had been blown at twenty past seven, had given the enemy ten minutes in which to take their positions at leisure. By the crater they saw young men dying in quantities that they had not dreamed possible. They had not fired a shot.

The excess of it made them clutch each other's arms in disbelief.

'They can't let this go on,' said Jack, 'they can't.'

Shaw stood with his mouth open. He was unmoved by violence, hardened to the mutilation he had seen and inflicted, but what he was watching here was something of a different order.

Please God, let it stop, thought Jack. Please let them send no more men into this hurricane.

The padre, Horrocks, came and stood with them. He crossed himself and tried to comfort them with words and prayers.

Jack turned his face away from what he saw, and he felt something dying in him as he turned.

Shaw had begun to weep. He held his miner's hands to the sides of his head and the tears coursed down his face. 'Boys, boys,' he kept saying. 'Oh my poor boys.'

Horrocks was trembling. 'This is half of England. What are we going to do?' he stammered.

Soon they all fell silent. There was an eruption from the trench below and another wave went up into the pitted moon-like landscape, perhaps Essex or Duke of Wellington's, it was impossible to see. They made no more than ten yards before they began to waver, single men at first picked out, knocked spinning, then more going as they reached the barrage; then, when the machine guns found them, they rippled, like corn through which the wind is passing. Jack thought of meat, the smell of it.

Horrocks pulled the silver cross from his chest and hurled it from him. His old reflex still persisting, he fell to his knees, but he did not pray. He stayed kneeling with his palms spread out on the ground, then lowered his head and covered it with his hands. Jack knew what had died in him.

Stephen thought of the brief communion he had enjoyed as he stood for better position on the body of the man he had killed. Nothing was divine any more; everything was profane. In the roar about his head he could make out only one word with any clarity.

'. . . the fucking Lewis gun . . . fucking eaten alive.'

Still in the shattering noise, they had to break out and kill their killers. Two men got the Lewis gun to the rim of the crater, but were taken by a storm of bullets as they slowed to drag the clumsy ammunition bucket. The others were left with Stephen, trying to surrender. One man throwing a white handkerchief, climbing out, was hit with silent precision in the eye.

Stephen looked behind where a line of support troops were coming forward in extended order, organized and balanced, towards them. Thirty yards back they caught the range of machine guns which traversed them with studied care until every man had gone down in a diagonal line from first to last. There was no movement from the bodies.

He shouted in the ear of the man next to him who shouted back but all one could hear was 'Jesus' and the other 'Fucking gun'. Stephen threw both his Mills bombs a short way ahead, and, as they went off, ran backwards on his own to a ditch behind a small clump of elms into which he flung himself.

It was noon and the sun was very hot above him. No clouds swathed it, no breeze cooled him. The noise had not diminished. He became aware of an acute exhaustion. He wanted to sleep. He reached down for his water bottles, but both were gone.

In the fighting round the German trenches there was confusion. He saw men unsure of which way they should be advancing. The trench he had entered earlier in the morning had been retaken by the enemy. A new attack on them was rolling forward behind him.

He believed he had to go on. The sense of elation had left him, but some automatic determination seemed to have taken its place. First he had to drink or he would die. His tongue was swollen like an ox's; it was like two tongues in his mouth. He thought of the river Ancre, down the hill to his right. He had lost all his men so it made no difference where he fought. He stood up and began to run.

He saw men from a colonial regiment, Canadians he thought, go forward through a narrow gap down towards a ravine. In the forty minutes it took him to skirt the back of them he had seen a battalion laid horizontal on the field. Only three men reached the German wire, where they were shot.

He was running, raging, in a dream, downhill towards the river. He saw a familiar figure to his right. It was Byrne, bleeding in the right bicep, but moving.

'What happened?' he screamed.

'Wiped out,' Byrne shouted in his ear. 'Colonel's dead. Two company commanders. We're supposed to regroup and attack again with the Fusiliers.'

'On the river?'

'Yes.'

'What happened to you?'

'I went back and came again. The second wave were killed in the trench. You can't move for bodies.'

231

'Have you got water?'

Byrne shook his head.

Towards the German lines they came across boys sleeping in shellholes. Nights of wakefulness beneath the bombardment, the exertion of the morning had proved too much, even in the range of enemy guns.

Shellfire was beginning again and Byrne and Stephen lay down with a sleeping boy and a man who must have been dead for some hours. Part of his intestine lay slopped out on the scooped soil of the shellhole where the sun began to bake it.

On the left a sergeant's mouth was moving hugely as he tried to urge men forward to another assault on the German trench that ran down to the railway track.

'There's some of our mob,' said Byrne.

It was Harrington's platoon, or what was left of them.

'We must go with them,' said Stephen.

Once more in ragged suicidal line they trudged towards the pattering death of mounted guns. Bloodied beyond caring, Stephen watched the packets of lives with their memories and loves go spinning and vomiting into the ground. Death had no meaning, but still the numbers of them went on and on and in that new infinity there was still horror.

Harrington was screaming where his left side had been taken by a shell, fumbling morphine tablets in his trembling hands.

Sniper fire began from the clogged shellholes towards the trench, then one final heave forward. A boy was whipped backwards against a tree by the power of the blast into his shoulder, others were falling or diving to the ground their own guns had chewed.

Byrne made stealthy progress towards the screaming boy. He got in behind the tree, the bark of which was flaking under lateral fire. Stephen saw the white of a field dressing flap as Byrne began to bind the wounds. Stretcher parties were coming up behind them but were bringing long, waving lines of fire into their upright progress.

Stephen dropped his face into the earth and let it fill his mouth. He closed his eyes because he had seen enough. You are going to hell. Azaire's parting words filled his head. They were drilled in by the shattering noise around them.

Byrne somehow got the boy back into the shellhole. Stephen wished he hadn't. He was clearly going to die.

Harrington's sergeant was shouting for another charge and a dozen men responded. Stephen watched them reach the first line of wire before he realized that Byrne was with them. He was trying to force a way through the wire when he was caught off the ground, suspended, his boots shaking as his body was filled with bullets.

Stephen lay in the shellhole with the boy and the man who had died in the morning. For three hours until the sun began to weaken he watched the boy begging for water. He tried to close his ears to the plea. On one corpse there was still a bottle, but a bullet hole had let most of it leak away. What was left was a reddish brown, contaminated by earth and blood. Stephen poured it into the boy's beseeching mouth.

Wounded men all round him tried to get up and retreat, but only brought eruptions of machine gun fire. They sniped back doggedly from where they lay.

When there was no fire from no man's land, the Germans in the second trench sniped at the bodies on the wire. Within two hours they had blown Byrne's head, bit by bit, off his body so that only a hole remained between his shoulders.

Stephen prayed for darkness. After the first minute of the morning he had not sought to save his own life. Even when his body opened itself to the imaginary penetration of the bullets as he ran through the gap in the wire, he had felt resigned. What he longed for was an end to the day and to the new, unliveable reality it had brought.

If night would fall the earth might resume its natural process, and perhaps, in many years' time, what had happened during the daylight could be viewed as an aberration, could be comprehended within the rhythm of a normal life. At the moment it seemed to Stephen to be the other way about: that this was the new reality, the world in which they were now condemned to live, and that the pattern of the seasons, of night and day, was gone.

When he could no longer bear the smell of the flesh in his

shellhole, he decided to run, come what may. A small attack on his left was temporarily drawing the German machine guns towards it and when he judged the moment right, by luck or fate or superstition, he ran weaving backwards, with several others who could not wait for nightfall.

Close to collapse, he staggered downhill towards the river, to the drink he had craved since noon. He left his rifle on the bank and stumbled down into the water. He dropped his head beneath the sluggish flow and felt it rush down into the pores of his skin. He opened his mouth like a fish.

He stood on the river bed, trying to hold himself together. He trailed his hands with the palms turned up as though in supplication. The noise pressed against his skull on both banks of the river. It would not diminish. He thought of Byrne, like a flapping crow on the wire. Would they pour water down the hole of his neck? How would he drink?

He tried to calm his thoughts. Byrne was dead: he had no need of water. It was not his death that mattered; it was the way the world had been dislocated. It was not all the tens of thousands of deaths that mattered; it was the way they had proved that you could be human yet act in a way that was beyond nature.

He tried to move to the shore, but the current was stronger than he had thought, and as his body neared its final exhaustion, he lost his footing and was carried downstream.

He was surrounded by Germans in the water. A man's face next to his shouting foreign words. Stephen held on to him. Others clasped each other, fighting to get out. All around him the people who had killed his friends, his men. Close to, in their pitted skin and wide eyes, he saw men like himself. An old, grey-haired corporal screaming. A boy, like so many, dark-complexioned, weeping. Stephen tried to hate them now as he had hated them before.

The press of German flesh, wet in the river, all around him, their clogged tunics pressing him, not caring who he was. The whining mêlée of their uncomprehended voices, shouting for their lives.

There was a narrow bridge above the river, of rough British

234

engineering. The Germans tried to clamber on to it, but the British soldiers stamped on their hands. Stephen looked up at the lone figure of a British private, helmetless, looking down with disdain.

'Get me out,' he shouted. 'Get me out.'

The man held down an arm to him and began to pull. Stephen felt other arms on him in the water. They were tearing at him. The private fired into the river and Stephen was up on the bridge. A few of them looked at him in surprise.

'Prisoners,' said the man who had pulled him out. 'Why should we help them across the river?'

Stephen reeled off the bridge on to the far bank of the river and lay down in the marshy grass.

Isabelle, the red room, his grandfather's cottage . . . He tried to focus on fragments of definite memory, to fashion a possible future from the past. His mind fixed on the smell of a musty clerk's office at the East India Docks. For a minute or more he lived in the room above the wharf.

It was dusk, it was close to night, though the light lingered tauntingly, and with it the noise.

His curiosity began to return. He wanted to know what had happened. He had undertaken that morning to attack and he should move forward, wherever he was. Above him to the right was the big wood of Thiepval. He pulled himself upright and began to walk towards the German line. An impact took his head as though a brick thrown at great speed had struck his temple, and he fell to the ground.

The next face he saw was not the clerk, or Isabelle or his mother, as he half-expected, but one of Weir's tunnellers.

'Blimey, you're a long way from home. You must have come a good mile and a half,' said the man, unravelling a field dressing.

Stephen grunted. The man's homely voice was too much to remember; it was from another time.

'Tyson's the name. We were all volunteered, if you take my meaning. They stopped attacking up where we were. They sent our mob down here. All the stretcher-bearers got wiped out. The Ulsters have copped it up there. So did your lot.'

'What have I got?'

'Flesh wound, I'd say. Left leg. Not even a Blighty one after all that. I'll send Captain Weir over.'

Stephen lay back in the shallow shellhole. He could feel no pain in the leg.

Price was reading the roll call. Before him were standing the men from his company who had managed to return. Their faces were shifty and grey in the dark.

To begin with he asked after the whereabouts of each missing man. After a time he saw that it would take too long. Those who had survived were not always sure whom they had seen dead. They hung their heads in exhaustion, as though every organ of their bodies was begging for release.

Price began to speed the process. He hurried from one unanswered name to the next. Byrne, Hunt, Jones, Tipper, Wood, Leslie, Barnes, Studd, Richardson, Savile, Thompson, Hodgson, Birkenshaw, Llewellyn, Francis, Arkwright, Duncan, Shea, Simons, Anderson, Blum, Fairbrother. Names came pattering into the dusk, bodying out the places of their forebears, the villages and towns where the telegrams would be delivered, the houses where the blinds would be drawn, where low moans would come in the afternoon behind closed doors; and the places that had borne them, which would be like nunneries, like dead towns without their life or purpose, without the sound of fathers and their children, without young men at the factories or in the fields, with no husbands for the women, no deep sound of voices in the inns, with the children who would have been born, who would have grown and worked or painted, even governed, left ungenerated in their fathers' shattered flesh that lay in stinking shellholes in the beet-crop soil, leaving their homes to put up only granite slabs in place of living flesh, on whose inhuman surface the moss and lichen would cast their crawling green indifference.

Of 800 men in the battalion who had gone over the parapet, 155 answered their names. Price told his company to dismiss, though he said it without the bark of the parade ground; he said it kindly. They attempted to turn, then moved off stiffly in new formations, next to men they had never seen before. They closed ranks.

Jack Firebrace and Arthur Shaw waited for them and asked how they had done. The men walked on as though in a dream, and did not answer. Some of them spat or pushed back their helmets; most of them looked downwards, their faces expressionless yet grained with sadness. They went to their tents and lay down.

OUT IN HIS shellhole, looking up the hill towards Thiepval, Stephen lay, waiting for the darkness to be complete.

Michael Weir slipped in beside him. 'Tyson pointed out where you were. How's the leg?'

'It's all right. I'll be able to move. What are you doing here?'

'Volunteered. There's chaos in our front line. There aren't enough trains to get the men out. The field dressing stations are overflowing. The trench you started from is just a mass of bodies, people who never even got going.' Weir's voice was unsteady. He was lying against Stephen's injured leg. 'Two of the generals have committed suicide. It's terrible, it's terrible, it's –'

'Calm down, Weir, calm down. Move over that way a bit.'

'Is that better? What happened to you?'

Stephen sighed and lay back against the earth. The noise was diminishing. The artillery on both sides had stopped, though there were occasional outbreaks of machine gun fire and the sound of sniping.

'I don't remember,' he said. 'I don't know. I saw Byrne killed. I thought we'd done well at first. Then I was in the river. I don't know. I'm so tired.'

It was dark at last. The night poured down in waves from the ridge above them and the guns at last fell silent.

The earth began to move. To their right a man who had lain still since the first attack, eased himself upright, then fell again when his damaged leg would not take his weight. Other single men moved, and began to come up like worms from their

238

shellholes, limping, crawling, dragging themselves out. Within minutes the hillside was seething with the movement of the wounded as they attempted to get themselves back to their line.

'Christ,' said Weir, 'I had no idea there were so many men out there.'

It was like a resurrection in a cemetery twelve miles long. Bent, agonized shapes loomed in multitudes on the churned earth, limping and dragging back to reclaim their life. It was as though the land were disgorging a generation of crippled sleepers, each one distinct but related to its twisted brothers as they teemed up from the reluctant earth.

Weir was shaking.

'It's all right,' said Stephen. 'The guns have stopped.'

'It's not that,' said Weir. 'It's the noise. Can't you hear it?'

Stephen had noticed nothing but the silence that followed the guns. Now, as he listened, he could hear what Weir had meant: it was a low, continuous moaning. He could not make out any individual pain, but the sound ran down to the river on their left and up over the hill for half a mile or more. As his ear became used to the absence of guns, Stephen could hear it more clearly: it sounded to him as though the earth itself was groaning.

'Oh God, oh God.' Weir began to cry. 'What have we done, what have we done? Listen to it. We've done something terrible, we'll never get back to how it was before.'

Stephen laid his hand on Weir's arm. 'Be quiet,' he said. 'You must hold on.'

But he knew what Weir was feeling because he had felt it himself. As he listened to the soil protesting, he heard the sound of a new world. If he did not fight to control himself, he might never return to the reality in which he had lived.

'Oh God, oh God.' Weir was trembling and whimpering as the sound rose like damp winds scraping down a sky of glass.

Stephen let his exhausted mind slip for a moment. He found himself go with the sound into a world in which there was only panic. He jerked awake, pulled himself back with an effort into the old life that could not be the same, but which might, if he believed in it, continue.

'Hold me,' said Weir. 'Please hold me.'

He crawled over the soil and laid his head against Stephen's chest. He said, 'Call me by my name.'

Stephen wrapped his arm round him and held him. 'It's all right, Michael. It's all right, Michael. Hold on, don't let go. Hold on, hold on.'

PART THREE
ENGLAND 1978

IN THE TUNNEL of the Underground, stalled in the darkness, Elizabeth Benson sighed in impatience. She wanted to be home to see if there were any letters or in case the telephone should ring. A winter coat was pressed in her face by the crush of passengers along the aisle of the carriage. Elizabeth pulled her small suitcase closer to her feet. She had returned from a two-day business trip to Germany that morning and had gone straight into work from Heathrow without returning to her flat. With the lights out she could not see to read her paper. She closed her eyes and tried to let her imagination remove her from the still train in its tight-fitting hole.

It was Friday night and she was tired. She filled her mind with pleasant images: Robert at dusk with the strands of grey in his thick hair and his eyes full of plans for the evening; a coat of her own design made up and back from the manufacturer in its clinging polythene wrap.

There was a madman in the carriage who began to sing old music-hall songs. 'It's a long way to Tipperary . . .' He grunted and fell silent, as though an elbow had been applied under cover of the darkness.

The train started again, heaving off into the tunnel, the lights surging overhead. At Lancaster Gate Elizabeth fought her way through the coats and on to the platform. She was relieved to be up in the rain where the traffic moved with the sound of wet tyres on the leaves that had drifted in from behind the railings in Hyde Park. She bent her head against the drizzle, pushing on towards where she could see the green shopfront of the off-licence beam its vulgar welcome.

A few minutes later she laid the suitcase and the clanking plastic carrier bag on the step as she opened the front door to the Victorian house. The mail was still in the wire cage attached to the front door: postcards for the girls upstairs, buff envelopes for all five flats, a gas reminder for Mrs Kyriades and, for her, a letter from Brussels.

Up in her flat she ran herself a bath and, when she was comfortably immersed, opened the letter.

If Robert chose to write in addition to his brief, panicky telephone calls, it usually meant he was feeling guilty. Either that or he was genuinely detained by the business of the Commission and had not even been home to see his wife.

'. . . appalling amount of work . . . boring paper read by the British delegation . . . Luxemburg next week . . . hoping to be in London on Saturday . . . Anne's half-term . . .'

Elizabeth put the letter down on the bathmat and smiled. There were many very familiar phrases, and she was not sure how much of it she believed, but at least she still felt a surge of fondness for him when she read them. The warm water closed over her shoulders as she slid down into the bath. The telephone rang.

Naked and dripping on the sitting-room carpet, she pressed the receiver to her ear, half-wondering, as she always did, whether there was any electricity in the handset and whether the water on her ear would conduct a shock into her brain.

It was her mother, wanting to know if she would go down for tea the next day in Twickenham. By the time she had agreed to go, Elizabeth was dry. It hardly seemed worth getting back into the bath. She dialled a Brussels number and listened to the single European ring. It sounded twenty, thirty times unanswered. She pictured the jumbled sitting room with its piles of books and papers, its unemptied ashtrays and unwashed cups, in which the instrument let out its neglected bleat.

In the hallway of Mark and Lindsay's terraced house there were a pram and a pushchair round which greetings were

244

exchanged. Elizabeth, in a gesture that had persisted since college days, handed Mark a bottle of wine.

As she stepped into the double sitting room, in which the dividing wall had been knocked through, Elizabeth entered a routine so familiar that she found herself talking, smiling and behaving as though by predetermined programme. Sometimes when she went to see Mark and Lindsay they had invited other people. Tonight there was a couple from the next street and a man suspiciously on his own. Elizabeth found a cigarette alight in her fingers and red wine sliding down her throat.

They were her oldest friends, bound to her by shared experience. Although she often thought the three of them would not now become so close if they were meeting for the first time, the link was surprisingly emotional. Lindsay was an impulsive woman with a domineering tendency; Mark was a homely man of no clear ambition. In their twenties there had often been some other guest who tried to impress with self-important stories or who was anxious to claim positions of political integrity unavailable to the rest; but by now such evenings took a friendly, uninspiring course. For Elizabeth, at the age of thirty-eight, they were reminders of how little their lives had changed. Only the children had altered things. At some stage there would be an exchange between the others about behaviour and schools, and she would have to close her ears, partly through boredom, partly through an unacknowledged anguish.

Lindsay had also been through a phase of inviting unattached men when Elizabeth went to visit. For two or three years the previously settled threesome would be augmented by a variety of single men, desperate, divorced, drunk, but more often merely content to be as they were.

'Your trouble,' Lindsay once said, 'is that you frighten men off.'

'Trouble?' said Elizabeth. 'I wasn't aware that I was *in* trouble.'

'You know what I mean. Look at you. You're so poised with your smart dresses and your Anouk Aimée good looks.'

'You make me sound middle-aged.'

'But you know what I mean. Men are such timid creatures, really. You have to be gentle with them. Make them feel safe. To begin with, anyway.'

'Then you can do what you like?'

'Of course not. But look at you, Elizabeth. You have to compromise a little. Remember that man David I introduced you to? He's very kind, just your type. You didn't give him a chance.'

'You seem to be forgetting that I've got a boyfriend already. I don't need to go pop-eyed and flirtatious with Dennis or David or whatever he's called. I'm spoken for.'

'By the Eurocrat, you mean?'

'Robert is his name.'

'He's never going to leave his wife. You know that, don't you? They all *say* they will, but they never, ever do.'

Elizabeth smiled serenely. 'I don't mind whether he does or not.'

'Don't tell me you wouldn't rather be married.'

'I don't know. I've got a job to do, people to see. I can't suddenly devote my time to searching for a husband.'

'And what about children?' said Lindsay. 'I suppose you're going to say you don't want children either.'

'Of course I'd like children. But I think I need to know why.'

Lindsay laughed. 'You don't need to know anything at all. It's called biology. You're thirty-nine.'

'Thirty-eight in fact.'

'Your body tells you time is running short. You're no different from the millions of other women in the world. You don't need a reason for God's sake.'

'I think I do. I think one should have some sort of reason for doing something that, on the face of it, is quite unnecessary.'

Lindsay smiled and shook her head. 'Spinster talk.'

Elizabeth laughed. 'All right. I will try, I promise. I'll try my hardest to fall spontaneously and exotically in love with Dennis –'

'David.'

'With whoever you produce.'

After having apparently given up, Lindsay had that night made a final attempt: a man called Stuart. He had tangled fair hair and glasses. He revolved a large wine glass thoughtfully in long fingers.

'What do you do?' he said to Elizabeth.

'I run a clothing company.' She disliked being asked this question, thinking people ought to ask new acquaintances who they were rather than what they did, as though their job defined them.

'You say you run it. You're the boss, are you?'

'That's right. I started as a designer about fifteen years ago but I transferred to the business side. We formed a new company and I became the managing director.'

'I see. And what's this company called?' said Stuart.

Elizabeth told him and he said, 'Should I have heard of you?'

'We supply a couple of chain stores, but they put their own labels on. We do a small amount of what we like to call couture under our own name. Perhaps you've seen the name in that context.'

'And what exactly is "couture"?'

Elizabeth smiled. 'It's mostly what you'd call dresses.'

As the evening went and Stuart relaxed the defensive tone of his opening cross-examination, Elizabeth found that she quite liked him. She had grown accustomed to people's responses to her. Many of them assumed that there was a polar choice between marriage and work and that the more enthusiastically she had embraced her job, the more vigorously she must have rejected the idea of children or male partnership. Elizabeth had given up trying to explain. She had taken a job because she needed to live; she had found an interesting one in preference to a dull one; she had tried to do well rather than badly. She could not see how any of these three logical steps implied a violent rejection of men or children.

Stuart told her that he played the piano. They talked about places they had visited. He didn't give her a long exposition of capital markets or join in competitive argument with Mark; nor did he too obviously flirt or fawn. He laughed at some of the things she said to him though she noticed that there was an edge of surprise in his amusement, as though something about her had not predisposed him to expect her to be light-hearted. When he did not ask her for her telephone number she was relieved, though also fractionally disappointed.

As she drove the familiar route home, over the river, she let her mind play with the idea of what it would be like to be married. Just by the Fulham Road ABC they had built the pavement out into the road to make it impassable to heavy traffic. It always made her inhale, in an effort to make her car smaller as it squeezed between the bollards already crimson with the scraped paint of fatter vehicles. Perhaps if she was married her husband would do the driving. Some chance, to judge from the couples she knew.

It was one o'clock when she let herself into the flat. As she turned on the light in the sitting room she saw her still-packed suitcase. She went into the kitchen to make some tea but found she had forgotten to buy any milk on her way back from the tube. By the sink were her breakfast cup and plate from two days ago when she had left in a hurry to get to the airport.

She sighed. It didn't matter. Tomorrow was Saturday and she would sleep in as long as she liked. She could read the paper in bed with the radio playing softly in the background and with no one to interrupt her tranquil routine.

It never went quite as smoothly as she planned. To begin with, she had to dress and go out to the shop to buy some milk. Then, when she had settled back in bed with the paper and a pot of tea, the telephone rang twice.

There was then at last an hour of perfect solitude. The main article in the paper was prompted, as many others had been, by the sixtieth anniversary of the 1918 Armistice. There were interviews with veterans and comments from various historians. Elizabeth read it with a feeling of despair: the topic seemed too large, too fraught and too remote for her to take on at that moment. Yet something in it troubled her.

In the afternoon she drove down to Twickenham. The firm's accountant had advised that she should run a large car on the company. He said this would impress clients and be what he called tax-efficient. Elizabeth had bought a glistening Swedish saloon with boorish acceleration and a tendency not to start.

'You work too hard, that's your problem,' said her mother, pouring tea from a pot with small pink roses set, improbably, on trails of honeysuckle.

Françoise was in her middle sixties, a handsome woman with a lined gentle face on which the short-sightedly applied powder was sometimes visible in little patches on the cheekbones. She retained a certain dignity, given by her posture and the grave light of her blue eyes. Although her grey hair made her look like a grandmother, it was possible to see in her skin and the texture of her face the earlier ages she had lived through; a fairness lingered in the front of her hair; episodes of middle age, even childhood could be read in the open, only superficially marked, planes of her face.

Elizabeth smiled and stretched out her legs towards the fire. Her conversations with her mother ran on predictable lines, but only up to a point. Naturally Françoise wanted her daughter to be happy and not to look tired when she came to visit, but she did not assume, like Lindsay, that marriage was the way to achieve this end. She had herself married a heavy-drinking man called Alec Benson who was disappointed that Elizabeth was not a boy and had disappeared to Africa shortly after her birth in pursuit of a woman he had met in London. He had returned at intervals and Françoise patiently took him back when he needed a home. She had remained fond of him, but she hoped for something better for her daughter.

On the sideboard there was a photograph of Elizabeth at the age of three being held by her grandmother. It was a family axiom that she had 'adored' Elizabeth, who found it disconcerting that she had no recollection of her: she had died the year after the picture was taken. There she was in the photograph, unquestionably doting, though this unreturned love had a ghostly, unnerving quality for Elizabeth.

'I was reading an article about the anniversary of the Armistice,' she said to Françoise, who had been following her gaze.

'Yes, the papers are full of it, aren't they?'

Elizabeth nodded. If she knew little about her grandmother, she knew even less about her grandfather. Her mother had occasionally mentioned 'that awful war', but Elizabeth had paid little attention. It had reached a stage when it would be embarrassing to ask her mother about him because it would have revealed the state of her ignorance. But something about the war article had unsettled her: it seemed to touch an area of disquiet and curiosity that was connected to her own life and its choices.

'Do you still have any of your father's old papers?' she said.

'I think I threw most of them out when I moved. But there may be some things in the attic. Why do you ask?'

'Oh, I don't know. I was just thinking. I feel mildly curious. It must be something to do with my age.'

Françoise raised an eyebrow, which was as close as she came to enquiring about Elizabeth's personal life.

Elizabeth ran her hand through her hair. 'I feel there's a danger of losing touch with the past. I've never felt it before. I'm sure it *is* something to do with my age.'

What she described as a mild curiosity crystallized inside her to a set determination. Beginning with the contents of her mother's attic she would track this man down: she would make up for the lateness of her interest in him by bringing all her energy to the task. It would be one way, at least, of understanding more about herself.

ELIZABETH STRAIGHTENED HER hair in the mirror. She was wearing a suede skirt, leather boots and a black cashmere sweater. She pushed the thick dark hair back a little from her ears and turned her head sideways to insert two costume earrings the colour of oxblood. There was light mascara on her lashes; the paleness of her skin made her look less Gallic than Lindsay had been suggesting, but there was nevertheless something dramatic in her face which further make-up would have overstated. In any case, it was only Monday morning, time for the late walk to Lancaster Gate tube, her mouth still burning from the too-hasty coffee she had bolted as the radio told her it had turned half-past eight.

The train of the Central Line fitted its tube like a bullet in the barrel of a rifle. When it came to its customary sudden, dark and unexplained halt between Marble Arch and Bond Street Elizabeth could see the pipes and cables of the tunnel only inches from the shell of the carriage. It was the deepest hottest line in London, dug by sweating tunnellers on a navvy's day rate. They started again with mysterious smoothness and glided into Bond Street where a delayed crowd was waiting. Elizabeth got off at Oxford Street and hurried north through the pedestrians ambling three abreast, none of them looking ahead, then turned left into the area behind the shops.

Once a week regularly and sometimes more often she went to visit Erich and Irene, the principal designers for the company. Both had refused to move from their old office or even to change the name on the door when the new company had been formed five years earlier.

Since she was already late, it would make no difference if she stopped at the local Italian café. She ordered three coffees to take away and Lucca, the plump, grizzled attendant, tore up a Mars Bar box for her to balance them on as she made her precarious way to a door a few yards down with a brass name plate in the brick: Bloom Thompson Carman. Wholesale, Fabric and Design.

'Sorry I'm late,' she called as she stepped out of the lift on the second floor and made her way to the open door.

She put the improvised tray down on the desk in the area laughingly known as Reception and went back to close the concertina doors on the lift.

'I brought you some coffee, Erich.'

'Thank you.' Erich came out of an inner room. He was a man in his early seventies with wild grey hair and gold glasses. His cardigan had holes in the elbows so large that there were in fact no elbows. His chain-smoked Embassy and baggy eyes gave him an air of compressed weariness held at bay only by his nervous, ticking fingers that worked the round dial on the telephone, impatient at its slow returning grind, or skittered his gold scissors through bolts of unshaped cloth.

'Train got stuck in the tunnel as usual,' said Elizabeth.

She sat on the edge of a desk, moving magazines, pattern books, invoices and catalogues with her hip. Her skirt lifted over the black woollen tights on her knees. She sipped dangerously from the scalding styrofoam cup. The coffee tasted of acorns, earth and steam.

Erich looked at her sadly, his gaze travelling the length of her body, from the thick dark hair, over the line of her thigh and the revealed knee to the toe of the chestnut leather boot.

'Look at you. What a wife you would have made my son.'

'Drink your coffee, Erich. Is Irene here yet?'

'Of course, of course. Since eight-thirty. We've a big buyer coming at twelve, I told you.'

'Hence the Savile Row suit?'

'Don't bother me, woman.'

'At least brush your hair and take off that cardigan.'

She smiled at him as she went through into the workroom to see Irene.

'Don't say it,' said Elizabeth.

'What?' said Irene, looking up from a sewing machine.

'"Look what the cat's dragged in."'

'I wasn't going to,' said Irene. 'I'm far too busy for chit-chat.'

'Here's some coffee. Did you have a nice weekend?'

'Not bad,' said Irene. 'My Bob was taken poorly Saturday night. Only indigestion as it turned out. He thought it was appendicitis. What a fuss he made, though. How's your Bob?'

'My Bob? He didn't ring. I don't know. I had a letter, but it's not the same, is it?'

'You tell me. My Bob's never put pen to paper except on the Littlewoods coupon.'

'I thought he was an expert on archaeology.'

Irene raised an eyebrow. 'You shouldn't be so literal, Elizabeth.'

Elizabeth cleared a space at her desk and began to make telephone calls. There were meetings to arrange, a cloth warehouse to visit, buyers to placate. When Erich had arrived from Austria in 1935 he had left disappointed customers in Vienna who had been prepared to pay well for his exuberant designs. He had first employed Irene as a seamstress but had later become dependent on her as his own energy began to fail. Elizabeth had joined them fifteen years earlier when their order books were growing empty. It had taken time to stop the slide, but then the company had grown rapidly; its headquarters in Epsom employed fifteen people and had flourished at a time of economic difficulty. Inflation ate some of the profits before they were even banked: like Weimar, Erich said. He took a dim view even of success, but his own inspiration was almost exhausted, and most of the company's most successful designs came from younger people commissioned by Elizabeth.

At lunchtime they closed the office and went to Lucca's café.

'The lasagne is very good today,' said Lucca, poised with a stubby bookmaker's ballpoint over his small curling pad.

'Fine,' said Elizabeth. 'I'll have that.'

'Very good choice, Signora,' said Lucca. He liked to stand close to Elizabeth so that his vast belly pressed through his spattered white apron and the black cashmere on her shoulder. 'I bring you a little salad.'

There was always the implication in his manner that this was a particular gift to Elizabeth, made from tiny slices of fresh fennel and pieces of Italian wild mushrooms flown in that morning from Pisa, secretively prepared by himself for fear of arousing the envy of other diners, anointed with the extra virgin olive oil and gallantly omitted from the bill.

'Not too much onion, please,' said Elizabeth.

'I'll just have wine,' said Erich, lighting a cigarette.

'Lasagne for me too,' said Irene.

Lucca waddled away, his back view revealing a purple cleft of flesh at the top of his blue-checked trousers. He returned with a litre of dense, inky fluid and three glasses, only one of which he filled.

Elizabeth looked round the restaurant, which was filling with shoppers, workers, even tourists who had strayed north of the shops on Oxford Street.

These were the lines of her life, these were the things that concerned her. Order books and Lucca's salad; Robert's awaited calls and the criticism of Lindsay and her mother. Strikes and economic crisis. Trying not to smoke yet keeping the endless check on her weight. A planned holiday with three or four others in a rented house in Spain; a snatched weekend with Robert in Alsace, or even in Brussels itself. Her clothes, her work, her flat: its small orderly ways maintained by just one weekly visit from a cleaner while she was at work. No elaborate system of crèche, day-care and mother's help as exhaustively discussed by her married friends. London in approaching winter, the wail of traffic through the park and cold Sunday morning walks that issued into jovial meetings in the pubs of Bayswater that seemed to last an hour too long. And the sense of a larger life inside her, excited and confirmed by pictures she saw in galleries, books she read, but particularly by pictures; something unfulfilled, something needing to be understood.

Sometimes she went away on her own to wilder parts of northern England where she read or walked. She didn't feel self-pity because she could see nothing to feel sorry for; the mundane concerns and preoccupations of her life were interesting to her. She found bed-and-breakfast cottages and small pubs in guidebooks where she sometimes fell into conversation with the owners or with other guests, and sometimes just read by the fire.

Once in a village in the Dales a boy of no more than nineteen began talking to her at the bar of the pub. She was wearing her reading glasses and a thick grey-and-white speckled sweater. He had fair hair and an unconvincing beard. He was at university and had gone off walking in order to do some reading for his studies. He was awkward with her and used set phrases with signalled irony, as though referring to books or films they both knew. He seemed unable to say things without suggesting that they were quotations from someone else. After he had drunk two or three pints of beer he became calmer and told her about his studies in zoology and about his girlfriends at home. He implied a riotous love life. Elizabeth liked his enthusiasm and the pitch of excitement at which he appeared to be living, even in this primitive pub on a Yorkshire hillside with only the landlord's steak and kidney pie to come.

It was not until after dinner, when she made her way up the narrow stairs to her room and heard him following that it occurred to her that his interest was more than conversational. She almost burst out laughing as he took her arm with clumsy caution outside her door. She kissed him on the cheek and told him to get on with his books. When he knocked on the door an hour later, however, she let him in. She was feeling very cold.

He was overwhelmed with gratitude and excitement; he was not able to contain himself even for a minute. In the small and icy hours of the morning he tried again. Elizabeth, reluctant to be awoken from deep sleep after a long day's walk, submitted wearily. He did not want to talk to her in the morning; he wanted to leave as quickly as possible. She felt a little tenderness towards him. She wondered what function the episode had served in his life and in his mythology of himself.

She liked living alone, she liked being alone. She ate what she wanted, not proper meals but plates of mushrooms and baked potatoes, grapes, peaches, or soups she made herself. She filled glasses with ice cubes and lemon slices, then poured over gin, hearing the explosion of the ice, leaving hardly any room for tonic water. She had plastic tops that kept the wine drinkable from one day to the next.

In the cinema she could drown in the sensuous load of picture and sound without the distraction of company or conversation. In the worst films she wandered off from the story and inhabited the scenery in a plot of her own. She felt self-conscious about going unaccompanied in case she should meet a couple she knew hand-in-hand in the foyer on their evening out; so she generally went on Saturday afternoon, entering in the after-lunch daylight, emerging in the darkness with the full evening still ahead.

By the end of a weekend she did want to talk to someone. She had read articles in the paper or seen something on the television that had set her mind moving; she needed to test her response.

'What do you know about the War, Irene?' she said. 'You know, the First World War.'

'"Pack up your troubles" and all that stuff?' said Irene. 'Terrible business, wasn't it?'

'Did your father fight in it?' said Elizabeth, cutting the hairy, internal stalk from the centre of a quartered tomato.

'I don't think so. I never asked him. But he fought in something because I've seen his medals.'

'When was he born?'

'Well, he wasn't thirty when I was born, so he must have been born about eighteen-ninety-five I should think.'

'So he was the right age?'

'Search me. I don't know when the wretched thing was. You ask Erich. Men know all about these things.'

Erich poured what remained of the litre carafe into his glass. 'Even I am not old enough to have fought. I do remember it a little. I was a schoolboy.'

'But what was it *like*?' said Elizabeth.

256

'I have no idea. I don't think about war. In any case your English schools should have taught you all about it.'

'Perhaps they did. I don't seem to have been paying attention. It all seemed so boring and depressing, all those battles and guns and things.'

'Exactly,' said Erich. 'It's morbid to dwell on it. I've seen enough of that kind of thing in my own lifetime without raking up the past.'

'What are you suddenly so interested in ancient history for?' said Irene.

'I'm not sure it *is* ancient history,' said Elizabeth. 'It isn't very long ago. There must be old men alive now who fought in it.'

'You ought to ask my Bob. He knows everything.'

'I bring you coffee now?' said Lucca.

THE ROAD SWEPT down into Dover on a wide, banking curve that overlooked the locked, grey sea to her left. Some childish sense of joy came up in Elizabeth at the sight of the water; it was the start of holidays, it was the end of England. On a Thursday evening in winter, it was like breaking bounds.

She drove, as instructed, beneath towering gantries, up a ramp and down through narrow marked lanes, peering round the piece of paper that a man in a kiosk had slapped on to the middle of her windscreen. She was waved to the head of an empty file. She got out of the car and felt the sea wind whip her hair. There were two container lorries to her left and a dozen or so smaller goods vehicles between marked lines about the dock; it was not a popular crossing. In the shop she bought a map of north-east France, and another of the motorways of Europe that would help her on to Brussels.

In the trembling hold of the ship she gathered up her book, her spectacles and a spare sweater, in case she should decide to go on deck. She gratefully escaped the diesel fumes of the huge articulated trucks and climbed the steep stairs to the passenger decks.

She felt a little presumptuous. Having lived to the age of thirty-eight without giving more than a glance to the occasional war memorial or dull newsreel, she was not sure what she now expected to find. What did a 'battlefield' look like? Was it a prepared area of conflict with each side's positions marked down? Wouldn't buildings and trees get in the way? Perhaps the people who now lived in these places would be sensitive about them; they might resent the arrival of some morbid sightseer, come like a tourist who hovers with his camera at the edge of an air crash. More probably, she thought, they would know nothing about it. It was all a very long time ago. 'Battle of What?' they would say. The only person she could remember evincing an interest in these things was a boy she had known at school: a funny, gentle creature with a wheezy voice who was good at algebra. Would history be there for her to see, or would it all have been tidied away? Was it fair to expect that sixty years after an event – on the whim of someone who had shown no previous interest – a country would dutifully reveal its past to her amateur inspection? Most of France was now like England in any case: tower blocks and industry, fast food and television.

She pushed back her hair, settled her glasses and took out the book that Irene's Bob had given her to read. She found it hard going. It seemed addressed to insiders, people who already knew all the terminology and all about the different regiments; it reminded her of the aircraft magazines her father had bought for her during his final attempt to turn her into the male child he had wanted. Still, in some of the book's more matter-of-fact moments, the calmly given statistics and geography, there was something that held her attention. Most eloquent of all were the photographs. There was one of a moon-faced boy gazing with shattered patience at the camera. This was his life, his actuality, Elizabeth thought, as real to him as business meetings, love affairs; as real as the banal atmosphere of the cross-channel ferry lounge, known to every modern holiday-maker in Britain: his terror and imminent death were as actual and irreversible to him as were to her the drink from the bar, the night in the hotel ahead, and all the other fripperies of peacetime life that made up her casual, unstressed existence.

Although her grandmother had been French, she did not know the country well. She fumbled for words as the expressionless policeman thrust his hand through her car window at the dock and made some rapid, guttural demand. The big lorries shuddered on the quayside; no other cars seemed to have made this winter crossing to a cold, dark continent.

Out of Calais, she found the road south. Her mind turned to Robert. She pictured the evening they would spend in Brussels. He was good at finding restaurants where he would not see anyone he knew and could talk to her without being on his guard. It was not that anyone would have minded; the majority of diplomats and businessmen away from home for long periods made 'arrangements' for themselves. Robert was unusual in the double inconvenience of having both his wife and his mistress in England. The thought of this made Elizabeth laugh. It was typical of a certain impracticality in him. The reason he did not want anyone to see them was because he felt guilty. Unlike his worldly confrères, who entertained their women on one of numerous business accounts, introduced them to their friends and even, sometimes, to their wives, Robert pretended that Elizabeth did not exist. This was something she found less appealing, but she had plans for it.

She chose a hotel in the town of Arras, which Bob had told her was near to a number of cemeteries and battlefields. The hotel was down a narrow side street that issued into a quiet square. She went through iron gates and up a gravel path to the front door. She stepped inside. To the right was a dining room with low lights in which half a dozen people scattered singly among the many empty tables were taking dinner with an audible sound of cutlery on china. A stooped waiter eyed them from the entrance to the kitchens.

The reception desk was in a nook below the stairs. A woman with iron-coloured hair wound into a bun put down her pen and looked at her through thick glasses. There was a room with its own bathroom; someone would bring her case up later. Would she be taking dinner in the hotel? Elizabeth thought not. She carried the small case herself, down a long corridor in which the intermittent ceiling lights seemed to grow dimmer the further she went from the stairhead. At last she found the number on the door. It was a vast room in which a riotous wallpaper had been pasted over the original nineteenth-century distemper. A seraglio effect had been attempted with drapes from a canopy around the four-poster bed, though the oval china doorhandles and the marble-topped bedside tables remained unorientalized. The room had a smell of damp cardboard, or perhaps brown tobacco from an earlier decade, mixed with something sweeter, a pre-war aftershave or the attempted concealment of some half-remembered plumbing failure.

Elizabeth went out into the night. Back on the main street she could see the square and the station to her right and the top of a cathedral or substantial church ahead of her. Keeping the spire in view, she went through the narrow streets, looking for somewhere congenial to eat, where a woman on her own would not attract attention. She found herself eventually in a large square that looked a little like the Grand' Place in Brussels. She tried to imagine it full of British troops and their lorries and horses, though she was not sure if they had had lorries in those days, or, come to that, whether they still used horses. She ate in a crowded brasserie full of young men playing table football. Pop music thundered from a speaker perched above the door. Occasionally the noise was augmented by one of the youths revving a two-stroke motorcycle just outside.

She looked up Arras in the index of Bob's book and found references to staff headquarters, transport, and a number of baffling numbers and names of regiments, battalions and officers. The waiter brought herring with potato salad, both of which seemed to have come from a tin. He deposited a mock-rustic pitcher of red wine next to her glass.

So what did they do in a town, exactly? She had thought of wars being fought in the countryside, on open ground.

She drank some red wine. What did it matter anyway? It was just a stopover on the way to see Robert.

She read a few pages of the book and drank some wine. The combination of the two things awakened a small determination in her: she would understand this thing, she would get it clear in her mind. Her grandfather had fought in it. If she had no children herself she should at least understand what had gone before her; she ought to know what line she was not continuing.

The waiter brought a steak with a towering portion of frites. She ate as much as she could, plying mustard over the surface of the meat. She watched as the juice from it furred the edges of the potatoes, turning them red. She enjoyed the small physical details she noticed on her own; in company she would just have talked and swallowed.

The food and wine brought relaxation. She sat back against the red plastic-covered bench. She saw two of the thinnest and tallest of the young eyeing her from the bar and looked down quickly to her book in case they should interpret her idleness as encouragement.

Her small determination hardened into something like resolve. What did it matter? It mattered passionately. It mattered because her own grandfather had been here, in this town, in this square: her own flesh and blood.

THE NEXT DAY she drove to Bapaume and followed the signs for Albert, a town, Bob had told her, that was close to a number of historic sites and which, according to the book, had a small museum.

The road from Bapaume was dead straight. Elizabeth sat back in her seat and allowed the car to steer itself, with only her left hand resting on the bottom of the wheel. She had slept well in the seraglio, and the hotel's strong coffee and icy mineral water had given her a sense of strange well-being.

After ten minutes she began to see small brown signs by the side of the road; then came a cemetery, like any municipal burial ground, behind a wall, belched on by the fumes of the rumbling container lorries. The signs began to come faster, even though Albert was still some ten kilometres away. Through the fields to her right Elizabeth saw a peculiar, ugly arch that sat among the crops and woods. She took it for a beet refinery at first, but then saw it was too big: it was made of brick or stone on a monumental scale. It was as though the Pantheon or the Arc de Triomphe had been dumped in a meadow.

Intrigued, she turned off the road to Albert on to a smaller road that led through the gently rising fields. The curious arch stayed in view, visible from any angle, as its designers had presumably intended. She came to a cluster of buildings, too few and too scattered to be called a village or even a hamlet. She left the car and walked towards the arch.

In front of it was a lawn, lush, cropped and formal in the English style, with a gravel path between its trimmed edges.

From near to, the scale of the arch became apparent: it was supported on four vast columns; it overpowered the open landscape. The size of it was compounded by its brutal modern design; although clearly a memorial, it reminded her of Albert Speer's buildings for the Third Reich.

Elizabeth walked up the stone steps that led to it. A man in a blue jacket was sweeping in the large space enclosed by the pillars.

As she came up to the arch Elizabeth saw with a start that it was written on. She went closer. She peered at the stone. There were names on it. Every grain of the surface had been carved with British names; their chiselled capitals rose from the level of her ankles to the height of the great arch itself; on every surface of every column as far as her eye could see there were names teeming, reeling, over surfaces of yards, of hundreds of yards, over furlongs of stone.

She moved through the space beneath the arch where the man was sweeping. She found the other pillars identically marked, their faces obliterated on all sides by the names that were carved on them.

'Who are these, these . . . ?' She gestured with her hand.

'These?' The man with the brush sounded surprised. 'The lost.'

'Men who died in this battle?'

'No. The lost, the ones they did not find. The others are in the cemeteries.

'These are just the . . . unfound?'

She looked at the vault above her head and then around in panic at the endless writing, as though the surface of the sky had been papered in footnotes.

When she could speak again, she said, 'From the whole war?'

The man shook his head. 'Just these fields.' He gestured with his arm.

Elizabeth went and sat on the steps on the other side of the monument. Beneath her was a formal garden with some rows of white headstones, each with a tended plant or flower at its base, each cleaned and beautiful in the weak winter sunlight.

'Nobody told me.' She ran her fingers with their red-painted nails back through her thick dark hair. 'My God, nobody told me.'

AFTER DRIVING ROUND Brussels for almost an hour Elizabeth despaired of finding Robert's flat. The only time she had come close to the right street she had found herself obliged to follow a one-way system that took her directly away from it. She left her car on the edge of a building site and hailed a taxi.

She was looking forward to seeing him; she could feel herself becoming excited as the driver pressed through the traffic. She was also a little nervous because every time she saw Robert she was worried that he would not live up to her recollection. It was as though there was this pressure on him to justify the effect he had on her life. She was denied to other men, lived alone and was party to a continuing deceit; it was up to him to be worth it. Yet he was the most diffident of men, unable to make such claims for himself, offering no promises and always urging her to act in her own interests. Perhaps that was one reason why she loved him.

She paid off the taxi and rang the bell on the street door. His voice came through the intercom and the door opened with a raucous buzzing sound. She ran upstairs, her feet echoing on the wooden steps. He was at the door of his first-floor flat, a bear-like scruffy man, cigarette in hand, still in his suit, but with the collar loosened and the tie at half-mast. Elizabeth flung herself into his arms.

She felt as she often did for the first few minutes in his presence, disorientated and in need of reassurance. She explained about the car and, when he had finished laughing, he said they

265

had better go and get it and put it in the underground parking.

Half an hour later they were back at the flat and able to begin again. Elizabeth went to have a bath while Robert stuck his feet up on the coffee table and began telephoning restaurants.

She came back into the sitting room in a new black dress, ready to go out. He handed her a drink. 'I promise I didn't put any tonic in. I just showed it the label. You look wonderful.'

'Thank you. You look all right too. Are you going to wear that suit or are you going to change?'

'I don't know. I hadn't thought about it.'

'Don't tell me.'

He went and sat next to her on the sofa, clearing a space among the books and papers. He was a heavily built man, tall, with a deep chest and a heavy belly. He began to stroke Elizabeth's hair and to kiss her glistening lips. He slid his hand up her skirt and murmured in her ear.

'Robert, I've just got dressed. Stop it.'

'You'll spoil my make-up,' he said.

'I mean it. And get your hands off there. You should wait till later.'

He laughed. 'This way I can relax and enjoy dinner.'

'Robert!'

He laddered her stocking and smudged her lipstick, but she had time to repair the damage before they went out. He was right in a way, Elizabeth thought; it was easier to talk once this closeness had been re-established.

At dinner he asked her what she had been doing and she told him about work and her mother and how she had become intrigued by her mother's parents. As she talked, it seemed to become clearer to her. Her life had reached an age at which she should no longer be the last to die; there ought to be someone younger than her, a generation of her children who should now be enjoying that luxurious safety of knowing that grandparents and parents still lay like a barrier between them and their mortality. But in the absence of her own children she had started to look backwards and wonder at the fate of a different generation. Because their lives were over she felt protective; she felt almost maternal towards them.

She described her visit to Irene's house where she had met Bob, someone who, from Irene's description, sounded as though he was seldom out of the pub or the betting shop, and how she had found a small bird-like man with thick glasses and quick hands who offered her a choice of two or three books from a room full of shelves.

'But nothing had prepared me for what I saw. The scale of it. The memorial is as big as Marble Arch, bigger, and every inch of it is written on. It all looks so recent. The cleaner showed me a shell they had found in the wood last week.'

Robert refilled her glass several times while she talked, and when they left the restaurant and set off towards the Grand' Place she felt light-headed and relaxed. Brussels seemed such a solid town, a monument to the efficiency of Flemish labour, to the comfort of large meals produced with French imagination, and above all to the pleasures of peace.

She was tempted to feel that an uneventful life was not necessarily a frivolous one; that the worthy crafts of citizenship had to be seriously worked at before they could be passed on. They went down a narrow alley as it began to rain. She felt Robert's arm urging her on towards the shelter of a café he had chosen for a *digestif*. As they rounded the corner they found themselves suddenly in the Grand' Place. Elizabeth looked up and saw the gilt façades of the merchant buildings, glittering gold beneath the filmy drizzle, lit by the soft lights of the square.

On Sunday afternoon she began to feel the low pressure of imminent separation. Sometimes it seemed to her that she began to dread her return almost as soon as she arrived.

Robert had put a record on and was lying back on the sofa balancing the ash on the end of his cigarette as he listened to music.

'When are we going to get married?' said Elizabeth.

'Is there an ashtray under that paper?'

'Yes.' She passed it to him. 'Well?'

'Oh Elizabeth.' Robert sat up. 'The trouble with you is that you're so impatient.'

267

'Ah, that's the trouble with me, is it? There are so many theories. And I don't think two years is that impatient.'

'We will divorce, but I can't do it now.'

'Why?'

'I've told you. Anne's just started a new school. And Jane needs to make friends where we've moved and –'

'It's not fair on Anne.'

'Exactly. She's only ten.'

'And soon she'll have exams and then Jane will need cheering up, then you'll have a new job.'

Robert shook his head.

'And the year after that,' said Elizabeth, 'it will be too late.'

'Too late for what?'

'Too late for you and me.'

Robert sighed. 'It isn't easy, Elizabeth. I do promise you that we will divorce. I'll even give you a deadline if you like. Say within three years.'

'I can't depend on that,' said Elizabeth. 'I can't plan my life on such a slender promise.'

'Are you feeling broody?'

'I wish you wouldn't use that word. I'm not a chicken. When I see a small child my guts turn over inside me. I have to stop walking and take several deep breaths because my whole body is yearning so strongly. Is that what the word means?'

'I'm sorry, Elizabeth. I'm really sorry. I'm no good for you. You must give me up for good. You must find someone else. I promise I won't make it difficult for you.'

'You don't see the point at all, do you?'

'What do you mean?'

'It's you that I want. You're the man I love. I don't want anyone else.'

Robert shook his head. He seemed moved by her conviction, but helpless. 'In that case I don't know what to suggest.'

'Marry me, you fool, that's what you should suggest. Follow the instincts of your heart.'

'But my heart is so torn. It's torn by Anne. I couldn't bear to hurt her.'

Elizabeth felt she should have foreseen his response. She

became more conciliatory. 'I would look after her,' she said softly. 'I'd care for her when she came to stay.'

Robert stood up and went to the window. 'You've just got to give me up,' he said. 'You know that, don't you? It's the only answer.'

Despite her furious endeavour to the contrary, she cried when she said goodbye to him in the underground parking. She began to feel dependent and helpless and despised herself for it. His arms seemed big when they folded her to his chest.

'I'll ring,' he said, shutting her in behind the driver's door.

She nodded and moved the car off to do blurred battle with the teatime traffic.

On Thursday evening Elizabeth went down to Twickenham to see her mother, and while Françoise was busy in the kitchen she went up to the attic where there were several trunks full of documents, photographs and books. She didn't tell her mother the reason for her search; she said she was looking for an old diary of her own.

The attic was not tall enough to stand up in, and Elizabeth had to crouch beneath the roof, though the builder had installed electric light by which she could make out the size of the task ahead of her.

There were five leather trunks and six black tin ones, in addition to several cardboard boxes, only a few of which seemed labelled. Most seemed to have been filled at random: there were Christmas decorations and old games with important bits missing packed in with bundles of letters and receipts.

She began with the leather trunks. She had no idea that her mother had been such a keen theatre-goer. There were bundles of programmes from the West End and magazines in which actors she had seen recently on television in grizzled character roles were shown on the stage thirty years before, their bright eyes rimmed with black, their wrists trailing lacy cuffs and their neatly trimmed hair glistening with matinée appeal.

In another trunk was a box, labelled THE ESTATE OF ALEC BENSON, which contained various probate papers. There had been no money, though there had been some interesting debts. Unknown to his wife he had bought a share in a horse-transporting business in Newmarket, and the sale of this had covered some of what he owed. The rest of his trunk was a jumble of prospectuses and letters from various companies he had bought, sold or invested in; most were based in Kenya and what had then been Tanganyika. They had in common a lack of capital and a certain El Dorado optimism. Later the documents came from Rhodesia and South Africa. There were sheaves of carefully preserved golf cards. Score 79, handicap 6, net 73. 'Let down by putting,' read a scribbled note at the bottom of one from Johannesburg dated 'Aug 19, 1950'.

In the first of the metal trunks Elizabeth came across a khaki battledress top. She pulled it out and held it up to the light. It told her nothing. It seemed in good condition, the rough serge unmarked and the stripes on the sleeves neatly sewn. There was also a tin helmet, in equally good condition, the webbing inside still in place and the exterior only slightly chipped. In the bottom of the trunk was a small leather writing case, and in this was an unused pad and a mono-chrome snap of a group of soldiers sitting in shirtsleeves on an armoured vehicle. A scribbled note on the back said: 'Tunisia, 1943 – The Fearless Five (Jarvis absent).'

Wrong war, wrong man. After all she had seen, after all the names on that great arch, they had come back for more barely twenty years later. If she herself were to have a boy, what guarantee was there that he too would not spend years of his adult life in this hellish perversion?

She moved, crouching, down the attic, to the row of metal trunks. Inside the first there was more rubbish: some of her old toys, and more bills and business letters relating to the purchase of the house.

Elizabeth dwelt on some of these because although they were trivial in themselves they touched her. The lines of debt and interest, drawn up on thick blue bond with red margins and figures entered with a manual typewriter and counter-signed in firm black ink, spoke of nugatory sums at kindly rates of interest, yet how fearsome they must have seemed in their time, how constant an obstacle to peace of mind. Above all to Elizabeth they did represent a family, however fissile and unsure, a house and a child with the presumed determination of the parents, of her mother at least, to make one more effort to improve upon the past. And with that slim debt to some mutual society had gone concomitant sacrifices of her personal ambition, of travel and a better life. Yet still somehow it was difficult to see her own life as the pinnacle of previous generations' sacrifices.

In the third metal trunk, towards the bottom, was a parcel, looped and tied in a bow with string. The dust from it dried the skin on her fingers and set her teeth on edge. She pulled open the knot and the parcel fell apart limply, dropping its guts into her hands. They were papers and letters and a notebook. There were also some coloured ribbons, three medals and a hip flask. It all seemed to date from an earlier time than the contents of the other trunks.

Among the papers were some handwritten in French. One had an address in Rouen. Elizabeth found herself reading it guiltily. It was hard to follow what it meant. The handwriting was of a dense, ornate kind, the ink was faded and Elizabeth's French was not good enough for the idiomatic language. There was a second letter in the same hand with an address in Munich.

At the bottom of the pile were two books. The first was a military handbook for officers. On the flyleaf was written Captain Stephen Wraysford, April 1917. Elizabeth opened it. Among instructions to officers was one that told him he should be 'blood thirsty and forever thinking how to kill the enemy and help his men to do so'. Something about the way the word 'bloodthirsty' was split in two made Elizabeth shudder.

The other was a notebook with pages ruled in thick blue lines. It was full of inky writing that spread in clusters over the printed lines from a red margin on the left.

It posed even more of a problem for Elizabeth than the letters. It appeared to be written in Greek script. She looked through it, puzzled. If it had belonged to a foreigner, someone unconnected with her family, what was it doing with this small parcel of her grandfather's belongings? She slipped it into the pocket of her skirt and tied the rest of the papers back into their bundle.

Her mother was reading a book in the sitting room.

Elizabeth introduced the subject with a small subterfuge. 'I couldn't find the diary I was looking for. It had an old address in it from years ago. When I moved flats you let me leave a lot of stuff up there, do you remember?'

'Yes I do. I wish you'd get rid of some of it.'

'I will. While I was looking for the diary I came across a little packet of what must have been your father's papers.'

'I thought they'd all been thrown away. There used to be a whole lot of them, but they got lost when I moved house.'

'What sort of things were they?'

'There were boxes full of notebooks that he'd kept from the time he first went to France. I think there were twenty or thirty of them. But I couldn't understand them because they were in some sort of code.'

'There's one up there in the attic. It looks as though it's written in Greek.'

'That's it,' said Françoise, putting down her sewing. 'There were lots more. I always thought that if he'd wanted anyone to understand them he would have written them in plain English.'

'What was he like, your father?'

Françoise sat up in her armchair, a slight flush colouring her cheeks. 'I wish you could have known him. He would have loved you. I wish he could just once have seen you and stroked your face.'

The following Saturday Elizabeth went down into the Underground station and sat on a train as it hurtled, clanked and rolled its electric way along the bed of the pipe inserted through the glutinous clay beneath the city. At Stratford she emerged into the winter daylight and took a bus onwards. She cursed the glistening Swedish saloon, which had refused to start.

Bob and Irene's house was in a square with half a dozen naked plane trees on a plot of grass behind iron railings. At one end was a sandpit with a red and orange construction for

272

children's climbing games, its gaudy surfaces sprayed with words formed from scripts known only to the sprayer. To Elizabeth they looked like angry warnings from a fundamentalist scripture. It was too cold for children to be playing in the garden, but a woman with a woollen scarf round her head was being dragged over the sparse and muddy green by a thin alsatian, which stopped and crouched heavily at the sandpit.

Elizabeth hurried to the house and pressed the bell. She saw the top of Irene's head as she bent to restrain her barking terrier in the half-open door. With threats and cajolings to the dog, and reassurances to Elizabeth, Irene managed to clear enough room for them both to get into the hallway and for her to close the door after them.

They went into the sitting room at the front of the house and Elizabeth sat down while Irene went to make tea. The room had dark brown wallpaper, though most of it was concealed by pictures and shelves that contained glass cases with stuffed birds and collections of china cups and saucers. There were two tailor's dummies, one dressed in a nineteenth-century velvet purple dress, the other draped and trailed over its otherwise naked torso with antique lace. There were a number of small tables about the room with brass curios and figures on them.

'I hope Bob doesn't mind me using him like a reference library,' said Elizabeth as Irene returned with the tea.

'I shouldn't think so,' said Irene. 'He's probably pleased to be asked. Were those books helpful?'

'Yes, they were. I told you about the memorial I saw, didn't I? The thing is I've become obsessed by the subject now and I want to know more. I've found this notebook of my grandfather's – at least I think it's my grandfather's, it was in with some of his things. It's written in a language I don't understand and I wondered if Bob might know, what with his archaeology and everything.'

'Egyptian hieroglyphics and all that?'

'Well, it's not Egyptian, but –'

'I know what you mean. He certainly used to know a lot about languages. He's done courses on them. I don't think he speaks any, but he'd probably recognize what it was, especially if it's an old one. Not very interested in the modern world, Bob. I gave him one of them record sets so he could learn French for our holidays one year and he never opened it.'

When Bob was persuaded at Irene's third attempt to come in from the garden, he shook hands with Elizabeth and poured himself a cup of tea. She told him about her visit to France and he nodded his head, sipping noisily, as he listened. He was shorter than his wife, with a bald skull and round tortoiseshell glasses. While she talked he rested his head on one side and occasionally scraped his chin on his upraised shoulder. Once she had explained the reason for her second visit his movements became wakeful and eager.

'Can I have a look at the offending article?' he said, holding out his hand.

Elizabeth passed over the notebook, guiltily, not sure of the propriety of allowing something her grandfather had written so many years ago to come under the scrutiny of this strange little man.

'I see,' he said, rasping through the pages like a bank clerk telling notes. Elizabeth feared that the dry old paper would crack. 'Wrote a lot, didn't he? Have you got any more of these?'

'No, this is the only one left.'

'I think we'll have to go through to my study. We'll be back in a jiff, Irene.' He stood up quickly and beckoned Elizabeth to follow him along the dark hallway to a room at the back of the house overlooking the garden where the last of the afternoon sun had drained away to leave only the black shapes of a wheelbarrow and a damp bonfire down by the wooden fence.

'I brought back those books you lent me,' said Elizabeth.

'Thank you. Just leave them on the side there. I'll shelve them directly I've finished this.'

Bob made a number of sucking and humming noises as he snapped the dry pages back and forth. 'I've got an idea what this is about,' he murmured. 'I've got an idea . . .' He went and pulled a book from one of the shelves that filled the room from floor to ceiling. They were arranged alphabetically, with

274

punched marker tape stuck on at intervals to announce the change of subject. Bob sat down again in a deep leather armchair; Elizabeth, at his invitation, was in the wooden chair at the desk.

'. . . but on the other hand, it doesn't quite add up.' Bob put the notebook down on his lap. He pushed his glasses up on to his forehead and rubbed his eyes. 'Why do you really need to know what all this means?'

Elizabeth smiled sadly and shook her head. 'I don't know, I really don't. It's just a whim, really, a vague idea I had that it might explain something. But I don't suppose there's anything interesting in it. It's probably just domestic lists, or records of things he's supposed to be doing.'

'Probably,' said Bob. 'You know you could have it looked at by an expert if you want. If you took it to a museum or a university department with someone who specializes in this kind of thing.'

'I wouldn't want to trouble them with it if it's so trivial. Couldn't you do it for me?'

'I might be able to. It depends on how much is private code. For instance, suppose you kept a diary and you referred to Irene in it as Queen Bess, shall we say. Someone might get as far as decoding the words Queen Bess, but they'd still be none the wiser, would they?'

'I suppose not. I don't want you to spend too much time on it, Bob. Why not just –'

'No, no, it would interest me. I'd like to work it out. The script is not of the language it's written in, I can tell you that. This is Greek script, but the words are not Greek. I think the words themselves are of a mixed language, perhaps with some private terms thrown in.'

'You mean the original language may not even be English?'

'Exactly. When they decoded Linear B they spent years thinking they were trying to decode Greek, but they weren't. Not Attic Greek at any rate. Once they'd got that sorted out, it fell into place. Not that this is as difficult as Linear B, I can assure you.'

Elizabeth smiled. 'How do you know so much about these things?'

'I had to do something to keep up with Irene. She was making all the money in the days when business was good. I just had my job at the works here. I did some studying in my spare time. It's surprising what you can learn if you just spend some time reading. I'll tell you what. If I can't sort it out within two weeks, you take it to someone else.'

'Are you sure you don't mind?'

'No. I'll enjoy it. I like a challenge.'

THERE WAS A call from Stuart, the man she had met at Lindsay's house. Elizabeth was surprised but not displeased to hear from him. He asked her to go out to dinner and she agreed. There was always a small feeling of guilt on her part when she went out with other men. No amount of rationalization about how 'unfaithful' Robert was to her could take it away, though it never stopped her going.

They went to a Chinese restaurant which Stuart insisted was of a more authentic kind than could usually be found in England. He had worked for a year in Hong Kong and had learned some Chinese there. He ordered half a dozen dishes and said a few words in Mandarin, which the waiter made a show of understanding. Elizabeth listened with interest as he explained each dish. They had the same glue-like consistency she was familiar with from Paddington takeaways, but Stuart was adamant that they were more authentic. She wished they could have wine instead of tea.

He asked if she would like to go back to his flat afterwards. It was in a mansion block in St John's Wood, not far from the restaurant. Elizabeth was intrigued by him and curious to see what sort of place he lived in. Her eyes moved quickly over the woodblock flooring, the tasteful rugs, the loaded bookshelves. There were only three pictures on the pale grey walls, but all of them were elegant and suitable – somewhere between art and decoration.

As she drank coffee, he went over to a grand piano and switched on a red-shaded light beside it.

'Will you play something?' she said.

'I'm very out of practice.'

He took some persuading, but eventually rubbed his hands together and sat down.

He played a piece that was vaguely familiar to Elizabeth; it had a fragile tune whose effectiveness depended on no more than two or three notes. The way he played it, however, very gently but with subtle timing, was touchingly good. Even as she heard it, Elizabeth felt that the little phrase would stay with her.

'Ravel,' he said when he had finished. 'Lovely, isn't it?'

He talked to her about Ravel and Satie and compared them to Gershwin. Elizabeth, who had thought of them as quite different kinds of composers, was impressed.

It was midnight when she finally rang for a taxi. She went downstairs happily humming the tune he had played. On the way home she had treacherous thoughts about Robert. She always told him that he made her unhappy by not leaving Jane; she promised him he would be happier with her. As far as she knew she was passionately sincere in all her protestations. However, she conceded as the taxi crossed the Edgware Road, it was just possible that she had chosen someone unobtainable for that very reason: that he did not threaten her independence.

Part Four

FRANCE 1917

UNDER THE COVER of a fading twilight, Stephen Wraysford narrowed his eyes against the drizzle. The men in front were invisible beneath the bulk of their clothes and the quantities of kit they were carrying. They looked as though they were bound for an expedition to the pole, explorers to the furthest regions. Stephen wondered what force impelled him, as his legs moved forward once more.

It had been raining for three weeks, drizzling, then surging into a steady downpour, then lifting for an hour or so until the clouds came in again over the low horizon of Flanders in its winter light. The men's coats were saturated, each fibre of wool gorged on water, and their weight added twenty pounds to what they carried. They had marched up from their billets into the rear area and already the skin on their backs was rubbed raw by the movement of the webbing beneath the load. Repetitive marching songs and chants had brought them to the support lines, but then as darkness fell they saw it was another three miles to the front. Slowly the songs and conversations died as each one concentrated on lifting his feet from the mud that began to suck at them. Their worlds narrowed to the soaked back of the man in front.

The communication trench was filled with orange slime that covered their boots and puttees. The closer they went to the front line the more it began to smell. Within half a mile it had become no more than a zig-zagged cesspool, thigh-deep in sucking mud that was diluted by the excreta of the overrun latrines and thickened by the decomposing bodies that each new collapse of trench wall revealed in the earth beneath.

An irritated shout passed up and down the line: the front men went too fast, someone had fallen down. The danger was that they would end up in the wrong part of the line and have to start all over again. They had been here before, however; there was something automatic now in the way they could find their way in the darkness and take the right fork when the choice came; there was something of routine in their swearing and their violent protests. At its best it was like pride. They had seen things no human eyes had looked on before, and they had not turned their gaze away.

They were in their own view a formidable group of men. No inferno would now melt them, no storm destroy, because they had seen the worst and they had survived.

Stephen felt, at the better moments, the love for them that Gray had demanded. Their desperate courage, born from necessity, was nevertheless endearing. The grimmer, harder, more sardonic they became, the more he cared for them. Still he could not quite believe them; he could not comprehend the lengths to which they allowed themselves to be driven. He had been curious to see how far they could be taken, but his interest had slackened when he saw the answer: that there were no boundaries they would not cross, no limits to what they would endure.

He saw their faces wrapped in woollen comforters, their caps sticking out beneath their helmets, and they looked like creatures from some other life. Some wore cardigans and waistcoats sent from home, some had strips of cloth or bandage wound around their hands in place of gloves mislaid or stolen from their packs by the less scrupulous. Any cloth or wool they could find in the villages had been pressed into service as auxiliary socks or as extra layers about the head; some had Flemish newspapers stuffed inside their trousers.

They were built to endure and to resist; they looked like passive creatures adapting to the hell of circumstances that oppressed them. Yet, Stephen knew, they had locked up in their hearts the horror of what they had seen, and their jovial pride in their resilience was not convincing. They boasted in a mocking way of what they had seen and done; but in their sad faces wrapped in rags he saw the burden of their unwanted knowledge.

Stephen knew what they felt because he had been with them and he himself did not feel hardened or strengthened by what he had seen; he felt impoverished and demeaned. He shared their conspiracy of fortitude, but sometimes he felt for them what he felt for himself, not love but pitiful contempt.

They said that at the very least they had survived, but even this was not true. Of their original platoon only he, Brennan and Petrossian were still at the front. The names and faces of the others were already indistinct in his memory. He had an impression of a weary group of greatcoats and grimed puttees, of cigarette smoke rising beneath helmets. He remembered a voice, a smile, an habitual trick of speech. He recalled individual limbs, severed from their bodies, and the shape of particular wounds; he could picture the sudden intimacy of revealed internal organs, but he could not always say to whom the flesh belonged. Two or three had returned permanently to England, the rest were missing, buried in mass graves or, like Reeves's brother, reduced to particles so small that only the wind carried them.

If they could claim survival it was by closing ranks and by the amalgamation of different units with conscripted reinforcements. Gray became battalion commander, replacing Barclay, and Stephen took over his company. Harrington made the long journey home to Lancashire, leaving part of his left leg on the bank of the Ancre, where the crows wheeled in delight.

It was night when they arrived at the front line. The men they were relieving passed out thigh-length rubber boots that had been in continuous service for eight months. The decayed pulp of the interior was a mash of whale oil and putrid rags that could accommodate feet of almost any size. None of them stayed quite calm in the hours of darkness. The bursts of light as shells exploded could be viewed as comforting in their remoteness, but there were always noises and shapes close to the trench itself that excited the old reflex. Stephen sometimes thought it was the only way they could be sure they were still alive.

The dugout which acted as company headquarters was a roofed hole in the second trench. Though small, it had an improvised bunk and a table. Stephen unloaded some of the kit he had brought up the line: a sketchbook, bars of chocolate and cigarettes, a periscope and a knitted waistcoat he had bought from an old woman. He was sharing with a young red-headed subaltern called Ellis who liked to read in bed. He was no more than nineteen or twenty, but he seemed composed and cooperative. He smoked incessantly but refused all offers of drink.

'When we have our next leave, I want to go to Amiens,' he said.

'It's miles away,' said Stephen. 'You won't get that far.'

'The adjutant said we could. He said it was all part of the new efficiency. Officers should have a decent time off in the place of their choice.'

'I wish you luck,' said Stephen, sitting down at the table and pulling a whisky bottle towards him.

'Won't you come too?'

'Me? I shouldn't think so. It's just a railway junction.'

'Have you been there?'

'Yes. I was there before the war.'

'What's it like?'

Stephen poured a drink. 'It's got a fine cathedral, if you like architecture. I didn't care for it myself. It's a cold building.'

'Well, I'm going anyway. Let me know if you change your mind. The CO said you spoke very good French.'

'Did he? I'm going to see if everyone's settled in.' Stephen drained the glass. 'Do you know where the tunnel head is?'

'It's about fifty yards that way.'

There was a hole in the ground roughly where Ellis had said. Stephen asked the sentry when the shift was due to come up.

'About half an hour, sir.'

'Is Captain Weir with them?'

'Yes.'

'If he comes up before I get back, tell him to wait for me.'

'All right, sir.'

Stephen went along the trench, twice tripping on the outstretched legs of men who had scraped sleeping holes for

284

themselves in the front wall. He wondered if it would really be possible to get to Amiens. It was almost seven years since he and Isabelle had left on the night train. Surely now it would be safe to return. After occupation and bombardment by the Germans, after the passage of almost seven years, surely the place could hold no disquieting reminders.

Michael Weir was emerging from the tunnel as Stephen arrived. There passed a moment of physical awkwardness between them when neither offered to shake hands. Weir's company had been sent back to its original position soon after the initial attack on the hot July morning. He was delighted when, some months later, Stephen's battalion also returned.

'Good rest?' said Weir.

'Yes. Fine. What's happening underground?'

'We've had a new consignment of canaries. The men are delighted. They were worried about gas.'

'Good. Come and have a drink if you like. It looks pretty quiet. We've got a patrol going out later but it should be all right.'

'Have you got whisky?'

'Yes. Riley always seems to get it from somewhere.'

'Good. I've run out.'

'I didn't think that was possible. Can't you just order some more?'

'Apparently I've been through my ration.'

Weir's hands were shaking as he took the bottle and filled his glass in the dugout. Ellis watched silently from the bunk: he was frightened by Weir's dishevelled appearance and his inability to talk sensibly until the liquor had put some strength and reason into him. He looked too old to be crawling underground with explosive charges, especially in those trembling fingers.

Weir gulped at the drink and shuddered as it ran down inside him. He found it more and more difficult to last out the long underground shift, even with the help of what he took with him in his hip flask. Increasingly he found reasons for instructing someone else to take the men down.

Weir had been on leave to England. He arrived at dusk at his

285

parents' Victorian villa in Leamington Spa and rang the front-door bell. The maid opened it and asked who he was. His telegram had gone astray; they were not expecting him. His mother was out, but the maid told him she thought his father would be in the garden. It was an October evening, three months after they had attacked on the Ancre.

Weir took off his greatcoat and left it on a chair in the hall. He dropped his kitbag on the floor and made his way through to the back of the house. There was a large flat lawn with laurel bushes and a giant cedar in one corner. He saw the gnats in the damp air ahead of him and felt his boots sink into the short-cropped lawn. The packed grass gave luxurious support to his steps. The air was thick with garden scents at evening. The denseness of the silence pressed his ears. Then he heard a door bang in the house, he heard a thrush; then a motor lorry backfiring in the quiet suburban street.

On the left of the lawn was a large greenhouse. Weir could make out a trickle of smoke coming from the door. As he approached it he caught the familiar smell of his father's pipe tobacco. He stood in the doorway and looked inside. His father was kneeling beneath a shelf on which small boxes of seeds were neatly laid out. He appeared to be talking to someone.

'What are you doing?' said Weir.

'Feeding the toad,' said his father, without looking up. 'Quiet now.'

From an old tobacco tin on the ground beside him, he took a small dead insect, pinched it between finger and thumb and pushed his hand slowly forwards under the shelf. Weir could see the polished seat of his trousers and the back of his bald head, but little else.

'That's it, that's my beauty. He's a champion, this one. You should see the size of him. We've not had an insect in here for weeks. Come and have a look at him.'

Weir went over the uncemented paving that his father had laid down the middle of the greenhouse and knelt on the gravel next to him.

'You see there? In the corner?'

Weir heard a fat croak from the direction his father indicated. 'Yes,' he said. 'A fine specimen.'

286

His father backed out from under the seed boxes and stood up. 'You'd better come on in then. Your mother's at choir practice. Why didn't you let us know you were coming?'

'I sent a telegram. It must have got lost. I didn't know until the day itself.'

'Well, never mind. We've had your letters. Maybe you'll want a wash after your journey.'

Weir looked across at his father's portly figure as they walked over the lawn. He wore a cardigan over his shirt, still with its stiff collar from the day at the office, and a dark, striped tie. Weir wondered if he was going to say any word of greeting. By the time they reached the French windows to the sitting room it was clear that the moment had passed.

His father said, 'I'll get the maid to make up a bed if you're stopping.'

'If that's all right,' said Weir. 'Just for a night or two.'

'Of course it's all right.'

Weir took his kitbag upstairs and went to the bathroom. The water roared in the pipes, stalled, gurgled with an airlock that shook the room, then thundered from the wide mouth of the tap. He dropped his clothes on the floor and sank into the bath. He expected that he would soon feel at home. He went to his old room and dressed carefully in flannel trousers and checked shirt: he was waiting for the moment when the familiar wash of normality would come over him and he would be restored to his old self; when the experiences of the last two years would recede into some clear perspective. He noticed that the clothes were too big on him. The trousers rested on his hip bones. He found some braces in a drawer and hitched them up. Nothing happened. The polished mahogany of the chest looked alien; it was hard to imagine that he had seen it before. He went to the window and looked down on the familiar view, where the garden ended by the cedar tree and the corner of the next-door house with its rear terrace and long drainpipe blocked the skyline. He remembered afternoons of childhood boredom when he had looked out at this view, but the familiar recollection did not bring back any sense of belonging.

When he went downstairs he found his mother had returned.

She kissed him on the cheek. 'You look a bit thin, Michael,' she said. 'What have they been feeding you on over in France?'

'Garlic,' he said.

'Well no wonder!' She laughed. 'We got your letters. Very nice they were, too. Very reassuring. When was the last one we had?'

'About a fortnight ago. You'd moved, you said.' Weir's father was standing by the fireplace, loading another pipe.

'That's right,' said Weir. 'We moved up from Beaucourt. We're moving again soon, up towards Ypres. Near somewhere called Messines, where we were at the start. I'm not really supposed to tell you too much.'

'I wish we'd known you were coming,' said his mother. 'We had our tea early so I could go to choir practice. There's a bit of cold ham and tongue if you're hungry.'

'That would be nice.'

'All right. I'll get the maid to set it out in the dining room.'

'You're too late for my tomatoes, I'm afraid,' said his father. 'We had a champion crop this year.'

'I'll ask the girl if she can find a bit of lettuce.'

Weir ate the meal alone in the dining room. The maid set a place with a glass of water and a clean napkin. There was a slice of bread and butter on the sideplate. He swallowed quickly, the sound of his own chewing magnified by the lack of conversation.

Afterwards he played cards with his parents in the sitting room until ten o'clock when his mother said it was time for her to go to bed.

'It's nice to see you all in one piece, Michael,' she said, as she gathered her cardigan around her and went to the door. 'Don't you two sit up talking all night.'

Weir sat facing his father across the fireplace.

'How's the office?'

'It's all right. The business doesn't vary as much as you'd think.'

There was a silence. Weir could think of nothing to say.

'We'll ask some people over if you like,' said his father. 'If you're stopping till the weekend.'

'All right. Yes.'

'I expect you'd like a bit of company after all . . . after, you know.'

'France?'

'Exactly. Make a change.'

'It's been terrible,' said Weir. 'I've got to tell you, it's been –'

'We've read about it in the paper. We all wish it would hurry up and finish.'

'No, it's been worse. I mean, you can't imagine.'

'Worse than what? Worse than it says? More casualties, are there?'

'No, it's not that. It's . . . I don't know.'

'You want to take it easy. Don't get yourself upset. Everyone's doing their bit, you know. We all want it to end, but we just have to get on with things in the meantime.'

'It isn't that,' said Weir. 'It's . . . I wonder if I could have a drink?'

'A drink? What of?'

'A . . . glass of beer, perhaps.'

'We haven't any in. There might be some sherry in the cupboard, but you wouldn't want that, would you? Not at this time of night.'

'No. I suppose not.'

Weir's father stood up. 'You get yourself a good night's sleep. That's the best thing. I'll ask the maid to get some beer tomorrow. We've got to build you up after all.'

He put out his hand and patted his son on the back of the left bicep. 'Good night, then,' he said. 'I'll lock up.'

'Good night,' said Weir.

When he could no longer hear his father's footsteps upstairs, he went to the corner cupboard and took out the two-thirds-full bottle of sherry. He went out into the garden and sat on a bench where he lit a cigarette and raised the bottle in his trembling hand.

'I WANT YOU to do the runes. Tell my fortune,' said Weir.

Stephen smiled at him. 'You're a hopeless devil, aren't you? He wants me to tell him he's going to survive,' he said to Ellis, who was watching from the bunk.

'Go on,' said Weir. 'Don't pretend you don't believe in it. It was you who introduced me to it.'

Stephen stood up and walked to the gas curtain that hung over the entrance to the dugout. 'Riley,' he shouted. 'Get me a rat.'

While they waited, Stephen took a pack of cards from the wooden shelf by the door, some stubs of candle and some sand. He made the shape of a pentangle on the table, placing several cards face down and linking them with trails of sand. He lit the candles and placed them at five equidistant points. He could feel Ellis's eyes boring into him from behind.

'This is voodoo I invented to pass the long hours. Weir likes it. It makes him feel that somebody cares about him. It's better to have a malign providence than an indifferent one.'

Ellis said nothing. He could not understand the relationship between the two men. The officer from the tunnel appeared to be always on the point of collapse while his own senior officer, Wraysford, seemed so calm that he was capable of being cruel to Weir, of saying anything without the other man protesting. Weir came shaking to the dugout for whisky and reassurance; he apparently depended on Wraysford's cold-ness. Yet on occasions, late at night, Ellis had had the impres-sion that there was another aspect to the men's surly friendship. He looked down and saw Wraysford's sunken eyes, black in the candlelight, and they seemed to be fastened on to Weir's nervous conversation; they were locked on to Weir as though he depended on him for some quality he lacked. It was almost, Ellis once thought, as if he really cared for him.

Riley came in carrying a rat by its tail. 'Coker got him, sir. The cheese on the bayonet trick.'

Ellis looked at Riley with distaste. He was a very smart little man, always perfectly turned out. Ellis admired this in him, but found him obsequious and inclined to break the rules.

'Have a drink, Riley,' said Stephen. 'Have some of this chocolate.'

Riley hesitated under Ellis's gaze but accepted.

'Ellis?' said Stephen. 'You going to risk a drink tonight? We wouldn't have to carry you to bed. You could just lie there.'

Ellis shook his head. The shellfire was starting up outside. He could not yet distinguish between the howitzers and the guns, between the different sizes of the enemy artillery. He had studied the effects of shellblast in training, however. He had seen the destructive powers demonstrated on maps and on prepared ranges; he had drawn diagrams of the conical delivery of shrapnel and the compacted blast of mortar. What he had not seen until the week before was the explosive effect on soft tissue, on the pink skin of two privates in his platoon who had been gathered up into a single sandbag by one of the others: he had watched the small joints of meat being dropped into the bag. When he heard the sounds of shellfire again he began to worry. The start he felt when the explosion went off was bearable; it was like a wave breaking, noisy but brief. Worse than that was the undertow of fear as the sound retreated. It seemed to suck and draw at him, leaving him a little weaker every time.

'They know what they're aiming at tonight all right,' said Riley. 'They've had planes over all week apparently.'

Stephen did not look up from the table. 'Turn the lantern off now,' he said. 'He likes this bit,' he said to Ellis. 'It makes him feel afraid.'

He placed a small wooden figure he had carved in the

middle of the pattern on the table. Its rough shape was caught by the flickering light of the candle flame. From his pocket he took a knife with a single, carefully sharpened blade. He sank it into the rat's chest, between the forefeet, and dragged it down. He held the rat in his other hand and shook out the guts on to the table.

Weir, despite everything he had seen, was fascinated. The pile of spleen and liver lay greenish-red and warm in the sandy grains of the wood. Stephen stuck the knife into the cavity again and scraped out what remained. Weir leaned over the table and examined it.

'What does it mean?' he said.

Stephen laughed. 'How should I know? It's just a dead rat. Is that the bowel there? Yes, I think so. It's been eating . . . What's that? Is it flesh?'

'What was the name of those two men in your platoon?' said Weir.

'For Christ's sake,' said Ellis. 'This is disgusting. I'm going out. You should be ashamed of yourselves. This is what the bloody ignorant men do. You should be setting an example.'

'Who to?' said Stephen. 'You?'

Ellis got off his bunk and stood up. Stephen pushed him back. 'Sit down and watch.' Ellis perched reluctantly on the edge of the bed.

Stephen poked his knife into the guts. 'The reading is doubtful,' he said. 'It suggests a sound future provided you have nothing to do with women or with priests. If you do, then you could encounter problems.'

'What card is a priest?'

'A ten,' said Stephen. 'Ten for the ten commandments. Queen is a woman.'

'And what should I hope for?'

Stephen pushed the knife into the mess on the table. 'Peace. Even numbers. And your own number – four. You were born in April, weren't you?'

'Yes.'

'I'm going to turn the cards over now,' said Stephen. He inserted the tip of the knife under the card nearest him and flipped it over. It was an eight. 'Good,' he said. The next card

292

was the four of hearts. Weir looked delighted. Stephen levered the next card slowly up. It was the two of clubs. 'I think the Man Upstairs is on your side, Weir,' he said. The fourth card was the ace of hearts. 'Peace,' said Stephen. 'The ace represents power and stability. This is the best horoscope you could have.' He reached out his knife for the final card and flipped it over with a flourish. It was the four of diamonds.

'You fixed it,' said Weir in a voice that hoped for a denial.

Stephen shook his head.

'You knew what cards were on the table and you just made it up that that was what I needed.'

'Did you see me fix the pack?'

'No, but it's obvious you did.'

'I don't know why you make me go through this absurd performance if you're not going to believe the results. Does Coker want his rat back, Riley?'

'I doubt it, sir.'

'You'd better get back. I'll clear this up. Light the lantern on the way out, will you?'

There was a long silence after Riley left. Ellis took up his book and lit another cigarette. Weir stared at the tracks of the sand on the table as though mesmerised.

'Why are you so anxious to survive?' asked Stephen.

'God knows,' said Weir. 'It's all I have, my life. In these conditions you just want to hold on to it. Perhaps I will do something with it later, perhaps it will all come clear.'

Stephen scrubbed the top of the table with a brush and a bucket the previous occupants had left behind. He felt vaguely ashamed.

Ellis looked down from his bed. 'Most people in this war want to survive so that we can win it. We are fighting for our country.'

Weir looked up wide-eyed in the light of the relit lantern. Somehow he had managed to smear rat's blood on his cheek. His mouth hung open incredulously. Stephen smiled.

'Well?' said Ellis. 'Don't you agree? That's what we are fighting for, isn't it? That's why we tolerate it when we see those brave men suffer and die. We know they've done it for a good cause.'

Stephen said, 'I went out on patrol the other day with a boy in your platoon, Ellis, and he was smoking some cigarettes called "Golden Future". Where did he get those from? They smelt like the stables in summer.'

'They come up with the rations,' said Ellis. 'They have some very inventive names. "Glory Boys", "Rough Riders". But you haven't answered my question.'

Stephen poured more whisky. He seldom drank more than two glasses, unless it was to keep Weir company. This night he had already drunk half a bottle. Perhaps it was merely to irritate Ellis. He could feel his tongue lying heavy in his mouth; his jaw had gone soft, so the words were difficult to frame.

'Weir, you love the place, don't you?'

'I thought it stank when I went on leave,' said Weir. 'Those fat pigs have got no idea what lives are led for them. I wish a great bombardment would smash down along Piccadilly into Whitehall and kill the whole lot of them.'

'Even your family?'

'Particularly my family. Particularly them. I tried to explain to them what it was like and do you know, my father was bored. He was actually bored with the whole thing. I would especially like a five-day bombardment on their street. And on the people who went on strike for more money in the factories when we were dying on a shilling a day.' Weir's voice was shaking. 'I would like to see them all walk into the enemy guns in long thin lines. For one shilling.' Saliva ran down his chin.

'What about you?' said Ellis to Stephen. 'Are you as embittered as this man?'

Stephen had a false eloquence lent by drink; it could have led him to adopt any opinion with fluency. He said, 'I can't remember the country. Should we fight for fields and hedges and trees? Perhaps we should. Perhaps if they're filled with the affections that people have brought to them, then they are worth dying for. And the mill towns where I used to visit factories, those sloping streets, and London with its docks and buildings – perhaps those bits of stone and mortar are worth more than the enemy's bits of brick, in Hamburg or Munich.

294

Perhaps if the fields and hills have been loved by enough people we should lie down and be killed for them, we should just let the bullets and the shells dismember us so that the green hills are undisturbed.'

'Are you saying the land itself is worth more than the people and our way of life?' said Ellis.

'No.'

'Then what are you fighting for?'

Stephen said, 'If I am fighting on behalf of anyone, I think it is for those who have died. Not for the living at home. For the dead, over here. Wilkinson, Reeves, and his brother, who disappeared. Disappeared to nothing. Byrne, caught on the wire. I am fighting for him.' His voice thickened and he clenched his fists. 'And all those others. I knew them. Studd and what-was-his-name, the fair-haired man with him, they were always together. Christ, I can't even remember his name.'

Weir said, 'Don't worry about it. As long as you know who the men are now.'

'Yes, I do, of course I do. That platoon still exists in some way. Petrossian and . . . Brennan, of course. And the new men. There's one called Goddard. There's Barlow and Coker. And lots of others. They're all right. What was Brennan's friend called? He bled so much. Douglas. You don't lose so many underground.'

'We've lost our fair share. Tyson at Beaumont Hamel as well as the people in the tunnels. But I'm not going to die.'

Weir's eyes took on a blue gleam as the night progressed, ignited by hope and intoxication. What remained of his hair stuck out above his ears in thin, fair wisps. His voice rose higher in his excitement.

'And don't look so sceptical. Don't tell me you never believed in any sort of magic power,' he said.

Stephen was drunk enough to be confessional. His temporary fluency had gone, but was replaced by honesty. 'I used to when I was a boy. We used to try to raise dead spirits. I tried to find fortune tellers at fairs. I wanted to believe that I had some important destiny. I wanted to have a make-believe world because I couldn't bear to live in the real one.'

The dugout shook with the impact of a nearby shell.

Weir looked surprised. 'Even then?'

'Gray told me one day when I was in hospital that this was quite common among children who had . . . what was his phrase? "Had the normal magic of their childhood taken from them" . . . something like that.'

'What the hell does Gray know about it?'

'One of his Austrian doctors told him.'

Ellis, who was still listening from his bed, said, 'What happened when you were wounded?'

'I began to believe in something.'

'In what?'

Stephen rested his chin on his hands. His speech was slurred, with long silences as he struggled to shape his thoughts. In the spaces between the words there was a screaming of shells. 'I heard a voice. There was something beyond me. All my life I had lived on the presumption that there was no existence beyond . . . flesh, the moment of being alive . . . then nothing. I had searched in superstition . . .' He waved his hand. 'Rats. But there was nothing. Then I heard the sound of my own life leaving me. It was so . . . tender. I regretted that I had paid it no attention. Then I believed in the wisdom of what other men had found before me . . . I saw that those simple things might be true . . . I never wanted to believe in them because it was better to fight my own battle.' With a burst of fluency, he said, 'You can believe in something without compromising the burden of your own existence.'

Weir looked at him uncomprehendingly. Ellis coughed. 'So what do you believe in?'

'A room, a place, some self-grounded place.' Stephen's head was close to the table and his voice was almost inaudible. 'Just a room. Where it is understood.'

Ellis said, 'I think you have a long way to go before you can call yourself a proper Christian.'

Stephen raised his head from the table. His eyes slowly filled, then brimmed with rage, the uncontrolled temper of a farm boy. He stood up and went unsteadily to the bunk. He took Ellis by the shirt and hauled him down.

'Look here, I'm sorry, I meant no offence.' Ellis was

alarmed by Stephen's expression. 'You're drunk, leave me alone.'

Stephen breathed in deeply. He let his hands fall to his sides. 'Go and look after your men,' he said softly. 'It's three o'clock. Go and talk to the sentries. You know how frightened they'll be.'

Ellis pulled on his coat and backed out of the dugout. Stephen watched him go, then turned back to Weir. 'That's right, isn't it, Weir? He should go and see that they're all right?'

'Who? Ellis? You should have kicked him. Let me sleep in his bunk till he gets back. I'm on my own since Adamson was wounded.'

Jack Firebrace and Arthur Shaw lay curled together in their dugout. There were ten men in a space twenty-five feet wide and five feet high. Once they had inserted themselves there was no chance of movement. Jack had grown used to sleeping all night on one side; with Arthur Shaw's bulk in position, he could not turn over. He was lulled by the sound of Shaw's deep, raucous breathing; he had become accustomed to the contours of his body. He slept as well with him as he had ever slept in London with Margaret, shutting his ears to the sound of the trains rattling past the back window.

In the morning he wrote a letter home:

Dear Margaret, Thank you very much for the parcel which arrived safely, it was most acceptable. We can always do with a few more Oxo cubes and the cake was much appreciated by all. We have been in much better billets recently and I am in very good health. We have proper dugouts – not just for the officers! It really is the lap of luxury, I can tell you, and we have all done a good bit of sleeping.

We are doing some digging too. I think the infantry accepts us more now and what we are doing is very important for the next big attack. Yes, there is to be another one.

It is dangerous of course and there have been some gas alarms, but we all feel better now we have had a new lot of canaries. I think there are enemy mines but we haven't met them yet. I tell you all this, but you are not to worry about me. If you worried then I should regret having written it.

The infantry always want us to do some of their fatigues but we do enough underground. We're not building anybody's trench for them, I can tell you. We did give a hand burying some telephone cables, but that's all. Now some of them are sent on fatigues to help us. That's more like it!

They marched us five miles back for a bath and we had had one the day before. There was a good bit of groaning, I can tell you. What's the point of getting clean if you can't change your clothes, which are full of 'visitors'. But it was a good bath with plenty of warm water and a warm shower-bath. Then the men were all very happy because we had some rest and there was a place with beer. We got a good strafing from the sergeant when we got back but it was worth it.

You say you've got no news and I must be bored with what you send but this is not so. We long for word from home. That's all we think of: home, home, home.

I think of the boy a good bit too. I must say I am finding it difficult to keep bright. We have divine service on Sunday and the sermon is always interesting. Last week the padre told the story of the Prodigal Son, how a rich man had two sons and one of them went to the bad, but when he came home his father killed the fatted calf for him. I would have wanted to do the best for John, but it is not to be.

I am doing my best to be merry, and you must not worry about me. Please thank Miss Hubbard for her good wishes. Write to me soon. Your affectionate, Jack.

THE MINES WERE driven far under the ground into a blue clay. At the heads of the deeper ones the men enlarged chambers where they could rest and sleep without needing to go back above the ground. They bore the stench of their packed, unwashed bodies for the sake of the warmth and safety. Any minute was better that was not spent beneath the endless dripping sky; no night was unbearable that offered shelter from the freezing winds that stiffened their waterlogged tunics and trousers into icy boards. The smell was hard to breathe, but it was no better above ground where the chloride of lime seemed not to relieve but to compound the atmosphere of putrefying flesh, where the latrine saps had been buried or abandoned and men preferred to inhale the toxic smoke of braziers than the smell of faeces.

While the principal deep mines, which had been under construction for two years, were gradually enlarged and driven out towards the ridge, Weir's company were working on a shallow tunnel from which they could listen for enemy counter-mines. One morning they heard sounds of German activity above them. There appeared to be an underground ladder nearby from which men were jumping. The noise of their boots could be heard stamping along the tunnel overhead. Weir ordered his tunnel to be evacuated, but two or three men had to be left in listening posts at all times to be sure that the Germans would not undermine the actual trench. There were no volunteers for this job, so he had to make a duty rota. They took candles with them so they could read books as they listened. Only twenty men had been down and back by the time the explosion they most dreaded shook the earth. With a large camouflet the Germans blew their tunnel. The two listeners were buried under thousands of tons of Flanders soil.

Weir was in the trench when the explosion went off, drinking tea with Stephen and explaining his difficulties. He went white as the earth rocked under them. The hot liquid spilled unremarked over his shaking hand.

'I knew it,' he said. 'I knew they'd blow it. I've got to get down there. It was my idea to put them there. Oh God, I *knew* this would happen.'

He looked frantically to Stephen for sympathy, then brushed past him on his way to the tunnel ahead.

'Just a minute,' said Stephen. 'You may have lost three men down there, but if the enemy's got a tunnel under this trench I'm going to lose half my company. You'd better be bloody sure where their tunnel's going.'

'You come and see if you're so concerned. I have to think of my own men first,' said Weir.

'Take one of your men and get him to report back to me.'

Weir was so angry that he had stopped trembling. 'Don't you tell me what to do. If you're so worried about your men then you –'

'Of course I'm worried about them. If they think there's a mine under them they won't stay put for twenty-four hours. There'll be a mutiny.'

'Well, come down and bloody well see for yourself then.'

'It's not my job to crawl around underground.'

Stephen was following Weir along the trench to where he kept the tunnelling supplies. He picked up a canary in a small wooden cage and turned to face Stephen.

'Are you frightened?' said Weir.

Stephen hesitated, glancing at the cage. 'Of course not. I merely –'

'Well, come on then.'

Stephen, who had not often felt himself out-argued by Weir, saw that he had little choice.

'It'll only take an hour,' said Weir, more placatingly now

that he could see Stephen weakening. There was a pause. 'You got wounded last time, didn't you? So now I suppose you're afraid to go down.'

'No,' said Stephen, 'I'm not frightened of going underground.'

Weir passed him a helmet with a lamp on it and a pick. 'It's very narrow there, and we'll need to clear some debris when we get to the explosion.'

Stephen nodded silently. He instructed the nearest man he could see to tell Ellis where he had gone, then followed Weir to the head of the tunnel.

A piece of tarpaulin was stretched over a wooden frame built back only a couple of feet from the front wall of the trench. The excavated clay was taken away in sandbags and dumped well to the rear so that enemy planes could have no idea where the digging was being done. The opening was not much more than a rabbit hole.

Weir turned to Stephen, his face set in anxiety. 'Follow me as fast as you can.'

Beneath the parapet of the trench was a vertical shaft into the darkness of the earth. The horizontal wooden rungs were several feet apart. Weir scrambled down with practised ease holding the handle of the canary's cage in his teeth, but Stephen had to feel ahead for each slat of wood with his feet.

Eventually he reached a wooden platform where Weir was waiting.

'Come on, for God's sake. This is it. It's only a shallow tunnel.'

Stephen, breathing hard, said, 'Shouldn't you have sent the stretcher-bearers?'

'Yes, they're ready, but they won't come unless an officer has told them where to go.'

Weir went forward at a crouch into the darkness, carrying the cage in his left hand. Stephen followed three or four paces behind. The bird was chirping, though whether from fear or happiness he could not say. Stephen shuddered at the sound. He thought of the surface of the earth above them: a pattern of round shellholes that made up no man's land, each one

301

half-filled with water, in which the rats played and feasted on the unrescued corpses; then thirty feet or so of packed, resistant clay, down which the moisture could still permeate from the world above them.

Weir had gone on to his hands and knees as the height of the tunnel decreased to about three feet. The sides of it pressed in on them and Stephen found it hard to see the beam of Weir's lamp ahead of him. His own seemed to illuminate only the nails on the soles of Weir's boots and the occasional glimpse of cloth on his slowly advancing rear.

As they went further, Stephen felt the clay stick to his crawling hands. He wanted to put out his arms to his sides and push back the flanks of the tunnel to give them space to breathe. As long as Weir's body was between him and the cage, however, any fear he felt from the enclosing weight of the earth was tolerable. Anything was bearable provided he did not have to come too close to that bird.

Weir's breath was coming in fast, loud gasps as he pushed onwards, using one hand to pull himself and one to drag the cage. Stephen felt a piece of rock slit the skin of his left hand. There was nothing he could do. The earth above them was poisoned by the spores of gas gangrene, a horse disease implanted by the copious manure used by farmers; he hoped it had not sunk so deep below the surface. He pressed on, trying to put his weight on the outside of his hand. The tunnel was now so narrow that they had to try to enlarge it with their picks. There was no room to bring sufficient leverage, however, so their progress was very slow.

Weir suddenly stopped, and Stephen heard him swearing.

'This is it,' he said. 'This is the end. There should be another thirty feet. They've blown the whole bloody thing. They'll both be dead.'

Stephen came up and saw the wall of earth in front of them. He felt a sudden panic. If the tunnel behind them should also now collapse . . . He moved his feet reflexively and began to manoeuvre to turn round: such an explosion must surely have weakened the whole structure with its flimsy supporting timbers.

From his haversack Weir took a round wooden disc which

he pressed against the side of the tunnel. Then he took out a stethoscope and plugged it into a teat on the surface of the disc and listened. He raised his finger to his lips. Stephen had no intention of interrupting. He listened carefully himself. It was curiously quiet. There was something unsettling about the silence: there were no guns.

Weir tore the stethoscope from his ears. 'Nothing,' he said.

'Is that thing effective?'

'Yes, it's good. A scientist in Paris invented it. You can never be sure, of course.'

'Who was in there?'

'Shaw was one. The other was called Stanley, I think. He was new.'

'And how do we get them out?'

'We don't. If we try to dig out this stuff we'll just bring in the roof. We send down some men to timber it, and if they can get through, so much the better. But I want to close this tunnel now.'

'And if they don't get to them?'

'We say a prayer. We're all buried in the end.'

'Do you want to say a prayer now?'

Weir's face was so close to his that Stephen could smell the stale alcohol on his breath. 'I don't know any prayers,' he said. 'Do you?'

'I could invent one.' The canary let out a small living sound. Stephen ached with fear. Words came from his lips. 'Into your hand, oh God, we commend the souls of these two men. May they rest in peace. Let this not be in vain. In Jesus Christ's name. Amen.'

'Let's go,' said Weir. 'You'd better let me lead the way. I'll try and get past you. Move back a bit that way, that's it, push up against the wall.'

Stephen flattened himself to try to let Weir pass over him. As Weir's body pressed against him his trailing pick caught against the clay above. A lump of it fell on him. The space dislodged a much heavier fall which smashed down on to his right arm. He let out a cry. Stephen instinctively tried to pull back to where the tunnel was wider in case the whole thing collapsed. Weir was swearing and groaning.

'My arm's broken. Get me out, get me out. Quick or the whole thing's going to come down.'

Stephen went back to him and began to lift the fallen earth very carefully off his body. He pushed it back towards the face of the blocked tunnel. Weir was moaning in pain.

'Get it off, get it off. We've got to get out.'

Stephen, through grinding teeth, said, 'I'm doing my best. I've got to be gentle.' He was lying on top of Weir, his head towards Weir's feet, as he cleared the debris from his arm. He then had to wriggle back over Weir's body, forcing his face down into the earth with his weight. He finally got back so they were lying face to face, Weir's feet towards the wall, Stephen's towards the way out. Weir spluttered on the clay in his mouth.

'Can you make it?' said Stephen.

'I've broken my arm. Maybe a rib too. I'll have to crawl on one hand. You take the bird.'

Stephen reached back to the cage. Its flimsy wooden frame had been crushed in the fall of earth; it was empty.

'The bird's gone,' he said. 'Let's go.'

'Damnation,' said Weir. 'We can't leave it. We'll have to find it and take it back. Otherwise if the Boche find it they'll know we –'

'For Christ's sake, they know there's a tunnel anyway. That's why they blew it.'

Weir spat through his pain. 'You cannot under any circumstances leave a bird free. Ever. It's in the handbook. I'd be court-martialled. Find the bird.'

Stephen crawled back over Weir's prostrate body. He felt himself close to tears as he searched the murk of the clay with the feeble light of his helmet. A little to the left of the hole made by the fall he saw a gleam of yellow. Gently, he reached out his hand towards it.

He could feel his heart pummelling the floor of the tunnel; his clothes were sodden with sweat. It ran down into his eyes. He held his hand steady, the fingers opening in the gloom as he moved towards the bird. Please God, he muttered, please, please . . . When his hand was no more than six inches from the canary he made a lunge for it. The bird took off and its wings brushed the back of his hand as it flew past him. Stephen screamed. His body convulsed and his legs kicked back into Weir's thighs.

'For Christ's sake! What's the matter? You're going to bring the tunnel down.'

Stephen lay face down, panting, with his eyes closed.

'Keep still,' said Weir. 'For God's sake keep still. It's up near me now.'

Stephen lay quietly, saying nothing. Weir made no movement. Stephen heard him make little whistling noises. He was trying to soothe the startled bird, or trick it into his hand. Stephen was still facing the wrong way. Weir's body was blocking his exit back to the light.

He felt Weir make a sudden movement. 'I've got it,' he said. 'It's in my hand.'

'All right. Let's go. You start off and I'll follow.'

'I've only got one hand. I can't take the bird.'

'Well, kill it. It's only a canary. Come on. I want to turn round. I'm getting cramp. I want to get out of here.'

There was a silence. Weir made no movement. Eventually he said, 'I can't kill it. I can't do it.'

Stephen felt a strange weight in his stomach. 'You must kill it,' he said. His voice came softly through his dry mouth.

There was another silence. Then Weir said, 'I can't do it, Wraysford. I can't do it. It's just a tiny bird. It's done nothing wrong.'

Stephen, trying to keep control of himself, said, 'For God's sake kill it. Just squeeze it in your hand. Bite its head. Anything.'

'You do it.'

'No! It's too risky passing it back to me. It might escape.'

Weir rolled over on to his back and held his left fist towards Stephen. The bird's head appeared between the forefinger and thumb. 'There it is,' Weir said. 'I'll hold it still while you take your knife and just cut its throat.'

Stephen felt Weir's eyes boring into him. He reached into his pocket and found his knife. He opened the blade and reached up over Weir's knees. Weir, straining up on his back was able to meet his gaze as Stephen's head appeared between

305

his shins. The two men looked at each other over the tiny yellow head between them. Stephen thought of the lines of men he had seen walking into the guns; he thought of the world screaming in the twilight at Thiepval. Weir looked steadily at him. Stephen put the knife away in his pocket. He fought back the rising tears. Weir might let the bird go. It might touch him.

'I'll take it,' he said.

'You'll need both hands to dig and crawl,' said Weir.

'I know.'

With his handkerchief Stephen made a sling for the bird. He tied three corners together and left an opening.

'All right. Put it in there and I'll tie it up.'

With teeth clamped very tight together he held out both hands to Weir, who released the bird into the handkerchief. Stephen jumped as he felt the battering of wings against the palms of his hands. He managed with fumbling fingers to bring the fourth corner of the handkerchief into the other three and tie it. He put the knot between his teeth and crawled back over Weir's body.

They began their slow retreat, Stephen pushing back the loose earth and enlarging the tunnel where he could. Weir fought his way with his left hand.

In the narrow darkness Stephen felt the feathery weight beneath his face. Sometimes the bird beat its wings and struggled, sometimes it lay still in fear. He saw in his mind the stretched skeleton of the lower wing, the darting movement of the head, and the black, relentless eyes. He tried to turn his mind away from it by thinking of other things, but no other thought would lodge in his mind. It was as though his brain had closed down, leaving only one picture: the fossil shape of a bird, a pterodactyl ribbed in limestone, the long cruel beak with its prehistoric hook and the bones fanned out, their exiguous width and enormous span, particularly the underside of the breakable wing, with its sinewy feathers plugged into the bird's blood at one end, then stretched over the delta that would flap and bang in his face as the frantic creature, in the storm of its true hostility, would bring its vast plucking beak into his eyes.

The small canary suspended from his mouth made feeble

movements and its yellow feathers protruded from the hand-kerchief to brush softly against his face. He closed his eyes and pushed onwards. He longed for the mud and the stench, for the sound of shells.

Behind him, Weir crawled as best he could. He asked Stephen to stop as he tucked his arm into the front of his shirt for support. He shouted in pain as the two bones momentarily rubbed together.

They reached the ladder and were able to stand up. Stephen took the handkerchief from his mouth and handed it to Weir.

'I'll climb up and send a couple of your men down to help you. You hold on to this.'

Weir nodded. He was very pale, Stephen noticed. Then Weir gave the wide, empty-eyed grin that worried Ellis so much. He said, 'You're a brave man, Wraysford.'

Stephen raised his eyebrows. 'You just wait there.'

He climbed the shaft of the mine with growing pleasure. Up in the mud, in the yellow light, beneath the rain, he stretched his arms and breathed deeply on the chloride of lime as though it were the finest scent from the rue de Rivoli.

He found Ellis waiting nervously near the tunnel head.

'Ah, Ellis, get a couple of sewer rats down there, will you? Captain Weir's broken his arm.'

'Where have you been, sir?'

'Helping out the sappers, you know. You have to show willing. If you ask nicely they'll even build a dugout for you.'

'I was worried, sir. Couldn't you have sent someone else?'

'That's enough, Ellis. Just get two men down there. I'm going for a walk. Nice day, isn't it?'

Down the line he could hear CSM Price issuing orders for a fatigue party to begin trench repair work. Stephen smiled. When the fields of Europe were no longer needed for human use and were allowed to sink back into the fires of creation, Price would still be making lists.

'OF COURSE YOU can go,' said Colonel Gray. 'This is supposed to be a civilized war now. And we shall know where to find you. Just don't let young Ellis here lead you astray, that's all.'

Stephen nodded. 'Thank you, sir.'

Gray picked up his book and swung his feet back on the desk. He was already a page further into Thucydides by the time Stephen and Ellis left the house that was acting as battalion headquarters.

The next day the train took them into a countryside almost buried by the debris of conflict. To begin with Stephen had found it strange to look up from a shelled trench and be able to make out normal country life a few miles back from the line, but after almost three years of fighting the ground had become littered with the light-industrial detritus of war. Petrol cans, shell cases, wooden boxes, tins, the packages of all kinds of supply goods and ammunition lay on either side of the tracks.

After ten minutes they saw their first green tree, the first trunk not blasted and blackened by shells, but still covered with brown bark and crowned with branches in which pigeons and thrushes were gathered.

Ellis offered him a cigarette. Stephen took the packet and looked at it. '"The Flag". How do you get these things, Ellis?'

'I'm trying to see how many different brands I can get through. Apparently there's some called "Kitchener's Small Size" that I haven't had yet.'

The cheap smoke filled the compartment.

Since Ellis had first mentioned Amiens, Stephen had allowed himself to weaken slowly. He had thought he would never return, but he had come to believe that what had happened there was so long ago and was an experience of so peculiar a kind that it had no real bearing on the life he was living. Perhaps there was something dangerous about revisiting places from an earlier time, but he did not feel open to any sentimental feeling. He had only a certain curiosity to see what had happened to the town. Gray told him it had been 'knocked about' by shells.

'Tell me something, sir,' said Ellis. 'You know those cards the other night. Did you –'

'You don't have to call me sir, you know. As for the cards . . . what do you think?'

'I think you fixed them.'

Stephen smiled. 'Of course I did. Even Weir knows that.'

'So why does he want you to do them?'

'Because he's frightened.'

Ellis looked puzzled.

'Yes, it's strange, I suppose. Weir doesn't believe in anything. He needs something to sustain him. He tries to believe that his own survival is something to fight for. Something to die for, you might almost say.'

'And the cards help him?'

'Perhaps. He's a very scared man. He can probably trick himself.'

'I see,' said Ellis. He spoke with a clipped, abrupt voice. 'And when did he first get the wind up?'

Stephen said very gently, 'I don't think it's fear in that sense. He's not afraid of gas or shells or being buried. He's frightened that it doesn't make sense, that there is no purpose. He's afraid that he has somehow strayed into the wrong life.'

'I see,' said Ellis doubtfully.

The train rattled on towards Amiens and Stephen felt his pleasurable anticipation increase. Ellis was not the man he would have chosen as a companion but he was determined to be kind to him. Weir was resting in a rehabilitation centre near Arras. He had hoped for a trip home, but injuries like his had been viewed with suspicion since the early days when the infantry had taken to sticking their arms in the rapidly unwinding winch gear in the hope of serious damage.

Ellis took out a writing pad and began a letter home. Stephen gazed from the window. The sounds of war were leaving him. Unlike Weir, who stood imprisoned by imaginary shell sounds in the quiet bedroom of his parents' house, Stephen found himself able to forget.

What had he been like seven years ago? What world had he lived in, what heightened, dazed existence? It had seemed coherent at the time; the powerful feelings it had set loose in him, inflamed each day by the renewed pleasure of his senses, had appeared to make up something not only comprehensible, but important. In his life at that time he felt he had come close to understanding, even proving something, though what that thing was he could no longer say.

'What are you going to do in Amiens?' he asked Ellis.

'I don't know. I've never been on leave before. I don't know how much of normal life goes on. I'd like to go to a theatre, perhaps. What ought I to do?'

Stephen shrugged. 'Most people want to get drunk first, then go to a brothel.'

Ellis frowned. 'I don't think I should like that.'

Stephen laughed. 'Which? The getting drunk?'

'No, the . . . other.'

'I think you're supposed to. The army thinks it's good for your health to go with a woman regularly. The brothels are sanctioned by the military police.'

'Well, will you go?' said Ellis challengingly.

Stephen shook his head. 'No. I've no interest at all.'

'Well then. Neither shall I,' said Ellis.

'Who are you writing to?'

'My mother.'

Stephen smiled. 'I probably asked you at the wrong moment in that case. But I shall definitely go to a bar. You must let me buy you some champagne. That's how we'll start.'

Stephen did not at first recognize the station as the train slunk in. He was braced for memories, but none came. On the platform he looked up at the vaulted roof and then down towards the concourse. He and Isabelle had left from another platform on the far side of the station. He remembered a green door he had stared at from the carriage window as they waited to depart. He looked across the tracks and saw it, just as it had been.

It was mid-afternoon when he and Ellis emerged on to the cobbled forecourt of the station. It was an overcast day but with the first signs that the six-month winter might be starting to relax its grip. It had stopped raining, and the breeze did not sting them with cold.

They walked up towards the cathedral. Some of the old buildings bore the marks of shellfire. Only a few miles behind Allied lines, Amiens had suffered according to the tide of the war. The recent Allied advances had made it safe for the first time: there were no bombardments, and the local businessmen were trying to profit from the new calm in the Somme region. Shops were reopening; the eight o'clock curfew on bars and restaurants was lifted.

Stephen looked with fierce interest at the streets he remembered. Despite the occasional missing wall or patch of blackened masonry, they remained for the most part unchanged. He had not actively recalled them in the seven years he had been away; he had thought little about the town. Yet as he walked up the familiar ways, the streets remembered themselves in his mind.

At a corner was a half-timbered building through whose open window Isabelle had once heard a tune that had excited her, though not her husband's friend Bérard. To his right, down a narrower passage, was the restaurant to which he had so often gone for lunch. Perhaps his favourite seat would still be in the window; it was possible the same Parisian would be behind the bar.

'Ellis, do you mind if we go down here? There's a café I remember.'

'As long as it has champagne. Is it the Gobert? That's the one that was recommended to me.'

'I can't remember what it's called. It was run by a man who used to have a café in the Place de l'Odéon in Paris.'

They stood outside and Stephen peered through the window. The wooden stalls had gone. There was a bare counter on one side, and on the other some cheap-looking tables and chairs. He pushed open the door, a light piece of wood with netting over the glass that grated on the stone floor as it turned. There was no one inside. They went up to the bar, behind which were some under-stocked shelves.

A bald man with a lined, exhausted face and a greasy apron came stiffly downstairs and through a small door at the end of the room. He had a cigarette attached to his lower lip. He grunted a greeting. Stephen ordered two beers.

'Do you know what happened to the man who used to own this place?' he said.

'He's in Germany. A prisoner. They were rounded up in nineteen-fourteen.'

'Who were?'

'All the men in Amiens. When the Germans occupied the town.'

Stephen took the beer. 'You mean every man in the town was taken to Germany?'

The man shrugged. 'Only the stupid ones. And the cowards. The rest made their own arrangements.'

Stephen said, 'And what about you?'

'I was too old to be of interest to them.'

'What's he saying?' said Ellis.

'He says the man who used to run this restaurant was deported to Germany. It's a bleak little place, isn't it? It used to be very lively, full of students and so on.'

Stephen put down his beer glass among the uncleaned rings on the zinc counter. He had suddenly understood what had happened to all the students who used to shout out their orders and fill the air with their strong cigarette smoke. Those who had not died at Verdun would now be gathering for the attack on the river Aisne under their inspirational new general.

'Let's go,' he said. 'Let's find somewhere else.'

'Why? I was just beginning to –'

'It's too sad. Come on.' Stephen left some coins on the counter.

It was beginning to grow dark outside and Stephen was anxious not to blight Ellis's first leave with his own thoughts.

'You pick somewhere,' he said, 'and I'll buy the drinks.'

They walked past the cathedral, which was sandbagged to the level of the lower windows. The stone was intact, though some of the glass was missing. Stephen noticed how many of the women in Amiens seemed to be in the black clothes of mourning.

They stopped in a bar called Aux Huîtres, though there were no oysters for sale inside. It was full of soldiers of all nationalities: English, French, Belgian, Portuguese. Stephen bought champagne and filled Ellis's glass. He raised his own and they drank each other's health. Stephen had a desire to reach oblivion quickly. He was finding it harder than he had thought to adapt to this relatively normal world. It was the presence of so many soldiers that was disconcerting. He knew that many of them had been waist-deep in mud, crawling among the rats the day before. He looked at their polished belts and smoothly shaved faces. If they could laugh so genially now, of what other deceptions could they not be capable?

The women of Amiens who were not mourning for their dead husbands seemed well disposed towards the foreign soldiers. They accepted drinks and sat at the tables where they made attempts to understand the stilted French of the English officers.

Before he had finished his second glass, Stephen found that Ellis had volunteered him to help with some interpreting. There was an embarrassed major of about thirty who was drawing down lungfuls of pipe smoke to conceal his confusion as a fellow-officer from a Scots regiment tried to forge some intimacy between him and a loud Frenchwoman who was drinking red wine.

'Tell her he's keen to show her round his dugout,' said the Scot.

Stephen translated, then replied, 'She says she thinks he's a very handsome fellow and wonders if he would like to take her to dinner somewhere.' This was rather more forthright than what the woman had actually said.

The major tried to make a stammering answer of his own, but his French went no further than, 'Est-ce que possible pour,' after which he returned to his pipe with various chivalrous gestures in the direction of the woman.

'I think she'd like a drink,' said Stephen.

'I see. I'm terribly sorry, I –'

'Don't worry, I'll get her one. You carry on chatting.'

The Scot then attempted to explain why what Stephen had said was funny on the grounds that in the army 'chatting' meant trying to kill lice; he did not know the word for lice or for kill, so relied on insect-like gestures of his fingers and a smashing motion of his fist on the table. The woman shook her head in confusion, so he took a lighter and held it against the seam of his tunic, then lay on his back on the floor kicking his legs in the air.

Stephen returned to find the woman laughing uproariously. Ellis looked up at Stephen a little uncertainly, but on seeing him smile back, also began to laugh and bang the table. Others from around the bar looked over tolerantly in their direction. Stephen closed his eyes and drank quickly. He had bought a bottle of Old Orkney whisky at the bar, a tumbler of which he now washed down with the champagne. When he opened his eyes again, he felt a melting of warmth towards the other men. He was relieved.

The Scot said, 'Tell her he'd like to take her to Paris for the weekend on his next leave. He wants to go to the Moulin Rouge.'

'Moulin Rouge,' echoed the woman, laughing. 'Very good.'

She was congratulated on her English. She said to Stephen, 'Tell him I learned English from a general who was staying in the town.'

'She says she thinks you'll soon be promoted to the rank of general.'

The major shook his head in modest embarrassment. Something of his gaucherie reminded Stephen of Weir, and he felt a pang of pity for his absent friend. He wished he had been there, poor, strange Weir, who was so unworldly and yet, in the last way he wanted, experienced beyond dreams.

It was clear that it was the Scot himself who, under the

guise of helping his English friend, was hoping to impress the woman.

'Ask the lady if she lives in Amiens, will you? Ask her if she's a spare room for two well-behaved officers of one of the finest Highland regiments.'

The woman looked towards Stephen enquiringly. She had brown humorous eyes and a rosy colour to her skin. 'Well,' she said, 'I suppose he wants to sleep with me.'

Stephen checked a smile. 'I rather think so.'

The woman laughed. 'Tell him to find a house with a blue light. Or red, if he wants something cheaper. I will offer three men a first-class dinner, a room with clean sheets and fresh eggs and coffee in the morning, all for a reasonable price. But nothing else, I'm afraid. You can come if you like.'

'Thank you. Are there bars in the town where the local people go to drink? Not the soldiers, just the people who have always lived here.'

'Yes, there are two or three up that way, towards the rue de Beauvais, or what's left of it.'

'Come on, pal,' said the Scot. 'What does she say?'

'She says there are facilities for what you want.'

'Good heavens,' said the major, exhaling powerfully, 'she sounds like the oracle at Delphi.'

The Scot suddenly looked unsure, and Stephen was worried that he had dampened his enjoyment. 'No, no,' he said. 'She was very friendly. She'll give you a bed for the night and . . . I'm sure she wants to carry on with the party.'

The Scot looked relieved. 'Good, that's fine. Let's get some more drinks. Anderson, it's your turn.'

Stephen leaned across and said quietly in Ellis's ear, 'I'm going out for a moment. It's too hot in here. Just in case I don't come back, will you be all right? Have you got money?'

'Yes, I'm fine. I'm enjoying myself.'

Stephen poured him a glassful of whisky, then put the bottle in his pocket. 'All right,' he said. 'I'll see you later.'

It was winter again on the street, though Stephen was glad of the cold air against his face after the heat and smoke of the bar. He pulled his coat round him and turned up the collar. A dog was sniffing at the kerbstones. It moved smartly down an alley, its white tail high over its back in the weak moonlight. It had business to do; most of the town had business to do, and although the shops were closed and dark, Stephen could see through their windows to the silent counters behind which were the draper's bolts of cloth or the pharmacist's bottles. There would be the same exchange of formalities at the baker's the next day; the regular 'good morning' from each customer to the owner and then to the other customers; the bread politely bought with thanks on both sides. A stoical eyebrow or shrug might indicate that all was not quite as it should be, but that was understood. For the rest, their lives would go on as before, for the simple reason that they had no choice. Next to the baker was a butcher offering three grades of horsemeat. In the roads and ditches of the support lines there was certainly no shortage of the raw material, Stephen thought, though he tried not to imagine the quality of the lowest grade.

He heard singing from a bar on the far side of the street, and crossed over to inspect it. He went through the door and found himself again surrounded by soldiers, though these were almost all British subalterns. Their young faces were flushed with drink and many of them made a noise somewhere between speech and laughter, a kind of roar. Having stepped inside, he could not turn round and leave without seeming offensive, so he pushed his way to the bar and ordered a drink.

One of the young officers was playing a piano in the corner, though not all the men were singing the same song. A young man's face loomed up close to his.

'I haven't seen you in Charlie's before. What's your regiment?'

Stephen felt the man take and inspect a button on his tunic. He seemed unimpressed. 'Seen any action, have you?'

'Some.'

'Poor old donkeys. Always under the guns, aren't you?'

'Yes. Usually our own.'

'Don't take it like that. I'm most awfully sorry. I think I'm going to be sick.'

The young man pushed past Stephen and staggered to the door.

316

'You'd better go and look after your friend,' said Stephen to a lieutenant next to him.

'Oh God, not again. Been sick, has he? He's got the wind up, that's his trouble. Excuse me.'

Stephen felt himself pushed backwards and forwards by the packed wave of bodies at the bar. They began to sing all together in loud, confident voices. Eventually he extricated himself, and managed to fight his way to the door. He walked briskly towards the rue de Beauvais.

He found a bar with white curtains in the window. A couple of men were standing at the counter, resting their feet on the rail. They looked at him suspiciously, but nodded and returned his greeting.

Stephen took a drink and sat in the window. It was quiet and cool, and he was able to collect his thoughts. He closed his eyes and tried to relish the quiet, the absence of guns, but his mind was still too alert. He wondered whether, if he drank some more, it would bring the necessary degree of relaxation. What he really needed, it occurred to him, was the closeness of human contact, not forced by the proximity of war, but given willingly, from friendship.

When he opened his eyes and looked up, he saw that a woman had come into the bar and was buying a bottle of some green cordial. She had her back to him and wore a dark scarf over her head. When she turned, holding the bottle in her hand, Stephen felt his stomach tighten as shock waves passed through him into the palms of his hands.

As the woman looked round, she saw his agonized expression, and put her head a little on one side, defensively, but also in some concern. Her eyes met his then slid away as his gaze locked desperately on to hers.

She made for the door of the bar in some embarrassment, taking quick short steps that rang out on the wooden floor. Stephen, his mouth hanging open, scraped back his chair and staggered out after her, leaving the barman to call out that he had left no money.

Stephen ran over the cobbles outside until he had drawn up alongside the woman.

'Excuse me.'

'Monsieur, please leave me alone or I shall call the police.'

'No, listen. Please. I think I know you. I mean you no harm, I promise.'

Reluctantly the woman stopped and looked cautiously at Stephen. His eyes scanned her face, with its wide-set eyes and strong bones.

'Is your name . . . Forgive me, this may seem ridiculous if I'm wrong. Is your name . . . Jeanne?'

The woman seemed reluctant, but admitted it.

'And your family name. Fourmentier?'

She nodded without speaking. There was a trace of her sister Isabelle in her manner.

Stephen said, 'Do you know who I am?'

She looked up and into his eyes. Her expression was of resigned weariness. 'Yes. I think I do.'

'Do you mind that I stopped you?'

She did not answer. At that moment the barman arrived with Stephen's hat. Stephen thanked him and gave him money.

When the two of them were alone again, he said, 'Could we talk somewhere? There are some things I'd like to ask you.'

'All right. Follow me.'

Stephen followed. There was nothing he wanted to ask her, there was nothing he needed to know. In the moment that he had seen her face and guessed who she was he had had to make a choice, either to ignore her or to acknowledge her. Without time to consider, he had instinctively chosen the latter, with all that it might entail.

Jeanne went into the Place de l'Hôtel de Ville and sat down on a bench. Stephen stood uncertainly in front of her.

'We can't talk here. I mean, couldn't we go indoors somewhere?'

Jeanne shook her head. 'I don't want to be seen with you in a bar.'

'What about your house? Couldn't we . . . ?'

'No, we can't go there. What do you want to ask me?'

Stephen sighed deeply. His exhaled breath made fragile statues in the gaslight. He pulled his coat across his chest.

He said, 'Perhaps I should tell you something of what

happened.' He saw that Jeanne distrusted him and thought it might allay her fears if he could show that he wished no harm to her or Isabelle. He gave a brief account of his life with Isabelle, though he knew Jeanne would have heard the story before. If he could confirm things she already knew then he could prove his reliability. Jeanne nodded at intervals with a slight, noncommittal movement of her head.

As he talked, it became clear to Stephen what it was that he wanted to know, and he was taken aback by the simplicity of it. He wanted to know if Isabelle still loved him. Looking into the eyes of her elder sister, he saw enough of Isabelle for a sense of her presence to be rekindled in him. With the sense of her came back his curiosity.

'Then I arrived back in France and there has been this war ever since. I have not moved very much, just a few miles up and down the line. The years have passed. Maybe one day it will end.' He felt his account finishing lamely. He didn't want to give Jeanne too much detail of his life in the war; he presumed that such things would be familiar enough to her from her own family and friends. Nor did he want to appear as though he were trying to win her sympathy, when his own experiences were typical of those of millions.

'And what of you?' he said. 'Do you live in Amiens now?'

Jeanne nodded. She pushed back the scarf from round her head a little, and he saw the shape of her large, brown eyes and the almost translucent whiteness of her skin. Her face was more strongly and simply constructed than Isabelle's, with none of the contradictory shades of character and colouring, yet in the texture of Jeanne's skin there was delicacy as well as strength. Her voice was low and soft.

'I have lived here for some time. I came here to . . . I came when I was asked to come, last November.'

'Are you married?'

'No.'

'Do you live alone?'

'No, I live with . . . friends.'

It was impossible to say whether her reticence was general or whether there was something specific she wanted to conceal. Stephen's own monologue had clearly not set her entirely

319

at ease. A shiver ran through him as the wind whipped into the square from the north. He saw Jeanne pull her cape around her. He would have to be more direct.

'I want to know about Isabelle. I want to know if she's well and if she's happy. I've no wish to make things difficult. I'm aware that you probably think badly of me for breaking up her marriage, and whatever life she has now – I have no wish to disturb it. After six years I just wanted to know if she's all right.'

Jeanne nodded. 'All right, Monsieur? Yes, she's all right. You must understand that what you did caused great suffering, to her husband and particularly to his children. It was a scandal. Of course Isabelle is not absolved from responsibility. Far from it – her life is ruined because people do blame her for what happened. But as for you, there are people in this town who would gladly shoot you for what you did.'

'I understand. I never undertook it lightly, it was always a serious matter for both of us. Do you understand the nature of Isabelle's marriage to Azaire? Did she talk to you about that?'

'Isabelle has talked to me about everything, Monsieur. I am her only friend and confidante and she has poured into me all the passion, all the details that a normal person would share between numerous others – sisters, friends and family. I know everything.'

'Good. It's not that her unhappiness with him exculpates me or her, but it's important that you know about it and understand how it motivated her.'

Jeanne said, 'I don't blame anyone. I took my position rather as you took yours. Isabelle trusted me and I had no choice but to return her trust. I have been faithful to her in everything. I can't turn back or qualify that.'

Stephen felt pleased by what Jeanne said. 'It's true,' he said, 'that loyalty can't be partial, it must be complete. I want to assure you that my loyalty is to Isabelle's happiness, not to my own or anyone else's. You must trust me.'

'I don't know you well enough to trust you. I know what my sister has told me of you and that, together with what I have seen for myself, disposes me to believe you. But there are

320

things better left undone or unsaid. I think we should say goodbye now.'

Stephen laid his hand briefly on her wrist to restrain her from going. 'Tell me, why do you live in Amiens?'

Jeanne looked closely at Stephen before she eventually said, 'I came to look after Isabelle.'

'Isabelle lives here? She's here now? And what do you mean, "look after her"? Is she sick?'

'I don't want to tell you too much. I don't want to lead you on.'

'It's already far too late,' said Stephen. He could hear his voice echoing in the still square. He swallowed, and tried to lower it. 'Tell me, is she in Amiens? And is she unwell? What happened?'

'All right. I'll tell you, provided you agree to let me go when I've finished. I'll tell you all that you need to know and then I shall go home. You mustn't follow me or make any attempt to reach me. Is that understood?'

'Yes. I agree.'

Jeanne spoke carefully, as though measuring out the optimum levels of truth that could be told. 'Isabelle returned to Rouen, to my parents' house. It was my suggestion. They were reluctant to take her back, but I insisted. After some months my father made a deal with Azaire, that she would return to him. No, listen. Let me tell you. She had little choice in the matter. My father would otherwise have thrown her out. Azaire promised to make a new beginning, to take her back as though nothing had happened. Grégoire, his son, pleaded with her. I think it was he who persuaded her. She came back to him, to his old house. There were other reasons, which I can't tell you. In the first year of the war the town was occupied by the Germans, as you probably know. Many men were taken away, including Azaire. Then . . . well, time passed, things happened. Isabelle stayed. The house in the boulevard du Cange was hit by a shell and the back part of it was destroyed. No one was hurt, but Isabelle moved to an apartment in the rue de Caumartin. Lisette was married and Grégoire was old enough to leave school. He's going into the army next year. Then last November there was a heavy bombardment, and the house in the rue de Caumartin was hit. Isabelle was injured, but she was lucky. Two people in the street were killed. She wrote to me when she was in hospital and asked if I would look after her, so I came from Rouen. She's out of hospital now, and she's quite recovered, though she won't be quite . . . fit again. I'm staying with her for a few more weeks.'

'I see.' So strong was the sense of Isabelle evoked by Jeanne that it was almost, Stephen felt, as though she were sitting on the bench between them. Yet clearly something, or perhaps a great deal, was being withheld.

'I want to see her,' he said. The words surprised him. At no moment when he had been encamped in slime and mud had he wished her to be more real to him than the indistinct memory that infrequently visited him; he had not wanted to see her actual skin, flesh or hair. Something Jeanne had said had altered that indifference. Perhaps it was his anxiety for her well-being that made it important for him to rely on the evidence of what he could see rather than on what he remembered or what was told him by Jeanne.

Jeanne shook her head. 'No, that's impossible. It wouldn't be wise. Not after all that's happened.'

'Please.'

Jeanne's voice became tender in response to Stephen's. 'Think about it. Think of all the disruption and pain that was caused. To go back now, to reopen all those things, would be quite insane.' She rose to go. 'Monsieur, I have told you perhaps more than I should, but I felt when I saw you that I could trust you. I also felt that there was some small debt owing to you. When Isabelle left you she gave no explanation, but I think you were honourable in your way. You did not pursue her or make her life more difficult than it was. I think you deserved at least to be told what I have told you. But my loyalty is now with Isabelle and, as you were saying, such things must be complete, they cannot be compromised.'

Stephen stood up next to her. 'I understand,' he said. 'Thank you for trusting me as much as you have. But let me ask you one thing. Will you at least tell Isabelle that I'm here? Tell her that I would like to see her, merely to wish her well in one short visit. Then she can decide for herself.'

Jeanne pursed her lips in great reluctance and began to shake her head. Stephen cut her off. 'That wouldn't be disloyal. It's simply allowing her to make up her own mind. It's still her own life. Isn't it?'

'All right. It's against my better judgement, but I'll tell her we've met. Now you must let me go.'

'And how will I know?'

'I'll meet you in the same bar at nine o'clock tomorrow evening. Now I must get back.'

They shook hands and Stephen watched the tall figure disappear across the square with the bottle of cordial clutched in her hand.

HE WALKED ACROSS the town towards the boulevard du Cange. He left the cathedral behind him, its cold Gothic shape fortified by the stacked bags full of earth, as though its spiritual truths were not in themselves proof against exploding metal, and descended to the banks of the canal where, in the warm evenings of his first visit to the town, he had watched the shirt-sleeved men casting their rods hopefully over the tamed, diverted waters of the Somme.

It had come alive again. What he had thought dead and reduced to no more than fossil memory was beginning to leap and flame inside him. He had never foreseen such a thing, even at the deepest moments of solitude, under the worst bombardments, when he had had to look for his most childlike, fundamental means of reassurance. At no stage had he drawn on the memory of Isabelle or of what had passed between them as a source of hope or meaning, or even as an escape from the pressing reality in which he found himself. Meeting Jeanne, however, had done something extraordinary to him: it had reduced the events of the last three years to something if not comprehensible, then at least contained.

He crossed to the southern end of the boulevard and began walking. He could not believe that the house would be there; it had the same unreliable quality as his memory of dying, when his life had lured him back with uncertain promises, or of his recollection of passages of battle, when time had seemed to collapse.

Then he saw the red creeper that grew up to the stone

balcony on the first floor; the formidable front door with its ornate ironwork; the grey slate roof that plunged in various angles over the irregular shape of the rooms and passageways it covered. Its solid, calm façade had an unquestionable solidity.

The taste of those days returned to his mouth. He could smell the polish on the wooden floors applied by the maid whose name was . . . Marguerite; the wine Azaire habitually served at dinner, a dry tannic red, not cheap but thick and dusty; then the sounds of footsteps, their deceptive ring seeming closer or further than they really were; the smell of pipe tobacco in the sitting room; and the clothes that Isabelle had worn, the hint of rose, their stiff cleanness and the sense she gave of having not merely dressed, but dressed up, as though in a costume that suited not the house but some other world she inhabited in her mind. They came back to him with pressing clarity, as did his own feeling at the time that Isabelle's withheld, inner life would in some way accord with his own. As he stood in the dark street, looking over at the house, he remembered too the rapturous urgency with which he had found that he was right.

He crossed the street to look more closely. The gates were locked and there were no lights inside. He walked on a little so that he could see the side of the house. A long sheet of tarpaulin was held in place at the back, and there were signs of repair work, with piles of brick waiting to be cleared. From what Stephen could see, it appeared that a large section of the rear of the house had been destroyed. They would have been using heavy guns in any case, and this must have been a direct hit, or possibly two. Stephen calculated that most of the main sitting room was destroyed, and several lesser rooms downstairs. Above them had been the back bedrooms, including the maids' quarters and the red room.

He sat down at the edge of the road, beneath a tree. He was overcome by the power of his memory. It was all clear again in his mind, as though he was reliving it. The ready-laid fire in the red room, the medieval knight, the clematis against the window . . . He tried to keep back the flood of complete recollection, yet at the same time he felt revived by it.

He stood up and began to walk away from the house, towards the town and then along the banks of the canal. He briefly wondered if Ellis would be all right on his own. There were plenty of billets in town, and friendly officers to show him where to go. He himself had no desire to sleep. He was close to the river gardens, the fertile enclosures through which he had punted one stifling afternoon with Azaire and his family and Monsieur and Madame Bérard.

Throughout the night he walked, occasionally stopping to rest on a bench in an attempt to clear his mind. When dawn came he was in the Saint-Leu quarter, where he heard the first signs of the day's activity as bakers lit their ovens and metal milk churns were brought clanking down the street on hand-pulled wagons.

At seven o'clock he ate fried eggs and bread in a café, with a bowl of coffee. He washed and shaved in a small room at the back indicated by the owner. He was so used to not sleep-ing that he felt no ill effects from the night. Perhaps he could find somewhere they were showing a film; if not, he would buy a book and read it in the gardens by the cathedral.

He passed the day in fitful expectation. During the after-noon he slept more deeply than he had expected in a room he took in a small hotel. In the evening he changed his clothes and prepared to meet Jeanne. As he walked towards the bar he noticed that his clean shirt, like his old one, had lice in it.

Shortly after nine Jeanne came into the bar. Stephen put down his drink and stood up. He pulled out a chair for her. He was barely able to go through the formalities of offering her a drink and asking after her health as his eyes searched her face for some indication of her news.

'And did you speak to Isabelle?'

'Yes, I did.' Jeanne, having declined the drink, sat with her hands folded on the table. 'She was surprised to hear that you were in Amiens. Then she was even more surprised to hear that you wanted to see her. She wouldn't answer until this evening. It's very difficult for her, Monsieur, for a reason you'll see. Eventually she agreed. I am to take you to the house this evening.'

Stephen nodded. 'All right. There's no point in delaying.' He felt quite cold, as though this were a routine matter, like a trench inspection.

'All right.' Jeanne stood up. 'It's not far to walk.'

They went down the dark streets together in silence. Stephen felt that Jeanne would not welcome questions from him; she seemed dourly set on her mission, about which she clearly had private doubts.

They came at last to a blue front door with a brass handle. Jeanne looked up at Stephen, her dark eyes glowing in the shade of the scarf wrapped round her head. She said, 'You must make of this what you will, Monsieur. Be calm, be strong. Don't upset Isabelle. Or yourself.'

Stephen was moved by her gentleness. He nodded his agreement. They went into the house.

There was a dim light in the modest hallway, which had a table with a bowl of daisies beneath a gilded mirror. Jeanne went upstairs and Stephen followed. They went along a small landing and came to a closed door at the end.

'Wait here, please,' said Jeanne as she knocked at the door.

Stephen heard a voice answering from inside. Jeanne went in. He heard the sound of chairs being moved and of low voices. He looked around him, at the pictures either side of the door, at the pale distemper of the walls.

Jeanne reappeared. 'All right, Monsieur. You can go in.'

She touched his arm in encouragement as she went past him and vanished down the corridor.

Stephen found his mouth had gone dry. He could not swallow. He put his hand to the door and pushed it open. The room was very dark. There was only one lamp, on a side table, beneath a heavy shade. On the far side of the room was a small round table, of the sort people might play cards on. On the other side he could see Isabelle.

He took a few steps into the room. This is fear, he thought; this is what makes men cower in shellholes or shoot themselves.

'Isabelle.'

'Stephen. It's good to see you.' Her low voice was the same he had first heard fill the room under Bérard's boorish prompting; it slid along each nerve of his body.

Stephen went closer so that he could see her properly. There was the strawberry-chestnut hair and wide eyes; there was the skin, if it had been bright enough to see it properly, in whose changing patterns and colours he had seen the rhythm of her inner feelings.

And there was something else. The left side of her face was disfigured by a long indentation that ran from the corner of her ear, along the jaw, whose natural line seemed broken, then down her neck and disappeared beneath the high collar of her dress. He could see that the flesh had been folded outwards. It had healed and dried; the ear had been well repaired. The altered line of the jaw, however, gave an impression of the great impact that must have struck her, and although the wound was closed, the sense of this force made it still seem immediate. The left side of her body was awkwardly held against the chair, as though it lacked independent movement.

Isabelle followed his tracking eyes. 'I was injured by a shell. I expect Jeanne told you. First the house in the boulevard was hit, then the place where we'd moved in the rue de Caumartin. It was unlucky.'

Stephen could not speak. Something had closed his throat. He raised his right hand with the palm towards her. It was supposed to indicate that he was glad she was alive, that he had seen much worse, that he felt sympathetic, and many other things, but it conveyed little.

Isabelle seemed to have prepared herself much better. She continued calmly, 'I'm happy to see you looking so well. You've gone a little grey, haven't you?' She was smiling. 'But it's good that you've survived this awful war.'

Stephen was grinding his teeth. He turned away from her, his fists clenched. He shook his head from side to side, but there was no voice. He had not expected this sensation of physical impotence.

Isabelle went on speaking, though her voice began to falter. 'I'm glad you wanted to see me. I feel very pleased that you've come. You mustn't worry about this injury. I know it's ugly, but it gives me no pain.'

The words went perilously on, addressing Stephen's back. Slowly he began to assert himself over the feelings that raged inside him. The sound of her voice helped him. He drew on all the strength of mind he had, and gradually assumed control of himself.

It was with relief and some pride that he heard a sound at last issue from his throat as he turned to face her. He was saying, like Isabelle, simple, empty things. 'I was fortunate enough to run into your sister. She's been very kind.'

He met her eyes and went over to the table, where he sat down opposite her.

'I was lost for words. I'm sorry. It must have seemed rude.'

Isabelle stretched out her right hand across the table. Stephen took it between both of his and held it for a moment. He withdrew his grip, not trusting himself to keep it there.

He said, 'Isabelle, would you mind if I had a glass of water?'

She smiled. 'My dear Stephen. There is a jug on the table in the corner. Help yourself. Then you must have some English whisky. Jeanne went out specially for it this afternoon.'

'Thank you.'

Stephen crossed to the table. After he had drunk the water he poured some whisky into the glass. His hand barely trembled and he was able to compel a smile as he turned back.

'You've kept safe,' she said.

'Yes, I have.' He took a cigarette from a metal case in his tunic. 'The war will last another year at least, perhaps more. I can hardly remember a life before it. We don't think about it, those of us who have survived.'

He told her how he had been wounded twice and how he had recovered on each occasion. Their conversation seemed quite passionless to him, but he was content that it should be.

Isabelle said, 'I hope you're not shocked by the way I look. Really, I was lucky compared to some others.'

Stephen said, 'I'm not shocked. You should see what I have seen. I won't describe it to you.'

He was thinking of a man he had seen whose face had been opened up by a bullet, a mere rifle shot. A neat triangle was made with its apex in the middle of his forehead and the two lower corners on the mid-point of each jaw line. Half of one eye remained, but there were no other features left except for some teeth buried at an angle; the rest of the face was flesh turned inside out. The man was conscious and awake; he could hear and follow instructions given to him by the medical officer. Compared to his wound, Isabelle's was discreet.

And yet he had lied. He was shocked by it. As he grew used to the light he could see where the skin at her left temple was stretched, so that it pulled the eye slightly out of shape. It was not the severity of it that appalled him, it was the sense of gross intimacy. Through her skin and blood he had found things no exploding metal should have followed.

Eventually, when some rapport was established, she ventured to tell him what had happened to her. She moved quickly over references to their life together, even to St-Rémy or other places they had visited.

'So I returned to Rouen, to the family house. It was like being a child again, but there was no innocence, no sense of many possibilities ahead. In some ways it was kind of them to take me, but I felt imprisoned by my failure. Can you imagine? It was as though I had been sent back to begin again because I'd been no good.

'My father gently introduced the idea of my returning to Amiens. I didn't think at first he could be serious. I imagined that Azaire would never want to see me again – to say nothing of the scandal. But my father is a shrewd negotiator. He dealt with it just as he had dealt with the marriage in the first place. He brought Lisette and Grégoire over to see me. I wept with happiness when I saw them again. Lisette had grown up so much, she was a young woman. She didn't need me to come back, but she was kind when she might easily not have been. And Grégoire pleaded with me. I was overcome by them. I couldn't believe they were so forgiving after what I'd done to their father. They just said it was forgotten. I think having lost one mother they would do anything not to lose another. And they forgave me. They forgave me because they loved me, just for who I was.

'Then there was the meeting with Azaire, which I dreaded. The strange thing was that he seemed quite ashamed. Because I'd left him for another man, I think he felt diminished. He was quite meek with me. He even promised to be a better husband. I couldn't really believe all this was happening. I had no wish to return. What decided me was how unhappy I was at home – something my father cleverly exploited.'

'You went back?' said Stephen. It did not make sense to him; it was inconceivable, unless there was some part of the story that Isabelle had withheld.

'Yes, Stephen, I went back, not willingly, but because I had no choice, and it made me very unhappy. I regretted it the moment I stepped back inside the house. But this time I knew I could never change my mind. I would have to stay. Within a few months what they call "society" had taken me back. I was asked to dinner by Monsieur and Madame Bérard. It was the old life, though even worse. But I was saved by the war. Perhaps that's why I'm philosophical about this.' She touched her neck with the fingers of her right hand. Stephen wondered what it felt like.

'That August British troops came through the town. I watched them, half-expecting to see you. People sang "God Save the King". Then things began to look bad. At the end of the month the army decided not to defend the town. They left us to the mercy of the Germans. I wanted to leave but Azaire was a town councillor and he insisted on staying. We waited for two days. It was agonizing. Eventually they arrived – they marched in down the road from Albert, up the rue Saint-Leu. For a moment or two there was a festival atmosphere. But then we learned of their demands. The mayor had two days to provide them with an enormous amount of food and horses and equipment. As a guarantee they wanted to be given twelve hostages. Twelve councillors volunteered. My husband was one of them.

'They'd come to the house on the boulevard du Cange and taken it over to accommodate a dozen German officers. My husband was kept in the council chamber that night. They were very slow producing all the food, and the Germans threatened to kill the twelve men. They trained a huge battery of guns on the town. The next day we heard that the hostages had all been freed, but then it turned out that the mayor had not paid enough money, so four of them, including my husband, were held. After three days of this uncertainty, the Germans agreed that their terms had been met, and all the councillors were free to return. But the city under this occupation was a different place.'

Isabelle moved quickly over the next part of the story. It did not reflect well on anyone involved.

All men of service age were required to present themselves for deportation. Many took the chance to leave town, but four thousand willingly gave themselves up. The Germans were embarrassed by their docility. They lacked the capacity to deal with such numbers. They released all but five hundred willing prisoners whom they marched out of town. By the time they reached the suburb of Longueau the less fearful saw that there were no effective restraints on them and went quietly home. At Péronne those who had not made their own arrangements were put in requisitioned French cars and driven to Germany. Azaire, who saw his duty as a councillor to lie with the men of Amiens, went with them. Although his age made him the object of several informal offers of release, he was steadfast in his determination to be with the wronged people of his town.

For Isabelle the city under occupation was certainly a different place; though to her in the house on the boulevard du Cange the occupation brought freedom.

The German officers were punctilious and good-humoured. A young Prussian called Max paid special attention to Isabelle's two-year-old daughter. He took the child into the garden and played with her; he persuaded his fellow-officers that care of the girl should excuse Isabelle from looking after their needs, which could be done adequately by the army servants. Isabelle was allowed, at his insistence, to keep the best room for herself.

When she recounted the story to Stephen, Isabelle made no mention of the child. It was for the baby's sake that she had agreed to return first to Rouen and then to Amiens: the child needed a home and family. She could not bring herself to mention the girl to Stephen, even though she was his daughter. She had kept her pregnancy a secret from him and had sworn Jeanne not to tell him. She believed that if he knew about the child it would make matters more painful and complicated between them.

For the same reason that she withheld the fact of the child's existence, however, she did tell Stephen about Max. She thought it would make things simpler and more final for Stephen if he knew.

The occupation lasted only a few days, but in the compressed time of war it was long enough for Isabelle to fall in love with this soldier who played with her infant daughter and made her own comfort his special charge. He was a man not only of great courtesy, but of imagination, stability and humour. For the first time in her life she felt she had met someone with whom she could be happy under any circumstances, in any country. He was dedicated to her well-being and she knew that if she returned that simple fidelity, no circumstances, no alterations, not even wars, could disrupt their simple, enclosed contentment. Compared to her passion for Stephen it was a muted affair, and yet it was not shallow; it made her profoundly content, and confident that at last she would be able to become the woman that she was meant to be, unhampered by restraint or deceit, and within a life that would be calm and helpful for her child.

Max appeared gratifyingly excited by what he described as his great good fortune. To Isabelle's modest surprise he seemed barely able to believe that she should return his feelings. His incredulity brought a lightness and brilliance to him in the short time they were together. The only darkness in Isabelle's mind concerned his nationality. At times when she lay awake at night she thought of herself as a traitor, not once or even twice now to her husband, but three times over, and most significantly, to her country and her people. She could not understand why she seemed to have attracted this strange fate when she remained in her own eyes such an uncomplicated creature, the same little girl who had wanted merely some love or attention, some natural human exchange as a child in her parents' house. Why was it that her simple desires had turned her into so extravagant an outcast?

This was the problem that stayed knotted, intractable, whichever way she drew it or examined it inside her. It brought misery to her when she dwelt on it; yet she had also a developed instinct for the practicalities of survival. Max was a man of flesh and blood, a good man, a human soul, and in the end this was more important than the accident of nationality, even at such a terrible time. Isabelle's natural feeling for the enduring, hard choices of daily living made her able to drive onwards to what she felt was right, regardless of what she thought of a larger, but ultimately theoretical consideration.

She corresponded with Max. She travelled secretly to Vienna to see him when he was on leave. Their long separations did nothing to diminish her feelings; they enforced her determination. This was her final chance to redeem herself and create a life for her daughter.

In June 1916 Max's regiment was moved to reinforce a previously quiet sector on the river Somme near Mametz. Isabelle received Stephen's letter from the line. For six months she could not bring herself to read a newspaper. The thought of Max and Stephen fighting was unendurable. She wrote to Max from hospital. The news of her injury redoubled his devotion. The more difficult it became, the more important they both knew that it was for them to honour the pledges they had made to each other.

'It isn't easy,' said Isabelle. 'These choices are all very, very difficult. But the longer the war goes on, the more determined we have become.'

She finished speaking and looked over at Stephen. He had said nothing during her account. She wondered if he had really understood it all. Because she had made no mention of the child, it had seemed much harder to explain than she had expected. She was aware that he seemed puzzled.

He had changed almost beyond recognition, she thought: certainly much more than he appeared to know. His hair was shot with grey, as was his untrimmed moustache. He was badly shaved, and he scratched his body all the time, apparently without knowing it.

His eyes had always been dark, but now they seemed shrunk. There was no light in them. His voice, which had once reverberated with meanings and nuances, with temper and emotions held in check, was now alternately toneless or barking. He seemed a man removed to some new existence where he was dug in and fortified by his lack of natural feeling or response.

Isabelle was greatly moved by the sight of these changes, but feared to reach out more than a hand to whatever world he now inhabited. She would shed tears for him when he had gone, but not until the practical business of his enlightenment had been completed.

Stephen took another cigarette from his case and tapped it slowly on the table. He smiled, surprisingly, a wide, sardonic movement of his lips. 'You've certainly not taken any easy path, have you?'

Isabelle shook her head. 'Though I didn't willingly ask to face any of these difficulties. They seemed to happen to me.'

'How's Lisette?'

'She's married. Much to my husband's irritation she married Lucien Lebrun. You remember, the man who organized the strike.'

'I remember. I used to be jealous of him. And is she happy?'

'Yes. Very happy, except that Lucien is in the army. Grégoire will join up next year if the war's still going on.'

'I would like to see Lisette. She was a nice girl.'

'She lives in Paris.'

'I see.' Stephen nodded. 'What's that noise?'

'It must be the cats. Jeanne has two of them.'

'It sounded like a child.'

They heard footsteps in the corridor. A door opened and closed.

Isabelle was aware that beneath Stephen's expressionless manner there was some powerful urge or desire.

He said, 'Isabelle, I'm glad of all these things you've told me. I don't wish to see you again now. This was all I needed to know. I wish you well with your German friend.'

Isabelle felt unforeseen tears welling up in her eyes. Surely he would not leave on this note of downcast generosity. She had not wanted to see him so broken.

He leaned forward across the table. He said with a slight catch in his voice, 'May I touch you?'

She looked into his dark eyes. 'You mean . . . ?'

'Yes.' He nodded slowly. He held out his right hand. She took it in hers, feeling the large, roughened fingers. Slowly, with a little tremor in her own grip, she guided it across her face and laid it on her jaw, just below the ear.

She felt his fingertips gently run down the cleft in her skin. She wondered if they were soft enough for him to feel the quality of her flesh or whether they were too calloused to register the different texture of what they touched.

She was overcome with desire as his fingers probed the abrasion. It was as though they were not on her cheek, but were opening the flesh between her legs; she felt again the soft intrusion of his tongue; she re-experienced the ecstasy of abasement and possession. Her skin flushed with blood; there was a melting in her belly and a hot gush of liquid. She was blushing with arousal, her skin beating and burning under her dress.

His head was quite steady, his eyes following the slow course of his hand through the turned furrow. When it reached the top of her dress, he left it for a moment, the fingers resting in the wound. Then he laid the back of his hand across the soft, unharmed skin of her cheek, as he had done so many times before.

He stood up and left the room without speaking. Isabelle heard him talking to Jeanne at the head of the stairs, then his footsteps going down. She covered her face with her hands.

IT WAS LATE afternoon and the light was already fading when Stephen arrived on the concourse of the station. He saw Ellis waiting at the head of the platform and walked over to him.

'What happened to you?' said Ellis nervously. He sounded annoyed.

'I met a friend.'

They found two seats on the train and Stephen looked out of the window as the station slid back behind them.

Ellis lit a cigarette. 'It's like that time of day on Sunday when you expect to hear the first bells of evensong,' he said. 'I'd give anything not to have to go back.'

Stephen closed his eyes. He no longer had strong opinions on what he wanted or did not want to do. The train would take them in its own time.

The next day he went to see Colonel Gray at battalion headquarters.

Gray put down his book as Stephen opened the door to his office, which was the converted parlour of a farm.

'Sit down, Wraysford. Did you have a good leave?'

'Yes, thank you, sir.'

'I'm afraid your company's going back to the front line tomorrow.'

'I don't mind,' said Stephen. He crossed his legs and smiled at Gray. 'We just go on and on. Until it's finished.' He liked Gray because he was direct. Only his penchant for strange psychological theories worried him.

Gray lit his pipe. 'I'm under pressure to put you in for a staff job,' he said. 'This time you'll have to take it.'

Stephen tensed himself. 'I haven't gone this far to abandon the men now.'

Gray spoke quietly. 'Which men?'

'The men I've been with for more than two years.'

Gray shook his head in silence and raised his eyebrows. Stephen swallowed and looked down at the floor.

'They're gone, Wraysford,' said Gray. 'They're all gone. You can't name more than two from your original platoon.'

Stephen licked his lips. There were tears in his eyes.

Gray said, 'You're tired.'

'No, I'm –'

'You're not shirking anything. I know you go on raids and patrols. I heard you were even down the tunnel with the miners. No, it's not that. You're tired in your mind, Wraysford. Aren't you?'

Stephen shook his head. He could not answer. It was so long since anyone had spoken to him with this degree of sympathy.

'It's nothing to be ashamed of. Good heavens, you've done as much as anyone in this battalion. The best you can do now is help brigade staff. They need your French. It's no use being fluent in a shellhole.'

'How long for?'

'A few months, that's all. There's a little trouble brewing in the ranks of our French allies. We need to know exactly what's happening because you can be sure they won't tell us themselves.'

Stephen nodded. He could see no line of profitable resistance.

'First there'll be home leave. And you're not going to get out of that this time, either.'

Gray's batman, Watkins, brought in tea and some walnut cake sent by Gray's wife in England.

They ate in silence for a moment, then Gray said, 'There was a bad incident with some enemy prisoners in B Company. Did you hear? It was after a long bombardment and the men were worn down. There was a raid and they took a dozen

Boche. When they discovered they had to escort them uphill five miles in the rain, they took them to the edge of a copse and killed them. The officer turned a blind eye.'

Stephen was aware that Gray was watching his response closely. It was possible, he thought, that Gray had even invented the story to test him. 'They should be charged,' he said.

'And I thought you were so hard towards our German friends,' said Gray, with the slight increase in Scots accent that meant he was intrigued.

'I am,' said Stephen, putting down his tea cup. Even in battalion headquarters it tasted of the petrol can it had been carried in. 'I find that the hardest part of my job, trying to get the men to hate them as much as I do. It's all right when we're in rest or reserve, but the closer we get to the front the more they start talking about "poor old Jerry". The worst thing is when they can hear them talking or singing, then I know we're in trouble. I remind them of their dead friends.'

'And what about you?'

'I have no difficulty in keeping the flame of hatred alive,' said Stephen. 'I'm not like them. I've learned to love the rule book, to be bloodthirsty in the way it prescribes. I only have to think of my men, of what they have done to them, of how they died.'

Stephen was agitated. He tried to calm himself in case he should say something injudicious. He was thinking of Brennan, whose brother had gone missing on patrol some days before.

Gray was nodding with intellectual excitement, like a surgeon who has found a gallstone that will be the talk of the medical papers.

'I don't think officers are supposed to live at a pitch of personal hatred for the enemy,' he said. 'They are supposed to be bloodthirsty, by all means, but with a clear head, and with regard to the safety of their men.'

'I have had that thought in my head all the time,' said Stephen. 'If you've seen what you and I did last July then you never wish to see the life of one of your men needlessly lost again.'

Gray tapped his teeth with his teaspoon. 'Would it please you to kill large numbers of the enemy – personally, with your own hands?'

Stephen looked down at the table. His mind was heavy with the thought of Isabelle and her Prussian. He pictured what he would do if he were to meet the man. He would find no difficulty, no awkwardness at all, in pulling the trigger on his revolver; he would not hesitate to take the pin from a grenade. He was not sure what Gray expected him to say. His thoughts were clouded, but a single strand was clear: that having come this far, with so many men dead, it would be insane to compromise or turn away. He told the truth as it then occurred to him. He said, 'Yes. A great number.'

'And yet you feel punctilious about a mere dozen prisoners who were shot by men whose lives they had made miserable.'

Stephen smiled. 'I know what they're like – the way they surrender as soon as they can no longer kill you in safety, all that "Kamerad" and souvenirs. But somehow there is a propriety. It sounds strange, but we have degraded human life so far that we must leave some space for dignity to grow again. As it may, one day. Not for you or me, but for our children.'

Gray swallowed, and nodded, without speaking. Eventually he said, 'We'll make an officer of you one day. First you must forget your hatred. Do you remember when I came to see you in hospital? I told you to stop playing with all that voodoo nonsense. Did you?'

'I do it on special request for Captain Weir. No one else.'

'You don't believe in it yourself?'

'I fix the cards. How could I believe in it?'

Gray laughed and brushed some crumbs from his mouth. 'And what do you believe in?'

'War.'

'What do you mean?'

'I want to see how it will end.'

'Anything else?' Gray had resumed his inquisitive doctor's expression.

'Sometimes,' said Stephen, who was too tired to be evasive, 'I do believe in a greater pattern. In different levels of experience; a belief in the possibility of an explanation.'

340

'I thought so,' said Gray. 'With most people it's the other way round. The more they see, the less they can believe.'

Stephen stood up. He said forcefully, 'I saw your face that July morning we attacked at Beaumont. I took my orders from you at the head of the communication trench.'

'And?'

'I looked in your eyes and there was perfect blankness.'

Gray, for the first time since Stephen had known him, seemed wrong-footed. He coughed, and looked down. When he could meet Stephen's eye again, he said, 'Those are intimate moments.'

Stephen nodded. 'I know. I was there. I saw the great void in your soul, and you saw mine.'

THEY BURIED ARTHUR SHAW and Bill Stanley, the man who had died with him. First they had to disinter them from their unscheduled burial place in the tunnel. It took working parties of four men three days to dig their way through, timbering as they went, until they got to the bodies. It was a dangerous exercise which Weir himself advised against; but since he was still resting behind the lines, the men were able to impress their willingness to find the bodies on the temporary company commander, a malleable character called Cartwright.

Jack Firebrace stood between Jones and Evans, their caps clasped in their hands as the padre read the prayers for the funeral service. Handfuls of earth were thrown in on top of the men. Jack felt unsurprised at what had happened. There had seemed to him no reason to suppose that his friend would survive any more than his son. When he heard the explosion in the German tunnel he waited for the news to come: two men had been down there, one had been Arthur Shaw. He merely nodded when Fielding told him. The random violence of the world ran supreme; there was no point in trying to find an explanation.

They sang a hymn, 'There is a green hill far away', which Jack knew Shaw had liked. Far away indeed, thought Jack, looking down to the yellowish mud around his boots. A bugle sounded. The men moved off heavily, lifting their feet from the earth. For the final time Shaw went back under the ground.

Jack's section was in reserve, billeted in a farm hut. Tyson, Shaw and he had clubbed together to buy a small primus stove, which was now his sole property. He invited Jones and Evans to a tin of Maconochie's stew, which Evans supplemented with some beans and a cake he had been sent from home.

'This is no good,' said Jack. 'We ought to be drinking his health.' He went to the door of the hut and tipped the mess of stew and beans out on to the ground.

When it was dark they found their way back through the support lines to a village where Fielding told them there was a friendly estaminet. They followed his instructions and came to a room in a cottage behind the main street.

By the time they arrived Jack found his hands badly in need of heat. The cuff of his uniform rubbed against the frozen veins and sent what felt like small electric shocks through his fingers. His body ached for warm water. The estaminet was crammed with men, standing round the walls and trying to push their way closer to the cooker at the end of the room, on which a deep pan of oil was spitting. Two women were throwing in handfuls of potatoes which they served with fried eggs, to the loud enjoyment of the men lucky enough to have found a place at the long table.

Jack pushed his way through to where a woman was handing out glasses of pale beer. Jack knew through watery experience that this was no way to get drunk. He asked for a bottle of white wine, and Jones commandeered some syrup from a man who was leaving. They drank the bottle quickly, while Evans shouted abusively at the old woman who was frying eggs. She swore back happily until eventually his turn came.

They bought more wine and drank it with the greasy potatoes, which tasted exquisite to them, fresh and hot and redolent of home. Jack wiped his mouth on his sleeve and lifted his glass. Evans and Jones were standing close to him in the crush.

'To Arthur Shaw,' said Jack. 'The best mate a man could have.'

They drank, and drank again, Jack with the rhythmic, slow determination he brought to his work at the tunnel face.

There was this memory of Shaw, this painful memory, kept in place by his sober, conscious mind. He would hack away that sobriety, bit by bit, until it all was gone, taking the memory with it.

The estaminet had to shut at eight-thirty, when the military police would come to make sure there were no men left there. With twenty minutes to go the speed of drinking increased. Evans began to sing, and Jones, whose Welsh forebears had gone to London many generations earlier, found enough Celtic memory in his veins to support him. Then they put up Jack Firebrace to do his music-hall turn.

Jack felt inspired as Evans called the room to silence. He launched into some familiar jokes and found that the men's initial resentment at having their conversations interrupted soon turned to loud appreciation. He looked forward to the punch line of each joke with professional calm, leaving little pauses to build the men's excitement. The drink made him unselfconscious and detached; he felt as though he had gone beyond the stage where he might slur his words or forget his place and had aimed instead at a new clarity. There was something disdainful, almost cruel in his confidence.

The men loved the jokes, though they had heard each one before. Jack's manner was persuasive; few of them had seen the old stories so well delivered. Jack himself laughed little, but he was able to see the effect his performance had on his audience. The noise of their laughter roared like the sea in his ears. He wanted it louder and louder; he wanted them to drown out the war with their laughter. If they could shout loud enough, they might bring the world back to its senses; they might laugh loud enough to raise the dead.

Jack drank more wine from a jug that an appreciative man passed up to him. He crossed the line from his state of particular calm, given by his complete loss of inhibition, into a raging incoherence, where he imagined that what he felt and what he wanted – this great release of laughter – could be brought on merely by urging, and not by his cold concentration on the means to that end. He began to repeat the crucial words of the jokes and to conduct the audience response with his arms. Some of the men looked puzzled, others started to lose interest in the entertainment and to resume the conversations they had broken off.

Jack always ended with a song. It was odd how the cheapest, simplest things were the best; these were the ones that enabled the men to think of home, each in his own mind. He began to sing, 'If you were the only girl in the world'. His voice rose, and he waved his arms in invitation to the men to join with him. Relieved that his stories were finished, many added their voices to his.

Seeing their faces, once more friendly and approving, Jack was moved and encouraged. The features of his dead friend came back. Shaw had been, in this strange alternate life, the only person in the world to him: his handsome head with its level eyes, his muscular back and huge, broken-nailed fingers. Jack could almost feel the supple shape of Shaw's body as it had curved to accommodate him in the narrow, stinking dugouts where they had slept. The words of the foolish song began to choke him. He felt the eyes of the growing audience, friendly once more, boring into him. He looked out over their red, roaring faces as he had once before looked out when singing this same song. At that time he had told himself that he had no wish to love any of these men more than any other, knowing what lay in store for them.

The hot, noisy room moved dizzily in front of his tear-filled gaze. I have made this mistake in my life, Jack thought: not once but twice I have loved someone more than my heart would bear.

With this hopeless thought in his mind, he fell forward off the chair into the arms of his friends Jones and Evans, who took him away into the night under the puzzled but indifferent eyes of his fellow men.

Two days later came the rare drama of divisional baths. Jack's company was marched three miles back from the front to an old brewery. Jack enjoyed the ritual and was amused at the optimism of a succession of young officers who were sure that this brief plunge would cure the hygiene problems of the men for good.

Jack had at first viewed the lice on his body as simple

parasites whose presumption had made him indignant. The way they dug their ugly fawn-coloured bodies into the private pores of his skin had revolted him. He took great pleasure in holding a lighted candle and working it slowly up the seams of his clothes where the insects lurked and bred. Usually their fiery deaths were silent, though occasionally he would hear a satisfying crackle. He would do Shaw's clothes for him too because Shaw did not have the necessary delicacy of hand and was liable to set fire to his underwear. If there was no candle available, a fiercely applied thumbnail was effective up to a point. There was a sense of relief when some of the creatures were gone, though it was like the crushing of a blood-gorged mosquito: Jack always felt they had no right to be there in the first place. The evident advantage in cutting back the numbers was the temporary relief it gave from the sour, stale smell the creatures left, though even this relief was qualified, since the odour was usually compounded or overwhelmed by stronger and more persistent bodily smells.

Jack, like most of the men, scratched almost all the time, unconsciously, and gradually less aware that he did so. Not all of them were resigned. Tyson had once been driven so frantic that the medical officer ordered him to have fifteen days' rest. The constant irritation had proved more wearing to him even than the sound of heavy guns or the fear of dying.

At the old brewery the men lined up and handed in their clothes. The underwear was thrown into a pile, a grey crawling heap that it fell to the most unfortunate refugees to pick up and take to the divisional laundry. The men joked at the women who had to perform the task. They wore gloves and carried handkerchiefs over their faces. Jones offered his gas mask to one thin, wretched Belgian woman who did not understand. They gave their tunics and trousers to others who, under the direction of Jack's platoon sergeant, carried them to the corner of the barn-like room where a Foden Disinfector, a machine that was dragged optimistically up and down the front line, was supposed to fumigate them.

Jack climbed into a tub with several men from his platoon. The water was still warm, though soapy from the previous occupants. They rubbed themselves all over and laughed at the feel of the heat on their skin. No showers had been provided for the men who dug the Underground in London; Jack had had to go home grimed with sweat and clay. Here, in the old beer barrels, there was a moment of friendship and relaxation such as he had barely known. Evans and O'Lone began to splash the water at each other, driving it up with the flats of their hands. Jack found he had joined in. He felt guilty for a moment towards the memory of his dead comrades, as though he were not being respectful, but the feeling passed. He would take any pleasure that helped.

Afterwards they stood shivering while the quartermaster checked the issue of clean shirts and underwear. With their outer clothes returned from the disinfector, they stood smoking in the weak sunlight of spring. The weather had begun to change. Though still cold with a deep chill at nights, the air during the day had thickened. Jack thought of the daffodils that would be coming out along the banks of the canal at home. He remembered how he had played with John, teaching him how to bait a line, or kicking a ball backwards and forwards for hours. He had hoped that this practice would make John better able to join in the games of the other boys in the street, though it seemed to make little difference. All Jack could see was the boy's cheeks flushed pink with excitement as he ran back towards him clutching the ball, which looked oversized against his narrow chest. He could hear his lisping, excited voice, cutting the foggy air with its unblunted innocence and glee.

He turned his mind away and looked down at his boots. He stretched his feet inside the clean socks. They formed up to march back to their billets. That evening they would be doing trench repair work in the front line. The difference between being in the front line and being in reserve, as Evans remarked, was that when you were in the front line at least you were allowed to be underground, beyond the reach of shells.

By the time they had reached their billets Jack felt the first irritation on his skin. Within three hours the heat of his body as he marched had hatched the eggs of hundreds of lice that had lain dormant in the seams of the shirt. By the time he reached the front his skin was alive with them.

THE NEXT MORNING there was a letter for Stephen from Amiens. He had never seen the handwriting before, but it had a family resemblance to one that had left notes to him in St-Rémy or messages for the delivery boys in the boulevard du Cange. He took it to his dugout and opened it alone, when Ellis had gone out to talk to the sentries. It was the first letter he had received since the war had started.

He turned the envelope round in the light, marvelling at his name on it. He opened it and felt the strange intimacy of the blue, crackling paper.

Jeanne wrote to say that Isabelle had left Amiens to go to Munich, where her German had returned home after being badly wounded. Max had had to pay an enormous sum to get her out through Switzerland. Isabelle had said goodbye to her and would never return to France. She was an outcast in her parents' family and in the town.

'When you asked me if I would write to you,' the letter concluded, 'you said you would like to hear about normal life. I don't think either of us expected that I would begin with such important news. However, since you asked for details of domestic life in Amiens, let me tell you everything is fine here. The factories are busy supplying uniforms to the army. Of course now that the men no longer wear red trousers, the clothes are not so exciting to make. Life is surprisingly normal. I expect to stay a little longer before returning to Rouen. If you would care to visit on your next leave, I can assure you that it would be acceptable to me. You could dine at the address you visited last time. The food supplies are not as good as in peacetime, but we probably do better than you soldiers at the front. With good wishes from Jeanne Fourmentier.'

Stephen laid the letter down on the rough surface of the table, in the grooves of which the rat's blood had dried. Then he rested his head in his hands. He had received an answer to the simple question that had intrigued him. Isabelle no longer loved him; or if she did, she loved him in some distant way that did not affect her actions or her feelings for another man.

When he looked into his reserves of strength he found that he could bear this thought. He told himself that the feeling they had had for each other still existed, but that it existed at a different time.

Once when he had stood in the chilling cathedral in Amiens he had foreseen the numbers of the dead. It was not a premonition, more a recognition, he told himself, that the difference between death and life was not one of fact but merely of time. This belief had helped him bear the sound of the dying on the slopes of Thiepval. And so he was now able to believe that his love for Isabelle, and hers for him, was safe in its extreme ardour – not lost, but temporarily alive in a manner as significant as any present or future state of feeling could be in the long darkness of death.

He put Jeanne's letter in his pocket and went out into the trench where Ellis came sliding along the duckboards to meet him.

'Quiet, isn't it?' said Stephen.

'Tolerable,' said Ellis. 'I've got a problem. I'm trying to get a working party to go out and bring back some bodies. It's pretty quiet, as you say, and we may not have a better chance.'

'So what's the problem?'

'My men wouldn't do it unless I went too. So I said I would. Then they insisted on having at least one miner with them, but the miners' CO says it's nothing to do with them and in any case they're fed up with doing our fatigues.'

Ellis's white, freckled face was agitated. He pushed the cap back from his forehead to show a puckered hairline from which the gingerish hair had started to recede.

Stephen smiled vaguely and shook his head. 'We should all go. It doesn't matter. It's only death.'

'Well, will you tell Captain Weir to get one of his sappers out with us?'

'I can ask him. Perhaps he'd like to come too, now that his arm's better.'

'Are you serious?' said Ellis crossly.

'I don't know, Ellis. There's something about you that makes me quite unsure. Get your working party ready for twelve o'clock. I'll see you in the next firebay.'

Weir laughed drily when Stephen made the suggestion.

'There'll be rum,' said Stephen.

Weir's eyes opened in interest.

Then when the moment came it brought a sudden fear and unreality. They could never be prepared to look at death in the crude form that awaited them. Stephen felt, as he had done before at moments of extreme tension, a dislocation in his sense of time. It seemed to stutter, then freeze.

At noon on the firestep in gas masks. Taste of death, smell of it, thought Stephen. Coker slashed sandbags into gloves. 'Wear these.' Firebrace and Fielding of the miners, Ellis, white like milk, Barlow, Bates, Goddard, Allen of the infantry; Weir taking rum on top of whisky, unsteady on the step of the ladder.

'What are you doing, Brennan?'

'I'm coming too.'

They tracked out towards a shellhole, the sun bright, a lark above them. Blue sky, unseen by eyes trained on turned mud. They moved low towards a mine crater where bodies had lain for weeks uncollected. 'Try to lift him.' No sound of machine guns or snipers, though their ears were braced for noise. 'Take his arms.' The incomprehensible order through the gas mouthpiece. The arms came away softly. 'Not like that, not take his arms *away*.' On Weir's collar a large rat, trailing something red down his back. A crow disturbed, lifting its black body up suddenly, battering the air with its big wings. Coker, Barlow shaking their heads under the assault of risen flies coming up, transforming black skin of corpses into green by their absence. The roaring of Goddard's vomit made them laugh, snorting private mirth inside their masks. Goddard, releasing his mask, breathed in worse than he had expelled. Weir's hands in double sandbags stretched out tentatively to a sapper's uniform, undressing the chest in search of a disc which he removed, bringing skin with it into his tunic pocket. Jack's recoil, even through coarse material, to the sponge of flesh. Bright and sleek on liver, a rat emerged from the abdomen; it levered and flopped fatly over the ribs, glutted with pleasure. Bit by bit on to stretchers, what flesh fell left in mud. Not men, but flies and flesh, thought Stephen. Brennan anxiously stripping a torso with no head. He clasped it with both hands, dragged legless up from the crater, his fingers vanishing into buttered green flesh. It was his brother.

When they got back to the safety of the trench Jack was angry that he and Fielding had been made to go, but Weir pointed out that there were three men from their company unburied. Goddard could not stop vomiting, though his stomach was long since empty. When he was not retching, he sat on the firestep, weeping uncontrollably. He was nineteen.

Michael Weir had a rigid smile. He told Fielding and Jack they were excused fatigues for a week, then went to Stephen's dugout in the hope of whisky.

'I wonder what my father would say,' he said reflectively. 'Of course they're all "doing their bit", as he put it.' Weir swallowed and licked his lips. 'It's just that his "bit" and mine seem so different.'

Stephen watched him and shook his head fondly. 'You know what I really dreaded?' he said. 'What frightened me was the thought that one of those men was going to be alive.'

Weir laughed. 'After all that time?'

Stephen said, 'It's been known.' He had a thought. 'Where's Brennan? Did you see him when we got back?'

'No.'

Stephen went along the trench looking for him. He found him sitting quietly on the firestep near the dugout where he and half a dozen others slept.

'I'm sorry, Brennan,' he said. 'That was a terrible thing for you. You needn't have come.'

'I know. I wanted to come. I feel better now.'

'You feel *better*?'

Brennan nodded. He had a narrow head, with thick, black greasy hair on which Stephen was looking down. When he turned his face up, its features were calm.

Stephen said, 'At least wash your hands, Brennan. Get some chloride of lime on them. Take some time off if you want to. I'll tell your sergeant you're excused fatigues.'

'It's all right. I feel lucky in a way. You know last July when I fell off the firestep when the mine went up and I broke my leg? Then watching you lot go over the top. I was lucky.'

'Yes, but I'm sorry about your brother.'

'It's all right. I found him, that's the thing. I didn't let him lie there. I got him back and now he'll have a proper burial. There'll be a grave that people can see. I can come and put flowers on it when the war's over.'

Stephen was surprised by how confident Brennan was that he himself would survive. As he turned to go, Brennan began to sing softly to himself, an Irish song that he had sung on the morning when they waited to attack. His voice was a grating, persistent tenor and he knew many songs.

All night he sang for his brother, whom he had brought home in his hands.

THERE WAS AN excited party of young officers in the dining room of the Hotel Folkestone in Boulogne. Many of them had been at the front no more than six months and had stories to tell their friends and families. The war was not going too badly for them. They had witnessed mutilation and death; they had undergone the physical discomfort of cold, wet and fatigue such as they had never thought themselves capable of enduring, yet they could still see this pattern of service at the front alternated with regular home leave as something tenable, for a short time at least. They drank champagne and boasted to one another of what they would do when they got to London. They had not been there for the great slaughters of the previous year and could not foresee the mechanized abattoir that was expected in the impassable mud of Flanders in the months to come. The horror of the entr'acte was bearable; they shuddered with the joy of survival, and chafed each other with the exhilaration of their relief. Their young voices rose like the squawl of starlings beneath the chandeliers.

Stephen heard them in his room on the first floor, where he was writing a letter to Jeanne. His hip flask, filled with the last of his whisky at Arras, was almost empty, and the ashtray was full. Unlike the men under his command, who wrote home daily, he had had little practice as a correspondent. The men's letters, which he read wearily, consisted of reassurances to those at home, comments on the contents of the parcels received, and requests for more news.

Stephen did not think Jeanne needed reassurance about his

353

well-being; neither would she enjoy details of trench life. While he compelled himself not to mention Isabelle, he thought it sensible to write about things common to both him and Jeanne. This meant talking about Amiens and how its people and buildings survived.

What he wanted to say to Jeanne was that she, apart from Michael Weir, was the best friend he had. Since he might be dead within the month, there seemed no reason not to say so. He wrote: 'It means a great deal to me to receive your letters, to have some contact with a sane world. I appreciate your kindness to me. Your friendship enables me to survive.'

He tore up the page and threw it in the wastepaper basket by his feet. Jeanne would not appreciate such things; it was precipitate and vulgar on his part. He needed to be more formal, at least for the time being. He rested his head on his hands and tried to picture Jeanne's long, wise face in his mind.

What was this woman like? What would she want him to say? He imagined her dark brown eyes beneath their arched brows. They were intelligent, sardonic eyes, and yet they had a quality of great compassion. Her nose was similar to Isabelle's but her mouth was wider, with a darker colouring in the skin of the lips. Her chin was sharper, though quite small. The strength of her features, the darkness of her colouring and the forbidding quality of her eyes, gave her a faintly masculine appearance; yet the beauty of her pale skin, not expressive like Isabelle's but quite even in its ivory colouring over her face and neck, spoke of extraordinary delicacy. He did not know how to approach her.

He wrote some details of his train journey to Boulogne and promised that he would write from England, when at least he would have something interesting to tell her.

When the boat arrived in Folkestone the next day there was a small crowd assembled on the quay. Many of the boys and women waved flags and cheered as the mass of infantry came up the gangplank. Stephen saw the looks on the faces of the crowd change from gaiety to bewilderment: for those come to greet sons or brothers these were the first returning soldiers they had seen. The lean, expressionless creatures who stepped ashore were not the men with gleaming kit and plump smiles who had been played aboard by the regimental bands. Some wore animal skins they had bought from local farms; many had cut pieces from their coats with knives to increase their comfort or to bind their cold hands. They wore scarves about their heads instead of caps with shining buttons. Their bodies and their clothes were encrusted with dirt and in their eyes was a blank intransigence. They moved with grim, automatic strength. They were frightening to the civilians because they had evolved not into killers but into passive beings whose only aim was to endure.

Stephen felt a hand on his arm. 'Hello. Are you Captain Wraysford? My name's Gilbert. I'm in charge here. Couldn't make it out with you chaps – bad leg, I'm afraid. Now look, you take these forms and when you get to the station I want you to liaise with the embarkation officer. All the men's names are here. Got that?'

Stephen looked at the man in bemusement. His body gave off an acrid, rotting smell when he came close to show him the forms.

On the station platform were further crowds of well-wishers. There were tables on which voluntary organizations were offering tea and buns. Stephen walked to the head of the platform and, when he was obscured from the throng by the bulk of the red-brick waiting room, dropped the thick bundle of forms into a liveried litter bin.

The train started with men lining the corridors, sitting on their kit, smoking and laughing, waving to the people on the platform. Stephen gave his seat to a woman in a blue bonnet.

Jammed up against the window of the compartment he could see little of England as it went past in flashing squares visible only occasionally beneath the angle of his armpit. The sight of his homeland had not brought any feeling of affection or deep welcome. He was too tired to appreciate it. All he could feel was the pain in his lower back from trying not to bang his head against the luggage rack above. In time, perhaps, he would appreciate the countryside and the sounds of peace.

'I'm getting out at the next stop,' said the woman in the

bonnet. 'Would you like me to telephone to your wife or your parents and tell them you're on your way?'

'No. No, I . . . don't think so. Thank you.'

'Where is your home?'

'Lincolnshire.'

'Oh dear, that's a long way.'

'I'm not going there. I'm going to . . .' He had had no plans. He remembered something Weir had once said to him. 'To Norfolk. It's very nice at this time of year.'

At Victoria Station Stephen pushed and fought his way out into the street. He wanted to see no more soldiers but to lose himself in the great blankness of the city. He walked briskly up through the park to Piccadilly, then slowly along the north side. He went into a well-stocked gentleman's outfitter near the foot of Albemarle Street. Many of his clothes had gone missing in transit a year before and he needed at least a change of shirts and underwear. He stood on the planed floorboards looking into the glass-topped cases with their extensive displays of coloured ties and socks. A man in a morning suit came down behind the counter.

'Good morning, sir. Can I help?'

Stephen saw the man's eyes run down him and register his uniform and rank. He also saw, beneath his formal politeness, an involuntary recoil. He wondered what it was about him that repelled the man. He did not know if he smelled of chloride of lime or blood or rats. He reflexively put his hand up to his chin but felt only a minimal scratch of beard that had grown back since he had shaved in the Hotel Folkestone.

'I want some shirts, please.'

The man went up a ladder and pulled out two wooden drawers which he brought down and laid out in front of Stephen. There were white, stiff-fronted shirts for evening wear and collarless cotton striped for the day. As Stephen demurred the assistant brought more drawers down with shirts of every colour and fabric they had in stock. Stephen gazed at the array of pastel colours, the great arc of choice that the man fanned out in front of him, their buttonholes finished by hand, the pleats of the cuffs nipped and pressed, their textures running from the rigid to the luxuriously soft.

'Excuse me, sir. I must just attend to this other customer while you make your choice.'

The assistant backed away, leaving Stephen confused by the decision and by the man's attitude to him. With the other customer, a large man in his sixties in an expensive overcoat and homburg hat, he was much more effusive. After several items had been charged to his account, the man wandered out of the shop, heavily, without acknowledging Stephen. The assistant's smile froze, then faded, as he returned. He kept a certain distance.

Eventually he said, 'I don't wish to hurry you, sir, but if you're not happy with our choice it would perhaps be better if you tried elsewhere.'

Stephen looked at him incredulously. He was about thirty-five with sandy hair receding on either side and a neat moustache.

'I was finding it difficult,' he said. His jaw felt heavy as he spoke. He realized how tired he was. 'Excuse me.'

'I think perhaps it would be better if –'

'You don't want me in here, do you?'

'It's not that, sir, it's –'

'Just give me these two.' He picked out the shirts nearest him. Ten years ago, he thought, he would have struck the man; but he merely offered him the money and left.

Outside, he breathed deeply on the thick air of Piccadilly. Across the street he saw the arches of the Ritz Hotel with its name lit up in bulbs. Women in trimmed fur coats and their escorts in sleek grey suits and black hats went through the doors. They had an air of private urgency, as though they were bent on matters of financial significance or international weight that would not even permit them to glance towards the ingratiating smile of the doorman in his top hat and gold frogging. They disappeared through the glass, their soft coats trailing behind them, oblivious to the street or to any life but theirs.

Stephen watched for a moment, then walked along with his service valise towards Piccadilly Circus, where he bought a newspaper. There had been a financial scandal and an accident at a factory in Manchester. There was no news of the war on the front page, though later, next to the readers' letters, was a report on Fifth Army manoeuvres and warm praise for the tactical expertise of its commander.

The further he walked, the more isolated he felt. He marvelled at the smoothness of the undamaged paving stones. He was glad that an ordinary life persisted in the capital, but he did not feel part of it. He would have been embarrassed to be treated differently from ordinary civilians by people in a country he in any case had not lived in for some time, but it seemed strange to him that his presence was a matter not just of indifference but resentment. He stayed the night in a small hotel near Leicester Square, and in the morning took a taxi to Liverpool Street.

There was a train to King's Lynn at midday. He had time to go to a barber and have a haircut and shave before he bought a ticket and wandered up the platform. He climbed on to a half-empty train and found a seat at leisure. The upholstery of the Great Eastern Railway was plush and clean. He sank into a corner seat and took out a book. The train jerked and clanked its way slowly out of the station, then began to gather speed as it left the low, grimed terraces of north-east London behind.

Stephen found he could not concentrate on the book. His head seemed too clogged and numb for him to be able to follow the simple narrative. Although there was some stiffness in his limbs he did not feel the ache of fatigue in any physical way; he had slept reasonably well in his small hotel room and breakfasted late. His mind, however, seemed hardly to function at all. He was capable of doing little more than sitting and staring at the landscape that went by. The fields were lit by a spring sun. The occasional narrow stream or river went quietly through them. On the rise of hills he could once or twice make out the grey spires of churches, or a cluster of farm buildings, but for the most part he saw only this flat, agricultural land, apparently uninhabited, whose deep, damp soil was going through the same minute rotations of growth and decay, invisible but relentless, as they had done for centuries beneath the cold, wet sky by day, by night, with no one to see.

Yet as the train clattered onward it seemed to sound a rhythm in a remote part of his memory. He dozed in the corner seat and awoke with a start, having dreamed he was in the Lincolnshire village of his childhood. Then he found he was still asleep: he had only dreamed that he had awoken. Again he found himself in a barn in a flat, pale field, with a train going by. A second time he awoke, in some fear, and tried to keep himself conscious; but again he found that he had only dreamed his awakening.

Each time his eyes opened he tried to stand up, to lever himself off the plush seat of the carriage, but his limbs were too heavy and he felt himself slide under again, just as he had once seen a man in his company slip on the duckboards of the trench into an uncovered sumphole where he had drowned in the clinging yellow mud.

At last he managed to catch himself in a moment of waking and force his legs up. He stood at the window and gazed at the fields.

It took some minutes before he could convince himself that he was not dreaming. The sensation felt no different, to begin with, from the half-dozen times he had thought himself awake, only then to find that he was still asleep and had dreamed it.

Gradually some clarity returned to him. He held tight to the frame of the window and breathed deeply. The sense of disorientation diminished.

I am tired, he thought, as he pulled a cigarette from its case. I am tired in my body and in my mind, as Gray pointed out. Perhaps Gray, or one of his Austrian doctors, could also explain the curious sequence of hallucinating dreams.

He straightened out his uniform and pushed his hair into place where he had ruffled it in sleep. Pulling back the door of the compartment, he wove his way down the swaying carriage to the restaurant car. Only two tables were taken and he was able to seat himself by the window. The steward waddled down the aisle with a menu.

Stephen was surprised by the choice. It had been years since he had been confronted with such variety. He asked for consommé, then sole, and steak and kidney pudding. The waiter offered him the wine list. His pocket was filled with English banknotes he had bought with his pay in Folkestone. He ordered the most expensive wine on the list, which was six shillings a bottle.

The steward hovered with a ladle full of boiling soup, most of which he deposited into the crested plate, though by the time he had finished, the starched white cloth bore a long trail of brown. Stephen found the soup too strong to be pleasant; the taste of fresh beef stock and seasoning confused him. He had not eaten lunch or dinner in Amiens and his palate had grown used to Tickler's plum and apple pudding, bully beef and biscuits, with only an occasional slice of cake sent out from England to Gray or Weir.

The little fillets of sole with the delicate film of veins and intricate white layering of flesh were too subtle for him to taste. With some ceremony the steward then poured an inch of wine into the crystal glass. Stephen swallowed quickly and told him to pour. While he waited for the steak and kidney pudding, he drank properly. He found the taste of it over-powering. It was as though his whole head had been filled with small explosions of scent and colour. He had not tasted wine for six months, and then only a rough, unlabelled white. He put the glass down quickly. Water at the front tasted simply of water if it had come up with the rations, or something worse if it had been sieved from shellholes; tea had an equally straightforward flavour – of petrol, from the cans in which it was carried. But when he drank this wine it felt as though he were drinking some complex essence of France itself, not the visceral inferno of Picardy, but a pastoral, older place where there was still hope.

He was evidently even more tired than he had thought. He ate as much of the steak and kidney pudding as he could. He passed over the dessert and smoked a cigarette with coffee. At King's Lynn he took a branch line along the Norfolk coast towards Sheringham, which he thought was the place Weir had recommended. However, he found as the small train puffed along that he was impatient with travelling. He wanted to be outside in the clear, peaceful air; he longed for an inn with a soft bed. At the next station, a village called Burnham

Market, he hauled his valise down from the luggage rack and jumped out on to the platform. He was able to walk into the village itself, which was bisected by a road on either side of which was a plush, well-kept green. Most of the houses that overlooked it had been built in the eighteenth century; they were spacious but modest and were interspersed with half a dozen shops, including a chemist, a chandler and a place that sold equipment for horses.

Behind a huge chestnut tree was a long, low-built inn called The Blackbird. Stephen went into it and rang a bell on a counter at the foot of the stairs. No one answered, so he went into the stone-flagged bar. It was empty, though there were still uncollected beer glasses from lunchtime on the tables. It had a dark, cool atmosphere given by the floor and the heavy wooden beams.

He heard a female voice behind him and turned to see a plump woman in an apron who smiled a little uncertainly as he met her eye. She told him she was only the cleaner and the landlord was out for the afternoon, but she could let him have a room if he would sign the register. She showed him upstairs to a small bedroom with a mahogany chest of drawers and an old wooden bedstead with a fat white eiderdown on it. There was one ladder-backed chair by the door and a washstand with a china jug and basin. Just by the door was a small bookshelf with half a dozen well-read volumes on it. Beyond the chest was a window that overlooked the green at the front of the hotel where the chestnut tree's white blossom blocked out the sky. Stephen thanked the woman and threw his valise on to the bed. It was the kind of room he had wanted.

When he had unpacked he lay down on the bed and closed his eyes. He wanted to sleep, but his eyelids were flickering too much. Each time sleep seemed near his body jolted him back from it. Eventually he fell into a half-waking state, like the one he had found on the train, in which brightly illuminated scenes from the last two or three years occurred at random in his mind. Incidents and men he had forgotten recurred with vivid immediacy, and then were gone. He tried to pull himself back from the lurid sequence of memories. He kept

361

seeing Douglas falling off the stretcher on the slippery floor of the trench as a shell landed; he could hear the lifeless thump of his passive body. A man he had forgotten, called Studd, came back to his mind, his helmet blown back and his scalp raked by machine gun bullets as he bent to help another man who had fallen.

Stephen climbed off the bed. His hands were shaking like Michael Weir's during a bombardment. He breathed in deeply, hearing the air catch in his chest. It seemed to him extraordinary that he should be feeling the shock now, when he was safe in a tranquil English village.

The thought of his surroundings stirred him. It was a long time since he had been in England. Perhaps it would be good for him to walk outside and look at it.

His boots echoed on the uncarpeted wooden steps as he went down, hatless, into the hall and out into the air.

He heaved his shoulders up, then let them drop in a long, broken sigh. He began to walk along the green, then turned down a lane that led away from the village. He tried to relax himself. I have been under fire, he thought; but now, for the time being, it is over. Under fire. The words came back. How thin and inadequate the phrase was.

The hedgerows were deep and ragged where he walked, covered with the lace of cow parsley. The air had a feeling of purity as though it had never been breathed; it was just starting to be cool with the first breeze of evening. From the tall elms he could see at the end of the field there was a sound of rooks, and a gentler calling of wood pigeons close at hand. He stopped, and leaned against a gate. The quietness of the world about him seemed to stand outside time; there was no human voice to place it.

Above him he saw the white moon, early and low above the elms. Over and behind it were long jagged wisps of cloud that ran in ribbed lines back into the pale blue of the sky, then trailed away in gestures of vaporous white.

Stephen felt himself overtaken by a climactic surge of feeling. It frightened him because he thought it would have some physical issue, in spasm or bleeding or death. Then he saw that what he felt was not an assault but a passionate affinity.

It was for the rough field running down to the trees and for the path going back into the village where he could see the tower of the church: these and the forgiving distance of the sky were not separate, but part of one creation, and he too, still by any sane judgement a young man, by the repeated tiny pulsing of his blood, was one with them. He looked up and saw the sky as it would be trailed with stars under darkness, the crawling nebulae and smudged lights of infinite distance: these were not different worlds, it seemed now clear to him, but bound through the mind of creation to the shredded white clouds, the unbreathed air of May, to the soil that lay beneath the damp grass at his feet. He held tightly on to the gate and laid his head on his arms, in some residual fear that the force of binding love he felt would sweep him from the earth. He wanted to stretch out his arms and enfold in them the fields, the sky, the elms with their sounding birds; he wanted to hold them with the unending forgiveness of a father to his prodigal, errant but beloved son. Isabelle and the cruel dead of the war; his lost mother, his friend Weir: nothing was immoral or beyond redemption, all could be brought together, understood in the long perspective of forgiveness. As he clung to the wood, he wanted also to be forgiven for all he had done; he longed for the unity of the world's creation to melt his sins and anger, because his soul was joined to it. His body shook with the passion of the love that had found him, from which he had been exiled in the blood and the flesh of long killing.

He lifted his head, and found that he was smiling. He walked in peace along the road for perhaps an hour, though he had no track of time. The evening stayed light as far as he went, the fields in their different shades and the trees in lines or clumps or alone where a chance seed had dropped.

As the road fell and turned a corner he found himself coming into a small village. There were two boys playing on a big green space beyond a ditch that separated it from the road. Stephen went into a pub opposite and found himself in what looked like a private parlour. An irritable old man asked him what he wanted. He fetched beer from an unseen barrel in a back room; with the pint mug he brought a smaller glass containing some cinnamon drink. Stephen took both glasses outside and sat on a bench by the green, watching the boys at play until the sun at last went down and the white moon glowed.

STEPHEN WENT BACK a day early to France so that he could visit Jeanne in Amiens. His transfer to brigade staff had been delayed by a fortnight, and he was to rejoin his company at the front in the meantime. He thought the return to the war might be made easier if he had spent a night in France before going on to whatever billet Gray had meanwhile allocated him.

Amiens station had the look of an old landmark to him, though he found to his surprise when he counted that this was only the third time he had actually arrived at it. The first time had led to extraordinary and unseen consequences and so, in a way, had the second. On this occasion there would certainly be no Isabelle; perhaps there would be no drama or reverse at all. He hoped so.

Jeanne had decided to trust him, and he felt grateful to her. There was no need for it, but it showed generosity and imagination on her part, he thought, unless it was only pity. He found it difficult to know what kind of feelings he awakened in people now, but even if Jeanne's impulse was merely one of charity to an uncouth soldier, he would not turn it away. She was a kind woman. He wondered why she had not been married: she must be thirty-eight or nine, almost too old to have children.

He had sent a telegram from Boulogne, and had awaited her reply. She would be happy to see him that evening, she said, at any time.

He walked up through the town, still with his awkward

service valise. He was wearing one of the new shirts he had bought in London, with new underwear. As far as he could tell, the lice that had plagued him had perished in the bonfire he had made with his old clothes in Norfolk. As he passed through Liverpool Street on his return, he asked the barber to remove his moustache. He had begun to feel almost like the young man who had arrived at the boulevard du Cange.

He crossed the square with the café in which he had met Jeanne and came to the small house in which she had been lodging with Isabelle. He rang the bell. As he waited he tried to remember what Jeanne looked like, but no picture came to his mind.

'Come in, Monsieur.' Jeanne held out her hand.

Stephen found himself once more in the modest hallway, though it seemed more brightly lit this time. Jeanne opened a door on the right into a sitting room. It had a shiny wooden floor and a circular table with freesias in a glass bowl. There were armchairs on either side of the marble mantelpiece.

'Are you tired after your journey?'

'No, not at all. I feel very well.'

Stephen sat in the chair that Jeanne indicated for him, and looked up at her. He did remember the strong features of her face and her pale skin; when he looked at them they made him calm. In the set of her eyes and the turn of her head there were occasional flickers of Isabelle, something impetuous that was transformed and stilled in the gravity of Jeanne's demeanour.

Jeanne said, 'She told me you stared a lot.'

Stephen apologized. 'These years in the mud – I've lost my manners.' He was glad that the subject of Isabelle had come up so soon. At least they could then dispose of it.

'Have you heard from Isabelle?'

'Yes,' said Jeanne. 'She's very happy. Max is badly hurt, but he's going to survive. She asked me to thank you for coming to see her. I think it meant a good deal to her. She has been very unlucky – or very foolish, as my father would say. All her decisions have been difficult ones. To see you again and to know that you at least wished her well, I think that sustained her.'

'I'm pleased,' said Stephen, though he did not feel pleasure.

It confused him to think the role he now played in Isabelle's life was to offer minor reassurance. 'I'm pleased,' he repeated, and in that moment of small insincerity he thought he felt the last presence of Isabelle leave him, not by going into false oblivion, as she had the first time, but into simple absence.

He turned to Jeanne. 'How long will you stay in Amiens? Isn't your home in Rouen?'

Jeanne looked down at her hands. 'My father's old and would like me to stay and look after him. Although my mother's still alive, she's not well and is less attentive than he would like.'

'So you will go back?'

'I don't know,' said Jeanne. 'I've been a dutiful daughter. But I'm drawn to the idea of independence. I like it here in Amiens, in this little house.'

'Of course.' Stephen thought of her age again. 'What about your other sisters? Couldn't they look after him?'

'No. They're all married. Now, Monsieur, we're going to have dinner in about an hour. I'll have to go and see how it's coming along. I'm not sure if you'd like to rest, or have some apéritif . . . I'm not used to this sort of thing.' She waved her hand. 'It's somewhat unconventional.'

'Nothing in the world is conventional at the moment.' Stephen smiled. 'I'm grateful that you understand that. In the meantime, yes. I'll have a drink.

Jeanne smiled back at him. It was the first time he had seen her smile, and he believed it was the most extraordinary expression he had seen on a human face. It began with a slow widening of the lips, then the pale skin of her face became radiant, not with blood as Isabelle's might have done, but with an inner light that made it shine. At last it reached her eyes, which developed squares of brilliance as they narrowed into trusting humour. It was not just her expression, Stephen thought, but her whole face that had changed into something forgiving and serene.

She said, 'There is something Isabelle sent me out to buy when you came before. It smells horrible. It's called Old Orkney. It's an English drink.'

Stephen laughed. 'Scottish, I think. I know it well.'

Jeanne brought the bottle and a jug of water. Stephen poured a little into a small crystal glass and looked around the room while Jeanne went to the kitchen. He could hear the sound of pans and cutlery; a smell of herbs and wine caused a sudden rush of hunger in his stomach. He lit a cigarette and searched the elegant little room for an ashtray. There were a number of small ceramic and china dishes, but he dared not risk them and flicked the ash into the fireplace where he rubbed it in with his foot. For all his new lice-free clothes, he felt lumpish and awkward in this tidy, feminine room. He wondered if he would ever refind his ease and naturalness in normal surroundings, or whether he had now evolved into a creature whose natural habitat was corrugated-iron ceilings, wooden walls and food hanging in rat-proof parcels from the rafters.

Jeanne had made soup that she served from a bowl on a table at the end of the room. It was supposed to be a fish soup in the manner of Dieppe, near her home in Normandy, she explained, but she had not been able to find all the ingredients she needed in Amiens. Stephen remembered how irritated Isabelle had once been when he said that Amiens was not noted for its cuisine.

'I expect the war has affected supplies,' he said.

'I'm not sure,' said Jeanne. 'It may be that the Amiénois are just not interested in food. Would you like to pour the wine? I don't know if it's good, but it's one I've seen my father drink.'

Stephen was still not sure whether Jeanne viewed him as a refugee whom someone public-spirited should foster, or if she had simpler motives of friendship. He questioned her as they ate.

She was not generous with information. Her manner had a pleasant shyness about it, as though she felt that the evening was not really permitted by the rules of etiquette and at any moment someone might come in and forbid it to continue. Stephen gathered that she had been kept at home by a sense of duty to her father, who seemed able to impose his will on her as he had on Isabelle. She had resisted his choice of husband more successfully than her younger sister, but he had retaliated by forbidding hers. As he had scared away Isabelle's soldier, so he had frozen from contention a widowed man who would have taken Jeanne away from him.

Jeanne spoke in very measured sentences; there was something strict in her manner that was relieved by the humour that glimmered behind it in her eyes and in the sudden movements of her long, thin fingers.

Stephen continued to feel a sense of tranquillity in her presence. He found himself happy to listen to her talking, and when she questioned him he was able to reply with a sense of proportion, even when talking about the war.

Then, as it grew late, he began to feel the dread of his return. From the first time as a child when he had been taken from the fields and made to go back to the institution in which he was living, he had feared the moment of separation more than anything: it was abandonment. The return to the trenches was something he could not bring himself to contemplate. As the time grew nearer he lost the ability to talk any more.

Jeanne said, 'You're thinking of your return, aren't you? You've stopped answering my questions.'

Stephen nodded.

'It won't last for ever. We are waiting for tanks and for the Americans, that's what General Pétain says. We must all be patient. Think of your next leave.'

'Can I come here again?'

'Yes, if you like. Count the days and the weeks. Keep yourself safe. It sounds as though with your new job you won't be in action so much. Be careful.'

Stephen said, 'You may be right.' He sighed. 'But it's been so long, so very long. I think of the men I was with and –'

'Then you must stop thinking about them, the ones who have died. You did your best for them and there's nothing more you can do. When it's over you can remember them. Now you must concentrate on getting yourself through it. Another casualty won't help those who have died.'

'I can't do it, Jeanne, I can't do it. I'm so tired.'

Jeanne looked at his pleading face. He was close to tears.

'I have given everything,' he said. 'Don't make me go on. Please let me stay here.'

Jeanne's smile came again. 'This is not the talk of a man who led his soldiers on the Ancre. A few weeks behind the lines, where there's no danger. You can manage that.'

'It isn't the danger. It's the effort. I can no longer bring my mind to it.'

'I know.' Jeanne put her hand on his. 'I understand. But you must be strong. I've made up a bed for you because I thought you might want to stay. I'll wake you in good time in the morning. Come on now.'

Stephen followed her reluctantly to the door. He knew he would go back the next day.

THE ASSAULT ON the Messines Ridge was planned hard and in detail. Veterans of the previous July were mean with the human life at their disposal.

'I've good news for you,' said Gray when Stephen reported back to him. 'There's time before your new appointment for you to organize a large raid on the enemy trenches. It's part of the new, cautious regime of knowing our enemy. Reconnaissance.' He tried unsuccessfully to still the twitchings of a smile.

'I see,' said Stephen. 'And will it make much difference to our grand strategy if we discover we are facing the Forty-First Regiment rather than the Forty-Second?'

'I very much doubt it,' said Gray. 'But my orders are to contribute to the intelligence gathered along the line. I think your company is coming out of reserve this week. It's good timing for a front-line soldier like you.'

'Thank you, sir.'

Gray laughed. 'All right, Wraysford. Relax. What I actually want you to do is lead an attack on the canal to the left. We need to get a foothold there. It's just a local attack. You go up at dawn with the rest of the battalion. We have support from our Black Country friends later in the day. Is that a bit more to your liking?'

'It seems a more useful way of dying than while examining the cap badges of the men opposite.'

'Good man, Wraysford. Keep going. I knew you would.'

'And how do *you* keep going, sir?' said Stephen.

Gray laughed. 'It's my Scottish blood. We've barely started yet.'

The men went up the line once more, through the long communication trench and into the mired slit of land beneath the sandbags. Apart from raids and patrols, they had not attacked for nine months, and there was nervousness and argument among the men who were detailed to place the scaling ladders against the trench wall. All morning was the sound of hammering and sawing as the wood was cut and positioned at intervals against the parapet. Stephen had the impression that for all their forebodings of the big offensive in Belgium that was reportedly so dear to Field Marshal Haig, they had somehow thought they would not themselves be involved in another trudge into the hurricane of guns.

Jack Firebrace watched the preparations when he came back from his shift underground, and they brought back memories he had until then successfully closed down. He remembered how he had prayed for the men who would go over on that summer morning and how he had trusted in their safekeeping. This time he had no prayers to offer.

He went into the large dugout at the head of the deep mine where his company was temporarily sleeping. He made tea and drank it with Evans, then took out his sketchbook. Since Shaw's death there were no more pictures of him. Jack had taken to drawing Stephen instead. From the moment he had pitched into his arms, back from the dead, Jack had been intrigued by him. Now he had made drawings of his large, dark head from many angles and in many poses – with his big eyes open in incredulity or narrowed in determination; of the smile with which he chafed his own officer, Captain Weir; of the blank, remote expression, as if his memory had failed, with which he had dismissed Jack when he had gone to report for sleeping on duty. He could not remember John's face well enough to draw it.

The wait for the attack was short, but no less difficult for that. Stephen talked to the platoon commanders who would go first up the wide-spaced ladders into the uncertain world beyond.

'You mustn't waver,' he said. 'What is waiting for you can't be changed, but if you hesitate you will needlessly endanger the lives of others.'

He saw Ellis licking his lips. There was sweat on his pale forehead. The bombardment was starting up and it was beginning to shake the earth from the roof of the dugout.

Stephen spoke with the calm of experience, but it did not help him. The fact that he had done this before was no guarantee that he could do it again. When the moment came he would have to confront the depths of himself once more, and he feared that he had changed.

The bombardment was only for a day. It was trained, so the artillery had assured them, with scientific precision based on accurate aerial reconnaissance. There would be no uncut wire, no unharmed concrete redoubts spraying lazy waves of death over the turned fields.

Weir came to his dugout at midnight. His eyes were wild and his hair disarrayed. Stephen felt dismayed at the sight. He did not want to catch the other man's fear. He did not want him to breathe over him.

'This noise,' said Weir. 'I can't bear it any more.'

'You've been saying that for two years,' said Stephen sharply. 'The truth is you're one of the most resilient men in the BEF.'

Weir pulled out cigarettes and cast his eyes round hopefully. Stephen reluctantly pushed a bottle towards him.

'When are you going over?' said Weir.

'Usual time. It'll be all right.'

'Stephen, I'm worried for you. I have this foreboding.'

'I don't want to hear about your foreboding.'

'You've been a marvellous friend to me, Stephen. I'll never forget when we lay in the shellhole and you talked to me and –'

'Of course you'll forget it. Now just be quiet.'

Weir was trembling. 'You don't understand. I want to thank you. I just have this premonition. You remember last time we did the cards and you –'

'I fix the cards. I cheat. They don't mean a thing.' Stephen could not bear the conversation.

Weir looked startled and downcast. He drank deeply. 'I know I shouldn't be saying this, I know it's selfish of me, but –'

'Just shut your mouth, Weir.' Stephen was shouting, his voice caught with the beginning of sobs. He put his face close to Weir's. 'Just try to help me. If you are grateful or something then try to help me. Christ Jesus, do you think I want to do this? Do you think my life was made for *this*?'

Weir recoiled under Stephen's indignant saliva.

He began to protest, but Stephen was now rolling with anger. 'All those boys of eighteen and nineteen who walk out in the morning and I have to go with them and watch. Just please for once try to talk about something else.'

In his oblique and drunken way Weir was as passionate as Stephen. 'This is something that has to be said, and I don't care if it's tactful. There are things more important than that. I want to thank you and to say goodbye, in case –'

Stephen took him by the lapels and lifted him to the door of the dugout. 'Fuck off, Weir, fuck off out of my way and leave me alone.' He pushed him and sent him sliding face down in the mud. Weir clambered up slowly, glanced back reproachfully at Stephen as he picked the slime and filth from his front, then made his solitary way along the duckboards.

Alone, as he had wanted to be, Stephen began the journey down into himself that would end at dawn. He looked carefully at his body and remembered the things his hands had touched; he looked at the prints of his fingertips and laid the back of his hand against the soft membrane of his lips.

He lay down on the planks of the bed and felt the touch of the woollen blanket against his face. It was a feeling he remembered from childhood. He closed his eyes tight and thought of his earliest memories of his mother, of the feeling of her hands, the sound and scent of her. He wrapped himself in the cloak of his remembered world, hoping he would be safe in it where no shells or bullets could reach him. He swallowed, and felt the familiar feeling of his tongue and throat. It was the same flesh he had had as an innocent boy. Surely they would not let anything happen to it now. His renewed love of

374

the world made the prospect of leaving it unbearable.

An hour before dawn Riley came to him with water he had boiled for shaving. Stephen was pleased to see the smart little man with his obsequious manner. He had also been able to brew a large pot of tea. Stephen shaved carefully and put on the belt that Riley had shined for him.

When he went out into the trench he found that the rations had come up on time and some of the men had cooked bacon for breakfast. He had to move carefully in the dark, watching his feet on the duckboards. He found CSM Price checking the kit. Price's methodical manner helped him; it was as though it was just an ordinary day. Then he spoke to Petrossian, the corporal in his old platoon. His familiar, swarthy face looked up at Stephen as though in hope of delivery. Stephen looked away. He came to a group of men who had not been over the top before, Barlow, Coker, Goddard, and some others huddled by a ladder. He stopped to talk to them and even in the darkness he could see the strange look on their faces. It was as though the skin had been drawn tight across them so that they glowed. They were incapable of responding to his words; each had gone down alone into himself, where time had stopped and there was no help.

The artillery began to lay down the barrage in no man's land. They could see the earth spitting and leaping over the height of the sandbagged parapet. Stephen checked his watch. Four minutes to go. He knelt on the firestep and prayed, a wordless yearning.

It had happened so fast. The long bombardment before the July attack had been almost intolerable, but it had at least given the men time to get ready. On this occasion it seemed that only a few hours earlier he had been having dinner with Jeanne and now he was preparing to die. It made little difference that this was, by comparison, a small attack: there were no degrees of death.

He rose from his knees and went back into the next firebay where he could see Ellis looking down at his watch. He went up to him and put his arm round his shoulders. Ellis's stricken face encouraged him; from somewhere he found a smile of reassurance to go with the squeeze he gave his shoulders. At the head of the communication trench stood Price, with a clipboard. He held out his hand to Stephen, who shook it. Price would not be going over, though he would count the cost.

Stephen looked up to the sky where the first light was cracking the clouds. He let out a long sigh that shook him to his boots. 'Oh God, oh God,' he breathed, shuddering down his spine. Where now was the loving unity of the world? With one minute to go the realization struck him as it struck all the men: that there was no way back. He threw a glance of longing down the clogged communication trench, then turned to face the front. A whistle blew, and clumsily the men began to clamber up the ladders, weighed down by their heavy packs, into the metal air.

Stephen watched their foolish, crab-like movements and felt his heart seize up with pitying love for them. He pushed his way through to follow.

The men ran as fast as they could over the broken ground; there was no repetition of the slow march ordered for the previous year. Their own machine guns were putting a barrage over their heads where it met the defensive fire of the enemy. Stephen was aware of the density of sound as he lowered his head, trying to take what protection he could from his steel helmet. He had to swerve over fallen bodies and leap small craters in the mud. He could see that the advancing line in front had reached the enemy trench. His own company, which was in support, began to regroup in shellholes about fifty yards short.

Stephen slid down a ten-foot drop into the slime, where he saw Goddard and Allen, the latter holding a field dressing over his bicep. Coker was looking over the rim of the shellhole, supported on another man's back, trying to see through field glasses what signals were coming from the troops in front.

He jumped down into the mud. 'Can't see a thing, sir,' he screamed at Stephen through the noise. 'No signals, nothing. They seem to be through the wire. There's Mills bombs going off in the trench.'

Stephen felt a throb of hope. It was possible that for the first time in his experience the artillery had actually cut the wire

376

and his men would not be playthings for the enemy machine guns.

Petrossian stumbled into the shellhole. He was black with the slime of mud and whatever decomposing filth he had encountered in previous shelters, but he was not bleeding.

'Signal from B Company, sir,' he shouted. 'They're in.'

'All right. Let's go.'

Stephen clambered up the edge of the shellhole and waved a flag. The ground began to move and disgorge men for a length of a hundred yards or more. The noise in front of them redoubled as German fire began from their support trench. Though the men in B Company tried to cover them, their rifle fire could not cope with the machine guns. The last fifty yards became a hopping, dodging exercise as men weaved through fire and leapt over fallen bodies.

Stephen followed two others through a hole in the German wire and jumped down into a crowded firebay. No one knew what was going on. There were groups of German prisoners along the duckboards wearing nervous smiles, looking relieved to be taken, but anxious that something might go wrong for them at this late stage. They plied the men of B Company with souvenirs and cigarettes. Their trench was a source of wonder to the British men, with its huge, deep dugouts and crafted parapets. They stared in rapt curiosity at the long-imagined privacy that they had finally violated.

Stephen managed to get the prisoners into an undamaged dugout where he left Petrossian in charge with three other men to guard them. He knew Petrossian would be relieved not to have to advance further and would take pleasure in killing them if necessary. He went along the trench and found Ellis, damp with sweat, and blank-eyed as though the battle was taking place in some other world.

There was still fighting in the trench to their left where it adjoined the canal, though after half an hour they saw more German prisoners being brought up, and the sounds of fire died down.

Ellis looked at Stephen expectantly. 'What now?'

'We'll get support at midday from that wood on the right,

from what Gray calls our Black Country friends. We have to secure the canal end, then press on to the second trench.'

Ellis smiled uncertainly. Stephen grimaced. 'We've started shelling their second line now,' he shouted as he heard the whine above him. 'Keep your helmet on and your fingers crossed.'

There was frantic movement in the trench as men piled up sandbags so they could fire over the rear of the trench towards the German support line. Many were hit in the head and fell back as they tried to find space to fire. Lewis gunners were looking for a secure post from which they could concentrate their aim, but for the time being it was hard to know whether they could move on before the counterattack came back at them.

Gradually the artillery began to find its targets. There were shouted reports of shellblasts on the trench lip, with men and earth thrown upwards together. From behind the lines the German artillery began a heavy reply. There was no communication with battalion headquarters, and in the noise and increasing carnage of the battle the only way Stephen could think of to impose order was to follow the original plan. He climbed up on to the improvised firestep. From what he could see the enemy was preparing for a further retreat to its reserve trench. If only there was some way of communicating with the artillery they could catch them as they went.

Through a series of yelled and half-heard orders, a second attack began. It was less coordinated than the first, without the distinct waves, but the men who had survived were dizzy with exhilaration as they wove onwards to the second line. With no room for rifles, they went into the trench with bayonets and fists. Some were crushed by their own artillery, who were late to be informed of the second advance, and some leapt straight into death below. Stephen crashed through the wire and landed on the body of a German corporal whose legs had been removed by a shell. He was alive and trying to haul himself to safety. They tried to gather in knots and push both ways along the trench so that their rear was always guarded, but new arrivals meant they could not throw grenades over the traverses for fear that they would be killing their own men. There was no alternative but for men to go blind round each corner. The fate of the first two or three was a good indicator to those who followed. Stephen watched the men go on madly, stepping over the bodies of their friends, clearing one firebay after another, jostling one another to be first to the traverse. They had dead brothers and friends on their minds; they were galvanized beyond fear. They were killing with pleasure. They were not normal.

By late morning they had secured the support trench. Stephen sent a detachment down to the canal to dig in against counterattack. All they had to do now was hold the line until reinforcements arrived at noon to protect their other flank.

Stephen could not bear the sight of Germans and tried to get the prisoners back as quickly as possible. Despite the continuing shellfire there were enough volunteers to escort them. To have taken two lines in a morning was thought by most men to be the limit of their likely good fortune. After five hours of exertion they were desperate for rest. Stephen enviously watched their tired departing backs.

The intensity of fire diminished for a moment, then built up again, mostly on the right flank, which was coming under attack from unseen machine gun emplacements and from rifle grenades. Stephen had not had time to taste the moment of significant advance before their position was besieged. The dog-toothed construction of the trench made it impossible to know what was happening more than a few yards away, but to him the sound of the counterattack was ominous.

He became aware of a concertina movement coming down the trench from the right as the furthest firebays were either being excavated or merely silenced. At noon he climbed a ladder on what had been the parapet and looked up to the wood for reinforcements. There was no one there. He jumped down into the trench and found a periscope. He looked back over no man's land and could see nothing except a distant line of prisoners being taken back. He closed his eyes and sighed quietly in the storm of fire. He might have known. He could have guessed.

A platoon commander called Sibley shouted in his ear. He wanted to know when the reinforcements would arrive.

'There are none. They're not coming,' bellowed Stephen.

379

'Why?' mouthed Sibley.

Stephen said nothing.

An hour later the Germans were back in the trench at the far end and there was hand-to-hand fighting. Shortly afterwards B Company were ordered by their commander to retire to the enemy front-line trench which they had taken in the morning. As they went up over the parapet they came under fire from German machine guns that had re-established themselves in the support trench.

The noise was making it impossible to think. Stephen was aware of Ellis screaming at him. 'We're going down, we're going down!' his lips said silently.

Stephen shook his head.

Ellis put his lips to Stephen's ear. 'B Company's gone.'

'I know. I know.' Stephen did not explain. His company's job was to occupy; B Company had been detailed to assault and were entitled to take their own view of when to move. He could not have made Ellis hear, but he wanted to stick to the orders given him by Colonel Gray.

A sergeant with blood-spattered face pushed past them, and was followed by another surge of men who were being squeezed back down the trench from their unprotected right flank. The counterattack was now also coming head-on in an advance from the reserve trench. Two Lewis guns were not able to keep them back. It only needed an attack from the canal end and they would be completely encircled. Stephen rapidly calculated the possibility of a retreat. There were now so many Germans in the trench that they would be able to resume their positions on the parapet and shoot his men in the back as they ran.

Ellis was weeping. 'What do we do?' he wailed. 'I want to save my men. What do we do?'

In his mind, Stephen saw only one outcome: his company's bodies stacked like sandbags one on another. It was not what he had chosen, but it was all that was left to them.

'What do we *do*?' Ellis moaned against the noise.

'We hold the line, we hold the fucking line.' Stephen's tongue and teeth were visible in the silently screaming cave of his mouth.

380

In the desperation of trying to save their own lives, the men fought over each yard of trench. Stephen joined them, firing rapidly at the advancing lines of grey.

Just before three o'clock he was aware of a Yorkshire voice in his ear and an unfamiliar face. He looked with puzzlement into the man's eyes. It was a lieutenant from the Duke of Wellington's Regiment. He shouted to Stephen that his men had regained control of the far end of the trench.

Within another hour they had cleared their way back to the canal. Further reinforcements came up with trench mortars and more machine guns. The German counterattack was temporarily over, and its stragglers withdrew to their reserve position.

Stephen climbed down on to the duckboards and went along to a dugout where he found a major of the Duke of Wellington's.

'You look all in,' the major said cheerfully. 'Your orders are to withdraw. We were sent up to cover you. Something went wrong before. Another triumph of planning.'

Stephen looked at the man's face. He looked so young, he thought, yet he had performed some kind of miracle.

'And what are you going to do?' he asked.

'Cover your withdrawal, then get the hell out of it.'

Stephen took the man's hand, then went outside.

They got the dead and wounded out first and what was left of the company was back in its own trench by nightfall. Ellis had been killed by machine gun fire. The small groups of survivors dragged themselves over the mud they had crossed in the morning. They did not ask about the fate of their friends; they were intent only on reaching somewhere they could lie down.

STEPHEN'S NEW JOB seemed to consist of going over maps and trying to ascertain which battalion was where. He was billeted in a pleasant house in the village, though was occasionally required to spend the night in a dugout in the reserve line. Even this was a great improvement on what he had known.

There was some urgency about the work since the attack on the Messines Ridge was imminent. Stephen took sardonic pleasure in confirming that Weir's tunnelling company was due for a rest shortly beforehand. Their work would be done and someone else could blow the mines.

The brigade major, a man called Stanforth, reminded him in manner of Colonel Barclay. He had a tendency to shout for no good reason, and he spoke in abbreviated sentences that were supposed to communicate urgency. If anything unforeseen happened he at once showed how much he was in command by issuing forceful and complicated orders, even though the hitch would usually sort itself out unaided.

The day he arrived Stephen had the unpleasant duty of writing to Ellis's mother, who had already been officially informed of her son's death. He chewed the pen in his office for an hour or more before he could begin. It was a summer day with blackbirds and thrushes at play in the garden of the house.

He made many false starts in which he tried to describe something of the attack or of the times he had spent with Ellis in the dugout or in Amiens. In the end he wrote only formal words of condolence.

Dear Mrs Ellis, I am writing to offer you my deepest sympathy on the loss of your son. As you will have been told, he was lost during an offensive action on the morning of June 2nd. He was killed by enemy machine gun fire while organizing the defence of a German trench bravely captured by the men under his command. He is buried with Lieutenant Parker and Lieutenant Davies. The grave has been properly marked and the position notified to the Graves Registration Committee.

During the last conversation I had with him he told me he had no fear of death and felt fully equipped for any task he might be called upon to perform.

In every circumstance his consideration for the welfare and comfort of his men came first.

His men loved him, and I am expressing not only my own sympathy but theirs too. In dying for what the Empire now seeks to uphold, he was among many who paid a great price. We commit the souls of our brothers who have fallen to the mercy and safekeeping of God.

When he read the letter back to himself, Stephen underlined the word 'every'. 'In *every* circumstance . . .' It was true. In a few months Ellis had won the respect of his men because he was not afraid, or, if he was, he did not show it. He had become a good soldier, for all that it had helped him.

Stephen was tired of writing such letters. He noticed how dry and passionless his own style had become. He imagined what effect the letter would have on the distraught widow who opened it. Her only son gone . . . He did not wish to contemplate it.

FOR THE LAST week before the attack, Jack's company was switched to the deep mines below the Ridge where they laid tons of ammonal in specially prepared chambers.

Two days before the attack itself the work was completed, and Jack emerged exhausted into the sunlight. Evans, Fielding and Jones came up after him. They stood in the section of the trench at the tunnel head and congratulated one another on their efforts. They were instructed to report to Captain Weir before being officially dismissed, and they made their way along the duckboards towards his dugout.

'There's a rumour of home leave for you, Jack,' said Fielding.

'I don't believe it. They'll make us dig to Australia first.'

'There's certainly no more digging we can do here,' said Evans. 'It's a warren under there. I'd be happy just to get back down the line into a nice soft bed with a glass or two of that wine inside me.'

'Yes,' said Fielding, 'and maybe one of those French girls to follow.'

Jack was beginning to think that the worst of the war might be over for him. He allowed himself to picture the hallway of his house in London with Margaret waiting for him.

Weir came along the boards to meet them. He looked happier than usual. He was wearing boots and a tunic and a soft cap. As he came closer to them, Jack noticed that some of the sandbags on the parapet had not been properly replaced from the day when the infantry had gone over them. He tried to warn him that he was not properly covered. Weir climbed on to the firestep to let a ration party go past and a sniper's bullet entered his head above the eye causing trails of his brain to loop out on to the sandbags of the parados behind him.

His body seemed for a moment unaware of what had happened, as though it would carry on walking. Then it fell like a puppet, its limbs shooting out, and the face smashing unprotected into mud.

Word reached Stephen the next night from an intelligence officer called Mountford. He was in his dugout in the reserve line where he was acting as liaison between headquarters and the men who would be in the second wave in the morning. Mountford delivered the news briefly. 'I believe he was a friend of yours,' he said. He could see from Stephen's face that there was little to be gained from staying.

Stephen sat still for a minute. The last time he had seen Weir had been to push him head first on to the floor of the trench. That had been his final gesture. For some minutes he could think of nothing but Weir's hurt, reproachful expression as he picked the mud from his face.

Yet he had loved him. Weir alone had made the war bearable. Weir's terror under the guns had been a conductor for his own fear, and in his innocent character Stephen had been able to mock the qualities he himself had lost. Weir had been braver by far than he was: he had lived with horror, he had known it every day, and by his strange stubbornness he had defeated it. He had not conceded one day of his service; he had died in the line of battle.

Stephen rested his elbows on the rough wooden table. He felt more lonely than ever in his life before. Only Weir had been with him into the edges of reality where he had lived; only Weir had heard the noise of the sky at Thiepval.

He lay on the bed, dry-eyed. Soon after three in the morning the mines went up and shook the bed where he lay. 'The explosion will be felt in London,' Weir had boasted.

The telephone rang, and Stephen went back to the chair at the desk. Throughout the small hours of the morning he relayed messages. By nine o'clock the Second Army was on the Ridge. Elation edged the voices he spoke to: something, at last, had gone right. The mines had been colossal and the infantry, using methods copied from the Canadians, had stormed through. Celebration seeped into the wires.

Stephen was relieved at noon. He lay down on the bed and tried to sleep. He could hear the unrelenting bombardment continue on the German lines. He cursed his fortune that he could not go in behind it. Now, to answer Gray's hypothetical question, now he would have taken life without compunction. He envied the men who could fire down on to the hopeless enemy, men with a chance to sink bayonets into unguarded flesh, men with the opportunity to pour machine gun bullets into those who had killed his friend. Now he would have gone killing with a light heart.

He tried to think that victory on the Ridge would bring pleasure or vindication to Weir, but he could not imagine it. He was merely an absence now. Stephen thought of his puzzled, open face, its chalky skin patched red with blood vessels broken up by drink; he thought of his balding skull and shocked eyes that could not contain his innocence. He thought of the pity of the flesh gone back underground without knowledge of another human body.

All that night and the next day he lay unmoving on the bed. He did not speak when Mountford came back to try to rouse him. He turned away the food that was brought to him. He cursed himself for his last act of impatience towards Weir. He hated the selfishness of his feeling, because he felt more sorry for himself than for his dead friend. He could not help it. Like all the others, he had learned to dismiss death from his thoughts; but he could not shake off the loneliness. Now that Weir was gone there was no one who could understand. He tried to make himself cry but no tears would come to express his desolation or his love for poor mad Weir.

On the third day Colonel Gray came to see him.

'Success at last,' he said. 'Those tunnellers did a wonderful job. Mind if I sit down, Wraysford?'

Stephen was sitting on the edge of the bed. He had made an

386

effort to stand up and salute when Gray came in, but Gray had waved him back. He gestured to the chair at the table.

Gray crossed his legs and lit a pipe. 'The Boche didn't know what hit them. I was never a great believer in the sewer rats, giving the enemy little craters to fortify, but even I would be forced to concede that they did their job this time.'

He carried on talking about the attack for a few minutes, apparently taking no notice of the fact that Stephen did not reply.

'Our chaps were in reserve,' he went on. 'Not needed. Some of them were a bit disappointed, I do believe.' He sucked on the pipe. 'Not many, though.'

Stephen ran his hand back through his unkempt hair. He wondered whether Gray had been sent or whether he had decided of his own accord to visit him.

'Stanforth,' said Gray. 'He looks like a typical English staff officer, doesn't he? Fat, complacent, ill-informed. Forgive me, I have nothing against the English, as you know, Wraysford. The appearance is misleading in his case. He's a very thorough planner. I believe he has saved many lives in this attack.'

Stephen nodded. A sense of interest was beginning to penetrate the blankness of his grief; it was like the first, painful sensations of blood returning to a numbed limb.

Gray kept on talking and smoking. 'There's a rather delicate matter coming up concerning our noble French allies. They are experiencing difficulties. A certain, how can one put this, reluctance is spreading. The removal of the dashing General Nivelle has helped. Pétain appears a little more thrifty with their lives, but it's alarming. We understand that two-thirds of the army has been concerned in some way, with perhaps one division in five seriously affected.'

Stephen was curious to hear what Gray said. The French army had performed better than the British in comparable circumstances and shown formidable resilience. Mutiny seemed unthinkable.

'Stanforth will ask you and Mountford to go with him. This is a completely informal meeting. The French officers concerned are on leave. It's just something that's been arranged by friends.'

'I see,' said Stephen. 'I'm surprised this is allowed. We hardly ever meet the French.'

'Quite,' said Gray, with a small smile of triumph. He had made Stephen speak. 'It's not allowed. It's just lunch with friends. And while I'm here. You look a bloody mess. Get a shave and a bath. I'm sorry about your sapper friend. Now get up.'

Stephen looked at him blankly. His body was without energy. His gaze fastened on to the pale irises of Gray's eyes. He tried to draw strength from the older man.

Gray's voice softened when he saw that Stephen was trying to respond. 'I know what it means when you're left alone, as though no one else has shared what you have. But you're going to have to proceed, Wraysford. I'm going to recommend you for an MC for your part in the action at the canal. Would you like that?'

Stephen stirred again. 'No, I certainly would not. You can't give tin stars to people when there are men who gave their lives. For God's sake.'

Gray smiled again and Stephen had the feeling as often before that he had been played like an instrument. 'Very well. No decoration.'

Stephen said, 'Recommend one, but give it to Ellis or one of those men who died. It might help his mother.'

'Yes,' said Gray. 'Or it might break her heart.'

Stephen stood up. 'I'll go back to headquarters and change.'

'Good,' said Gray. 'If you falter now you'll rob his life of any purpose. Only by seeing it through can you give him rest.'

'Our lives lost meaning long ago. You know that. At Beaumont-Hamel.'

Gray swallowed. 'Then do it for our children.'

Stephen pulled his stiff limbs out from the dugout and into the summer air.

When he looked about him to the trees and the buildings that were still standing, and to the sky above them, he could still feel something of the binding love he had experienced in England. He was able to compel himself to act, though he feared that the reality he now inhabited was very fragile.

388

He wrote to Jeanne almost every day for a time, but then found he had nothing to say. She replied with accounts of her life in Amiens and told him what the French newspapers said about the war.

He went in a car with Stanforth and Mountford to Arras where they met two French officers called Lallement and Hartmann in a hotel. Lallement, the older of the two, was a plump, worldly man. In peacetime he had been a lawyer attached to the Civil Service. He ordered numerous wines with lunch and ate several partridges, which he tore apart with his hands. The juice ran down his chin and on to a napkin he had tucked into his collar. Stephen watched in disbelief. The younger officer, Hartmann, was a dark, serious-looking young man of perhaps twenty years old. His expression was inscrutable, and he seemed unwilling to say anything that might embarrass his senior officer.

Lallement talked mostly about hunting and wildlife. Stephen translated for the benefit of Major Stanforth, who surveyed the Frenchman with some suspicion. Mountford, who could speak French, asked him about morale in the French army. Lallement assured him, as he wiped the gravy from his chin, that it had seldom been better.

After lunch Lallement questioned Stanforth, through Stephen, about his family in England. They had a friend in common, an elderly Frenchwoman who was related to Stanforth's wife. From there Lallement turned his questioning to the British army and how they viewed the state of the war. Stanforth was surprisingly frank in his replies and Stephen found himself tempted to censor them. He presumed Stanforth knew best, and in any case Mountford might have noticed any alterations.

Stephen, who was not used to intelligence-gathering operations, even such informal ones, wondered when they were going to find out about the collapse of French morale and the extent to which the armies were affected. By teatime he had given a detailed account of the movements of most of the divisions in their part of the BEF and a picture of the low state of the men's spirits, which successes at Vimy and Messines had lifted only for a time. Depression had begun to sink into the army's bones, particularly among those who knew of the prospects of the major offensive at Ypres.

Lallement wiped his mouth finally on his napkin and suggested they go to a bar that a friend had told him about near the main square. They stayed till ten o'clock, when Stephen was dispatched to find the driver of Stanforth's car. He found him asleep on the back seat. By the time they said goodbye to the French it had started to rain. Stephen looked back at Lallement and Hartmann standing together beneath the dripping colonnade.

He visited Jeanne again in August and September. They went for walks about the town, though he resisted her suggestion that they should spend an afternoon in the water-gardens.

She told him she was worried by his listlessness. It was as though he had given up hope and was allowing himself to drift. He said it was hard not to, when the attitude of the people at home to what they had endured was one of indifference.

'Then be strong for my sake,' she said. 'I am not indifferent to what happens to you or to any of your friends. I am not impatient. I will wait for you.'

He was encouraged by her. He told her what he had felt when he was on leave in England, when he had stood by the field.

Jeanne said, 'You see! There is a God, there is a purpose to it all. But you must be strong.'

She took his hand and held it tightly. He looked at her pale, imploring face.

'Do it for my sake,' she said. 'Go back, go where they ask you. You are lucky. You will survive.'

'I feel guilty that I have survived when all the others are gone.'

He returned to brigade headquarters. He did not want to be on the staff. He wanted to be back with the men in the trenches.

He managed only to exist.

His life became grey and thin, like a light that might at any moment be extinguished; it was filled with quietness.

PART FIVE

ENGLAND 1978–79

'ANY PROGRESS?' SAID Elizabeth to Irene during her weekly visit.

'Not really,' said Irene. 'He says it's proving more difficult than he thought. He's still working at it, but your grandad seems to have covered his tracks pretty well.'

Two months had passed since Elizabeth had given Bob the diary and she decided she would have to find other ways of making contact with the past. From his officer's handbook she discovered which regiment her grandfather had been in, and attempted to trace its headquarters.

After a series of telephone calls and unreturned messages she found that the regiment had ceased to exist ten years earlier, when it had been amalgamated with another. The headquarters were in Buckinghamshire, where Elizabeth drove one Saturday afternoon.

She was met with suspicion. Her car was searched thoroughly for bombs and she was made to wait for an hour before a young man eventually came to see her.

He was the first soldier Elizabeth had ever met. She was surprised by how unmilitary he seemed. He had the attitude of most clerks and small officials: regimental documents were held somewhere, hard to reach, confidential; there was not much chance.

'The thing is, you see,' said Elizabeth, 'that my grandfather fought in this war and I would like to find out more about it. People don't always appreciate what sacrifices were made for them – still are made for them – by the armed forces. All I would need is a list of names of people in his . . . battalion, company, whatever it was. I'm sure an organization as efficient as the Army must keep good records, mustn't it?'

'I'm sure everything's in order. It's a question of access. And confidentiality, as I've explained.'

They were sitting in a little wooden guardhouse near the main gate. The corporal folded his arms. He had a pale, unhealthy-looking complexion and short brown hair.

Elizabeth smiled again. 'Do you smoke?' She held the packet across the table.

'I'll tell you what I'll do,' he said, leaning across to accept a light. 'I can let you have a look at the regimental history. That should give you some names at least. Then you can follow it up from there. Of course, I don't suppose there's many of them still alive.'

'We must waste no time then,' said Elizabeth.

'You wait here. I'll have to go and get you a pass.'

He left the room and a very young man with a rifle came to stand guard, in case, it seemed to Elizabeth, she should attack.

The corporal gave her a piece of card with a safety pin, which she attached to her chest, and took her inside a large brick building. He let her into a room with a plain deal table and two hard chairs. It looked to Elizabeth like the kind of place in which interrogations took place. He handed her a heavy volume bound in red cloth and stood in the corner watching her as she leafed through it.

Prominent among the names revealed by the regimental history was that of a Captain, later Colonel, Gray. Elizabeth wrote down various other names on an envelope that was in her bag. There was apparently no chance of the corporal's finding, let alone revealing, any addresses. She thanked him effusively and drove back to London.

That evening she rang Bob to see if he had made any progress with the notebook. She said, 'I've got a few names of people I think must have been in it with him, but I've no idea how to get in touch with them. There's someone called Gray, who seems to have been important, but he must be incredibly old if he's still alive.'

She heard Bob whistling pensively at the other end. 'Have

394

you thought of *Who's Who?*' he said. 'If this Gray got some sort of gong or went on to do something in civilian life he might be in there.'

Elizabeth found a three-year-old copy of *Who's Who* in the public library in Porchester Road and worked her way through the details of the fifty-two Grays included. They had distinguished themselves in a range of business activities and public service but few of them had even been born before 1918. Over the page was one last Gray.

'**GRAY, William Allan McKenzie,**' she read. 'Senior Consultant, Queen Alexandra's Hospital, Edinburgh, 1932–48; *b* Calcutta 18 Sept. 1887; *s* of Thomas McKenzie Gray and Maisie Maclennan; *m* 1910, Joyce Amelia Williams, *d* of Dr A R Williams; one *s* one *d*. *Educ:* Thomas Campbell College; St Andrew's University. BSc. 1909.'

Her eye ran on down the small print until it came to the words 'Served War of 1914–18'. The details tallied.

At the foot of the entry was an address and telephone number in Lanarkshire. The only problem was that the book was three years old, and even then he had been, Elizabeth calculated . . . eighty-eight.

As she had remarked to the corporal, there was no time to waste. She hurried back to her flat and made for the telephone. It rang before she could get to it.

'Hello.'

'It's me.'

'What?'

'Stuart.'

'Oh, Stuart. How are you?'

'I'm fine. How are *you?*'

'Oh, you know. Fine, thanks. Quite busy.' Elizabeth paused so that Stuart could tell her why he had rung. He said nothing, so she chattered a bit more. Still he said nothing when it was his turn to speak. Eventually she said, 'Well. Was there something, you know . . . in particular?'

'I didn't know I needed a reason to ring.' He sounded affronted. 'I just rang for a chat.'

It was not the first time he had rung for a chat and then said nothing. Perhaps he was shy, Elizabeth thought, as she talked on about what she had been doing. She found it difficult to say goodbye to people without at least pretending that they would soon be meeting, and she found by the time she put the receiver down that she had invited Stuart to dinner.

'You must come round some time,' she said.

'Must I?' he said. 'When?'

'Well . . . God. What about Saturday?'

It didn't matter. She liked him. She would have time to cook something. Meanwhile she pulled the envelope from her bag and started to dial the Scottish number.

As her finger returned to zero she pictured a cold, grey farmhouse in Lanarkshire where an ancient telephone would ring thunderously on the hall table and a very old man would have to lever himself from an armchair several rooms away and make painful progress down the corridor, only to be confronted with a complete stranger asking him questions about a war he had fought in sixty years ago.

It was ridiculous. Her nerve failed her and she cut off the line.

She went into the kitchen and poured some gin over three ice cubes and a slice of lemon. She added a dribble of tonic, lit a cigarette and went back into the sitting room.

What was it all for? She wanted to find out what had happened to her grandfather so that she could . . . what? Understand more about herself? Be able to tell her notional children about their heritage? Perhaps it was just a whim, but she was determined. The worst that could result from the telephone call was embarrassment. It didn't seem a very fearful price.

She dialled again, and heard the number ring. Eight, nine, ten times it rang. Fourteen, fifteen. Surely even the lamest old man would by now have –

'Hello?' It was a woman's voice. For some reason Elizabeth was surprised.

'Oh, is that . . . is that Mrs Gray?'

'Speaking.' The voice had a slight Edinburgh accent. It sounded distant and very old. Joyce Amelia.

'I'm very sorry to bother you. My name is Elizabeth Benson. I have a rather peculiar request. My grandfather fought in the same company as your husband in the First World War and I'm trying to find out something about him.'

Mrs Gray said nothing. Elizabeth wondered if she had heard.

'I know it's a very odd thing to ask,' she said. 'And I really am sorry to trouble you. I just didn't know who else to ring. Hello? Are you there?'

'Yes. I'll go and fetch my husband. You'll have to be patient. And do speak up. He's a wee bit deaf.'

Elizabeth felt her palms prickle with nervous excitement as Mrs Gray set down the receiver with a heavy bakelite report. She pictured it lying on the hall table, beneath the draughty wooden staircase. She waited for a minute, then another minute. Eventually a quavery but loud voice came on the line.

Elizabeth explained again. Gray could not hear her, so she went through it for a third time, shouting out her grandfather's name.

'What do you want to know about all that for? Good heavens, it was years ago.' He sounded annoyed.

'I'm sorry, I really don't mean to be a nuisance, it's just that I'm anxious to get in touch with someone who knew him and to find out what he was like.'

Gray made a snorting sound at the other end.

'Do you remember him? Did you fight with him?'

'Yes, I remember.'

'What was he like?'

'Like? Like? What was he like? God knows. You don't want to go into all that now.'

'But I do. Please. I really need to know.'

There were more noises from Gray's end of the line. Eventually he said, 'Dark-haired. Tall. He was an orphan or something. He was superstitious. Is that the chap?'

'I don't know!' Elizabeth found herself bellowing. She wondered if Mrs Kyriades was enjoying the conversation through the wall. 'I want you to tell me!'

'Wraysford. God . . .' There was some more snorting. Then Gray said, 'He was a strange man. I do remember him. He was a tremendous fighter. Quite unbelievable nerve. He never seemed very happy about it. Something worried him.'

Elizabeth said, 'Was he a kind man, was he a good friend to the other men?' She did not think she had the army terminology right, but it was the best she could do.

'Kind? Dear me.' Gray seemed to be laughing. 'Self-contained I would say.'

'Was he . . . funny?'

'Funny? It was a war! What an extraordinary question.'

'But did he have a sense of humour, do you think?'

'I suppose so. Pretty dry, even to a Scot like me.'

Elizabeth could sense Gray beginning to recall; she pressed him. 'What else do you remember? Tell me everything.'

'Never wanted to go on leave. Said he had no home to go to. He liked France. I remember visiting him in hospital when he'd been wounded. Must have been nineteen-fifteen. No, nineteen-sixteen.'

Gray spent some minutes trying to date the visit while Elizabeth fruitlessly interrupted.

'So is there anything else? Did he have any friends? Anyone I could speak to now who would remember him?'

'Friends? I don't think so. No, there was some sapper. I can't remember his name. He was a loner.'

'But a good soldier.'

The line crackled as Gray considered.

'He was a terrific fighter, but that's not quite the same thing.'

Mrs Gray's voice came back on the line. 'I'm sorry, but I'm going to have to take my husband away now. He isn't used to this kind of thing and I don't want him to get tired out. Do you understand?'

'I do,' said Elizabeth. 'I'm very grateful to you both. I do hope I haven't been a nuisance.'

'Not at all,' said Mrs Gray. 'There's a man my husband used to write to. His name was Brennan. He was in a Star and Garter home in Southend. It's not far from London.'

'Thank you very much. You've been very kind.'

'Goodbye.'

There was the sound of a receiver rattling in its cradle.

In the silence Elizabeth could hear the thump of music from the flat upstairs.

THE SWEDISH SALOON had again failed to start, and Elizabeth was compelled to take the train from Fenchurch Street, one of British Rail's recent corridorless variety, with new orange plush on the seats. She brought a cup of coffee down the rocking carriage, wincing as the boiling fluid seeped out from under the lid and on to her hand. When it was cool enough to drink, she found its taste merged into the atmosphere of diesel fumes and cigarette ends, so it was hard to tell where one ended and the next began. The heating was turned up full and most of the people in the carriage seemed on the point of unconsciousness as they looked out of the window at the flatlands of Essex sliding past the window.

Elizabeth had telephoned the matron of the home, who told her that Brennan was barely worth visiting, but that he would see her if she came. She felt excited by the prospect of actually meeting someone from that era. She would be like a historian who, after working from other histories, finally lays hands on original source material. She had an unclear picture of Brennan in her mind. Although she knew he would be old and, to judge from what the matron had said, decrepit, she still envisaged him in uniform, with a gun.

It was raining when she emerged from the station in Southend. She opened the door of a blue Vauxhall taxi on the forecourt. The car moved off over the glistening streets, along the front with its long dejected pier and crumbling Regency hotels. As they went up the hill, the driver pointed out towards the sands where a cockle boat was fishing with an attachment that looked like a giant vacuum hose trailing over the edge.

The home was a large Victorian building of red brick just visible beneath the pattern of fire escapes. Elizabeth paid the driver and went inside. There were stone steps leading up to a reception desk. Huge, high-ceilinged corridors led off in either direction. The receptionist was a plump woman with a mauve cardigan and tortoiseshell glasses.

'Is he expecting you?'

'Yes, I think so. I spoke to the matron, Mrs Simpson.'

The receptionist dialled two digits on the telephone. 'Yes. Visitor for Brennan. All right. Yes.' She put the phone down. 'Someone'll come for you,' she said to Elizabeth. She picked up the magazine she had been reading.

Elizabeth looked down and brushed a crumb from her skirt.

A woman in a nurse's uniform came up and introduced herself as Mrs Simpson.

'You're for Brennan, aren't you? If you'd like to step into my office a moment.'

They went a few yards down the corridor and into a small over-heated room with filing cabinets. There was a calendar on the wall with a picture of a kitten in a basket. On top of a table was a spider plant whose green and white shoots trailed down almost to the floor.

'You haven't been here before, have you?' said Mrs Simpson. She was a surprisingly young woman with peroxide hair and red lipstick. The uniform sat oddly on her.

'What you have to understand is that some of the men have been here almost all their lives. This is all they know, all they remember.' She stood up and took out a file from the cabinet. 'Yes. Here we are. He was admitted in nineteen-nineteen, your Mr Brennan. Discharged nineteen-twenty-one. Returned nineteen-twenty-three. He's been here ever since, paid for by the government. No surviving family. Sister died in nineteen-fifty.'

Elizabeth calculated. He had been there almost sixty years.

'They're very ignorant, most of the old-timers. They haven't kept up at all with what's been happening in the world. We do encourage radio and newspapers but they can't follow them.'

'And what exactly is wrong with Mr Brennan?'

'Amputation,' said Mrs Simpson. 'Let me see. Yes. Injury sustained during final offensive, October nineteen-eighteen. Shellblast. Left leg amputated in field hospital. Returned to England. Hospital Southampton. Moved to North Middlesex, then Roehampton. Admitted September nineteen nineteen. Also shellshock. Do you know what that means?'

'Psychological damage?'

'Yes, it's a catch-all expression. Soft in the head. Some of them got over it, some of them didn't.'

'I see. And will he know who I am? I mean, if I explain why I've come?'

'I'm not sure I've quite made myself clear.' Mrs Simpson's genteel voice took on an exasperated edge. 'This man lives in a world of his own. They all do. They have no interest in the outside world at all. Some of them can't help it, of course. But everything's done for them. Meals, toilet, everything.'

'Does he have many visitors?'

Mrs Simpson laughed. 'Many visitors? Oh dear. His last visitor was . . .' She consulted the file on her desk. 'His sister. In nineteen-forty-nine.'

Elizabeth looked down at her hands.

'Well, I'll take you along to see him, if you're ready. Don't expect too much, will you?'

They walked down the green linoleum of the corridor. The brickwork was tiled to waist height on either side, then met high overhead in a semi-cylindrical shape from which hung yellow lights on long plaited flexes.

They turned one corner, then another, past piled laundry baskets, past a pair of swing doors from behind which came a sudden burst of cabbage and gravy before the more general smell of disinfectant reasserted itself. They arrived at a blue-painted door.

'This is the day room,' said Mrs Simpson. She pushed open the door. There were a number of old men sitting round the edge of the room, some in wheelchairs, some in armchairs covered with pale brown plastic.

'He's over by the window.'

Elizabeth went across the room, trying not to breathe too deeply on the hot stagnant air, which smelt of urine. She approached a small man in a wheelchair with a rug over his thighs.

She held out her hand to him. He looked up and took it.

'Not that one,' said Mrs Simpson from the doorway. 'Next window.'

Elizabeth let go of the man's hand with a smile and moved down the room a few paces. There was an orange and brown patterned carpet over the centre of the floor. She wished she hadn't come.

The little man in the wheelchair was like a bird on its perch. He had thick glasses bound on one side with sticking plaster. Elizabeth could see his blue eyes watering behind them.

She held out her hand. He made no movement, so she took his hand from his lap and squeezed it.

She felt self-conscious and intrusive. Why on earth had she come? Some vanity about her imagined past, some foolish self-indulgence. She pulled up a chair and took Brennan's hand again.

'My name is Elizabeth Benson. I've come to visit you. Are you Mr Brennan?'

Brennan's blue eyes rolled in watery surprise. She felt him hold on to her hand. He had a tiny head. The hair was not so much grey as colourless. It lay flat and unwashed against his skull.

She made to take her hand away, but she felt him try to hang on to it, so she left it in his, and moved her chair up closer.

'I've come to see you. I've come to see you because I think you knew my grandfather. Stephen Wraysford. It was in the war. Do you remember him?'

Brennan said nothing. Elizabeth looked at him. He was wearing a striped woollen shirt with the top button done up but no tie, and a hand-knitted brown cardigan. He was so small, with one leg missing; she wondered how much he weighed.

402

'Do you remember the war? Do you remember those days at all?'

Brennan's eyes were still awash with surprise. He could clearly not grasp what was happening.

'Shall I just talk for a minute or so? Or shall we sit quietly for a bit?'

He still did not answer, so Elizabeth smiled at him and laid her other hand on top of his. She shook her head so that the hair that had fallen on to her cheek was held back over her ear.

Brennan started to speak. He had a little high voice like a girl's. It came up through a weight of phlegm Elizabeth could hear moving on his chest; after every few words he took thin sips of air.

'Such fireworks. We was all there, the whole street. There was dancing. We was out all night. Barbara and me. My sister. She fell down. In the blackout it was. Had to put it up every night. Fell off a ladder.'

'Your sister fell off a ladder?'

'There was a song we all sung then.' He took an extra gulp of air and tried to sing it for Elizabeth.

'And do you remember anything about the war? Can you tell me anything about my grandfather?'

'The relief of Mafeking that was. They give us such a bad tea. I can't eat it. It's muck. It was that bloody Hitler.' His hand was warm between hers.

A tea-trolley was brought into the room and made its clanking, metal way towards them.

'All right, Tom. You got a visitor then?' boomed the woman who pushed it. 'What are you doing with a pretty girl like this? You up to your old tricks I expect. I know you, you old scoundrel. Leave it there, shall I?' She put a cup on the small table near Brennan's elbow. 'He never drinks it,' she said to Elizabeth. 'You like a cup, love?'

'Thank you.'

The trolley rattled off. Elizabeth sipped the tea. She felt her gorge rebel against the extraordinary taste and quickly put the cup back on the saucer.

She looked round the room. There were perhaps twenty men in the stifling atmosphere. None of them were talking, though one was listening to a small radio. They all stared ahead of them. Elizabeth tried to imagine what it must have been like to spend sixty years in such a place, with nothing to differentiate one day from the next. Brennan began to talk again, looping from one random recollection to another. As Elizabeth listened she could see he believed he was living in whatever era he was recalling: that time became the present for him. Most of his memories seemed to come either from the turn of the century or from the early forties and the Blitz.

She pressed him once more with her grandfather's name; if he did not respond she would leave him alone and not meddle any more with things that did not concern her.

'My brother. I brought him back all right. Always looked after him, I did.'

'Your brother? Was that in the war? Did he fight with you? And my grandfather? Captain Wraysford?'

Brennan's voice piped up. 'We all thought he was mad, that one. And the sapper with him. My mate Douglas, he was my mucker, he said, "That man's strange." But he held him when he died. They was all mad. Even Price. The CSM. The day it ended he ran out with no clothes. They put him in a loony bin. They bring me this tea, I say I don't want that. My brother's good to me, though. Caught some good fish too. I like a nice bit of fish. You should have seen the fireworks. The whole street was dancing.'

His grip of time gave way again, but Elizabeth was moved by what she had heard. She had to look away from Brennan, down to the orange and brown carpet.

It was not what he said that was important. He had told her that her grandfather had been strange, whatever that might mean in such a context; he told her they thought he and some friend of his were mad, and – though this bit was unclear – that he had comforted a dying man. She didn't feel inclined to press him for clarification, however. Even if he had been lucid enough to give it, she felt it would have made no difference. It was not what Brennan said; it was the fact that some incoherent part of him remembered. By hearing his high voice in the tiny mutilated body, she had somehow kept the chain of experience intact.

404

She sat, feeling great tenderness towards him, holding his hand, as the limited range of what he could recall began to play itself again. After another ten minutes she stood up to leave.

She kissed him on the cheek and walked quickly across the cavernous room. She said she would visit him again, if he liked, but she could not bear to look back at the small body in the chair where it had perched for sixty years.

Outside the high Victorian walls, she ran towards the sea. She stood on the road that overlooked the water, breathing gulps of salty air in the rain, digging her fingernails into the palms of her hands. She had rescued some vital connection, she had been successful in her small errand; what she could not do, which made her curse and wring her hands, was restore poor Brennan's life or take away the pity of the past.

'IT'S FOR YOU,' said Erich, wearily proffering the telephone receiver with its tangled flex to Elizabeth. 'It's a man.'

'A man,' said Elizabeth. 'Erich, you're so precise.' It was Robert. He was going to find himself unexpectedly in London that evening and wondered if she would like to come to see him in his flat.

'I'm sorry it's such short notice,' he said. 'I've only just found out. I don't suppose you're free.'

Elizabeth was going to the cinema and then to a party somewhere in south London. 'Of course I'm free,' she said. 'Shall I come round at about eight?'

'I'll see you then. We'll stay in, shall we? I'll buy some food.'

'Don't worry. I'll get it,' she said with a swiftness based on experience of Robert's shopping.

When she had disentangled her earlier arrangements, she went through into Erich's room to see if she could help him.

'So,' he said, the sound causing half an inch of ash to tumble down the front of his cardigan, 'the errant knight is paying a call.'

'I do wish you wouldn't listen to my conversations.'

'If you use the office as a centre for your social life how can I help it?'

'It's not such a very busy life, is it? One man once a month. There must be worse. Cheer up, Erich. I'll buy you lunch.'

Erich sighed. 'All right. But we won't go to Lucca's. I'm fed up with that man. You see the same trays of sandwich filling

406

in there day after day. I think he just smears a new layer of mashed sardine over what's already in there. The bottom inch must have been there since Lucca came to London in nineteen-fifty-five.'

'How do you know that's when he came?'

'We immigrants, you know, we stick together. We're frightened of your bloody police and your Home Office regulations. The year you arrive is important.'

'Does the Home Office give you a course in how to run a sandwich bar? I mean, all these Italians from different parts of their country, all of them grew up with wonderful food and they came here and they all produce the same egg mayonnaise, the same mashed sardines in stale rolls, the same coffee that tastes of acorns, when in Italy it's like nectar. Do the immigration people give them a complete kit or what?'

'You have no respect for us wretched refugees, do you? Be careful or I'll insist you take me to the best restaurant in London.'

'Anywhere you like, Erich. It's my pleasure.'

'My God, that man puts you in a good mood, doesn't he? It's like ringing a bell. It's like Skinner's rats.'

'Don't you mean Pavlov's dogs?'

'No, I'm an Anglo-Saxon these days. Skinner will do for me. Get back to work, will you? I'll come through at one, not a minute before.'

Erich was quite right, Elizabeth thought, as she went back to her desk. Robert rang; she jumped. His voice made her happy. It was better to have some source of happiness than none, though, wasn't it? She had pushed and pulled him and tried to change her mind; she had analysed her own feelings and guessed at his; she had done everything she could to make him leave his wife, but nothing had changed. She had resigned herself to not thinking about the future. The grim conversations and the tearful partings would come back soon enough.

Robert had a small top-floor flat in a block off the Fulham Road. While he waited for Elizabeth he tried to remove traces of his family, though it was difficult to obliterate them completely. The flat had an open kitchen attached to the sitting

407

room with a bamboo curtain dividing them. On the wooden unit between the rooms there were two Chianti bottles with red candles stuck in them which gave it the air of a Chelsea bistro from the sixties, as Elizabeth frequently pointed out. They could not be thrown away because Robert's daughter liked them.

Half a dozen of his wife's dresses hung in the wardrobe, and there was some of her make-up in the bathroom cabinet.

He could at least remove her photograph from the sideboard and bury it beneath the tablecloths in the drawer. Each time he did this he felt a pang of superstitious guilt, as though he had stabbed her effigy. He wished her no harm; he recognized in her the qualities of dedication and generosity he feared that he himself lacked, but with Elizabeth he could not help himself.

Many of his male colleagues assumed it was an arrangement of convenience, a light-hearted sideshow of the kind the majority of them enjoyed. Robert knew that Elizabeth also thought so, however hard he tried to convince her to the contrary. When he protested that he was not that kind of man, she laughed at him. He had been unfaithful to his wife for one ill-advised night before he met Elizabeth, but with her, as he tried to explain, it was different. He believed he had married the wrong woman. He didn't want to reclaim some notional freedom, he just wanted to be with Elizabeth. He had been addicted to her initially in a physical way: a week without her body made him vague and irritable. Then the mocking confidence of her character had intrigued him. If, as she sometimes claimed, he used her just as an amusing diversion, why was it not more enjoyable? Why was there so much anguish in what his colleagues nudgingly hinted must be such fun?

He heard her ring at the intercom as he was straightening the cushions on the sofa.

'What on earth is this?' said Elizabeth, fingering his sweater.

'I had time to change out of my suit, so I –'

'Where did you get it?'

'I bought it this afternoon. I thought it was time I smartened myself up.'

'Well, you can get rid of that for a start. And are those flared trousers? Robert, really.'

'There's not a single man in Europe that doesn't have slightly flared trousers. You can't buy any other sort in the shops.'

She went into the bedroom and found some old corduroy trousers and an inoffensive sweater. Robert pretended to protest when she took control of small aspects of his life, but privately he was pleased. He admired her for knowing about such things and he was flattered that she cared enough about him for it to matter.

Properly dressed, he made drinks and stood with his arm round Elizabeth as she set about cooking the food she had brought. This was the time he liked best, when everything was anticipation and the evening had not really begun.

While they ate he talked about his work and the people he had met in the course of it. Elizabeth urged him on with questions. He feared boring her, but she clearly liked the sardonic way he described the various meetings and dinners he had attended.

They managed to spend an evening and a night of enclosed harmony without discussing the difficult decisions that awaited them. Robert was glad, and Elizabeth too, when she left with a light step in the morning, seemed elated.

ON SATURDAY AFTERNOON Françoise telephoned to say she had found twenty more notebooks in the attic, and Elizabeth went down at once to fetch them. She had nothing to do that evening, so she would have a long bath, not bother with dinner, but study the notebooks and see if she could make any headway where Bob had failed.

She lit the fire in the sitting room to warm it up while she was in the bath. She wondered whether some law would prevent the Gas Board from going on strike. Almost everyone else had at one stage during the winter, lining up to take their turn. If they stopped the gas, would the army take over the supply? She could always go and stay with her mother, who had oil-fired heating, though she would have to take Mrs Kyriades with her, otherwise she wouldn't last a day in the cold . . .

Elizabeth brought her mind back to the notebooks. She curled up in her dressing gown on the sofa and opened the first one. It had a date, 1915, in the front cover. They were all dated, she discovered, from 1915 to 1917. The one she had given Bob had been from 1918, she thought. In some of them were lines of English. 'Arrived back at Coy HQ at ten. Still no word from Gray abt attack.' Elizabeth felt a leap of excitement at the word 'Gray'. Again she had touched the past. It had stopped being history and had turned into experience.

She flicked through the books at random. There seemed to be an almost complete and sequential record, though she noticed that after a long entry on June 30th 1916 there was nothing for two months. Had something happened?

She settled her reading glasses and picked up another note-book. There was a ring at the doorbell.

She went crossly into the hall to answer the intercom from the street. 'Hello?' she said abruptly.

It cracked and fuzzed. 'It's me.'

'Who?'

'Stuart of course. It's freezing.'

Elizabeth was dumb. Stuart. God. She had asked him round.

'Come up. I was just . . . in the bath. Come on up.' She pushed the button on the intercom and left the door of the flat open as she dashed into the bedroom. She ripped off her glasses, tore the combs from her hair and wrapped the dress-ing gown more modestly about her. She could hear him knocking at the open door. He must have run up the stairs.

She proffered her cheek. 'I'm sorry. I'm running a bit late.'

'Hmm,' he said. 'I thought I couldn't smell any enticing aromas on the stairs.'

'Come in, come in. I'm sorry it's such a mess.' The note-books were open all over the floor; her breakfast coffee cup was still on the table. Short of actually having her clothes hanging in front of the fire to dry she could hardly have made it clearer that she was not expecting anyone.

Stuart appeared not to notice. 'I brought you this,' he said, handing her a bottle of wine. She peeled off the paper.

'Lovely,' she said. 'Muscadet. Is that very special? I don't know anything about wine.'

'I think you'll find it's pretty good.'

'You'll have to excuse me while I get dressed. I'm sorry to be so chaotic. Help yourself to a drink from the side there.'

Elizabeth cursed steadily under her breath as she dressed. She pulled on a knee-length navy wool skirt she had just bought, woollen tights and boots. She thought about the top. She didn't want to look too dowdy, but on the other hand she was going to have to go out into freezing night to buy some food. She took a polo neck from the drawer and an old leather jacket from the wardrobe. There was no time to make up. Stuart would have to take her au naturel. Terrifying thought, she murmured, as she quickly brushed her hair. This was not the kind of thing that Lindsay, who thought her so poised, would ever have imagined happening to her. She quickly fastened a pair of red earrings as she went through to the sitting room.

'Ah, what a transformation. Magnificent. You –'

'Look, I've just realized I forgot to buy any pasta. We're having pasta and I forgot the pasta. Would you believe it? So I'm just going to slip out. Is there anything you'd like while I'm there? Cigarettes? Turn on the television. Have another drink. I won't be a minute.'

She managed to get out of the front door before Stuart had a chance to protest. She ran to the supermarket on Praed Street and hastily collected all she would need to make a quick dinner. She had more wine at home if Stuart's bottle was not enough for both of them. It was some red wine Robert had brought; she wasn't sure if Stuart would approve, but her shopping bag already looked suspiciously full.

'Just thought I'd buy a few other things while I was there,' she explained to Stuart as she puffed through into the kitchen. She poured herself some gin and started cooking.

'What's this?' said Stuart, standing in the doorway, holding out his hand to her. 'It looks like a buckle from a belt.'

Elizabeth took it. '*Gott mit uns*,' she read from the lettering on it.

'God with us,' Stuart translated. 'I found it on the carpet.

'Just something I got in a junk shop,' said Elizabeth. It must have fallen out of one of the notebooks, but she didn't want to discuss it.

Once dinner was on the table Elizabeth began to relax. Stuart hadn't seemed to mind the chaos of her arrangements; in fact he had hardly seemed to notice. He was complimentary about the food and took charge of the wine himself, making sure their glasses stayed full.

'So, tell me all about yourself, Elizabeth Benson,' he said, sitting back in his chair.

'I think I already have. This time and last time. Between the two I think I've covered the ground. You tell me some more about your work. You're a marketing consultant, didn't you say?'

412

'That's right, yes.'

'What does it entail?'

'How long is a piece of string?'

'You know what I mean. Do people come to see you and ask how to sell their products? Is that what it is?'

'That's part of it. It's rather more complicated than that.'

'Well, go on. Tell me. I'm sure I can follow.'

'We are in the skills business. We like to see ourselves as beneficent jailers. We have a set of keys for all occasions. The keys unlock the potential of a business. We have to teach people how to use them, which key fits which lock. But above all we have to teach them how to ask the right questions.'

'I see,' said Elizabeth, with a slight hesitation. 'So you give advice and sales go up and you take a percentage. Is that it?'

'It's more a question of seeing how each part of a business can relate to the other parts. So suppose you're in product development and Bloggs is in sales, then unless you're asking the right questions you may be pulling in different directions. I always say our main aim is to teach people not to need us.'

'And how do I know when I don't need you?'

'That's a very good question.'

'Is it one of the questions you would have taught me to ask?' Elizabeth felt a twitch at the corner of her mouth, which she tried to quell.

'It's not quite that simple.'

'I thought it might not be. Anyway. I thought you were a musician.'

Stuart ran his hand back through his hair and resettled his glasses. 'I am a musician,' he said. 'It's just that I don't make a living from it. You don't make a living from being a cook, but you're still a cook, aren't you? Do you follow?'

'I think so. You play the piano very well anyway.'

'Thank you.'

'I'm afraid it's only ice-cream. I meant to make something, but I didn't have time. Is that all right?'

As she made coffee in the kitchen and tried to spoon the frozen ice-cream from its carton without snapping the shaft off the spoon, Elizabeth was struck, not for the first time, by the thought that her life was entirely frivolous.

It was a rush and slither of trivial crises; of uncertain cash-flow, small triumphs, occasional sex and too many cigarettes; of missed deadlines that turned out not to matter; of arguments, new clothes, bursts of altruism and sincere resolutions to address the important things. Of all these and the other experiences that made up her life, the most significant aspect was the one suggested by the words 'turned out not to matter'. Although she was happy enough with what she had become, it was this continued sense of the easy, the inessential nature of what she did, that most irritated her. She thought of Tom Brennan, who had known only life or death, then death in life. In her generation there was no intensity.

She took the coffee and the ice-cream back into the sitting room. Stuart had put a record on, a Beethoven piano concerto, and was listening to it with closed eyes.

Elizabeth smiled as she put his ice-cream down in front of him. She had made up her mind about Stuart. She had been impressed by his piano playing and flattered by his attention, but the way he spoke was intolerable.

They sat on the sofa afterwards and he explained to her, still with his eyes closed, how the piece of music was constructed and where, in his view, the soloist was going wrong.

When the record finished Elizabeth made to go and change it, but Stuart caught her by the forearm and pulled her back.

'Sit down, Liz. I have something to ask you.'

'Sorry?'

'I want you to listen carefully. I don't know what you'll make of me and I'm not sure it matters too much. I'm going to tell you a story.'

As Elizabeth started to interrupt he held up his hand to silence her.

'Once upon a time there was a very attractive girl. She had lots of friends, a very good job, a flat in town, and everyone envied her. Then, as time went on, her friends got married and had babies and this girl became a very attractive woman. But she didn't get married. The older she got, the more she pretended it didn't matter to her, but the more, deep down inside, she longed for children and a husband. Part of the problem was that the more she pretended, the more she frightened men

414

off. Because they, poor little creatures, believed her when she said she was happy.'

Elizabeth looked down at the floor. An unhealthy curiosity was fighting the embarrassment that ran in waves up and down her spine. Stuart himself showed no trace of self-consciousness. He looked straight ahead.

'Then one day she met a man who was not frightened at all. He was kind to her and funny and friendly. And when she really thought about it, she knew, deep down, that this was what she had always wanted. And they moved to the country and she had lots of children and they all lived happily ever after.'

Elizabeth swallowed. 'And?'

Stuart turned round to face her. 'I'm asking you to marry me. I know it's unorthodox. This is only the third time we've met and I haven't even bothered to seduce you. I'm such a sweet old-fashioned thing. You're a very unusual woman. I think you'll find, if you accept my offer, that I'm an equally unusual man.'

Elizabeth stood up. She took a cigarette and spluttered as she inhaled it. 'It's very . . . nice of you. I'm flattered by the thought, but I'm afraid you've got the wrong person. I have a boyfriend. I –'

'He's married, isn't he? Let me guess. You see him once a month for hasty sex and a tearful farewell. He says he'll leave his wife, but we all know he won't, don't we? Is that what you want? Is that your future?'

Elizabeth's voice took on a frozen edge. 'You shouldn't talk about people you don't know.'

Stuart stood up and threw his arms open expansively. 'Come on, we're both adults, we both know the score. I'm sorry if I intruded on a private sorrow, but this is a very important matter. I have money. Did I mention that? Or is it the sex thing? Do you want a trial run?'

'I *beg* your pardon?'

'Well, at least give me credit for not having seduced you.'

'What on earth makes you think you could have?'

Stuart shrugged suggestively. 'I'm sorry, Liz. I've gone too far. I'm going to leave you now. Let's say I've planted a seed.

415

You just do me the favour of watering it from time to time. Think about it.'

He took his coat from the hook in the hall and came back into the room. 'Thank you for a marvellous evening,' he said. 'And will you water it, that little seed?'

'I . . . won't forget. I certainly won't forget.'

'Good.' He smiled and kissed her on the forehead, then let himself out.

ELIZABETH WAS IN a condition of shock for some days. The presumptuousness of what Stuart had said to her felt, in retrospect, like an unwanted physical intimacy; it was as though he had forced himself on her.

She went for long walks in Hyde Park and breathed deeply on the cold January air. She worked till late in the office. She bought, and read, two books about the war her grandfather had fought in. She made resolutions for the New Year. She would smoke less, she would visit Tom Brennan once a fortnight, if he wanted, or, if he didn't, she would visit someone else of his generation. Somehow she would repay the debt; she would complete the circle.

For the first of her New Year visits to Tom Brennan she hoped she might find out some more about her grandfather. She understood enough about his state of mind not to expect a long recollection, or even an anecdote, but she hoped for some reference at least.

She was wearing fewer clothes this time, knowing what the central heating was like in the rest room. In view of his complaints about the food, she took Brennan a cake her mother had baked. She was struck as she packed it by how much it was like sending a parcel to a man in the trenches. She took half a bottle of whisky as well; at least that was something he wouldn't have been sent from home. She also, feeling ashamed as she did so, put two mothballs in her handkerchief, so she could hold it to her face and breathe in camphor rather than the cloying smell of urine.

He was in the same place at the window. He put his hand in hers and they sat happily together. Elizabeth asked him what he had been doing in the past few weeks and what he had done the years before that. His answers bore no relation to her questions. He talked about Mafeking night, he talked about his sister in the blackout and how she had fallen off a ladder. He told her he didn't like the food they gave him.

Occasionally she could tell that a particular question had registered with him, because his eyes showed alarm behind the thick lenses of his spectacles. He would mumble a few words, then either fall silent or resume with one of the stories he knew. Elizabeth began to suspect that she had already heard most of his repertoire.

This time she didn't press him on the subject of her grand-father. She had made the first vital connection. If he had anything else to say it would come in time; in fact it was more likely to come out when he became familiar with her visits.

She left him with the cake and whisky and said she would be back in two weeks' time. The matron, Mrs Simpson, passed her in the doorway.

'I didn't think we'd see you again,' she said. 'Any joy?'

'Well . . . not joy exactly. I don't know if he liked seeing me. But I liked seeing him again. I left him a little parcel. Is that allowed?'

'It depends what's in it.'

Elizabeth had a feeling the whisky would be forbidden. She left before she would have to see it being confiscated.

At home that night she did some calculations. It was a task she had been putting off, because she feared the result. With the help of last year's diary she was able to work out when her last period had been. It had definitely been in progress on the sixth of December because she remembered being late for a lunch that was marked for that day when she had had to make a detour to find a chemist. It was now January 21st. The last time she had seen Robert was not recorded in her diary, but it had been in the week before Christmas. She remembered the decorations in the shops. In fact he had come over on his holidays a day early, which was how he had managed to squeeze her in. She had had to go to work the following day, so it must have been a weekday. She narrowed it down to the 21st or the 22nd. Either day was halfway through the cycle which, if she remembered rightly, was the dangerous time. She tried to remember what precautions she had taken. She had been on the pill for four years continuously and her doctor had advised her to stop taking it. They had then used a variety of means. Both of them were careful, Robert neurotically so in her opinion.

The next morning she bought a pregnancy testing kit from the chemist in Craven Road. It was a flat, rectangular piece of plastic with two windows. She took it to the bathroom, then, five minutes later, as instructed, looked at the windows. The blue line across each was firm and assertive. It was not just positive, it was bursting with life.

She passed a day in which her feelings oscillated between joy and despair. Twice she began to tell Irene her secret and twice discretion made her change the subject. She went out for lunch on her own and found her eyes brimming with tears as she ate. Already she felt an absurd passion for the invisible thing inside her.

In the evening she telephoned Robert. There was no reply, but she left a message on his recently acquired answering machine telling him to ring at once.

She ran a bath and slid beneath the water. She gazed at her lower belly and wondered what microscopic events were taking place there. She was frightened of the physical changes and worried about what people would say; but much more than anxiety she felt exhilaration. Her telephone rang and she sprang from the bath and went dripping through to answer it.

It was Bob.

'I've cracked it,' he said. 'I'm sorry it's taken me such a long time. It was perfectly straightforward, really, once I'd figured out how the old codger's mind worked. Greek letters, French language and a bit of private code. Elementary, my dear Watson. I can't swear I've got every name right, of course. I've marked the odd query. But it all seems to add up.'

When she had overcome her disappointment that it was not

Robert, Elizabeth said, 'That's marvellous, Bob. Thank you very much. When can I pick it up?'

'Come over at the weekend if you like. I put a couple of pages in the post this morning. I just did the last two in the book because they were the ones I'd worked on first. They should be with you in the morning if the Post Office isn't on strike as well. You never know, do you?'

'No. Quite. Well, I'll look forward to getting those tomorrow.'

'Yes,' said Bob. 'They're a bit gloomy, you know. Pour yourself a drink first.'

'You know me, Bob. And thanks again.'

Robert didn't ring till after midnight, when Elizabeth was asleep. She told him straight away that she was going to have a baby. She was too sleepy to break the news gently, as she had intended. 'I won't tell anyone who the father is. These things can be kept secret,' she said.

Robert was shocked.

'You could sound a bit happier about it,' she said.

'Give me time,' he said. 'I'm happy for you, and in time I'll be happy for myself and the child. Just give me time to get used to it.'

'I will,' said Elizabeth. 'I love you.'

The next day was a Saturday and in the morning there was a package from Bob.

Elizabeth put it aside till after breakfast, then opened it carefully with a knife. Bob had re-used a brown envelope from an old catalogue or circular, sticking a white label with her name and address over his own.

Inside were two large sheets of thin, crackling white paper. Elizabeth was very excited. From the moment she saw the black ink of Bob's careful script, she knew that she had found what she wanted.

Gray's old voice barking down the line from Lanarkshire had been good; the glimpse of memory through the chaos of Brennan's recollection had been thrilling. But finally she had what she wanted: the past was alive in the spidery letters in her slightly shaking hand.

She read:

I don't know how the days pass. The anger and the blood have gone. We sit and read. There is always someone sleeping, someone strolling. Food is brought. We don't read real books, only magazines. Someone is eating. There are always others unaccounted for or absent.

Since Weir??? died I have not been very close to reality. I am in a wilderness beyond fear. Time has finally collapsed for me. I had a letter from Jeanne this morning. She said two months have passed since we met.

Men come out from England like emissaries from an unknown land. I cannot picture what it means to be at peace. I do not know how people there can lead a life.

The only things that sometimes jolt us back from this trance are memories of men. In the set of the eyes of some conscripted boy I see a look of Douglas or [name illeg. Reeve?]. I find myself rigid with imagining. I can see that man's skull opening as he bent down to his friend that summer morning.

Yesterday a signaller came up to talk and his gestures reminded me of W. I had a clear picture of him, not sprawling in the mud as I last saw him, but emerging from his burrow in the ground, wild-eyed. The image lasted only for an instant, then time collapsed and drifted past me once again.

I have been summoned to see Gray tomorrow. Perhaps he will feel the same.

We are not contemptuous of gunfire, but we have lost the power to be afraid. Shells will fall on the reserve lines and we will not stop talking. There is still blood, though no one sees. A boy lay without legs where the men took their tea from the cooker. They stepped over him.

I have tried to resist the slide into this unreal world, but I lack the strength. I am tired. Now I am tired in my soul.

Many times I have lain down and I have longed for death. I feel unworthy. I feel guilty because I have survived. Death will not come and I am cast adrift in a perpetual present.

I do not know what I have done to live in this existence. I do not know what any of us did to tilt the world into this unnatural orbit. We came here only for a few months.

No child or future generation will ever know what this was like. They will never understand.

When it is over we will go quietly among the living and we will not tell them.

We will talk and sleep and go about our business like human beings.

We will seal what we have seen in the silence of our hearts and no words will reach us.

PART SIX
FRANCE 1918

STEPHEN PUT AWAY his pen and notebook. It was night-time. There was moonlight on the hills above the village. He lit another cigarette and turned the pages of a magazine. There was a pile by the chair of others he had already skimmed. His eyes scanned each page but barely read.

He went outside into the yard behind the little house. Chickens scattered in front of his footsteps.

He went into the lane and began to walk. The road was half made up. He felt the puddles and the loose stones beneath his feet. He went as far as the main road and looked around him. The guns were soft and distant; they rumbled like a train going through an embankment.

He stood and breathed deeply on the air. He could hear an owl's call. He went slowly up and down the lane. The owl reminded him of childhood; it was a noise boys would make with their hands. His own seemed so long ago that it felt as though someone else had lived it for him.

Back in the billet he found Mountford sitting at the table, playing cards with a lieutenant called Tylecote. He declined their offer of a game, but sat in a daze and watched them move the greasy pictures over the wooden surface.

In the morning he went to see Colonel Gray in battalion headquarters two miles away.

Gray sprang up when Stephen went into the room. 'Wraysford! How good to see you again. Civil of you staff men to pay us a call.'

Gray had changed little in appearance. He gave the

impression of an enquiring terrier with its head on one side. His moustache and hair showed patches of white, but his movements were still swift and certain.

He pulled back a chair and gestured to Stephen, who sat down.

'Do smoke,' he said. 'Now then. Are you enjoying yourself with your wee maps and lists?'

Stephen breathed in deeply. 'We . . . exist.'

'Exist? Good heavens, that's not the sort of talk I'm used to from a front-line man like yourself.'

'I suppose not. If you remember, sir, I didn't ask to be transferred.'

'I remember very well. In my view you were battle-weary. Mind you, most people were never allowed to reach that stage. A bullet saw to that.'

'Yes. I've been lucky.' Stephen coughed as the cigarette smoke went down into his lungs.

Gray looked out of the window and swung his feet up on to the desk. 'Our lot have done pretty well, you know. Terrible casualties on the Somme, but who didn't? Otherwise not too bad. Both battalions are pretty much back to full strength.'

'Yes I know,' said Stephen. He smiled. 'I know quite a lot about troop strengths in this area. More than when I was fighting.'

Gray nodded his head quickly up and down and tapped his teeth with a pen. 'Tell me,' he said, 'when the war is over and the regiment puts up a memorial, what words will we inscribe on it?'

'I don't know. I presumed there would be a divisional memorial. The regiment would list the actions it was in, I suppose.'

'Yes,' said Gray. 'It's a proud list, isn't it?'

Stephen did not answer. He felt no pride in the unspeakable names.

Gray said, 'Well, I've good news for you. Your staff attachment is finished. You're coming back.' He paused. 'I thought that's what you wanted.'

'I . . . yes, I suppose it is.'

'You don't look very pleased.'

'I can't be pleased by anything that carries on this war. But I'm not displeased. I'm indifferent.'

'Now listen to me. Quite soon we are going to attack. On a long front we are going to move rapidly forward into Germany. Parts of the line have already started to advance, as you know. If you want to lead your old company, you can. The temporary OC will become your second in command.'

Stephen sighed and said nothing. He wished he felt pleased or excited.

Gray stood up and came round the desk. 'Think of the words on that memorial, Wraysford. Think of those stinking towns and foul bloody villages whose names will be turned into some bogus glory by fat-arsed historians who have sat in London. We were there. As our punishment for God knows what, we were there, and our men died in each of those disgusting places. I hate their names. I hate the sound of them and the thought of them, which is why I will not bring myself to remind you. But listen.' He put his face close to Stephen's. 'There are four words they will chisel beneath them at the bottom. Four words that people will look at one day. When they read the other words they will want to be sick. When they read these, they will bow their heads, just a little. "Final advance and pursuit." Don't tell me you don't want to put your name to those words.'

Stephen laughed. 'I really don't mind what –'

'Go *on*.' Gray growled at him like a dog. 'There must be one of those words you like the sound of.'

Stephen said, 'I suppose so. "Final."'

Gray shook him by the shoulders. 'Good man. I'll tell the men you're on your way.'

THE WORK OF the tunnellers reached its climax with the explosion at Messines Ridge. Weir's company was absorbed by the three RE field companies attached to the division in which Stephen served. The work was less arduous and less interesting:

Jack Firebrace wrote:

Dear Margaret, These are just a few lines while I have a moment. Thank you for the parcel which got here yesterday, though it was slightly damaged. Did you put in razor blades?

We are on road repair work again. It is very hard work, though most of the men think it better than tunnelling. We have to fill big holes with stones and what they call fascines, which are bundles of spoil, masonry and suchlike, from damaged houses.

What with the mire and the rain and all the dead animals, it is a sorry business. We feel sorry for the dead horses, such beautiful animals so badly knocked about and they didn't ask for any part of it.

We still do a bit of digging. The CO says we've made our contribution to the war, but that it's going to become a much faster business fought above the ground now. We'll see about that. We have started to advance now and there is a real feeling that one more push and it will be over.

We are all keeping cheerful and bright. Evans has had a new pack of cards and I am quite the star turn at brag now. I have also done some more sketching.

Trusting you are keeping well and that I will see you again soon. From your loving husband Jack.

Before he rejoined his company, Stephen took two of the days owing to him in leave and went to Rouen, where Jeanne had moved during the German spring offensive.

It was a hot Sunday afternoon when he arrived. There was a festive atmosphere in the streets. Old motor cars were taking families for a drive. Others had four-in-hands, carts or bicycles – anything to keep their promenade moving. There were numbers of small boys running on the cobbles and shouting to the drivers of the vehicles.

Stephen moved through the crowd in some puzzlement. Following Jeanne's instructions, he came to the cathedral and turned into the medieval part of the city where she had taken a room until she could return to Amiens.

She sat him down in one of the two armchairs and looked at him. He had grown very thin and his skin had become lined and leathery about the eyes. Their expression was no longer guarded; to Jeanne it seemed vacant. He had not lost any hair, even at the temples, but there were now streaks of early grey almost everywhere in it. His movements had a dreamlike quality, as though the air about him were very thick and had to be pushed slowly back. He smoked without seeming to know that he did so and dropped ash on his clothes.

This was the man who eight years earlier had so stirred her younger sister. Isabelle had told her nothing about their love-making, but she had given Jeanne a strong physical sense of him by referring to his shoulders, his eyes, and the deft movements of his hands. The man Jeanne saw was different; it was hard to believe it was the same person. This thought made her feel easier in her mind.

They went for a walk in the town and then to the museum, where they sat in the gardens.

'What happened to you in the spring?' said Stephen. 'I had no letters for a time.'

'I did write,' said Jeanne. 'Perhaps they got lost in all the commotion. To begin with the town was filled with refugees from others places as the Germans advanced. Then we were bombarded and the mayor gave the order to evacuate the town. I stayed for a time because I didn't want to come back to Rouen. They used to shell at night using flares to guide their fire. It was frightening. I went to the cathedral to help them take out the stained-glass windows. We wrapped them all up in blankets. Eventually I had to leave, but I didn't tell my parents where I'd gone. I managed to find these rooms with the help of a friend I'd known when I was a girl. My parents don't know I'm here.'

'Would they be angry?'

'I don't know. I think they've almost given up hope with their daughters. They heard that Isabelle had gone to Germany. They had a letter from an old friend of Azaire's in Amiens, a man called Bérard. He said he thought they ought to know.'

Stephen sang softly, '"And the little boat sailed away-y-y."'

'What was that?'

'I knew that man. He used to visit when I was there. He was a bully, a preposterous little man, full of his own importance. But he seemed to have some sort of power over people.'

'I wrote to Isabelle and told her what had happened. She wrote back and told me that when the place was first occupied by the Germans this man Bérard offered the commandant his house to live in. He thought they would be staying there for the whole war. When they moved on after a few days he was left feeling shamefaced. According to Isabelle he tried to make up for it afterwards by making very belligerent noises.'

'But he didn't join the army?'

'No. Perhaps he was too old. Isabelle said she was happy, though Max is not well. He had to have his leg amputated and he has not recovered his strength. She's very devoted to him.'

Stephen nodded. 'Poor man. I'm sorry.'

'Now what about you?' said Jeanne. She took his hand and squeezed it in her affectionate, sisterly way. 'You're looking very distracted and pale. I worry about you. I told you that, didn't I? I don't suppose you're eating properly either.'

Stephen smiled. 'I'm all right. The food was much better in the job I've just finished. There was plenty of it, too.'

'Then why are you so thin?'

He shrugged. 'I don't know.'

Jeanne's dark eyes lit up with seriousness as she pressed his hand and made him look at her. 'Stephen, you mustn't give up. You mustn't let yourself go. It's nearly over. Any day now we'll advance and you'll be free to resume your life.'

'Resume? I can't remember my life. I wouldn't know where to look for it.'

'You mustn't talk in this way.' Jeanne was angry. Her pale skin showed, for the first time since Stephen had known her, a pin-point of blood in the cheeks. With her left hand she lightly beat the wooden bench on which they were sitting to emphasize what she said.

'Of course you won't resume whatever it was you were doing in Paris, drifting around as a carpenter or whatever it was. You'll do something better, you'll do something worthwhile.'

Stephen turned his eyes slowly to her. 'You're a dear woman, Jeanne. I would do what you say. But it's not the details of a life I've lost. It's the reality itself.'

Jeanne's eyes filled with tears. 'Then we must make it come back. I'll bring it back for you. I'll help you to find whatever it is you have lost. Nothing is beyond redemption.'

'Why are you so kind to me?' said Stephen.

'Because I love you. Can't you see that? From all that's gone wrong I want to make something good. We must try. Promise me you'll try.'

Stephen nodded slowly. 'We will try.'

Jeanne stood up, feeling encouraged. She took his hand and led him through the gardens. What else could she do to invigorate him, to bring him back to the reality he had lost? There was one thing, naturally; though the complications might outweigh the benefits. It should happen spontaneously or not at all.

They had dinner early in a restaurant on their way back to her lodgings and she made Stephen drink wine in the hope that it would cheer him. Glass after glass of red Bordeaux went down his throat but brought no light into his dead eyes.

On the way home Jeanne said, 'Please be very quiet as we

431

cross the courtyard. I don't want the concierge to know there's a man staying the night in my rooms.'

Stephen laughed for the first time. 'You Fourmentier girls. What would your father say?'

'Be quiet,' said Jeanne, glad that she had made him laugh.

It was a hot night, and it was not yet dark as they walked. A small band was playing in one of the squares where the cafés were starting to put on their lights among the plane trees.

Stephen went with elaborate care over the paving of the courtyard and made no sound until they were safely back in Jeanne's lodgings.

'I've made up a bed for you on the sofa in the corner. Do you want to go to bed now or would you like to sit up and talk? I think I have some brandy. We could take it on to the little balcony there. But we must keep our voices down.'

They sat in two wickerwork chairs on the narrow strip which gave a view over a dry, sandy garden.

'You know what I want to do for you?' said Jeanne. 'I'm going to make you laugh. That's going to be my project. I'm going to banish your Anglo-Saxon gloom. I'm going to make you laugh and be full of joy, like a proper French peasant.'

Stephen smiled. He said, 'And I'll tell stories and slap my thighs like a Norman farmer.'

'And never think about the war. And those who have gone.'

'Never.' He drained the brandy in a gulp.

She took his hand again. 'I'll have a house with a garden at the back with rose bushes and flowerbeds, and perhaps a swing for children to play on – if not my own, then visiting children. The house will have long windows and be full of the smell of wonderful meals in the kitchen. And the sitting room will have freesias and violets. And there will be paintings on the wall, by Millet and Courbet and other great artists.'

'I'll visit you. Perhaps I'll live there with you. It will shock the whole of Rouen.'

'We'll go boating on Sunday, and on Saturday we'll go to the opera, then to dinner in the big square. Twice a year we'll have parties in the house. They'll be full of candles, and we'll hire servants to take round drinks on silver trays to all our friends. And there will be dancing and –'

432

'Not dancing.'

'All right, no dancing. But there'll be a band. Perhaps a string quartet or a gipsy violinist. And those who *want* to can dance, somewhere in a separate room. Perhaps we'll have a singer.'

'Perhaps we could persuade Bérard.'

'A good idea. He could sing some German lieder he had learned from the commandant and his wife. The parties would be famous. I'm not sure how we'd pay for them.'

'I'll have made my fortune by some invention. Your father will have left his millions to you.'

They drank some more brandy, which made Jeanne feel dizzy, though it seemed to have no effect on Stephen. When it grew cold they went inside and Stephen said he would like to sleep. She showed him his bed and fetched him a carafe of water.

In her bedroom Jeanne undressed. She felt encouraged by Stephen, though she could see he was making efforts for her benefit. It was beginning. She walked naked across the floor to take her nightgown from the back of the door.

It opened just before she reached it, and she saw Stephen outside in his shirt with bare legs.

He recoiled. 'I'm sorry, I was looking for the bathroom.'

Jeanne had grabbed reflexively for a towel that lay on the chair, and tried to arrange it modestly over her body.

Stephen turned and began to move back into the sitting room.

Jeanne said, 'Stop. It's all right. Come back.'

She put the towel on the chair and stood quite still.

There was no light in the room, but the brightness of the autumn night made it easy to see.

'Come and let me hold you,' she said. The slow smile rose up and illuminated her face.

Stephen walked slowly into the room. Jeanne's long thin body stood to welcome him. Her pale arms were held out, pulling up the round breasts that rode like mysterious white flowers on her ribcage in the uncertain light. Stephen went and knelt at her feet. He put his head against her side, beneath her ribs.

She was hoping that his forced lightness of spirit would still be with him.

He put his arms round her thighs. The soft hair that grew up between her legs was long and black. He laid his cheek against it for a moment, then put his face against her side. She felt him begin to sob. 'Isabelle,' he was saying, 'Isabelle.'

WHEN STEPHEN RETURNED to his company in the forward area there were celebrations. The men were guardedly hopeful that their next attack would be their last, and after the events on the Ancre and the advance on the canal Stephen had acquired a reputation for survival. Even the conscripted men who had joined since he had been away were aware that he was regarded as a lucky charm. Exaggerated rumours reached them of the witchcraft he performed in his dugout.

The engineers and tunnellers came up infrequently to do trench maintenance. A long tunnel out into no man's land was periodically inspected and repaired. Its furthest point provided an entrance to a useful if dangerous listening post close to German lines, apparently still undiscovered by the enemy. Men positioned in it had heard talk from the German front line. It had been of retreat.

Enemy shelling followed a pattern. It was accurately aimed at the rear area, with little danger to the front line, and stopped for an hour at lunchtime. The British reply observed the same formalities, so Stephen was able to eat peacefully on his first day back. Riley had heated up some tinned stew, but had managed to find a fresh cabbage to enliven it.

Cartwright, the officer commanding the engineers, came to see him in the afternoon. Although he was regarded as a weak character by the infantry, he had a sense of grievance that made him a tenacious arguer.

'As you know,' he said, 'we have an agreement to help each other, though as far as I can see there has been little give and take about it.' He had a pale face with a receding chin; he favoured familiar domestic phrases and proverbs in the hope that they would make his arguments seem more palatable.

'Now I've received an order that my men are to enlarge the listening post at the end of the main drive. That's all well and good, but the last men I had down there said they heard what sounded like enemy work going on just above them.'

'I see. So you're saying you want some of my men to go down with you.'

'Yes. I think we're entitled to it.'

'I thought all the digging had stopped.'

'You never know with our friends the Boche, do you?'

'I suppose not. It seems a bit unnecessary, but –'

'I thought that since you'd been away you'd like to see what's been going on for yourself. After all, the work is done for the protection of your men.'

'You're as bad as Weir. Why are you always so keen to get us underground?'

'Because we dug you proper drains here and made this dugout.' Cartwright gestured to the wooden walls and the bookshelf above the bed. 'You don't think your men could have done this, do you?'

'All right,' said Stephen. 'I'll come and inspect it, but I can't be away for more than an hour. One of your men will have to bring me back.'

'I'm sure that can be arranged. We're going down at midday tomorrow.'

The autumn light showed the blackened, splintered stumps of what had once been trees. The floor of the trench was for once reasonably dry when the men assembled at the tunnel head.

Jack Firebrace, Evans and Jones were among six experienced tunnellers who handed out helmets, lamps and Proto breathing sets to the infantry. Cartwright said to Jack, 'You're to escort Captain Wraysford back after he's inspected the work, Firebrace.'

'Aren't you coming?' said Stephen, putting an electric torch in his pocket.

'Wouldn't do to have us both down there,' said Cartwright.

436

Stephen looked up at the sky above him. It was a clear, pale blue with a few high clouds. The tarpaulin-draped entrance to the burrow was dark.

He was thinking of the first time he had gone underground with Hunt and Byrne to protect Jack Firebrace. He remembered the pale light of panic in Hunt's face and the impact of his own wounds. He himself had changed since then; he could no longer be sure that he would be as calm in the narrow tunnels that awaited them. He rested his hands on the wooden revetting that held the front wall of the trench and breathed in deeply. There were no distinct worlds, only one creation, to which he was bound by the beating of his blood. It would be the same underground as here in the warm air, with the birds singing and the gentle clouds above them.

He clambered in after the tunnellers and felt the splintering wood of the ladder against his hands. The drop was vertical and the rungs were far apart. Stephen hesitated as he lowered his feet into the darkness, but was forced to continue by the boots that kept treading down close by his fingers. The light at the top of the tunnel was obscured by their large, descending bulk, and eventually narrowed to something like a distant window pane, then to nothing.

He heard Jack's voice below him telling him how much further he had to go. Eventually he jumped off the ladder and fell to the earth on a platform about ten feet square where Jack and two of the infantry were waiting with lamps. When the others had arrived some timber was lowered down. Jones and Evans took it from the end of the dangling rope and prepared to carry it forwards into the tunnel.

Three tunnellers led the way, with the other three at the back and the six reluctant infantry in between. The tunnel was at first high enough to stand up in and they made good progress over the dry, chalky floor. After about fifty yards, the senior miner, a Scottish lieutenant called Lorimer, told them they were to be quiet from then on. They were coming to a long lateral gallery from which led various tunnels going towards the enemy. To begin with they would all go down the main one, which led to the forward listening post; later, when the men were working to enlarge it, the infantry would be required to go into a parallel tunnel to protect them. They would be able to take a miner with them to show the way. All were equipped with lamps.

They went down on their knees to get into the main section and Stephen saw the anxious glances being exchanged between his men. The air had a dense, damp quality. They strained and gasped as they went through a small opening, but then found they could half stand again and proceeded at a crouch. Stephen noticed the solid horizontal planks attached to verticals at distances of about five feet. From what he could see it had been well done. In the accustomed scamper of the tunnellers there was no fear or sense of the unusual.

The six infantrymen, led by a lieutenant called Crawshaw, were struggling to keep up with those in front. Stephen could hear them gasping. They carried rifles, which made it difficult for them to use their hands to steady themselves.

It seemed a strange way, Stephen thought, in which to have passed the war, like rodents in a separate element. It had shielded them from the impact of the big attacks and the sight of bodies piling up, but the world the miners inhabited had its own ingrained horror.

He would go just as far as the main chamber, then insist on getting back to his men. They would be grateful that he had made the gesture, which would secure the continued cooperation of the tunnellers in the jobs they found most wearing.

The tunnel became narrower and they were obliged to go down on all fours again. The front men suddenly stopped, causing the others to crush together behind them in the darkness.

'I think they've heard something,' Crawshaw whispered into Stephen's ear. 'No one move.'

The men lay huddled in the tube of earth as Evans fumbled in his pack and squeezed through them to get up to his three colleagues at the front. After a whispered consultation, Evans squirmed forward to a piece of dry wall and stuck a flat disc against it, into which he plugged a stethoscope. Crawshaw raised a finger to his lips and made a downward motion with both hands. The others lay flat on the floor of the tunnel.

Stephen felt a stone against his cheek, and tried to shift his head. He was lodged up against the leg of someone he could not see and had to stay where he was. He could feel his heart moving slowly against his ribs.

Evans lay tight against the tunnel wall, like an unwashed and unqualified doctor listening for signs of hostile life.

Stephen closed his eyes. He wondered whether, if he stayed in this position long enough, he might drift off to a final sleep. The agitation of the other men prevented him from sliding into his own thoughts. He could sense their fear through the tension of the bodies that pressed against his. It was their passivity that made it difficult; even against the guns they had some chance of riposte, but beneath this weight they were helpless.

Evans eventually pulled the stethoscope out of his ears and folded it back into his pocket. He shook his head and pursed his lips. He whispered his report to his lieutenant, who in turn put his mouth to Stephen's ear.

'Can't hear anything. It may have been shellfire from the surface. We're going to press on.'

The men on the floor of the tunnel stirred and dragged themselves back again into their crouching positions in which they could again advance deeper.

Stephen could feel himself sweating. He could tell by the stench from the bodies packed in round him that he was not the only one. Trench conditions had improved, but not to the extent of providing the men with means of washing, even in hot weather.

The roof of the tunnel began to lift a little, and the smaller men, such as Evans and Jones, were able to walk upright. They came to a junction where the miners' lieutenant, Lorimer, issued instructions. The main digging party would proceed straight to the listening chamber; the others would go into one of the fighting tunnels alongside, the entrance to which he was now able to point out.

Stephen smiled to himself as he saw the expressions on the faces of his men. They exaggerated their reluctance into comic grimaces, but he knew from his own experience that it was real enough. He was glad he was going into what, presumably, would be the largest section of tunnel. He had no fear of going forward provided he felt he could get back. What had frightened him underground with Weir was when the earth fell behind them and he had for a moment thought he would not be able to turn round.

Crawshaw checked that his men had their grenades and rifles. He himself carried a revolver, which he waved dangerously towards the tunnel entrance. Stephen guessed he was trying to show them how fearless he was. Perhaps they believed him.

He watched them depart. He remembered the feelings of tenderness he used to have for the men when they went into battle or on patrol; he used to imagine their lives and hopes, their homes and their families, the little worlds they carried on their backs and in their minds. He could remember this compassion, but he no longer felt it.

His own party was about twenty-five yards short of the main listening chamber when Lorimer again came to a halt and raised his finger to his lips.

Stephen inhaled tightly. He was beginning to regret having come down. Either Lorimer was nervous, and was turning a routine inspection into something protracted and unpleasant, or else there was real danger. Evans had taken his listening set into the adjacent tunnel. Jack Firebrace was summoned by Lorimer to place his ear against the wall.

Jack covered the other ear with his hand and closed his eyes for better concentration. For half a minute they all stood motionless. In the light of a miner's lamp, Stephen stared with minute intensity at the grain of a piece of timber about six inches from his face. He traced the tiny lines and indentations. He imagined how it would curl beneath a plane.

Jack pulled back his head from the wall and wheeled to face Lorimer. His urgent whisper was audible to all of them.

'There's footsteps, going back towards their lines. They've got a tunnel west and about ten feet up.'

Lorimer's face tightened. He said nothing for a moment, then, 'Retreating, did you say?'

'Yes.'

'Then I think we should press on and do our work.'

440

'Yes,' said Jack, 'but they may have laid a charge. I mean, there are any number of reasons why –'

'We'll wait for five minutes,' said Lorimer, 'then we'll proceed.'

'For God's sake,' said Stephen. 'You don't risk the lives of all these men to –'

The air was driven from his chest before he could complete the sentence as an explosion drove them backwards into the tunnel walls; it was as though the soil in front of them had been hurled back by some violent, compacted earthquake. Stephen's head struck wood. By the jagged light that burned into the earth he saw the flailing limbs and flying parts of cloth and kit, helmets, hands and spitting chalk that ricocheted round the hollow tube, taking the human detritus with it in a roar of condensed fury.

He lay on the tunnel floor beneath the fields, and still he was not dead. He was aware of earth in his eyes and nose, and of weight. He tried to move but felt himself pinned down, as though the earth had wrapped him in heavy, comfortable blankets and was urging him to sleep. The noise of the explosion seemed trapped in the narrow tube. He pictured his way back sealed off, and a flicker of panic rose in his belly, but died again beneath the heaviness of his pinioned state. The captive sound eventually diminished.

He listened for it to be replaced by the familiar sound of human agony, of men whose limbs had been removed from them or whose brains were going free from their skulls. He heard nothing at first. Then, as the last pieces of displaced earth settled in the tunnel, he heard a long thick sigh; it was a sound he had never heard before, but he knew that it was the noise of several men expiring simultaneously.

He envied them the peaceful exhalation, breath and spirit gone. He tried to move a leg, and found that he could. He flexed his shoulders and arms and felt a raw, sharp pain in the upper right arm. He tried to swallow, but could not gather enough saliva in his dry, earth-filled mouth.

After a few minutes it became clear to him that he was not seriously injured. His legs seemed unharmed. His right arm was damaged, but that would not matter, he thought, unless he needed to dig his way out and the efforts of one arm were not enough. He needed to move the debris from on top of him, then he could see if there was anyone else alive. He tipped his head back as far as he could, and saw that most of the roof of the tunnel was intact above him. It was the old good luck, the contemptible voodoo of survival.

With his left hand, he began to scrape and push at the earth on top of his legs. Eventually he reduced the weight sufficiently to be able to kick some of it away. He flexed and stretched his legs and found that apart from bruises they seemed to have escaped injury. He rolled his upper body, as though trying to throw off bedclothes, and managed to sit up. He stopped and breathed suddenly from the pain in his arm. He spat several times to clear his mouth. Gradually he gathered enough saliva to be able to swallow, and then to speak. He called out in the darkness. There was a lamp on its side: the glass was cracked but it was still alight.

He heard nothing. He manoeuvred himself on to all fours and began to crawl forwards with the lamp. He had been at the back of the group of men when the explosion had gone off; any survivors would therefore be in front of him. There were four miners, who were supposed to do the enlargement work on the listening chamber, and two other infantry. Stephen wondered how far spread the blast had been. Perhaps some of the others in the parallel tunnel had been further from the impact.

As he moved forward he came to a solid wall of detritus. Above it there were still small particles of earth dripping down like rain from where the roof had been blown away. It looked as though a further fall might occur at any moment. Stephen turned round and looked behind him. The way back appeared to be open. Although he would have to go on all fours for the first ten yards or so, he was reasonably certain he could fight his way back to the second lateral gallery where the men had dispersed. From there it would be simple enough, he presumed, to go back into the main gallery and thence to the foot of the shaft.

Something moved in the crush of earth ahead of him. He could see nothing. Then he heard a tiny scraping sound.

442

He followed it with his hands and found that he was touching a piece of material. It was attached to an arm or leg of some kind. Movement was there.

With a growing heaviness of heart, Stephen saw that he would have to try to rescue its owner. He knelt down and began to pare at the weight of earth with the fingers of his left hand.

His right arm was of no use. Doggedly he worked away at the fall of soil, pulling it back with his hand until it had formed a pile, then kicking it away, and spreading it out with his leg on to the floor behind him.

He examined his progress with the lamp. Eventually he made a hole around the piece of material, which was a sleeve. He stuck his hand in and squeezed the arm. He could feel it all the way to the shoulder. The sound of a human voice, in pain or greeting, came to him from the wall of earth.

Stephen shouted words of encouragement. He rested for a moment, then peeled off his tunic from his sopping shirt. As he freed his right arm he saw the black stain of blood on it.

He resumed his digging work. He worried that the earth he took out was supporting other matter which would then fall into the space, closing it up even more heavily.

After an hour he had made a space round the shoulders and head of the man. A piece of timber had collapsed diagonally above him, holding the main weight of the roof off his head, which lay in a protected space. He had been very lucky. Stephen was now close enough to speak to him.

'Hold on,' he said. 'Just keep still. I can get you out.'

He thought it unlikely that he could, because of the weight that had clearly fallen on the man's legs, which were shot out ahead of him towards the original face of the tunnel, but he kept digging and clearing and gasping through his efforts the automatic words of encouragement.

Jack Firebrace, entombed in his heavy burial place, felt his life come and go as the air thinned in the cavity about his head. The pain from his crushed legs swept up and down his spine and made him faint, then gasp back into consciousness, then drift away again. He tried to move them because he felt the

443

agony would keep him from dying. If he could feel the pain then he would be conscious and therefore still alive.

In this state he recognized the voice of the man who had once pitched naked into his arms with a dry imprecation, himself on the verge of dying. He could feel the weak hand picking at the soil that trapped him, and he felt a sense that it was right that he should be rescued by someone he had himself saved; he felt confident that Stephen would deliver him.

Jack's struggle was with himself. He narrowed his efforts to the battle against the soft, rolling waves of sleep that were his body's natural response to the pain in his legs. His head at least could move, and he thrashed it from side to side in an effort to stop it clouding over.

Stephen's soothing voice came in his ear. Jack felt a hand grip under his armpit and try to pull him.

'It won't work,' he said. 'My legs are trapped.

'Can you hear me?' said Stephen.

'Yes.'

'Who are you?'

'Jack Firebrace. The one supposed to get you back safe.' Jack was surprised that he was able to talk so well. The restored human contact had revived him.

'What happened?' said Stephen.

Jack grunted. 'Camouflet probably. They were right above us. They've got our tunnel well marked down. They must have been waiting for weeks.'

'Will there be more?'

'God knows.'

'How badly are you trapped?'

'My legs have gone. I can't move them. My arms are all right. I can help you if you make enough space. I'm . . .'

'What's the matter? Are you all right?'

The effort of speech had made Jack faint. 'Yes. Don't talk now. Dig.'

'What if we bring down more?'

'Chance it,' gasped Jack.

Stephen pulled off his shirt and resumed his toil. Jack felt him crawl in alongside in the space he had cleared. He told him to try to support the earth above them by using bits of timber that lay in the wreckage. For hours Stephen worked on one-handed under Jack's instructions. He was able to create a miniature self-contained chamber within the fallen earth. Jack helped him push and heave the timbers into place above them; he used his hands to pull back more debris until his body was clear to the waist.

Eventually Stephen said, 'I must rest. Even if it's only for a few minutes.'

He lay down in the nest they had made and fell asleep at once, his head resting on Jack's chest. Jack felt the rise and fall of his breathing. He envied him his sleep, but dared not join him for fear that he would not wake up.

He had said nothing to Stephen, in order not to raise his hopes too far, but he assumed a rescue party would have been dispatched from the trench. Even if they sensibly waited to be sure that there were no further enemy camouflets, they could not be long in arriving.

There was no time in the darkness, but Jack estimated they had been underground about six hours, for about five of which he had been trapped and Stephen had been working to free him.

He pictured Cartwright organizing the rescue party in the bright summer day above them. He made a vow that if he made it up to the surface he would never go underground again. He would pass the rest of his days in the air, with the feeling of sun or rain on his face. He found that he was drifting again: his mind began to follow itself in slow, dreamy circles.

He decided he would have to wake Stephen. If not, he was going to die. He took him by the shoulders and shook him, but Stephen fell back on to him. He slapped his face, and Stephen groaned, then fell asleep again. The weariness of four years seemed to have overtaken him.

Jack began cursing. He thought of the vilest things he could say and shouted them at Stephen. He slapped him again. Nothing would penetrate his fatigue.

Then from behind them, back towards their own line, there came the sound of another explosion. Jack closed his eyes and crouched against the ground. He expected a core of soil and flame to come leaping down the tunnel, driven by the power of the blast.

Stephen was awake. 'Christ. What was that?'

Jack could make out Stephen's anxious face in the light of the lamp.

'Another one. Back towards our line. They've got us marked out all right.

'What does it mean?'

'Nothing. We must try to get out.'

What it really meant, Jack thought, was that it might now be impossible for a rescue party to reach them. It depended on precisely where the explosion had come.

It also meant that if Stephen had gone back without trying to rescue him he could have been safely back above the ground some hours ago.

He said kindly, 'You'd better try and pull me out. I'll be more use to you then than if I'm stuck here.'

Stephen resumed his delicate work, trying under Jack's instructions to build a wooden tent over his legs. It reminded him of the construction they had put over the legs of the gassed boy opposite him in the hospital. He had to clear and build at the same time. Jack helped him force the earth out behind them.

As Stephen worked he thought about the second explosion and the damage it might have done. He felt the death he had wanted come closer to him. Still he could not embrace it.

Eventually the weight on Jack's legs was small enough for Stephen to pull him free. In the end he came out like a cork from a bottle, though with a bitter scream as the crushed flesh was dragged against the debris round it.

He lay trembling on the floor of the tunnel while Stephen tried to comfort him. If only they had brought some water. It had occurred to him as they left that a bottle would be useful, but he was only supposed to be underground for an hour.

'How bad is it?' said Stephen when he gauged that Jack could speak.

'I think both legs are broken. And my ribs. There's an awful pain in here.' He touched his chest.

'There's a bad cut on your head. Do you feel pain there?'

'Not really. But I feel weak. I feel dizzy, as though I've been hit.'

'I'm going to have to carry you,' said Stephen.

Jack said, 'That's right. Like that time I caught you.'

'I'll do my best for you, I promise. Do you think we'll get out?'

'It depends on where the earth fell.'

'I think I should look for other survivors first.'

Jack said, 'You'd better understand. This'll be difficult. There'll be no one else. We can search if you want to, but I've seen what happens underground. Two of us surviving's a miracle.'

Stephen put on his shirt and tunic and manoeuvred Jack on to his shoulders. He was not a big man, but the weight of him on Stephen's back as he went at a crouch down the tunnel made him have to stop every few yards. Jack was biting the fabric of Stephen's tunic to keep himself from screaming.

They got back to the junction with the second lateral gallery and sat down against the wall. Jack was trembling all over. A fever had started in him, and he had an urge to sleep. Stephen panted in lungfuls of the warm, thin air and tried to shift his position to give respite to the muscles of his back.

When they had rested a little, he said, 'Which way did we come? I'm lost.'

'It's quite simple. I'd better explain in case I . . . in case you lose me. Imagine a three-pronged fork.' Jack put all his strength into making himself clear. 'The middle prong leads to the listening chamber at the tip. We were halfway up it when the camouflet went off. The two prongs either side are the fighting tunnels. A lateral section joins the three prongs at their base. That's where we are now. This is where Lorimer sent us to our separate tunnels.'

Stephen looked around at the anonymous tube beneath the ground with its bits of wood and earth.

'To get back,' said Jack, 'we go straight ahead, back down the shaft of the fork. Halfway back, that's where we first stopped to listen. It's very narrow, you remember. Then when the handle of the fork ends, where it would meet the hand, is the main lateral gallery. We cross that and it's only a short way to the shaft.'

He lay back against the wall, exhausted by his explanation.

Stephen said, 'All right. I understand. What I'm going to do is leave you here while I go and look in the fighting tunnels for survivors.'

'You don't need to go into that one,' said Jack pointing to the left. 'They all went into the right-hand one.'

'Are you sure? I think I'd better check the other one.'

Jack breathed in tightly between his teeth. 'You must understand. I've got a fever now. If you leave me for long I won't survive.'

Stephen saw the anguish in Jack's face. It was not the physical pain: he was weighing his own life against the chances of saving any of his friends. 'I don't want to be alone for long,' he said.

Stephen swallowed. His instinct was to make it back to the foot of the shaft as fast as possible, but he imagined what the others in the tunnel must be thinking, if any of them were alive. They would be begging him to come to them. It was not fair to leave them without a chance. Something about Jack's blue face did not in any case make him hopeful.

He took Jack's arm. 'I'll go very quickly up this one, the empty one. Then I'll come back and see how you are. Then I'll look quickly up the other one. I promise I won't be more than ten minutes in either.' He searched his pockets to see if he had anything to give him that might make things easier. He found some cigarettes and a piece of chocolate.

Jack smiled. 'No flames allowed. Gas. Thanks for offering.'

Stephen left him and took the lamp into the left of the two fighting tunnels. It was not as well supported as the main one. He could see where they had hacked it out with their picks. In a way it was more like a passageway, a thoroughfare that would emerge in light and understanding.

He made quick progress in the shambling crouch he had seen the miners use. He came to the end of it and saw the evidence of the explosion. It had not been so bad as in the central tunnel, but a good deal of earth had come down. He could not tell how much further the original face of the tunnel had been.

For a moment he stopped. There was no danger. It was quiet. He sighed and ran a hand back through his hair. He became aware of himself and his circumstances as the immediate imperative of action lifted. He would not go back until he was sure that he and Jack were the only survivors. If by searching he brought death closer, it would not matter; there would be some decorum in their dying deep beneath the country they had fought so long to protect.

He shouted out in the darkness. He went up to the blockage and pulled some loose earth away. He put his lips to the hole and shouted again. The debris was compacted so tight that the sound did not penetrate. Anything beyond it that had been living would long ago have been crushed to death.

He turned and made his way back to where Jack was lying. He knelt down beside him. Jack's eyes were closed, and for a moment Stephen thought he was dead. He felt for his pulse beneath the coarse cuff of his shirt. He had to dig between the tendons with his fingertips, but he found some small beat where life still ran.

He slapped him gently in the face to bring him round. Jack stirred and looked up.

He said, 'Don't leave me again. Don't go.' His voice was dry but Stephen could hear the weight of feeling in it.

'There'll be no one alive,' said Jack. 'That's where the main blast was, in that tunnel. We got it through the wall.'

Stephen looked at him. He was in pain and he was frightened of dying, but there was no reason to disbelieve him. He knew about working underground.

'All right,' said Stephen. 'We'll try and get out. Are you strong enough? Do you want to rest some more?'

'Let's try now.'

Stephen stretched himself, then bent down once more. He levered Jack's upper body on to his shoulder, and supported him beneath the thighs with his left arm. He carried him as he would have done a sleeping child. Jack held the lamp over Stephen's shoulder.

After a few yards Stephen had to stop. His own damaged right arm could not support the weight and his left, naturally weak and further tired by digging, was dropping Jack's legs.

He propped Jack against the side of the tunnel, then knelt in front of him and manoeuvred him on to his left shoulder. With both arms wrapped round him he could keep him on for bursts of ten yards at a crouch. Jack fainted each time Stephen stood him up, so after the first three attempts Stephen took his rest kneeling, with Jack still on his shoulder, and his own face pressed to the soil. He closed his eyes against the sweat that ran down from his forehead. He cursed his life and the shards of chalk that pierced his knees.

After an hour of the slow, dragging bursts they reached the end of the tunnel. There was nowhere to go; in front were only thousands of tons of France.

Stephen swore at Jack. He meant the words to be beneath his breath, but they escaped. Jack stirred on his shoulder, and Stephen laid him down on the ground.

'You've brought me the wrong fucking way.' He was exhausted. He lay panting with his face down.

Jack was stirred from his delirium by the impact of being set down. He shook his head and tried to concentrate.

'We went straight, didn't we?' He peered back behind them. There was still a lamp hanging from the roof that Evans had put there on their way through.

It was a terrible sign. Jack looked ahead of them again. He said softly, 'This is the right way. This is not the end, this is where the second explosion went off. We're about twenty yards short of the main gallery.'

Stephen let out a groan and closed his eyes. Now death had him, he thought; now he would go with it.

They stayed where they were for an hour. Neither man had the energy to move. There was one way out and it was closed to them. Jack would shortly die of his wounds; Stephen would die of thirst and starvation.

By his side was his revolver. When hope was finally gone he would fire: up through the palate, into the coiled mess of consciousness and memory. There was a perverse appeal in the thought that he would complete what no enemy had managed.

When they had grown used to their despair, they began to

450

talk again. Stephen asked Jack if his company would try to send more men down to rescue them.

'I don't think so,' said Jack. 'They'd find it difficult to shift this amount of spoil even if they did. They'd have to blow it out and that would risk bringing in the roof and making it worse. Also it's too close to our own line for comfort. They'll say a prayer at the service on Sunday and put us down as missing.'

'You can't blame them. The war's almost over.'

Jack said, 'Are you afraid to die?'

'I think so.' Stephen was surprised to hear himself say it. 'I was lucky that I didn't feel fear above the ground, except at the obvious moments. Now I feel . . . alone.'

Jack said, 'But you're not alone. I'm here. I'm someone.' He shifted his weight against the rubble. 'What's your first name?'

'Stephen.'

'Shall I call you that?'

'If you want.'

There was a pause, then Jack said, 'It's strange, isn't it? That I should be with you at the time I die. Of all the people I've known in my life that it should be you.'

'Who would you choose to be with?' Stephen found himself interested even though he was weighed down by the thought of his own death. 'Which human being out of all those you have met would you choose to hold your hand, to hold close to you in the beginning of eternity?'

'To be with, like that, always, do you mean?'

'Yes. The other half of you.'

'My son,' said Jack.

'Your son. How old is he?'

'He died two years ago, of diphtheria. His name was John.'

'I'm sorry.'

'I miss him. I loved him so much.' In the darkness of the tunnel Jack's voice came up unexpectedly in the lament he had denied himself at the time of John's death; so close to his own time of dying, he was freed from restraint. 'I loved that boy. Every hair of him, every pore of his skin. I would have killed a man who so much as laid a hand on him. My world was in his face. I was not so young when he was born. I wondered what my life had been about until he came along. It was nothing. I treasured each word he gave me. I made myself remember each thing he did, the way he turned his head, his way of saying things. It was as though I knew it wouldn't be for long. He was from another world, he was a blessing too great for me.'

Stephen said nothing, but allowed Jack to sob quietly into his hands. Jack did not seem resentful, even in his grief. His flat, guileless face with its narrow eyes looked wonderstruck, incredulous that such a love had been permitted him.

When he was calmer, Stephen said, 'You talk almost as though you had fallen in love.'

'I think I did,' said Jack. 'I think it was almost like that. I was jealous of him. I wanted him to love me. I would watch the way the women played with him. I was pleased that he was happy, but I knew that really it was our games that were best. I knew it was the times with just the two of us that were the best, the purest things on earth.'

Jack talked about the boy's innocence and how it had changed him. He could not find the words for it, and began to weep again.

Stephen put his arm round his shoulders. 'It's all right,' he said. 'I'll get you out from under here. Somehow I will get you out and you'll have other children. John won't be the last.'

'No. Margaret's too old now. She couldn't have another.'

'Then I will have them for you.'

When Jack had composed himself again, he said, 'I don't suppose you'd choose to die with me beside you. I'm not much good to you.'

'You'll do very well,' said Stephen. 'Who knows? Our own choices might not be so good as those that are made for us. I've met men I would trust in the mouth of hell. Byrne or Douglas. I would trust them to breathe for me, to pump my blood with their hearts.'

'Did you love them best? Would they be the ones you'd choose?'

'To die with? No. The one time I've felt what you describe was with a woman.'

'A lover, you mean?' said Jack. 'Not your own flesh and blood?'

452

'I think she was my own flesh and blood. I truly believe she was.'

Stephen seemed to go into a trance. Jack said nothing. Then, as the minutes passed, he tried to rouse himself.

'We must find a way out of here,' he said. 'Back to the shaft's no good, so we should go forwards.'

'What's the point? There are just the tunnels there that end in blank walls.'

'It would give us something to do, rather than just wait to die. We could try to make a noise. If you can manage to carry me again. Take off your breathing set. That's just getting in the way. And take mine off too. Leave them down there.'

Stephen knelt down and helped Jack on to his shoulder. He tried to conceal his despair. Clearly it was pointless for them to go back the way they had come; they had seen two of the three forward tunnels blocked. The third one, according to Jack, had taken the worst of the blast so was not likely to lead them miraculously into clean air and sunlight.

There seemed to Stephen something frivolous about their hope as they laboured back into the darkness. They were facing death and they could find nothing better to do. He felt they should have passed the time more constructively; they should have readied themselves in some way for the end instead of indulging this boyish hope.

It seemed to please Jack, however. When they reached the crossroads at the second lateral gallery Stephen set him down and flopped to the ground beside him. His chest rose and fell as he squeezed the air into his lungs. Jack had closed his eyes to overcome the pain from his legs which, Stephen noticed, had developed a cloying smell of blood.

Jack smiled when he opened his eyes again. 'Only one thing for it. Try the third prong of the fork. Where those other poor buggers went.'

Stephen nodded. 'Give me a moment to get my breath back. I suppose we might as well. At least then we'll know . . .'

He trailed off, still not quite able to say the obvious thing.

Jack did it for him. 'That it's the end.'

The thought did not perturb Jack. He was beginning to

welcome the idea of dying. While a primitive fear kept stirring in him, the pain of his body and the lost illusions of his life made him wish for the conclusion to come. He loved Margaret still, and would have chosen to see her, but she belonged to a different existence from the one he now inhabited with such unwanted intensity. She would die, in any event. The things on which he had based his faith had proved unstable. John's innocence, the message from a better world, had been taken from him. Any meeting he might have with Margaret and any rekindling of love he might feel would also prove illusory. Love had betrayed him, and he no longer wished to be reunited with his life.

He felt tranquillity at moments when his pain left him. There was no consideration beyond the body in the darkness of the tunnel; what was done by them in the earth with their hands and legs and voices was the boundary of it all. In the muscular efforts of Stephen to save him, the way he patiently submitted himself to the weight and the pointless striving, Jack felt a sense of rightness and calm.

They came to the beginning of the right-hand tunnel and Stephen had to go down on all fours to guide them through the ragged entrance. By the light of the fading lamp Jack looked up at the inadequately supported roof and was silently critical of the work of the men who had made it. It was not as high as a fighting tunnel ought to be. Soon Stephen was crouching. After a few more yards he needed to rest again.

It seemed to Jack that the sensible thing would be for Stephen to leave him while he pressed on in the hope of whatever miracle it was they were looking for; but Stephen did not suggest it. Stephen appeared to Jack to be filled with a kind of perverse determination; the harder their progress became, the more set he would be on carrying his ungainly burden.

The force of the explosion in the third tunnel had taken a different course. It appeared to have narrowed it by sucking it in from the sides. As Stephen went down on his knees to continue, he lifted Jack on to his back where he was able to hold the lamp. It swung to and fro, giving uneven flashes of light to their progress.

Jack let out a scream as a cold hand brushed across his face. Stephen stopped and Jack twisted the lantern to look. An arm was sticking out from the wall of the tunnel. The body to which it was attached was buried behind it.

They pushed onwards. Jack saw a trousered leg sticking out from the earth. They stopped to inspect it.

'It's Evans,' said Jack. 'I recognize his sewing in the cloth here. He was my mate. We did shifts together.'

'I'm sorry. We knew he'd gone, didn't we?'

'It doesn't matter,' said Jack. 'He's better off out of it. We've all gone now. Shaw, Tyson, Evans, Jones and me. The whole of our little group.'

As they crawled on Jack lost his sangfroid. He began to tremble and to brush imaginary hands from his face. He was in a gallery of ghosts. The souls of all who had died, his friends and their companions; the spirits of the men they had killed, the German bodies that had been hurled upward in the soil above the great mines they had laid: all the needless dead of the long war were clasping at his face with their cold hands. They reproached him for having killed them; they mocked him for being still alive.

He was trembling so much that Stephen had to put him down. He lay in the darkness sweating and shaking with fear, the pain of his leg momentarily forgotten.

'We are going to die now,' he said. There was no more composure in his voice, only a wretched, childlike fear.

Stephen sat opposite him and rested his head in his hands. 'Yes,' he said. 'I think this is the end.'

Jack closed his eyes and rolled on to his side. He wished that the fever he had fought to hold at bay would now come and make him sleep.

Stephen said, 'I don't mind dying. God knows, with all these men dead we couldn't ask for anything better. If I could have one wish before I went it would be for a small glass of water. The thought of streams and pools and gushing taps is all that's keeping me going, just the thought of them.'

Jack began to moan softly. Stephen had heard the sound many times; it was the low, primitive cry he himself had made when he was carried in to the surgeon. Jack was calling to his mother.

Stephen felt Jack's shivering body and his soaking shirt. He had nothing dry with which to cover him: his own clothes were saturated with the sweat of carrying and digging. He tried to make Jack comfortable, then left him and crawled up the tunnel.

He wanted to be on his own. He planned to find a place where he could lie down. There he would try to sleep and hope not to wake again.

He kept crawling forward till he came to a larger area, a space perhaps created by the blast. He rolled on his side and pulled up his knees to his chest. He prayed for oblivion and, despite the pain in his arm, he fell asleep.

For many hours the two men lay separated by a few yards, each in his own unconsciousness.

When Stephen awoke, the damp smell and darkness made him think he was in his dugout. Then he stretched and encountered the walls of his narrow tomb.

He cried softly to himself as his memory returned. He moved his injured arm, and as he searched for a grip with his left hand to lever himself up, he touched what felt like cloth.

He recoiled, thinking that, like Jack, he had discovered a corpse, some grim cadaver with whom he had been lying unaware for hours. But the material was coarser even than the weave of army clothes. He felt in his pocket for the electric torch he had been given at the tunnel head. In its weak beam he explored the material further with his fingers. It was a sandbag.

He sat up and pulled at it. He had to brace his legs against the side of the tunnel to shift the weight. Eventually he was able to work it back a few feet towards him. He saw that there was another one behind it. This part of the wall appeared to be built from sandbags. They were packed in too neatly and tightly to have been blown there by the blast, so presumably they had been placed there by the miners at some stage.

Sandbags, in his experience had only one function, which

was to absorb blast, whether from shells or bullets. Presumably they had felt this part of the tunnel to be particularly vulnerable. If so, then they must have known that there was a counter-mine nearby; and if that was the case, why had they continued to work there? He would have to ask Jack.

At the back of his mind was the shadow of a thought that there might be something behind the bags. Although it was probable that they were there for extra protection, it was just possible that they might lead into another tunnel. But if so, why had Jack not known about it?

Stephen crawled back to where he had left Jack. He found him curled up and shivering. He took him by the shoulder and tried to shake him awake. Jack shouted incoherently. It sounded to Stephen as though he was saying something about a shield.

Slowly Stephen was able to restore him to himself. He rocked him gently and called his name. He felt cruel bringing him back to the facts of his existence when any delirium must have been preferable.

Jack looked up at him imploringly, as though asking him to disappear. Stephen knew that to Jack his face was a reminder that he was still alive.

'Listen,' he said. 'I found a sandbag up there. What do you think that means?'

'A full one?'

'Yes.'

Jack shook his head weakly. He did not respond. Stephen took him by the wrists and squeezed them. He put his face close to Jack's, where he smelt the rotten air that he expelled from his lungs.

'Is it just to shore up the wall, or what? What do you people use them for? Come on. Answer me. Say something.' The flat explosion of his hand against Jack's face made a magnified sound in the narrow space.

'I don't know . . . I don't know . . . It's just a bag. We used to fill them when we dug the tube. The Central Line. Inside the big shield. We stopped at Bank.'

'For God's sake. Listen. Why sandbags in the wall? Here in France, in the war, not in the underground railway.'

'We got to Liverpool Street in nineteen-twelve. I was all in. Didn't work again.'

Jack went on about his work in the London clay. Stephen let go of his wrists so that his arms fell on to his lifeless legs. The pain of the impact seemed to startle Jack.

He looked up again with wild eyes. 'Behind the chamber. We packed them in behind the charge.'

'But it's a fighting tunnel,' said Stephen. 'Anyway, they go sideways.'

Jack let out a snort. 'Sideways? You're mad.'

Stephen lifted Jack's hands again. 'Listen, Jack. I may be mad. Maybe we both are. But we are going to die very soon. Before you go, just think very hard. Do that for me. I have carried you this far. Now do me this favour. Think what it might mean.'

He held Jack's eyes in his from what light remained in the lantern. He could see Jack fighting to be free of him, desperate to shake off his last contact with the living world. Jack shook his head, or rather allowed it to loll from side to side. He closed his eyes and lay back against the tunnel wall.

There was drool and foam at the corners of his mouth. His blank, unemotional face seemed to withdraw further. Then a flicker caught the edge of his eye.

'Unless . . . no . . . unless it's Kiwis. Could be Kiwis.'

'What are you talking about? Kiwis? What do you mean?'

'They lay the bags different, the New Zealanders. We stick them in a straight line behind the charge. They dig a little run at right angles to the main drive, then stick the charge in there. You don't need so many bags of spoil.'

'I don't understand. You mean they'd lay a charge not in the main tunnel but off to one side?'

'That's it. Better compression, they say. Not so much work, if you ask me. Not so many bags.'

Stephen tried to contain his excitement. 'What you're saying is that there could be explosive in there, behind all the sandbags?'

Jack finally looked him in the eye. 'It's possible. We don't come down so often these days and I know there was a Kiwi company here before us.'

'You mean they didn't tell you there was an explosive chamber?'

'They would have told the captain, but he wouldn't necessarily tell me. They never tell me anything. I've only been underground twice since we've been here.'

'And then because we're not going to blow any more mines we've just been using it as a fighting tunnel to protect the main listening chamber?'

'We haven't blown a mine for months. We only do fatigues these days.'

'All right. Just suppose there was explosive in a chamber behind those bags. Could we blow it?'

'We'd need a wires or a fuse. And it depends how much there was. Probably bring down half the country.'

'We've got nothing else to try, have we?'

Jack looked down. 'I just want to die in peace.'

Stephen knelt down and lifted Jack to a crouching position, then heaved him on to his shoulder and began to stumble back into the darkness, the torch gripped between his teeth. A new energy made him unaware of the ache of his limbs or Jack's weight, or even the torturing thirst in his mouth.

When they got back to the enlarged area where he had found the sandbags, he laid Jack down again. He desperately wanted Jack to survive so that he could tell him how to blow the charges.

Each sandbag was three feet long and two feet across. They had been packed densely with what Jack called spoil, the debris of digging, in order to maximize their ability to contain the blast. With only one good hand to pull them, Stephen worked very slowly, each drag of about six inches being followed by a rest.

He talked to Jack as he worked, hoping that his voice would stop him from slipping away. There was no response from the figure slumped on the ground. Although progress was measured in inches, he worked with a fury given him by hope. He had a picture in his mind of a great crater being blown into the field above them, and of him and Jack emerging from behind their shelter of sandbags to walk into the bottom of it, which, though thirty feet below ground level, would be open to the rain and the wind.

He was able to stand up in the enlarged area of tunnel and stretch his back from time to time. Each time he rested he bent over Jack and tried to rouse him with a mixture of force and cajoling. There was usually some response, though it was grudging and incoherent; he seemed to be delirious again.

Stephen went back to his work. He switched off the torch and laboured in the darkness. When he had cleared a dozen bags and stacked them in the main tunnel, it became easier to work because there was more space around him. He wanted to stop and make sure Jack was all right, but feared that the more time he wasted by not clearing the bags, the closer they would come to the end of Jack's life.

He pressed on. When his left hand was not strong enough he gripped the nozzle of a wedged bag between his teeth and worried it like a terrier. A piece of chalk broke one of his front teeth and drove into his gum, filling his mouth with blood. He was barely aware of the discomfort as he worked on and eventually came to the end of the pile of bags that had been so neatly and tightly stacked by the New Zealanders.

He went back to the tunnel and took the torch from the floor. Crawling back through the space he had cleared he held the light ahead of him. There were several stacks of boxes marked 'Danger. High Explosive. Ammonium Nitrate/ Aluminium'. They were piled against the forward wall of the small chamber, towards the enemy.

A small leap of excitement went through him. He stopped for a moment and found that his eyes were moist. He allowed himself to give in to the sensation of hope. He would be free.

He went carefully back and took Jack by the hand.

'Wake up,' he said. 'I'm through. I've found the explosive. We can get out. We can be free. You're going to live.'

Jack's eyes, with their heavy lids, opened over his narrow, uninquisitive gaze. 'What's in there, then?'

'Boxes of ammonal.'

'How many?'

'I didn't count. Maybe two hundred.'

Jack let out a snort. He began to laugh, but seemed to lack

460

the strength. 'That's ten thousand pounds. It takes one pound to blow up the Mansion House.'

'Then we'll have to shift them out and just leave however much we want.'

'One box would let them know we're here.'

'Help me, Jack.'

'I can't. I can't move my –'

'I know. Just encourage me. Tell me it can be done.'

'All right. Do it. Perhaps you can. You're mad enough.'

When Stephen had rested for half an hour, he crawled back into the hole.

The wooden boxes had rope handles. At fifty pounds each, they were the ideal weight to be lifted and stacked by a fit man with both arms. With only his left to use, Stephen struggled badly. The ones he pulled from the top of the pile had to be jerked clear, then held aloft to stop them banging into the ground.

After the first hour he had cleared six boxes and taken them back down to the fighting tunnel to a distance he imagined would make them safe from sympathetic detonation. He took out his watch and calculated. It would take him approximately thirty hours. As he became more tired and dehydrated his rests would become longer. He would need to sleep.

He looked at Jack's prostrate form on the tunnel floor and asked himself if the effort was really worthwhile. He expected Jack to die before he could finish. He could not be sure that he himself would last. At least he had found air in the explosive chamber. It was neither fresh nor plentiful, but a small trickle was penetrating from somewhere. It was possible that the explosion had smashed a ventilation pipe. There was a small pool of water on the floor in one corner which he sucked into his mouth, held, and spat back on to the chalky ground. It was too fetid to swallow, and in any case he would need it again.

In the middle of the boxes was a large wad of guncotton attached to a wire, which Stephen set to one side. When he had moved forty boxes he lay down next to Jack and slept. The time on his watch said ten past two, but he did not know if it was morning or afternoon or how long they had been underground.

He used the torch as little as possible. He worked with the instinct of an animal, brutal, stupid, blind. He did not think about what he did or why he did it. His life on the surface of the earth was closed to him. He would not have remembered Gray or Weir, could not have recalled the names of Jeanne or Isabelle. They had gone into his unconscious, and what he lived was like a bestial dream.

Sometimes he stumbled on Jack as he passed, sometimes he kicked him hard enough to make him respond. Occasionally he dropped to his knees and sucked at the puddle on the floor.

As he neared the end of the task he feared that he might die before it was completed. He slowed down and rested more. He checked his own pulse.

It took him three days to clear the chamber and when he finished he was too exhausted to think about setting off the single box that remained. He lay down and slept. When he awoke he at once went over to Jack and shone the torch in his face. His eyes were open and fixed ahead of him. Stephen shook him, certain that he was dead. Jack groaned in protest at being brought back to wakefulness.

Stephen told him he had cleared the chamber. To encourage him, he crawled into it, scooped a handful of water from the puddle, brought it carefully back in his hands and threw it in Jack's face.

'Tell me how to blow it, and you'll have as much water as you want.'

Jack's voice was almost inaudible. Stephen had to put his ear close to the dry lips. Jack told him they used electric leads.

'Can I do it with a fuse?'

'If you can make one. Must be long. So we can get clear.'

'Suppose I used the sandbags. Tore them into strips, then tied them together.'

'If they're dry. But it won't work without a primer. Ammonal burns but it won't explode without guncotton to set it off.'

Stephen went down to where he had stacked the bags; they were reasonably dry. He went back to where he had left his

462

tunic and took out his knife and a box of matches. He cut the end from a bag and emptied it, then struck a match. The ragged edge flared up and the denser parts burned slowly. It could not be relied on.

'Suppose I break a box of ammonal and lay a small trail of powder along the top of it. Would that help?'

Jack smiled. 'Be careful.'

'How far away do we have to be?'

'A hundred yards. Behind a solid wall. And it lets off gas. You'll need to get the breathing sets.'

Stephen calculated how long it would take him to cut and tie a hundred yards of sandbag. It was not possible. He could not use the dry guncotton because without it the ammonal would not detonate. He would have to lay a trail of explosive.

First he carried Jack back down the fighting tunnel to the lateral gallery. He put him a few yards up the left-hand fighting tunnel where he gauged he would be best protected. He collected the Proto breathing sets from the site of the second explosion and returned with them to Jack.

Then he carefully levered the top off a box of ammonal, first with the blade, then with the handle of his knife. He took the grey powder out in handfuls and placed it in a sandbag until it began to grow heavy. He carried it to the chamber and emptied a pile of it against the guncotton primer, which he placed inside the box that remained. Then he laid a trail about two inches wide back through the connecting run into the fighting tunnel. By this time the bag was empty and he went back to replenish it, then returned to where he had left off and continued, twice refilling the bag, before he came to where the rest of the ammonal was stacked. He ran the trail as far from it as possible. It was a chance he would have to take: he could not move it all again. He stopped the powder in the middle of the lateral gallery. He then emptied and cut up six sandbags for a fuse to get from himself to the start of the ammonal.

He sat down next to Jack. He fitted Jack's breathing set for him, then his own. Absurd hope made his heart pound.

'This is it,' he said. 'I'm going to blow.'

Jack made no response, so Stephen went into the gallery and knelt down by the end of the fuse he had made from the sandbags, which was about thirty feet long. He wanted to watch it burn through to the ammonal, then he would know they were going to be all right.

He paused for a moment and tried to find some thought or prayer appropriate to the end of his life, but his mind was too tired and his hand too eager.

He scratched the head of the match against the box and watched it flare. No thought of caution or fear was in his mind. He touched the sandbag and saw it flame. His heart leapt with it; he wanted to live. It made him laugh, mad-eyed and bearded, like a hermit in his cave.

The material spluttered and glowed, then caught and faded, then burned again. It went to about six feet from the end, then seemed to stop. Stephen cursed loudly. He clasped the torch. For Christ's sake. A spark flew from the dead fuse like electricity leaping in a void. It touched the ammonal and Stephen saw a sheet of flame rising to the tunnel roof. He turned and ran three steps back towards Jack, but before he got there he was pitched forwards by an explosion that tore out tunnels, walls and earth and hurled the debris up into the air above the ground.

The force of the blast rocked Lieutenant Levi on the firestep, where he was eating pea soup with sausage and bread dispensed from a company cooker that had travelled hundreds of miles since its first dispatch from Saxony.

A British bombardment had been focused on their front line for three days, presumably presaging a large attack. Levi had been vaguely wondering how soon it would be before he could resume his peacetime medical practice in Hamburg where he had begun to gain some reputation as a doctor specializing in children's ailments. He had resisted joining the army for as long as possible, but the heavy loss of life inflicted on his country had made it inevitable. He left the children in the hospital and went home to say goodbye to his wife.

'I don't want to fight the French,' he told her, 'and I particularly don't want to fight the English. But this is my country and our home. I must do my duty.'

She gave him a Star of David, a small gold one that had

464

belonged to several generations of her family, and put it on a chain round his neck. It was not just the Jewish quarter that was sorry to see Dr Levi go: a small crowd gathered at the station to see him off.

Since the German spring offensive had been halted and the enemy, reinforced now by the Americans, had been moving numbers of tanks up into their front lines, Levi assumed that with the bombardment under way it would be only a matter of weeks before he and his wife were reunited. The small shame he felt at the prospect of German defeat was easily outweighed by his pleasure at the thought of peace.

'You're a doctor at home, aren't you, Levi?' said his company commander, coming down the trench as the shock of the ammonal explosion began to subside.

'A children's doctor, but I –'

'All the same. You'd better go and have a look. We've got a patrol down there. Take two men with you. Kroger and Lamm. They're your best bet. They know all the tunnels here.'

'There are usually two explosions, aren't there? Hadn't we better wait?'

'Give it an hour. Then go down.'

Kroger and Lamm came to report to him thirty minutes later. Kroger was a refined and clever man who had refused promotion on several occasions. He came from a good family, but had principles about social justice. Lamm was of simpler, Bavarian stock, a handsome dark-haired miner of imperturbable temperament.

They took breathing apparatus, in case the explosion had released gas underground, as well as picks, ropes and other pieces of equipment Lamm told them might be useful. Lamm himself also took a small quantity of explosive.

'How many of our men were down there?' said Levi.

'Three,' said Lamm. 'They'd just gone on a routine patrol to listen for enemy activity.

'I thought we'd destroyed their tunnel three or four days ago.'

'We probably did. We're listening to see when they're going to attack. We don't expect them to be able to repair their own tunnel. We blew it in two places. They never heard us coming.'

Kroger said, 'Let's go, shall we? I'd rather be underground than sitting beneath this bombardment.'

They heard shells screaming overhead and detonating in the support lines behind them. Levi followed the others down an incline that slowly took them thirty feet beneath the ground. Although he felt safer where the shells could not reach him, he was not enthusiastic about the idea of being shut in beneath the earth. They had been issued with enough food and water to last for three days, so someone at least presumed it might be a lengthy operation.

They walked along the main gallery for ten minutes. It had electric light in the ceiling though the circuit had been broken by the explosion. The system had been built with considerable care and precision. Lamm and Kroger sang as they walked along. The tunnels followed a similar pattern to those built by the British, though the main lateral gallery of the German network was attached to the sewers of the nearby town. The listening post that they had created close to the British line was protected by a single fighting tunnel that ran about ten feet above the British works; from this they had been able to dig down and lay the two charges that had made most of the enemy system impassable.

They had not gone far up their own central tunnel before they came to a substantial blockage. Levi sat down while Lamm and Kroger explored it with their picks. An appalling thought had occurred to him. His brother, an engineer attached to the same company, had told him he expected to go down and inspect the system at some time to make sure they had effectively closed the British tunnel. He did not normally go underground, but would periodically inspect new works. Levi had not seen him for three days, which was not in itself unusual as their duties were quite different, and while he did not know that he was one of the patrol who had gone down, he did not know for sure that he was not.

'It's a very heavy blockage,' said Lamm. 'Our best bet is to leave it for the time being and go and see what's happened in the fighting tunnel. We can come back if we have to.'

Levi said, 'Do you know which men were in the patrol?'

'No,' said Lamm. 'Do you?'

'No, I don't. I know there are three. I'm just wondering if one of them's my brother.'

Kroger said, 'I'm sure the CO would have told you.'

'I doubt it,' said Levi. 'He's got other things on his mind. He's about to be organizing a full-scale retreat.'

'We'll just have to hope,' said Kroger. 'For all we know they're all alive anyway, just carrying on with their job.'

Lamm looked rather doubtful, as he slid his pick into a loop on the side of his pack and led the way back to the beginning of the tunnel. They climbed through the narrow entrance into the fighting tunnel and made their way forwards. It was narrower and darker, and they had to move at a crouch in places until they came to a section where the roof had been raised and timbered to the standard they expected from their diggers.

After fifty yards there was a great mess of exploded debris. The blast had blown the tunnel's sides out, hugely enlarging its circumference, though filling all the space with the earth and chalk. The three Germans looked doubtfully at one another.

'It's blown right through into the main tunnel,' said Lamm. 'This is the same blast area.'

'What I don't understand,' said Levi, 'is who set this thing off. What is it, anyway? I thought we'd knocked them out, and it can't be us, can it?'

'My guess,' said Kroger, 'is that it was an accident. There was a charge down here that wasn't used against their tunnel. It was left behind and it detonated. It's unstable stuff.'

'The other possibility,' said Lamm, 'is that it's an enemy action.'

'But how could they have got in again so quickly when we'd blown their whole system?' said Levi.

'Because they didn't get back in, they never left. We don't know how many men they had down there when we set off those charges. Some could have survived.'

'But surely they'd have suffocated by now.'

'Not necessarily,' said Lamm. 'They have ventilator pipes, air feeds. They're probably smashed by now, but you get air pockets and odd vents up to the surface. One of ours survived eight days with just a bottle of water.'

'God.' Levi was appalled. 'So behind this debris there could be not only three of our men dead or alive, but an unknown number of British, armed with explosives, living in holes or air pockets, like, like . . .'

'Like rats,' said Lamm.

They began to hack at the obstruction with their picks. Two of them worked while the third rested or cleared the mess they had made. They were able to keep going for five hours before all three of them slumped to the ground. They drank as little water as they could bear and ate some biscuits and dried meat.

Levi's younger brother was called Joseph. He had been the clever boy at school, always winning prizes for his Latin and mathematics. He had gone to be a scientist at university in Heidelberg. He emerged with a doctorate and was offered work by numerous firms as well as by the government. Levi found this garlanded figure with his bespectacled aloofness towards those who sought to load him with their favours hard to reconcile with the determined, asthmatic, but fundamentally comical figure he had known as a boy. Joseph had competed hard with his elder brother, but the difference in their ages had usually defeated him. Levi felt from the moment Joseph was born a great tenderness towards him, principally because he was the product of what he loved most in the world, his parents. He was anxious for Joseph to learn quickly what it was that made his parents so important and their way of doing things so admirable. His worst fear was that Joseph would in some way not understand the honour of the family, or would let it down. He thus felt no jealousy, only pleasure, when Joseph's prizes brought it the public renown he privately believed was its due.

Sometimes his younger brother exasperated him by what Levi saw as wilfulness. When they had so much in common, it seemed unnecessary for him not to follow his elder brother in everything but to make different decisions, cultivate different tastes, almost, it seemed to Levi, out of perversity. He thought that it was done to spite him, but did not allow it to destroy his fondness for the boy; he trained his irritation to be subservient to his continuing protectiveness.

It would be in some way characteristic of Joseph to have got himself into this narrow tunnel at the moment the charge had gone up. As Levi hacked at the wall with his pick he had a clear picture of Joseph's pale, strangely expressionless, face, lying with eyes closed, crushed by the weight of the world on his asthmatic chest.

In the pauses between work they could make out the noise of the bombardment overhead.

'The attack must be getting closer,' said Kroger.

'We're never going to get through this,' Lamm said. 'You can hear by the sound it makes how heavy the fall is. I'm going to have to try to blow it.'

'You'll bring the roof down,' said Kroger. 'Look.'

'I'll use a very small charge and I'll pack it in tight so the blast goes the right way. Don't worry, we'll get right back out of the way. What do you think?'

'All right,' said Levi. 'If that's the only way. But be careful. Use as small a charge as you can. We can always try again.'

He did not want Joseph to be killed in a fall caused by his own men.

It took Lamm two more hours to excavate the kind of hole he wanted. He wired the charge and paid out the line all the way back to the beginning of the incline that led up to the surface. He attached it to the detonator they had left there and, when Levi and Kroger were safe behind him, he sank the handle.

In his narrow tomb, where a hole no larger than a knitting needle brought air but no light, the noise reverberated in Stephen's ears. A tremor of hope went through him. They had sent the rescue party. Weir's old company wouldn't let them down: they had been slow to start but now they were on their way. He shifted his weight a little, though there was hardly room for manoeuvre in the space that was left to them. Against his head to one side was a solid piece of chalk that divided them from whatever remained of the main tunnel. It was the only feature by which he could orientate himself; the rest of the earth that had been displaced by the explosion of ammonal had trapped them on all sides.

'Are you still there, Jack?' he said. He stuck out a leg and felt Jack's shoulder under his boot. There was a faint groan.

He tried to rouse him by talking. 'Do you hate the Germans?' he said. 'Do you hate everything about them and their country?'

Jack had not been properly conscious since the blast.

Stephen tried to provoke him. 'They killed your friends. Don't you want to stay alive to see them defeated? Don't you want to see them driven back and humiliated? Don't you want to roll into their country sitting on one of our tanks? See their women looking up at you in awe?'

Jack made no response. As long as he was alive, Stephen felt there was some hope. If he was left alone, without the pretence of helping someone else, he would give way to the despair that ought, by any reasoned judgement of the facts, already to have overcome him.

He was not sure where the air was coming from, but towards the upper end of their space there was something breathable. He periodically changed places with Jack so that they could share it. He imagined some vent or pipe from the surface had been bent over by one of the explosions and was still delivering a tiny but vital current of air.

It was the darkness that worried him most. Since the explosion they had seen nothing. The torch had been blown from his hand and smashed. To begin with they were covered with earth, but slowly they had been able to remove it. The space in which they lay was about fifteen feet long and no wider than the span of their arms. When he first felt the size of it Stephen cried out in despair.

The obvious course of action was to lie still and wait to die. At some point in the exertion of digging he had lost his shirt, his tunic and his belt with the pistol on it. He still had on trousers and boots but had no way of killing himself unless he took the knife from his pocket and applied it to an artery.

He flicked the blade open in the darkness and laid it against his neck. He enjoyed the familiar feel of the single, scrupulously sharpened, blade. He found the pulse from his brain to his body, thudding silently beneath the skin. He was ready to do it, to end the panic of his entombment.

470

The little pulse beat against the fingertips of his right hand. It was oblivious to his circumstances. It beat as it had beaten when he was a boy in the fields or a young man at work; its unvarying blink saw no difference between the various scenes he had inhabited with such conviction and clarity. He was struck by its faithful indifference to everything but its own rhythm.

'Jack, can you hear me? I want to tell you about the Germans and how much I hate them. I'm going to tell you why you've got to live.'

There was no response. 'Jack, you have to want to live. You must believe.'

Stephen pulled Jack's body up closer to his. He knew the dragging would cause him pain.

'Why won't you live?' he said. 'Why don't you try?'

Shocked by pain back into half-consciousness, Jack spoke to him at last. 'What I've seen . . . I don't want to live any more. That day you attacked. We watched you. Me and Shaw. The padre, that man, can't remember his name. If you'd seen, you'd understand. Tore his cross off. My boy, gone. What a world we made for him. I'm glad he's dead. I'm *glad*.'

'There's always hope, Jack. And it will go on. With us or without us, it will go on.'

'Not for me. In a home, with no legs. I don't want their pity.'

'You'd rather die in this hole?'

'Christ, yes. Their pity would be . . . hopeless.'

Stephen found himself persuaded by Jack. What made him want to live was not a better argument, but some crude lust or instinct.

'When I die,' said Jack, 'I'll be with men who understand.'

'But you've been loved at home. Your wife, your son, your parents before them. People would love you still.'

'My father died when I was a baby. My mother brought me up. Surrounded by women I was. They're all gone now. Only Margaret, and I couldn't talk to her any more. Too much has happened.'

'Wouldn't you like to see us win the war?' Even as he asked the question Stephen thought it sounded hollow.

471

'No one can win. Leave me alone now. Where's Tyson?'

'I'll tell you a story, Jack. I came to this country eight years ago. I went to a big house in a broad street in a town not far from here. I was a young man. I was rash and curious and selfish. I was alive to dangerous currents, things in later life you look at, then pass by – because they're too risky. At that age you have no fear. You think you can understand things, that it will all make sense to you in time. Do you understand what I mean? No one had ever loved me. That's the truth of it, though I wasn't aware of it then. I wasn't like you with your mother. No one cared where I was or whether I should live or die. That's why I made my own reasons for living, that's why I will escape from here, somehow, because no one else has ever cared. If I have to I will chew my way out like a rat.'

Jack was delirious. 'I won't have beer yet. Not yet. Where's Turner? Get me off this cross.'

'I met a woman. She was the wife of the man who owned the big house. I fell in love with her and I believed she loved me too. I found something with her that I didn't know existed. Maybe I was just relieved, overwhelmed by the feeling that someone could love me. But I don't think it was only that. I had visions, I had dreams. No, that's not right. There were no visions, that was the strange thing about it. There was only the flesh, the physical thing. The visions came later.'

'They got the compressor in now. Ask Shaw. Get me off.'

'It isn't that I love her, though I do, I will always love her. It isn't that I miss her, or that I'm jealous of her German lover. There was something in what happened between us that made me able to hear other things in the world. It was as though I went through a door and beyond it there were sounds and signals from some further existence. They're impossible to understand, but since I've heard them I can't deny them. Even here.'

It sounded to Stephen as though Jack was choking. He wasn't sure if he was trying to stifle laughter or whether he was sobbing.

'Lift me up,' said Jack when he could breathe properly.

Stephen lifted him up in his arms and held him across his

lap. His inert legs dangled to one side, and his head fell back on his shoulders.

'*I* could have loved you.' Jack's voice had become clear. He made the choking sound again, and with his head now so close to his own, Stephen could hear that he was laughing, a thin, mocking sound in the cramped darkness.

As it became fainter, Stephen began to knock rhythmically with the end of his knife against the wall of chalk by his head to give the rescue party guidance.

Lamm's controlled explosion had made a hole in the fallen debris large enough for the three of them to go through.

Levi followed the other two with a mixture of eagerness and apprehension. They found the line of the main German tunnel but could see from the shattered timbering that there was further damage.

Kroger stopped the other two and pointed ahead. The base of the tunnel seemed to disappear into a hole. When they were as close to it as they dared to go, Lamm took a rope from his pack and secured one end round one of the timbers that was still upright.

'I'll go down and have a look,' he said. 'You two keep hold of the end of the rope in case the timber snaps.'

They watched him tread carefully into the abyss. Lamm called up to them every two or three steps he took. Eventually he found another level where he could stand. He tied the rope firmly round him and shouted up to the top for them to keep a tight hold. He held his lamp up and peered about him. A metal gleam came back from the murk. He bent down to look. It was a helmet. On all fours, he searched the earth with his hands. He touched something that was solid and bore no resemblance to chalk. It left a sticky feeling on his hand. It was a shoulder, wrapped in feldgrau, the grey of the German uniform. The rest of the body was attached to it, though from the waist down it was buried under debris. The head was also more or less whole, and Lamm could see from the features that this was the body of Levi's brother.

He inhaled and blew out again through puffed cheeks. He did not want to shout the news up to the others, but it seemed

473

unfair on Levi to withhold it from him. He lifted his lantern
and looked round the chamber again. He could see no further
evidence of bodies or activity. He felt the hands of the dead
man to see if he had a ring; he took the identity tag from his
neck but wanted something less bleak by which his brother
could identify him. The fingers were bare, though he found a
watch, which he put in his pocket.

He tugged twice at the rope and shouted that he was coming up. He felt the line go taut as Kroger and Levi added their
counterweight to his ascent. It was a drop of about twenty feet
and it took them several minutes to bring him up as his boots
scrabbled against the loose sides in an effort to find a proper
grip.

'Well?' said Levi, when they had all regained their breath.
Something about Lamm's handsome face troubled him; it was
unwilling to meet his gaze.

'I found a body. One of our men. He must have been killed
instantly.'

'Have you got his disc?' said Kroger. Levi had gone very
still.

'I have this.' Lamm held out the watch to Levi, who took it
reluctantly. He looked down. It was Joseph's. It was a present
that had been given to him on some family occasion by their
father: his bar mitzvah, he thought, or as a reward for
winning his place at university.

Levi nodded. 'Silly boy,' he said. 'So near the end.'

He walked a little way up the tunnel, away from the others,
so he could be alone.

Lamm and Kroger sat on the tunnel floor and ate some more
of the food they had brought.

An hour later Levi returned from his prayers. His religion
would not permit him to take the food Lamm offered him.

He shook his head. 'I have to fast,' he said. 'Meanwhile, we
should continue our search.'

Kroger cleared his throat. He spoke gently. 'I wonder if this
is wise. Lamm and I have been talking. We've seen the size of
the blast and Lamm tells me there is almost no chance that
anyone further into the tunnel than your brother could have

474

survived it. We've discharged our duty as a search party. We've established what happened and we can take your brother back to the surface and give him a proper burial. If we continue underground I think we would jeopardize our own lives for no real purpose. We don't know what may have happened above us. Honour has been satisfied here. I think we should go back.'

Levi rubbed his hand along his jawline where the beard was starting to grow. A period of mourning would mean that it would cover his face by the time he was next allowed to shave.

He said, 'I sympathize with you, but I don't agree. Two of our fellow-countrymen are somewhere beneath the earth. If they are dead we must find them so we can give them a proper burial. If they are alive, we must rescue them.'

'The chances are –'

'It doesn't matter what the chances are. We must complete the task.'

Kroger shrugged.

Lamm saw the practical problems of delay. 'It's hot down here,' he said. 'His body –'

'The flesh is weak. What remains of him is something that won't rot. I will carry him myself when the time comes.'

Lamm looked down.

'Don't be afraid,' said Levi. 'The men down here are from our own country. They don't want to be left beneath this foreign field. They must go back to the places they loved and died for. Don't you love your country?'

'Of course,' said Lamm. He had taken his orders. He saw no further need for discussion. He stood up and began to gather up the rope to carry on.

'I love the Fatherland,' said Levi. 'At a time like this, a death in my family, it binds me more than ever to it.' He looked challengingly at Kroger, who nodded unhappily, as though he thought Levi's fervour came from some temporary storm.

Levi took his shoulder. 'All right, Kroger?' He looked into Kroger's clever, doubtful face. He saw no real agreement, but at least there was acquiescence. Kroger went to help Lamm prepare to go down again.

Levi went with him, leaving Kroger at the top to rest.

475

Twenty feet below the floor of their main tunnel they began to hack with their picks at the debris from the blast. They did not know what they were searching for, but by clearing the earth that had been most recently displaced they hoped to see more clearly what had happened.

They took off their shirts as they warmed to the work. Their picks made hard reverberations where they struck the solid chalk.

Stephen took the glass from his watch so that he could feel the time in the darkness. It was ten to four when he heard the sounds of digging once more, though whether it was morning or afternoon he did not know. He estimated that he and Jack had been underground five or possibly six days.

He pulled Jack once more up to the tiny draught of air so he could take his turn. He lay with his fingers on his watch, timing the half-hour he would spend in the stifling end of the coffin. He made no movement in case it should increase his need for oxygen.

The fear of being enclosed still ran through him. He reasoned with himself that since the worst had happened, and he was now buried alive with no room to turn round, then he should no longer be afraid. Fear was in expectation, not in the reality. Yet still the panic was with him. Sometimes he had to hold his body rigid to prevent himself from screaming. He wanted desperately to strike a match. Even if it only showed the limits of his prison it would be something.

Then would come minutes of diminished life. His imagination and his senses seemed to close down, like lights being turned off one by one in a big house. Eventually only a dim blur persisted as some trace of will kept burning.

Through the hours he lay there he did not cease to protest in his mind against what was happening to him. He fought it with a bitter resentment. Although the strength of it came and went as his body flagged with thirst and fatigue, the bitterness of his anger meant that some light, however faint, stayed alive.

When his half-hour was up he crawled back and lay down alongside Jack.

'Are you still with me, Jack?'

There was a groan, then Jack's voice came up through layers of consciousness and found a lucidity it had not had for days.

'Been glad of these socks to rest my head on. I've had a new pair from home each week of the war.'

Stephen felt the knitted wool beneath Jack's cheek as he lifted him up.

'I've never had a parcel,' he said.

Jack began to laugh again. 'You're a joker, no mistake. Not one parcel in three years? We got two a week at least. Everyone did. And as for letters –'

'Quiet. Can you hear that? It's the rescue party. Can you hear them digging? Listen.'

Stephen manoeuvred Jack so that his ear was close to the chalk.

'They're coming,' said Stephen. He could tell from the sound of the echo how far away they were, but he made out to Jack that they were almost on them.

'Any minute, I should think. We'll be out of here.'

'You've worn army socks all the way through? You poor bugger. Not even the poorest private in the section had –'

'Listen. You're going to be free. We're getting out.'

Jack was still laughing. 'I don't want that. Don't want that . . .'

His laughter turned into a cough, and then into a spasm that lifted up his chest in Stephen's arms. The hacking, rattling sound filled the narrow space, then stopped. Jack let out a long final exhalation as all the breath left him and his body fell back in the end he had wanted.

For a moment Stephen held the body in his arms, out of respect for him, then moved it back to the airless end of the hole. He put his mouth close to where the draught of air had been and breathed in deeply.

He stretched out his legs and pushed the body a little further from him. He felt bitterly alone.

There was only the sound of digging which, he could now no longer deny to himself, was hopelessly distant, and the weight of the earth to keep him company. He found matches in his pocket. There was no one to forbid him his craving for light. Somehow he desisted.

He cursed Jack for dying, for not believing in the possibility of rescue. Then his anger faded and his mind narrowed its efforts to the distant rhythmic sound of pick on chalk. While the sound was there it was like the beat of his own pulse. He took his knife from his pocket again and began to knock the end as strongly as he could against the wall by his head.

After four hours of digging Levi and Lamm had made little impact. Levi called up to Kroger that he should come down and replace Lamm.

While he was waiting for Kroger to arrive, Levi sat down and rested. It had become a matter of honour for him to find his brother's companions. Joseph would not have wanted him to be the kind of man who allowed personal grief to deflect him. It was not so much his own honour as Joseph's that was at stake. His actions could restore some dignity to the broken body.

Above the rasp of his breathing, very faintly, he heard a tapping sound. He pressed his head against the wall and listened. It could have been a rat, he thought at first, but it was too rhythmic and too far underground. There was something about the quality of the sound that made it clear it was coming from a considerable distance: only a human being could have had the strength to make the noise carry.

Kroger jumped off the end of the rope and Levi called him over. Kroger listened.

He nodded. 'There's definitely someone there. Slightly up from here, I think, but roughly parallel. It doesn't sound strong enough to be a pick or a spade. I think it's someone trapped.'

Levi smiled. 'I told you we should carry on.'

Kroger looked doubtful. 'The question is, how are we going to get through? There's a lot of chalk between us.'

'We'll start by blowing it. Just a controlled explosion. I'll go up and send Lamm down in my place. He can lay a charge.'

Levi's face was set in determined enthusiasm. Kroger said, 'Suppose this noise is being made not by one of our men but by one of the enemy who's still trapped?'

Levi's eyes widened. 'I don't believe anyone could be alive

478

after all this time. And supposing it was, then . . .' He spread his hands wide and shrugged.

'Then what?' said Kroger briefly.

'Then it would be the man who killed my brother and his two companions.'

Kroger looked at him unhappily. 'An eye for an eye . . . You're not thinking about revenge, are you?'

Levi's smile faded. 'I'm not thinking of any specific action. My faith provides me with guidance for anything. I am not afraid to meet him, though, if that's what you mean. I should know what to do.'

'We should take him prisoner,' said Kroger.

'That's enough,' said Levi. He went to the foot of the rope and called out to Lamm to bring him up.

Lamm, who had been on the point of falling asleep, said nothing as Levi told him what he wanted him to do. He prepared a charge and slipped it into his pack, then went down the rope.

The mixture of chalk and soil proved difficult for him and Kroger to excavate. It took five hours before they had made a hole for the charge which satisfied Lamm. Levi changed places with him to help Kroger. They filled sandbags and packed them in tight behind the explosive.

Kroger stopped to drink some water and eat more of the meat and biscuit he had brought. Levi declined his offer.

He was beginning to feel light-headed with grief and fatigue, but he was determined to maintain his fast. He worked on furiously, ignoring the sweat that stung his eyes and the trembling of his fingers as he filled the sandbags.

He did not know what or whom he expected to find behind the wall; he felt only the compulsion to carry on. His curiosity was linked to his sense of loss. The death of Joseph could only be explained and redeemed if he could find the man still living and confront him.

They laid the wires and retreated to their safe place at the foot of the long incline back towards the surface. They could hear the sound of heavy shelling, varied by mortar and machine gun fire from the air above. The attack had begun. Lamm sank the detonator and the ground shook beneath their feet. There was a hot, breathy roar that ebbed, then flowed again. For a moment it sounded as though fireballs of earth and chalk were coming for them through the tunnel. Then the sound ebbed a second time and died in quietness.

They went back quickly through the low, timbered entrance, crawled, shuffled and ran back to the top of the dip into the earth below. A cloud of chalk made them cough and retreat for a minute until it had subsided.

Levi told Kroger to stay behind while Lamm went down with him. He wanted Lamm's assessment of the blast, and he doubted Kroger's wholeheartedness.

They went through the hole made by the explosion, digging and enlarging as they went. It had taken them right into the main British listening post. They examined the foreign timbering with quizzical interest.

'Listen.' Levi laid his hand on Lamm's forearm.

The sound of tapping was frantic and much closer than before.

Levi was so excited that he leapt into the air, banging his head against the roof of the chamber. 'We're there,' he said. 'We've made it.'

They had blown away what separated them. Now they had only to dig through and reach with their hands.

In his narrow space Stephen was rocked by the new explosion. He rolled on to his front and covered his head with his arms against the imagined fall of the world. But although the noise rebounded from the walls, they stayed secure.

He began to kick and buck within the confines of where he lay. The claustrophobia he had kept at bay now gripped him. The thought of men moving freely close at hand and the fear that they might not hear or reach him let loose his panic.

In his thrashing he dislodged earth that had been shaken by the blast. A heavy fall on his legs made him stop for a moment and hold himself tight in self-control.

He resumed his knocking with the butt of his knife and began to shout as loudly as he could. 'I'm here. Over here.'

He pictured the men of Weir's company, their cheerful faces grinning beneath their helmets as they hacked their way towards him. Who would they be? Which ones had been sent for him? He could remember no names or faces. There had been Jack, but he was dead alongside him. A vacant-looking man with fair hair, Tyson, but he had died long ago. And these small ones who never seemed to be standing upright, even in the open air, though perhaps they too had been underground with him when the first blast went off.

Stephen felt his mind become extraordinarily clear. It was filled with pictures of the normal world, the world inhabited by women, where people moved in peace and made love and drank, and there were children and commerce and laughter. He thought of Jeanne and of the astonishing smile that rose like a sunburst to her eyes. The hideous, cramped world of earth and sweat and death was not the only reality; it was a confining illusion, a thin prison from which he would burst forth at any moment.

His thirst and fatigue were forgotten; he was alive with a passion for the world, for the stars and trees, and the people who moved and lived in it. If they could not reach him, he would throw off the walls of the earth, he would scratch, eat and swallow his way out of them and up into the light.

'Keep going,' laughed Levi, a flame in his eyes. His skin was shining with sweat as he worked his pick into the wall, where they had peeled back the timbers.

Lamm screwed up his face under matted hair and squinted up at him from the light of the lantern.

'Go on,' shouted Levi, 'go on.'

He was close to delirium as he heaved his pick once more into the earth. In his mind he saw only the features of his dear brother Joseph. How much he had loved him and lived through him; how much he had wanted Joseph to be like himself, but better, to profit from his experience and make something that would honour the noble nature of his parents and their family before them.

Lamm worked on in an urgent rhythm, the slabs of muscle on his shoulders sliding back and forth beneath the drenched grey vest as the pick demolished the intervening earth.

Working ten yards along from Levi, he struck air. He was

481

through. He shouted out. Levi pushed him aside and began to dig frantically with his hands, throwing out the earth behind him like a dog. He called out to the trapped man. They were coming, they were with him.

It was Levi's work, not Lamm's, that had loosened the earth sufficiently at the end of Stephen's coffin for him to be able to crawl out of it, over the fallen body of Jack Firebrace.

On hands and knees he moved back among the debris his own explosion had made. About a yard further along he could see where the tunnel was still intact. It was here that Lamm had broken through. Levi pushed Lamm back and climbed into the British tunnel himself. Tricked by the echo of Stephen's tapping, he turned the wrong way, and began to walk away from him.

Gurgling and spitting earth from his mouth, Stephen clawed his way forward, shouting as he went. He could see light from some lantern swaying in the tunnel ahead of him. There was air. He could breathe.

Levi heard him. He turned and walked back.

As the tunnel roof lifted, Stephen moved up into a crouch and called out again. The lantern was on him.

He looked up and saw the legs of his rescuer. They were clothed in the German *feldgrau*, the colour of his darkest dream.

He staggered to his feet and his hand went to pull out his revolver, but there was nothing there, only the torn, drenched rags of his trousers.

He looked into the face of the man who stood in front of him and his fists went up from his sides like those of a farm boy about to fight.

At some deep level, far below anything his exhausted mind could reach, the conflicts of his soul dragged through him like waves grating on the packed shingle of a beach. The sound of his life calling to him on a distant road; the faces of the men who had been slaughtered, the closed eyes of Michael Weir in his coffin; his scalding hatred of the enemy, of Max and all the men who had brought him to this moment; the flesh and love of Isabelle, and the eyes of her sister.

Far beyond thought, the resolution came to him and he found his arms, still raised, begin to spread and open.

Levi looked at this wild-eyed figure, half-demented, his brother's killer. For no reason he could tell, he found that he had opened his own arms in turn, and the two men fell upon each other's shoulders, weeping at the bitter strangeness of their human lives.

THEY HELPED STEPHEN to the bottom of the rope and gave him water. They lifted him up, and Levi walked with his arm round him to the end of the tunnel while Lamm and Kroger went back into the darkness to bring out the body of Jack Firebrace.

Levi guided Stephen's slow steps up the incline towards the light. They had to cover their eyes against the powerful rays of the sun. Eventually they came up into the air of the German trench. Levi helped Stephen over the step.

Stephen breathed deeply again and again. He looked at the blue and distant sky, feathered with irregular clouds. He sat down on the firestep and held his head in his hands.

They could hear the sound of birds. The trench was empty.

Levi climbed on to the parapet and raised a pair of binoculars. The British trench was deserted. He looked behind the German lines, but could see nothing in front of the horizon, five miles distant. The dam had broken, the German army had been swept away.

He came down into the trench and sat next to Stephen. Neither man spoke. Each listened to the heavenly quietness.

Stephen eventually turned his face up to Levi. 'Is it over?' he said in English.

'Yes,' said Levi, also in English. 'It is finished.'

Stephen looked down to the floor of the German trench. He could not grasp what had happened. Four years that had lasted so long it seemed that time had stopped. All the men he had seen killed, their bodies, their wounds. Michael Weir. His

484

pale face emerging from his burrow underground. Byrne like a headless crow. The tens of thousands who had gone down with him that summer morning.

He did not know what to do. He did not know how to reclaim his life.

He felt his lower lip begin to tremble and the hot tears filling his eyes. He laid his head against Levi's chest and sobbed.

They brought up Jack's body and, when the men had rested, they dug a grave for him and Joseph Levi. They made it a joint grave, because the war was over. Stephen said a prayer for Jack, and Levi for his brother. They picked flowers and threw them on the grave. All four of them were weeping.

Then Lamm went looking in the dugouts and came back with water and tins of food. They ate in the open air. Then they went back into the dugout and slept.

The next day Stephen said he would have to rejoin his battalion. He shook hands with Kroger and Lamm, and then with Levi. Of all the flesh he had seen and touched, it was this doctor's hand that had signalled his deliverance.

Levi would not let him go. He made him promise to write when he was back in England. He took the buckle from his belt and gave it to him as a souvenir. *Gott mit uns*. Stephen gave him the knife with the single blade. They embraced again and clung on to each other.

Then Stephen climbed the ladder, over the top, into no man's land. No hurricane of bullets met him, no tearing metal kiss.

He felt the dry, turned earth beneath his boots as he picked his way back towards the British lines. A lark was singing in the unharmed air above him. His body and his mind were tired beyond speech and beyond repair, but nothing could check the low exultation of his soul.

PART SEVEN

ENGLAND 1979

ELIZABETH WAS WORRIED about what her mother would say when she told her she was pregnant. Françoise had always been strict about such things, to the extent that Elizabeth had not told her that her boyfriend was married. 'He works abroad,' she had been able to say, when Françoise had wanted to know why they had never been introduced.

She postponed the moment when she would have to tell her, but by March she was beginning to put on weight. Rather than work it into the conversation during one of her teatime visits to Twickenham, she decided to invite her mother up to dinner in London and make a celebration of the announcement. Part of the reason, she admitted to herself, was to wrong-foot Françoise, to put her on the defensive; but she hoped that her mother would share in her own happiness at the prospect. The date was fixed and the restaurant was booked.

Telling Erich and Irene was also awkward because her pregnancy meant she would be away from work for a time. Erich took the news as a personal slight against him and his son, who, he irrationally believed, ought to have been the father of Elizabeth's children, even though he was contentedly married to someone else.

Irene was also displeased. Elizabeth could not understand. Irene was one of her best friends: she took her side in everything. Yet with this most important news, she seemed unable to share Elizabeth's joy and excitement. She muttered a good deal about marriage and the family. A few weeks after

Elizabeth had first told her, Irene came into her room at work to apologize.

'I don't know why, but I was a bit put out when you told me about the baby. I expect it's just the old green-eyed monster. I'm very pleased for you, dear. I've already made these for it.' She gave Elizabeth a paper bag in which was a pair of knitted woollen socks.

Elizabeth hugged her. 'Thank you. I'm sorry I was so tactless. I really should have thought. Thank you, Irene.'

When people asked her who the father of the child was, Elizabeth refused to tell them. To begin with they were affronted. 'It's bound to leak out, you know,' said the ones who had not heard about Robert. 'You can't expect the child not to have a father.' Elizabeth shrugged and said she would manage. Those who did know about Robert presumed he was responsible. Elizabeth said, 'I'm not telling you. It's a secret.' Their irritation eventually died down, and with it their curiosity. They had their own business to attend to, and if Elizabeth was going to be silly about it, that was up to her. So, as she had thought, it was possible to keep a secret: people's nosiness was finally exceeded by their indifference; or, to put it more generously, you were allowed to make your own life.

Elizabeth was due to meet her mother on a Saturday evening. In the morning she finished reading the last of her grandfather's notebooks, translated by Bob's arachnoid hand. They went into considerable detail. There was a long account of his burial underground with Jack Firebrace and the conversations they had had.

Elizabeth was particularly struck by a passage, somewhat unclear in Bob's rendering, in which they appeared to have talked about children, and whether either of them would have them after the war. 'I said I would have his,' was how the exchange appeared to end. Much clearer was the paragraph in which Stephen recalled Jack's love for a son called John.

Having read all the notebooks as well as two or three more books about the war, Elizabeth finally had some picture in her mind of what it had been like. Jeanne, or Grand'mère as Elizabeth knew her, made several appearances towards the end, though the narrative gave away nothing of what Stephen

490

might have felt for her. 'Kind' was the tepid word most often applied to her in Bob's translation; 'gentle' made the occasional appearance. It was not the language of passion.

Elizabeth did some calculations on a piece of paper. Grand'mère born 1878. Mum born . . . she was not sure exactly how old her mother was. Between sixty-five and seventy. Me born 1940. Something did not quite add up in her calculations, though it was possibly her own arithmetic that was to blame. It didn't really matter.

She dressed and made up carefully for the evening. She tidied her flat and poured herself a drink as she waited for her mother. She stood in front of the fire and straightened the things on the mantelpiece: a pair of candlesticks, an invitation, a postcard and the belt buckle, which she had cleaned and polished so it shone with the glittering fervour it must have had when first cast: *Gott mit uns*.

When Françoise arrived she opened a half-bottle of champagne.

'What are we celebrating?' said Françoise, smiling as she raised her glass.

'Everything. Spring. You. Me.' She found the news harder to break than she had expected.

The restaurant she had chosen was one that had been recommended by a friend of Robert's. It was a small, dark place in Brompton Road that specialized in northern French cooking. It had benches covered in scarlet plush and brown smoky walls with oil paintings of Norman fishing ports. Elizabeth was disappointed when they first arrived. She had expected something brighter with a noisy clientele more appropriate to an evening of good news.

They studied the menu as the waiter tapped his pen against his notepad. Françoise ordered artichoke and sole Dieppoise. Elizabeth asked for mushrooms to begin with, then fillet of beef. She ordered expensive wine, Gevrey-Chambertin, not sure if it was red or white. They both drank gin and tonic while they waited. Elizabeth ached for a cigarette.

'Have you completely given up?' said Françoise, seeing her daughter's nervous hands.

'Completely. Not one,' Elizabeth smiled.

'And have you put on weight as a result?'

'I . . . well, a bit I think.'

The waiter arrived with the first courses. 'For you, Madame? The artichoke? And for you the mushrooms? Which of you ladies would like to taste the wine?'

When he finally left them and they had started to eat, Elizabeth said awkwardly, 'I have put on a little weight, I think, but it's not because of giving up smoking. It's because I'm expecting a baby.' She braced herself for the response.

Françoise took her hand. 'Well done. I'm delighted.'

Elizabeth, with tears in her eyes, said, 'I thought you'd be annoyed. You know – because I'm not married.'

'I'm just pleased for you, if it's what you want.'

'Oh yes. Oh yes. It's what I want all right.' Elizabeth smiled. 'You don't seem very surprised.'

'I suppose I'm not. I noticed that you'd got a little heavier. And that you'd stopped smoking. You told me it was a New Year's resolution, but you'd never managed to keep it before.'

Elizabeth laughed. 'All right. Now aren't you going to ask who the father is?'

'Should I? Does it matter?'

'I don't think it does. He's happy about it – well, happy enough. He's going to help support it financially, though I didn't ask him to. I think it'll be all right. He's a very nice man.'

'That's fine then. I won't ask any more.'

Elizabeth was surprised by how calmly Françoise had taken the news, even if she had guessed and therefore had time to prepare herself. 'You don't mind that your grandchild will be born to a woman who isn't married?'

'How could I mind?' said Françoise. 'My own mother wasn't married to my father.'

'Grand'mère?' Elizabeth was amazed.

'No. Grand'mère is not my real mother.' Françoise looked tenderly at Elizabeth. 'I've often meant to tell you, but somehow there seemed no need. It's so unimportant really. Your grandfather married Grand'mère, Jeanne, in 1919, after the war. But I was already seven years old then. I was five by the time they first met!'

492

'I *thought* it didn't add up! I was doing some sums after I'd been reading his notebooks. I put it down to my bad maths.'

'Are there references to someone called Isabelle in these books?'

'A couple, yes. An old girlfriend, I assumed.'

'She was my mother. She was Jeanne's younger sister.'

Elizabeth looked wide-eyed at Françoise. 'So Grand'mère was not really my grandmother?'

'Not in the flesh, no. But she was to all intents and purposes. She brought me up and she loved me like her own child. Your grandfather went to stay with a family before the war. He had an affair with Isabelle and they ran away together. When she discovered she was pregnant, she left him and eventually went back to her husband. Years later, during the war, your grandfather met Grand'mère in Amiens. She took him to see Isabelle again, but Isabelle made Grand'mère promise she would not tell him about the baby.'

'And the baby was you?'

'That's right. It was a silly subterfuge. I don't know. She just wanted to spare his feelings. He didn't find out until he was about to marry Jeanne. I was sent to Jeanne from Germany, where I had been living, because my real mother had died. She died of flu.'

'Of flu? That's impossible.'

Françoise shook her head. 'No. There was an epidemic. It killed millions of people in Europe just after the end of the war. Isabelle had always said that if anything should happen to her, Grand'mère was to bring me up. That was agreed between them when she first went to Germany with the man she had fallen in love with. He was a German called Max.'

'But didn't he want to keep you with him?'

'I don't think so. He was very sick from the war. He died himself not long afterwards. And I wasn't his child, after all.'

'And so you were brought up as though you were Stephen and Jeanne's child?'

'Exactly. Grand'mère was wonderful. It was like having a second mother. We were a very happy family.'

The waiter brought more food.

'Do you mind?' said Françoise after a minute. 'Does it

matter to you? I hope not, because it doesn't matter to me. Where there is real love between people, as there was between all of us, then the details don't matter. Love is more important than the flesh and blood facts of who gave birth to whom.'

Elizabeth thought for a moment. 'I'm sure you're right,' she said. 'It'll take me a bit of time to digest it, but I don't mind at all. Tell me about your father. Was he happy?'

Françoise raised her eyebrows and inhaled. 'Well, it was . . . difficult. He didn't speak for two years after the war.'

'What, not a word?'

'No, not a word. I don't know, I suppose he must at least have said "I do" when they got married. He must have said a few words, just to stay alive. But I never heard him speak then. And Grand'mère said it was two years of silence. She says she can remember when he first spoke again. It was one morning. He quite suddenly stood up at the breakfast table and smiled. He said, "We're going to the theatre in London tonight. We'll take the train at lunchtime." I couldn't believe my ears. I was only ten years old.'

'And you were living in England then?'

'That's right. In Norfolk.'

'And was he all right after that?'

'Well . . . he was better. He talked and was very kind to me. He spoiled me really. But he wasn't in good health.'

'And did he talk about the war?'

'Never. Not a word. From that day on it was as though it hadn't happened, according to Grand'mère.'

'When did he die?'

'Just before I got married to your father. He was only forty-eight. Like a lot of men of that generation, he never really recovered.'

Elizabeth nodded. 'Just a couple of years before I was born.'

'Yes,' said Françoise sadly. 'I wish he could have seen you. I wish so much he could have seen you. It would have made him . . . much happier in his heart.'

Elizabeth looked down at her plate. 'And Grand'mère? How did she manage?'

'She was a wonderful woman. She loved him very much.

She nursed him like a mother. She was the heroine of the whole story. You do remember her, don't you?'

'Yes, I do,' Elizabeth lied. 'Of course I do.'

'I'm sorry,' said Françoise. She held a napkin to her face. For a minute she couldn't speak. 'I didn't mean to cry in a public place. I don't want to spoil your happy day, Elizabeth. It would have meant so much to her too.'

'It's all right,' said Elizabeth. 'It's all right. Everything's all right now.'

In the course of the summer, Elizabeth attended the antenatal clinic of her nearest hospital. There was some concern about her age; she found herself referred to as 'elderly' by members of the staff. The concern never became a worry, however, because she was never seen by the same person twice.

'Thank you, Mrs Bembridge,' said the doctor who examined her at eight months. 'I'm sure you know the routine by now.'

'I beg your pardon?'

'Well, number four, should be second nature to you.'

It turned out he had been using the wrong notes. Elizabeth wondered who had been examined in the light of hers. They booked her into a bed on the day it was expected and told her not to go on an aeroplane in the meantime.

'Remember,' said the nurse. 'Most labours take a long time. Don't ring the hospital until the contractions are regular and painful. If you come in too soon we'll just have to send you away again.'

Irene told her of some classes that the daughter of a friend of hers had attended. Elizabeth signed up and went to a flat in Kilburn where a fierce woman told a group of half a dozen expectant mothers about the different stages of labour and the kinds of painkiller available. Elizabeth made a note to ask for an epidural at the earliest permissible moment.

The child rolled and kicked inside her. The skin of her abdomen was subject to sudden bulges and rippling distortions as it stretched and turned. Her back ached and, as the summer wore on, she longed for cold winter days when it would all be over and she could breathe again.

Sometimes she would sit naked on the edge of her bed with the windows wide open to catch any breeze that might be passing. She held the weight of the child in the palms of her hands beneath the swell of her belly, where a thin brown line had appeared, running down into her groin. Above the hip bones the skin had stretched into small white scars, though nothing as bad as she had occasionally seen on the ravaged abdomens of women in the changing cubicles of clothes shops. Most of the questions at the antenatal class had been concerned with what the women called getting their figures back, and the resumption of sexual relations with their husbands. Elizabeth found that neither question was at the front of her mind.

She was preoccupied by an intense curiosity about her child. While she felt protective and maternal towards it, she also felt a respect that sometimes bordered on awe. It was a separate being with its own character and its own destiny; it had chosen to lodge and be born in her, but it was hard not to feel that it had in some sense pre-existed her. She could not quite believe that she and Robert had created an autonomous human life from nothing.

After several days of complicated deceit, false trails and cunning use of his answering machine, Robert managed to arrange matters so he could join Elizabeth for the week before the birth. He intended to stay with her afterwards until she was fit enough to go down to stay with her mother. His wife believed he was travelling to Germany for a conference.

He had no desire to be present at the birth itself, but wanted to be on hand in case she needed him. He rented a cottage in Dorset, near the sea, where Elizabeth could relax for the last few days while he looked after her. They planned to return to London three days before the due birth date.

Robert was still edgy about the arrangement as they drove in Elizabeth's car through the Hampshire countryside. 'Suppose it comes early?' he said. 'What am I supposed to do?'

'Nothing,' said Elizabeth, twisting awkwardly round from the passenger seat to look at him. 'Just keep the baby warm. Anyway, first labours usually take about twelve hours, so even at the speed you drive we should be able to make it to the hospital in Poole or Bournemouth. Also first babies are seldom early. So let's not worry.'

'You've become quite an expert, haven't you?' he said, accelerating a little in response to her criticism of his driving.

'I've read some books. I haven't had much else to do this summer.'

The cottage was situated by a track on the side of a hill. It overlooked deep countryside and was about fifteen minutes from the closest town. The front door opened straight into the living room, which had a large stone fireplace and worn, chintz-covered furniture. There was an old-fashioned kitchen with a greasy cooker attached to a cylinder of gas, and cupboards with sliding glass doors. The back door led into a sizeable garden, at the end of which was a large chestnut tree.

Elizabeth was delighted by it. 'Do you see that little apple tree?' she said. 'That's where I'll set up my chair.'

'I'll do it,' said Robert. 'I'd better go and get some food before the shops shut. Do you want to come with me?'

'No, I've made a list. I'll trust you.'

'I was thinking in case you went into labour.'

Elizabeth smiled. 'Don't worry. It's not due for another eight days. Just stick a chair up there if you don't mind, and I'll be fine.'

As the last sound of the car vanished down the track, she began to feel short, sharp contractions. They were like the cramp she sometimes had in her leg at night, but situated in or near her womb.

She breathed deeply. She would not panic. She had been warned that there were often false starts over a period of weeks. They were named after the doctor who had identified them. Braxton Something. Nevertheless, there was no harm in finding a telephone directory and writing down the number of the nearest hospital.

She went into the living room and found what she wanted. There was a list of 'Useful Numbers' on a piece of paper stapled to the front cover of the directory. Both the hospital and a local doctor, only five miles away, were listed.

Relieved, Elizabeth went back into the garden and sat down

under the apple tree. There was another sharp contraction that made her gasp and put her hand on her belly. Then the pain receded. It drifted away and left her feeling calm and oddly powerful. The life was knocking inside her. By her own endeavours she would bring forth a child to carry on the strange history of her family. She thought of her grand-mother, Isabelle, and wondered when and how she had given birth. Had she been alone and frightened in her disgrace, or had someone – Jeanne perhaps – been there to help her? Elizabeth became quite anxious as she thought of Isabelle alone with this frightening pain. No, she told herself. She would have planned for it. Jeanne must have been there.

Robert returned an hour later with the shopping and brought a drink out to her beneath the tree. He sat at her feet and she ran her hand through his thick, tangled hair.

The airless heat of August had gone, and it was a warm September evening. 'In a few days nothing will ever be the same again,' said Elizabeth. 'I just can't imagine it.'

Robert took her hand. 'You'll manage. I'll help you.'

He cooked dinner under instructions she called out from the living room. It was dark by the time they ate, and there was enough chill on the air for them to light a fire. The smell of wood-smoke filled the room as it billowed out from the grate. By leaving the front door ajar, they were able to drive it back up the chimney, but the resultant draught eliminated the benefit of the fire.

Elizabeth went to fetch a cardigan, and, as she climbed the narrow stairs, felt another contraction. She mentioned nothing to Robert. He was sure to want to take her to the hospital where they would either keep her for days or, more probably, send her away again. She liked the cottage and she treasured the few days she was able to spend alone with Robert.

She slept badly that night. It was difficult to find a comfort-able position in which to lie. The cottage bed was deep and soft, with a heavy eiderdown. She was glad when the dawn came with a loud, discordant sound of birds. Later, she slept.

Robert looked at her sleeping face when he brought her tea in the morning. She was the most beautiful woman, he thought. He stroked back a strand of dark hair from her cheek. He felt sorry for her in the ordeal she was about to undergo. Her compelling confidence had not allowed her to understand how painful and exhausting it would be. He left the tea by the bed and went quietly downstairs.

He walked in the garden, up to the chestnut tree, and back to the house. It was a sunny morning, with the sound of a tractor coming from a nearby field. Although he was calm, he felt his life had entered a brief period over which he would have no control; it was as though it was on railway tracks, under its own momentum. He would be tested.

That night Elizabeth had more contractions. He saw her bent over in the living room as he came through from the kitchen.

'It's nothing,' she said. 'It's just a Braxton thing.'

'Are you sure? You look very pale.'

'I'm fine.' She spoke between clenched teeth.

They went to bed at midnight, and Robert fell asleep. At about three in the morning he was awoken by the sound of Elizabeth gasping in pain.

She was sitting on the side of the bed. He could just see her face in the moonlight that came in through the curtains.

'This is it, isn't it?' he said.

'I'm not sure,' she said. 'They're painful, but I'm not sure how regular they are. Have you got a watch? I want you to time them.'

Robert turned on the light and watched the second hand crawl round the face of his watch. He heard Elizabeth gasp again. Six minutes had passed.

'Well?' he said.

'I don't know. This might be it. It might be.' She sounded distraught. Robert wondered at what point the pain and fear would make her knowledge and instinct unreliable and compel him to follow his own judgement instead.

'Leave it for a bit,' she said. 'I don't want to go to hospital.'

'That's silly, Elizabeth. If you —'

'Leave it!'

She had warned him that she was likely to become

irritated. Many women used language they had barely heard before.

An hour passed, and the contractions became stronger and closer together. Elizabeth walked about the house, and he left her alone. He guessed she was trying to find some comfortable position in which to brace herself against the pain and she did not want him with her. He could hear her going through different rooms of the cottage.

He heard his name called, and ran to her. She was in the living room, resting her head on the sofa. 'I'm frightened,' she sobbed. 'I don't want it to happen. I'm frightened. It's so painful.'

'All right. I'm going to ring the doctor. And the ambulance.'

'No. Don't.'

'I'm sorry. I'm going to.'

'Not the ambulance.'

'All right.'

A man's voice answered at the doctor's. 'It's my wife you want. I'm afraid she's out on a call. I'll tell her directly she gets in.'

'Thank you.' Robert swore as he put down the receiver.

'It's coming! I can feel its head. Oh, God, it's coming. Help me, Robert, help me.'

Robert breathed deeply. His mind, under the pressure of the panic, became suddenly clear. The child was only flesh and blood; it was designed to survive.

'I'm coming, darling, I'm coming.' He went into the kitchen and then up to the bathroom. He grabbed armfuls of towels which he brought down and laid on the carpet beneath Elizabeth's knees as she leaned over the sofa.

'The towels,' she sobbed, 'you'll stain them.'

He gathered a pile of newspapers from the fireplace and spread them on top.

He went and knelt by Elizabeth. She had rolled up her nightdress to her waist. As she squeezed her eyes tight and moaned again, he saw blood and mucus pour from between her legs.

'Christ, it's coming, it's coming,' she said. She was beginning to weep again. Her upper body contracted and heaved once more, but produced only blood.

'Go away,' she shouted at him. 'Go away. I want to be alone.'

Robert stood up and went through into the kitchen, where he poured Elizabeth a glass of water. It was starting to grow light outside. From the window he could see down to a small cottage in the valley. He envied its inhabitants. He wondered what it must be like to be living a normal life, not on the edge of death and drama, but calmly asleep with the prospect of breakfast and an ordinary day ahead.

'Robert!' Elizabeth screamed, and he ran through to her.

He knelt down beside her in the blood.

'I don't know,' she moaned, 'I don't know if I'm supposed to push or not. I can't remember.'

He put his arm around her. 'I think if you want to, then you should. Come on, darling, I'm here. Come on, now. Push.'

Another huge spasm ran through her, and Robert saw the flesh divide between her legs. Blood spurted downwards and he saw, in the lamplight of the living room, the top of a grey skull begin to pulse and push at the unlocking entrance to her body.

'I can see the head, I can see it. It's coming. You're doing well, you're doing marvellously. It's almost here.'

There was a pause as Elizabeth leaned forward on the sofa, waiting for the next contraction. Robert looked down at the newspapers beneath her, one of which was open, appropriately he thought, at the Announcements.

Elizabeth gasped and he looked to where the top of the skull pushed and bore down again, demanding entrance. The body split and parted for it; the head emerged, whole, streaked with blood and slime, trapped around the neck by Elizabeth's divided flesh.

'Come on,' he said, 'come on, one last push and it's there.'

'I can't,' she said. 'I have to wait for a contr . . .' Her voice failed. He put his face close to hers and kissed her. Strands of hair clung to her cheek, struck down by sweat, as she buried her face in the chintz cushion of the sofa.

He took the baby's head between his hands.

'Don't pull,' she gasped. 'See if you can feel the cord round its neck.'

Robert gently probed with his finger, but feared to stretch the bursting flesh further. 'It's all right,' he said.

Then Elizabeth opened her eyes, and he saw them fill with a determination he had never seen in any human face before. She threw back her head and he could see the sinews of her neck rise up like bones. Her wild eyes reminded him of a horse that has finally scented home and clamps his teeth on to the metal bit: no power on earth could stop the combined force of muscle, instinct and willpower as it drove on to its appointed end.

Elizabeth screamed. He looked down and saw the baby's shoulders driven out behind its head. He reached down and took them in his hands. Now he was going to pull.

The baby's shoulders were slippery between his palms, but as he increased the pressure, it suddenly burst free with a sound like a giant cork being released. In a rush of blood it slithered down into his hands and let out a single bleat. Its skin was grey and covered with a whiteish substance, thick and greasy about the chest and back. He looked down to the angry purple cord that looped back beneath Elizabeth's blood-smeared legs, then to the baby's genitals, swollen with its mother's hormones. He blew into its face. It cried, a jagged, stuttering cry. It was a boy.

He could not speak, but he found a towel less bloodied than the others, in which he wrapped the baby. He passed it back beneath Elizabeth's knees into her hands. She sat back on her heels amid the newspapers and the blood, holding the child to her.

'It's a boy,' said Robert hoarsely.

'I know. It's . . .' She struggled on the word '. . . John.'

'John? Yes, yes . . . that's all right.'

'It's a promise,' she said. She was in a storm of weeping. 'A promise . . . made by my grandfather.'

'That's fine, that's fine.' Robert knelt with Elizabeth and the boy; he put his arm round both of them. They stayed in this position on the floor until they were disturbed by a knock at the door. They looked up. A woman with a briefcase had let herself in, then knocked because they had not heard her.

'It looks as though I'm too late,' she smiled. 'Is everyone all right?'

'Yes,' gasped Elizabeth. She showed her the baby.

'He's lovely,' said the doctor. 'I'll cut the cord.'

She knelt down on the floor. She looked up at Robert. 'It's probably best if you go and get a bit of fresh air now.'

'Yes. All right.' He stroked Elizabeth's hair and laid his fingers against John's cheek.

The sun was up outside. It was a fresh, clear morning, overpoweringly bright after the darkness and panic of the cottage.

Released from the need to be calm, Robert heaved his shoulders up and down and forced out several long, sobbing breaths.

He walked a few paces up into the garden, and then the joy overwhelmed him.

He felt it coursing through his arms and his legs; the top of his skull began to crawl and throb as though it would lift off his head. The feeling that rose up inside him was like taking flight; his spirit lifted, then, as the confines of his body would not contain it, seemed to soar into the air.

He found that in his rapture he had walked to the top of the garden. He stopped and looked down. His feet were ankle-deep in conkers, which had fallen overnight from the tree, the glossy fruit bursting from the spiky green shells. He knelt down and picked up two or three of the beautiful, shining things in his hand. When he had been a boy he had waited every year for this day. Now here was John, his boy, another chance.

He threw up the conkers into the air in his great happiness. In the tree above him they disturbed a roosting crow, which erupted from the branches with an explosive bang of its wings, then rose up above him towards the sky, its harsh, ambiguous call coming back in long, grating waves towards the earth, to be heard by those still living.

THE HISTORY OF VINTAGE

The famous American publisher Alfred A. Knopf (1892–1984) founded Vintage Books in the United States in 1954 as a paperback home for the authors published by his company. Vintage was launched in the United Kingdom in 1990 and works independently from the American imprint although both are part of the international publishing group, Random House.

Vintage in the United Kingdom was initially created to publish paperback editions of books acquired by the prestigious hardback imprints in the Random House Group such as Jonathan Cape, Chatto & Windus, Hutchinson and later William Heinemann, Secker & Warburg and The Harvill Press. There are many Booker and Nobel Prize-winning authors on the Vintage list and the imprint publishes a huge variety of fiction and non-fiction. Over the years Vintage has expanded and the list now includes great authors of the past – who are published under the Vintage Classics imprint – as well as many of the most influential authors of the present.

For a full list of the books Vintage publishes, please visit our website
www.vintage-books.co.uk

For book details and other information about the classic authors we publish, please visit the Vintage Classics website
www.vintage-classics.info